AUNT SOOKIE
& ME

AUNT SOOKIE & ME

THE SORDID TALE OF A
SCANDALOUS SOUTHERN BELLE

———

Michael Scott Garvin

ISBN: 1545568723
ISBN 13: 9781545568729
Library of Congress Control Number: 2017906389
CreateSpace Independent Publishing Platform
North Charleston, South Carolina

*From the award winning author of **A Faithful Son**.*

Huffington Post – "Garvin ultimately writes not about finding faith – but about finding himself – and maybe, in some ways, that is the same thing."

Janet Mason - Huffington Post

IPPY Awards – Gold Medal Winner – Independent Publisher's Award
"...A Faithful Son is bound to be a new all-time favorite and classic..."
Anita Lock, **San Francisco Book Review.**
Nominated for 2017 *Indie Reader Discovery Awards*
Winner of the **2016 Beverly Hills Book Awards**
New York Book Festival Finalist
5 Stars -San Francisco Book Review
5 Stars - Foreword Reviews
Best Fiction of 2016 - International Book Festival

The Novel Approach – Best of 2016

".... Zach's joy, pain, longing, and isolation are real and palpable throughout, and every piece of the story and setting only furthers the life and experience bled onto the page...." **<u>KIRKUS REVIEW</u>**

- Finalist on the Table of Honor - International Book Festival

"...A Faithful Son is a visceral experience, realistic and vibrant, wrought with the same craftsmanship as a painting resembling a photograph, or a window into another time and place. Michael Scott Garvin has populated his pages with vivid scenes filled with all the colors and sensations of nature, grounding narrator Zach's story in the inevitable passage of time in a

way that is particularly rural, attuned to the slow, even pace of life's wear upon the body and the soul..." **Patti Comeau** -

"...Garvin's debut is nothing less than stunning... in the flavor of Harper Lee's inimitable novels—To Kill a Mockingbird and Go Set a Watchman— Garvin, like Harper, has created a colorful cast amid chaotic and enlightening eras..." **San Francisco Book Review.**

"...Garvin avoids easy resolutions, caricatures, and shocking twists in the service of a strong story populated by believable characters. A Faithful Son is a highly recommended, enjoyable read for lovers of quality literature that needs no flash or hype to leave an impression." **Foreword Reviews**

Dedicated to my sisters,
Lori and Christi.

PROLOGUE

—————

THIS STORY IS MINE.

It belongs to me and me alone. Why I have chosen to lay bare such private matters to unfamiliar eyes is a mystery to me. Plenty of well-intentioned folks have warned me to keep such messy matters out of sight, hidden below my box springs.

The Sunday morning before we buried the frozen corpse beneath the vegetable garden, Aunt Sook looked me straight in the eye and said, "Folks who go around leavin' their screen door swung wide open for every passin' stranger and wild critter gets precisely what's comin' to them."

Old Sookie was a wise one. I suspect her sentiment was true. Opening my door to y'all may be plain foolishness, and there lies the rub.

I was planted on Sook's lap, plucking stray black hairs sprouting from her chin, while she painted my lips with apricot lipstick.

Peeking over the top of her bifocals, she declared, "Child, it ain't no one's concern how you live your life. It ain't no preacher's business, no politician's, and it certainly ain't no nosy neighbor's concern."

Stricken with the shakes, old Aunt Sook's trembling hand applied the waxy lip color like we was traveling on some unpaved road. She drew a crooked line on my upper lip from one corner, clear across my mouth and up the far side of my cheek. Yellow cataracts blanketed her eyes, like two blue marbles coated by lemon custard. As she applied a teal eye shadow to my upper lids with a foam-tipped stick, I listened to Sook's every word.

"Missy, you heed what I'm saying to you. A child with your peculiarities should just bolt her door tight and keep your private matters to yourself. Are you listenin'?"

"Yes, ma'am."

My aunt Sook's front door was always shut tight, locked, and bolted. I reckon I was the only living soul to possess my very own house key, strung about my neck on a tied shoelace. Jesus Christ himself, returning from heaven, could be knocking on Sook's door, but she wouldn't never unlatch her three deadbolts.

Sook pulled me in close and cupped my face in her quivering hands. Searching my eyes, she said, "Poppy, you gotta take a tight grip of what is rightfully yours, or someone else is likely to snatch it up. You understand, child?"

"Yes, ma'am."

Ain't no one ever gonna snatch up my story. This here story is mine to tell.

What are little boys made of?
Frogs and snails
And puppy dog tails.
That's what little boys are made of.

What are little girls made of?
Sugar and spice
And everything nice.
That's what little girls are made of.

CHAPTER 1

———————

Savannah, Georgia, 1968

I am Poppy Wainwright.

I am thirteen years of age. Some two years ago, by way of a dusty Greyhound bus, I came to reside on 22 South Digby Street in Savannah, Georgia. All my kin come from Mountain Home, Arkansas, but I was brought here to Savannah to reside with my aunt Sookie shortly after my grandma Lainey kicked the bucket.

Sook ain't my proper aunt. She's my late grandma's sister. After Grandma Lainey died of a weak heart, the officials of Mountain Home started shuffling me around like a deck of playing cards, determining who'd take possession of me. For reasons unclear, Sookie raised her hand and staked her claim. I reckon she drew the short stick.

My grandma Lainey and Aunt Sookie shared no sisterly affection, and I don't suppose God could have created two more opposite creatures. Any love the sisters might have ever felt was buried beneath quilts of grievances. Hurtful, poisonous words kept flesh wounds infected, and neither of the two stubborn women had a hankering to reach a forgiving hand across the divide.

My late grandma had long warned me that her older sis, Sook, was a blasphemous heathen with a wicked tongue. Sook said my grandma Lainey was a rigid, Bible-thumping imbecile.

My sweet grandma woke every morning with a kindly smile on her face, but I never once witnessed a grin turn at the corners of old Sook's mouth. Sookie cursed with ease and couldn't string a single sentence together without using the Lord's name in vain.

Sook's eyes had heavy lids, and her skin was as wrinkled as a river turtle's. She moved about like the slowest creature. Her pink and blistered scalp was sparsely covered with thin patches of gray and black hair, like some molting chicken. Gathered with bobby pins, the remaining wiry strands were pulled back into a tight bun. Her teeth were chipped and coffee stained, and her puffy face was round and spotted red. A pair of spectacles was roped around her neck on a silver chain and rode low on her nose. She had herself a pair of heavy udders that rested on her bloated belly like two sacks of flour, and she spent her days lounging in a raggedy, terry cloth house coat and a pair of soiled, green, fuzzy bed slippers. Sook had a crop of whiskers, rolled her own ciggies, and used a salad fork to clean crud from under her toenails.

My late grandma Lainey's face was as smooth as a porcelain doll's. She laughed with ease, and her complexion was as pale and perfect as a pearl. Soaking wet, my grandma couldn't have weighed more than eighty pounds, and her fragile bones pushed through translucent skin. At the dimming of the day, Grandma Lainey would sit at her upright piano and serenade me with her favorite hymns. Her pale green eyes were always upturned, focused on the glorious hereafter. Grandma wasn't much for this earth; she knew with certainty she was heaven bound.

"This life is only a resting place," Grandma Lainey declared, "before my final march on to glory."

The soft-spoken sort, Grandma carefully went fishing for her words, cautious not to make more than a ripple in the water. Only when she was quoting scriptures or sitting at her upright piano did I ever hear her volume rise to over a murmur. But Aunt Sookie entered a room like an angry storm, cussing like the foul-mouthed sailors loitering near the old Pirate's House. Aunt Sook spoke directly at a concern and didn't much care if her truth telling wasn't delivered wrapped in pretty ribbons and bows.

Before her passing, my grandma Lainey reminded me, "Poppy, propriety and discretion is the Lord's way. You must always carry yourself like a proper young lady."

Grandma was long widowed. My grandpa, Samuel Faulkner, had passed long before I was born. A banker by trade, he'd kept my grandma in silk and satin finery, even though he preferred the green felt of a poker table. Rumor had it Grandma lost her husband to both the guiles of another woman and the seductive lure of the playing cards. When Grandpa lost his position at the bank he squandered the last of their wealth at the tables.

After I was bussed here to Savannah, Aunt Sook declared, "Your Grandma Lainey was a fool who gave her money to that worthless, womanizing gambler from Mountain Home. And after Samuel passed on, she gave her heart to every pick-pocketing pastor this side of the Mississippi."

Sookie's disdain for my grandpa Faulkner burned as hot as a poker. "That man couldn't keep his pecker in his pants," she said. "The very last time I spoke to Lainey, she was bawling over the phone. I told my foolish sister the sure way to castrate old Samuel was to kick his secretary square in the jaw!"

For his final few years on this earth, my grandpa turned to gin for comfort, while grandma turned to scriptures for her constant companion.

As for Aunt Sook, she never seemed to go about hankering for a man. I remember Grandma telling me that her older sister hadn't ever taken her a husband.

"Sookie had herself a beau in her youth, a sweet young man, about nineteen years of age, who pledged his undying love to her," Lainey recounted the story. "But after he courted that vile creature for nearly nine months, the sweet boy opted to park his pickup on the tracks of an oncoming freight train. The young fella lost his life on the tracks that day, but he freed himself from a lifetime of grief living with my hateful older sister."

"Sookie was no good from the start," Grandma complained. "Being the firstborn and all, even our own sweet momma confessed, 'The first waffle should be made only to heat up the iron and then tossed out in the bin!'"

It seemed that years before I was born, the two stubborn sisters had planted themselves deep on opposite sides of a barbed wire fence, and forgiveness couldn't take root in such hard, barren soil. Even after the muddy earth had swallowed up my grandma Lainey, Aunt Sook still couldn't find a tender word for her deceased younger sister. I reckon some cuts are so deep that the flesh rots, withers away, and is left to the wind.

And so it was that five days after my grandma Lainey was buried deep in Arkansas dirt, I packed up my belongings in a single case and was put on a bus to Savannah by a county official in a pinstriped suit. With a safety pin, a smiling fella fastened a tag on my collar with my full name, the date of my birth, and my Greyhound's final destination.

It was a sweltering August afternoon when Sook came hobbling up to claim me at the bus depot. I stood small in front of her, no taller than May's corn.

Extending her quaking hand, she said, "Folks call me Sookie."

I replied, "Poppy. Poppy Wainwright."

She snickered, "You ain't no bigger than a peanut."

"Yessum. I'm still holdin' out for a growin' spurt."

"If you were a fish, I'd toss you back."

"Yessum."

"You comin' to stay with me for a spell?"

"Yes, ma'am."

"Good enough," she grumbled. "I reckon, I ought to extend my condolences on the passing of your grandma, but can't say I shed a single solitary tear. Your Grandma Lainey was a self-righteous nit-wit, and if I had the gumption, I'd drive myself up to Mountain Home and spit on her freshly dug grave."

I planted my feet firmly on the ground. Balling up my two tiny fists behind my back, I replied, "Well, my grandma Lainey said you're as spiteful as a jackass and meaner than a rabid dog."

Sookie eyed me suspiciously from my untied sneakers up to my pigtails. "Is that so?"

I gulped. "Yessum."

Sook shrugged her shoulders slightly. "It's true, I suppose."

With the tip of her walking stick, she scratched a straight line in the dirt, directly in front of my sneakers. "Missy, you're in Georgia now. I ain't got no time for the foolishness of Mountain Home."

I cleared a lump lodged deep in my throat. "Ma'am, I'm suspectin' my grandma Lainey's conclusions about you were correct." Gripping the handle of my leather satchel, I stepped clean over her line. "Shall we go?"

Sook shook her head and mumbled. "Missy, that saucy mouth is gonna land you in a heap of trouble." With a wave of her walking stick, we started down toward Digby Street.

So, these were the cards I was dealt. My grandma Lainey once said to me, "There ain't no sense goin' around hoping for aces when the deck is stacked against you with only sixes and sevens."

———

CHAPTER 2

GRACEFUL, GIANT MAGNOLIAS LINED BOTH sides of Digby Street. Their sprawling, heavy boughs reached to one another from across the lane, and their shading, green canopies provided cover year-round. On the clearest of summer days, only dappled sunlight breached the shade of the mighty magnolias. After a spring shower, water pooled in every upturned leaf, and a soft rain continued to drop from the canopies, well after the storm clouds had passed on.

Aunt Sookie's big old house sat on the corner of Digby Street and West Jones. The first time I ever set my sights on the decaying antebellum it had been entirely mummified with rolls of toilet paper. Draped in strands of white tissue, the grand old estate stood as ghoulish as a ghost covered in a linen bedsheet. Mischievous neighbor kids had selected old Sook's place for the TPing and had tossed rolls of paper up into the tallest treetops and along the gutter pipes. Front to back, over and under, the tissue weaved through the fence pickets and porch swings, from atop the TV antenna to the highest awnings, and hung like strands of crepe paper from the eaves and rooftop.

Arriving from the bus depot, Sook and I walked up the sidewalk and stood at the front gate.

With her quaking hand, Sookie sheltered her eyes from the hot summer sun and declared, "Those gawd-damned little fuckers did this in the dead of night."

Clutching the handle of my suitcase, I surveyed the spectacle. "Ma'am, it looks as though they got you good."

She scoffed, "Child, it ain't who fires the first cannon ball who is victorious in battle. This war has just begun."

It seemed the act of vandalism had occurred some several weeks earlier, while Sookie slept soundly. The deviant juveniles had crept under the cover of night and thoroughly toilet-papered Sook's ramshackle. Tissue paper wrapped about the columns, railings, and balconies. The ancient house seemed to be completely wrapped in the sheer gauze.

I asked, "Ma'am, can I help you clean up this mess?"

"No, no! Don't you touch nothin'," my aunt insisted. "Understand me? Do not remove a single solitary strand."

In protest, it seemed old Sookie had opted not to remove the rolls of tissue—an attempt to further rile her neighbors—some of whom were the parents of the exact children who had done the dastardly deed. My stubborn aunt had chosen to go about her business as usual, leaving the house cocooned in the crepe-like paper. However, what vengeful Sookie hadn't forecasted, after a few days under the sweltering Savannah sun and following a few summer rains, the soggy toilet paper formed a crispy shell all about her antebellum. Like some giant papier-mâché piñata, the goopy tissue had dried and hardened in the sizzling sun and now stuck to the English ivy-covered walls and window glass like a white paste, adhering like glue to the shingles and shutters.

Standing on the cobblestone in front of the sad sight, I said, "That's a heap of toilet paper."

"Yessum."

"How many rolls do you suspect they used?"

"Dunno." She shrugged her slight shoulders. "But, the gawd-damned little bastards better sleep with one eye open."

"Ma'am, who do you suspect did the papering?" I asked. "Do you know 'em?"

In a voice that seemed to arrive from somewhere down deep in her spiteful gut, she grumbled low, "Oh, yes, I know who they are. I know exactly who the little fuckers are."

Old Sook fought with the rickety gate latch, and we walked up the front path.

Mine was the last bedroom down the long hallway on the second floor. The vine-choked house had been a beauty in its day. With peeling, pale yellow paint and a raised porch wrapping the entire first floor, the grand estate stood as a living testament to a bygone era. A crooked white picket fence traveled the length of the front yard and up along the side yard on West Jones Street. French paned windows lined the upper floor. The rusted plumbing moaned behind the plastered walls, and the taps only gifted us a drizzle of lukewarm water in the mornings. The tangles of haphazard electrical wiring caused the dusty chandeliers and hallway sconces to flicker as the clothes washer whined through it cycles.

The decaying state of Aunt Sook's place was a growing concern for the surrounding neighbors. Anytime the ladies of the Society for the Beautification of Savannah came snooping around the front gate, Sookie would shoo them back off into the street. At one time, her house was the most prized historic antebellum in these parts, but the decomposing ramshackle kept the nosy society ladies up fretting at night.

Back at Mountain Home, my grandma's house was clean as a whistle. If she wasn't dusting something, she was walking room to room, sniffing out dust. Grandma would slide her finger along the credenza in the foyer, over the piano keys, and high above the armoire in the front sitting room, then examine her digit for a hint of a speck. Lainey's shelves of leather-bound books were arranged in perfect straight rows, and her freshly laundered towels smelled like lavender. The windows' flower boxes bloomed with marigolds and geraniums, and her green lawn was plush as a carpet. But Aunt Sookie's filthy, rambling house was a calamity. Sunlight had corroded the lace on the window curtains, and when you took a seat on a cushion, plumes of soot rose into the air like Oklahoma dust. The wood-paneled doors squeaked an off-pitch tune, and the old staircase grumbled low when one descended its treads.

There was no denying the big old house and its grounds were in fast decline. Choking English ivy and a coating of grime covered any remaining trace of elegance. The wooden shutters hung by their last penny nails, and warped wood siding buckled and cracked. Sookie's only lawn care was an ornery goat named Annabelle, who grazed on the always-growing dandelions and gypsum weeds that sprouted wild in the yard. Having mastered the backdoor knob with her hoof, Annabelle entered and exited the home at will.

Aunt Sookie was of the belief that the goat was Mother Nature's most perfect invention.

"A goat is a scrappy, self-reliant creature," Sook declared. "They tend to themselves. They'll gobble up pretty much anything placed in front of their snouts, and they ain't got no ax to grind with nobody. I got absolutely no use for a dimwitted dog or a treacherous cat. A poor hound can be beat with a stick, and he'll still come back sniffin' for another kick, out of some perverse sense of devotion. And felines don't have no conscience at all. It don't matter if it's a stray alley cat or a pampered house tabby, they'll scratch your eyes from their sockets if given the opportunity. But a goat is the loyal and independent sort."

Annabelle roamed the unkempt yard during the day and retired to her bed in the corner of the sitting room come nightfall. Her little pellet droppings littered the yard and down the hallways, scattered about on the worn oriental rugs. It seemed to me that the spiteful goat shared none of the loyalty of which Sookie spoke. If given the opportunity, I believed Annabelle would've taken aim at Sookie's ample backside, lowering her snout, taking off at a full gait, and ramming Sook to the far side of the moon.

On the sunny south side, protected with a perimeter of chicken wire, was Sook's bountiful vegetable garden. Perfect rows of carrots, radishes, onions, and peppers grew to ripe perfection, like her very own Garden of Eden. Tomato bushes, squash vines, a vast assortment of melons, lettuce, cabbage, and black-eyed peas grew under the warm Savannah sun.

My aunt Sook spent countless hours tending to her prized garden, laboring on her knees. While Sook hadn't the slightest interest in conversing with town folk, she would lavish every seedling with praise and encouragement as she toiled in her garden. Among her crops, she'd speak sweetly to every sapling and saved her acidic tongue for all her surrounding neighbors. With rich mulch and fertilizers, Sook worked the earth into the most fertile soil in all of Savannah. After we had buried the corpse deep under the garden bed, Aunt Sookie said it was just another nutritional supplement for the grub worms to feast on.

Coaxing a civil sentiment or kind compliment about my aunt Sook from her surrounding neighbors was an impossible task, but when it came to Auntie's vegetable garden, not a soul in Savannah could muster a single negative word. The neighbor ladies passing along on the sidewalk would peek beyond the yard's clutter and debris to admire Sook's meticulous green garden. Attempting to catch a glimpse, the envious neighbors stretched their necks up over the front hedge to sneak a look at the rows of golden corn stalks, collard greens, and meaty tomato bushes. From our side of the picket fence, Annabelle would follow the ladies' path along the sidewalk, snapping and spitting. The ornery goat seemed to enjoy threatening the tourists and blue-haired voyeurs.

It took a good spell for Sook and me to warm to each other. I reckon a person had to go looking hard to find any sweet spot in Sookie. If you crossed her, she was meaner than spit, and any soft places were calloused over with worn, leathered skin. But I had a hunch that in time I could manage old Sookie and melt her into something warm and mushy like a bowl of Grandma Lainey's mashed potatoes.

The house was a quiet place, and for those first few weeks Sook and I walked a wide path around each other. I stepped silent as a field mouse on the floorboards of the rambling antebellum. I suspected she was also content to keep well clear of me. With my ear pressed to the wall, I listened for any sign of my aunt. Her slow, shuffling feet in the hallways or the poking of her walking stick up the staircase provided the stretch of time to plot an opposite path and dodge the cantankerous old woman.

The day after arriving on the Greyhound, I sat across from Sook at a quiet supper table, waiting for either to bridge the silence. With my fork, I pushed an unidentifiable slice of burned beef around my plate.

"You'd best understand now, I'm no cook," Sook declared. "You'll have to fend for yourself in the kitchen. I can fry up a good egg and a digestible chicken casserole, but that just about sums up my culinary expertise." She took a bite and struggled to chew the dry morsel of mystery meat.

"Grandma insisted we say grace before each supper."

Agitated, Sookie drew in a deep breath and rested her fork near her plate. "I'm a nonbeliever, so if you're gonna go about quotin' scriptures, you best know you're preachin' to a deaf ear."

I paid her no never mind and bowed my head, pressed my palms together and mumbled through grace, while an amused Sook looked on.

"I suspect your Grandma Lainey led you to the church."

"Yes, ma'am."

Taking a bite of the charred chop, she chewed with furious intensity. "There's a steeple on every street corner in Savannah, so you can believe in whichever God you wish. Hell, there's so many damned churches, you can praise a new savior every Sunday. In time, I reckon, you'll be permitted to go exploring for salvation, but for now church will have to wait."

"Are you denying me the right to worship the Pentecost in a proper house of God?"

"Yes," Sook responded. "I suppose I am." She cleared her throat. "Missy, I ain't sure the citizens of Savannah are ready for a child with your proclivities. It's wiser for you to stay near the house for the time being, so I can keep my eye on you. I believe your great-grandma's Bible is in the bottom drawer in the foyer credenza. You can go searching for your redemption in its pages for now."

It was clear that I'd be left to my own devices to seek out nourishment for my body and sustenance for my soul. So I read the old Bible by lamplight and prepared home-cooked vittles for Aunt Sook and myself. For my services rendered, I earned a four-dollar weekly allowance.

On Sundays when payment came due, Sook begrudgingly counted out the coins in the palm of my hand and took the opportunity to remind me of every disappointment on the week's menu.

"Last night's supper was a lumpy mush," she griped. "The collard greens were indigestible; the broccoli gave me terrible gas, and that beef brisket was overcooked. It was like chewing on a gawd-damned work boot."

"You sure are the crotchety sort," I said. "Why so?"

She seemed to consider my question.

"I suspect it's cuz I'm older than dirt. Death is knockin' at my door. Just yesterday I was strollin' by the Bonaventure cemetery, and two fellas came chasin' after me with shovels."

"Ain't true," I laughed. "If you don't mind me askin', how old are ya?"

"Hmm, I ain't sure, but when I was a girl the Dead Sea was only feeling poorly."

———————

From the start, Aunt Sook laid down the strict law, forbidding me to travel past the front gate. She made it clear as crystal that straying into the city streets wouldn't be permitted.

"Child, you're too young to roam Savannah unattended. And I ain't sure Georgia will take kindly to your sort."

"But Sookie," I complained, "all the other kids are allowed to ride their bikes to the park, or to the Piggly Wiggly, or the ice cream parlor."

"No, no. I won't abide a juvenile delinquent gallivantin' around Savannah, unsupervised." She stood firm. "You're gonna stay put. If you have a hankering, I can escort you to the Piggly Wiggly."

I huffed and crossed my arms in protest. "Auntie, when can I be enrolled in a proper school?"

"We'll have to wait and see. Didn't your Grandma Lainey home-school you?"

"Yes, ma'am," I said, "but she promised I could attend a real school."

The crusty old woman tapped her quaking finger on her chin, considering my request. "Only time will tell. Perhaps next September you'll be permitted to enroll. But until then, you'll be taught right here at my side. I've got more knowledge in my pinky finger than those tightly wound teachers over at the elementary school."

For those first weeks, I remained in the confines of Sook's old house and inside the perimeter of the picket fence. Like the old goat Annabelle, I was held captive from the big world outside. If I was restless, I took myself to the shingled rooftop, where I could see all of Savannah. I observed the comings and goings of Digby Street. From my roof perch, I could spy some of the neighbor ladies chatting over the picket fences, exchanging recipes and gossip. I came to know my neighbors from a distance. A skinny blond lady in the white house with the yellow shutters entertained a handsome gentleman caller in the afternoons, when her husband was off to work. A rotund, elderly woman with blue, teased hair three houses down on the right buried empty whiskey bottles deep in her garbage bin when she thought no one was watching.

At the day's end, all the fathers sauntered out onto their porches and smoked cigars and read the evening paper. On Saturdays, the boys played kickball right down the middle of Digby, and a cluster of little girls gathered in circles under the shade trees and giggled among themselves.

I imagined their perfect lives being lived in the rows of perfect houses. At dusk, from my shingled perch, I conjured up the image of perfect families taking their proper places around their supper table while kind fathers bowed their heads and said grace. Behind the pulled window shades, I imagined perfect mothers tucking their young'uns into soft down beds and sleepy children dreaming big dreams that always came true.

I reckon, after a child has been abandoned by a struggling momma, we learn to dream more practical dreams, like choosing our Sunday shoes from the sales bin and never daring to wish for the loveliest pair in the storefront window. An occasional postcard from Poughkeepsie arrived in the box like a Christmas gift wrapped in pretty foil paper. Us kids who are left waiting, learn to listen to the whispering wind for a lost lullaby. The night cradles us to sleep, and hope wakes us the next morning like a hungry stomach. When a troubled momma leaves her babies behind, we learn to yearn for only what is placed in front of us at the supper table and not hunger for a single crumb more.

CHAPTER 3

—◆—

FROM MY ROOFTOP, I SPIED directly into the McAllister's kitchen window, right across the street. Mr. Carl McAllister was a respected lawyer in town, and Dixie, his wife, was a high-society lady who chaired the Society for the Beautification of Savannah. Because of her high position, poor Dixie was kept up late at night, fretting about my aunt Sook's dilapidated dump, which sat right outside her front window. Every week, Sookie would find another violation or citation in her mailbox with Dixie's signature, demanding repairs commence immediately on the historical home. But, Sook paid no heed to the notices and instead fed the yellow citations to Annabelle.

Dixie McAllister moved about like some boney bird, always nervous, always hesitant. A platinum bouffant balanced atop her tiny noggin, and her long, thin neck seemed to carry her compact cranium out in front of her, leaving her feet and torso following behind.

Carl and Dixie had a pair of fat-necked boys, Timmy and Tommy. The boys were identical twins who fought and fussed around the clock. A day didn't pass when I didn't witness Mr. McAllister chasing the boys about the house, swinging his leather belt, or Dixie hollering their names and throwing frying skillets at the roughens from her front porch.

The boys fought like two alley dogs. The tubby twins' hatred for each other had no bounds. So diabolical was their loathing for each other that a concerned Carl asked the local sheriff to escort the boys to the Savannah county jail and lock them up—all in an attempt to demonstrate to the identical demons what prison would feel like if they happened to kill the other during one of their brawls. But what Timmy and Tommy lacked in social graces, Dixie made up for with the boy's fancy, matching duds. Her twin hooligans were polished up like two matching bookends.

Sook told me that when Mrs. McAllister was pregnant with the boys, she had set her hopes on a pair of delicate little girls.

"When Dixie delivered those two no-neck little bastards, her heart broke into a million pieces. She was absolutely beside herself. After Dixie dried her tears, she decided to spare no expense and started dressing those ugly, fat baby boys in fancy matching ensembles. She paraded those dreadful mongrels around Savannah in identical rompers, hats, and booties." Sook shook her head disapprovingly. "Dixie McAllister spent too much time shopping for matching britches and suspenders and forgot to civilize those two rotten boys."

At thirteen years old, far past the age that any respectable boy would ever dress like his brother, the two were still trotted out in matching shirts, socks, britches, and bow ties. Every morning, we'd hear the awful ruckus coming from the McAllister's window as Dixie demanded that the boys dress in their matching getups. Thanks to Carl's stinging belt and Dixie's vigilant tenacity, Timmy and Tommy arrived at the school bus stop, a mirrored reflection of one another.

Because the McAllister twins were spitting images of each other, it was all but impossible to differentiate between the two, blubbery boys. One afternoon, from our front porch we watched as the twins squared off, taunting each other.

Finally, one boy grabbed the other about his fat neck, and they tumbled to the ground. In a dusty tangle of legs and arms with rusty elbows and blackened, soiled feet, they rolled in the dirt, punching, biting, flailing, and cursing.

It was then Aunt Sook confessed her fail-safe formula to distinguish one fat boy from the other.

"It took me some time, but I finally got those little bastards all sorted out," Sook remarked. "Timmy is the nose picker. When he ain't fightin' or fussin', he's always pickin'!"

Sure enough, after Dixie came out from the door, and separated the two fighting hooligans, one of the bloated boys went exploring his left nostril with his index finger.

"Good Lord, I can't even bear to watch," Sookie winced. "If that child goes digging any deeper, he's gonna tunnel himself all the way to Shanghai."

It seemed to me that old Sook and the McAllister twins reveled in their ongoing feud, antagonizing one another from a stone's throw distance across the lane. Like some nasty game of dodgeball, the eighty-four-year-old cripple and the pair of ornery eighth-graders torpedoed insults back and forth across Digby.

One afternoon from my window, I watched on as the two boys, high up in their treehouse, whistled over to Sook, who was busy watering her bean sprouts.

"Hey, you old coot!"

Sook searched the sky until she spotted the rascals held up in their tree fort, nestled in the highest branches of an old oak.

The other McAllister hollered, "Up here, you old, fat battleax!"

The two boys extended their stumpy middle fingers, flipping off old Sook with their twin birds. From my window seat, I could see each of their middle fingers had been fitted with a cardboard spool from an empty toilet paper roll.

Sookie returned the not-so-neighborly gesture by turning about, lifting up the back of her skirt, dropping her bloomers to the dirt, and flashing the boys a full view of her bare backside.

The twins cringed at the sorry sight.

It just so happened Mr. McAllister sauntered out onto his porch at the precise moment as Sook was advertising her wide ass like a billboard along the interstate.

He called out kindly, "Sookie Wainwright, I don't believe you've ever looked prettier than you do on this very mornin'!" He took a seat on his favorite lawn chair and perused his *Morning Daily Press.*

Driving back and forth to the Piggly Wiggly, my aunt made it a practice to run the two pedaling punks right off the road whenever they were out and about. Her Buick's bumper would kiss the spinning back wheel of one of the boy's identical bikes as they attempted to escape. Sookie would grip to her steering wheel, riotously laughing as she reveled in the boy's panic-stricken eyes.

One afternoon Sookie confessed, "Watching those worthless boys, I now understand why some critters eat their own young!"

———◆———

Being held captive at Sookie's, I still hadn't made the acquaintance of any of the neighbor kids. But I found me a hiding spot down low in the front myrtle hedge, where I could spy on them as they waited for the coughing school bus to turn onto Digby.

Kneeling down low in the bushes, I watched through the fence pickets the pretty girls all standing in a row, chewing bubble gum and twisting strands of their long hair. They clutched their school packs and whispered in one another's ears while the boys hunched low in a circle, shooting marbles in the dirt. When the bus arrived, all the kids boarded in single file and then traveled off to school.

Aunt Sook arrived back from town with a pile of thick, heavy textbooks from the library. Every morning by nine o' clock sharp, Sook was hollering after me, "Poppy, come on inside. It's time for your school lessons!"

Back at Mountain Home, my sweet Grandma Lainey would sit patiently near my side, and we worked through my American history quiz, English lessons, or some math equations. Together, we solved the exercises and answered the daily assignments. If I couldn't grasp a lesson, my understanding grandma would sit with me under the lamplight and work through each problem until she recognized the illumination of understanding in my eyes. But old Aunt Sook had no tolerance for my schoolwork, and within mere moments of sitting down at the breakfast table, she'd grow aggravated.

"Child, are you soft in the noggin?" She shook her gray head in frustration. "Your grandma Lainey was as stupid as a stump, and I'm thinkin' this branch didn't fall too far from the tree."

I stiffened my backbone and replied, "My grandma went on to college, and she said that you were lucky to scratch out a high school diploma."

Sookie stammered, "Book learnin' never interested me, no how." She tapped her forehead with her finger. "I was gifted with the kind of smarts that don't require all this nonsense." With that, she pushed the textbooks far across the table. "Besides, if you're wantin' to enroll in the school come next September, you'd best get to learnin' this nonsense."

One afternoon, after Aunt Sook closed the cover of my science book, she glanced over nervously in my direction. "Child, I ain't sure if your Grandma Lainey ever sat you down and discussed the nature of men and womenfolk, but I feel it's my duty to do so." Fidgeting with the dusty, plastic fruit bowl in the center of the table, she announced, "It may be an uncomfortable discussion, but we best be done with it."

I watched her move about awkwardly in her chair.

She retrieved a plastic banana from the table's centerpiece bowl in one hand and with the other formed a circle with her quivering thumb and index finger. "Poppy, this here, is the man." Sookie raised the yellow fruit. "And this hand, is the woman."

I interrupted, "Sookie, hold up. I know all about the birds and the bees."

The old woman exhaled, with a sigh of relief. "Thank the ghost of Jefferson Davis."

"Ma'am, when your momma is Miss Loretta Wainwright, you come to a clear understanding of the birds, the bees, and the entire barnyard. There's no need to illuminate any new light on that particular subject."

For those lonely first few weeks at Aunt Sook's, the grandfather clock downstairs was my constant companion. It tolled the lonesome hours. The swaying pendulum ticked off the passing seconds. I roamed from room to room and went about opening the heavy, fringed curtains, allowing sunshine in. It seemed the dusty parlors had been holding their breaths for decades, waiting on my arrival. The ancient rooms seemed to welcome my presence to Digby Street. Even Annabelle trailed close behind me as I wandered about the big old house, bringing light to every dark and dingy chamber.

After my school lessons, I was left to my own devices. I explored every inch of the sprawling house and grounds. Up in Sook's dusty attic, I rummaged through old cardboard boxes and crates. I discovered an ancient wooden chest. Inside, a satin and lace wedding dress was folded neatly and placed in tissue paper, like something cherished. I lost afternoons looking through picture albums with yellowing photographs of faces of those who had lived long before I was birthed. Cases were stacked upon cases of fine old-fashioned dresses, sequined gowns, and lace corsets. In a shoebox, I found stacks of old letters as fragile as tissue.

Later, I descended into the deep, dank basement, where the old, rusty furnace groaned. Discarded antiques were stacked to the trusses. Tiffany lamps and leather-bound books were stacked in piles, collecting mildew and grime. After I'd investigated every nook and cranny of the old house, I walked every inch of Sook's cluttered yard and explored the old shed out back, which housed Sook's jalopy and stored all her garden supplies.

At the dimming of the day, I'd return to my rooftop perch and recline on the shingles. Having fully explored the old house and its grounds, I grew restless of 22 South Digby Street—Savannah called to me from out past the front hedge, like some great adventure.

Like string stretched between tin cans, word spread to the neighbors of my confinement inside Sook's stuffy, decaying house.

One afternoon, the McAllister twins, who were doing chores on the front lawn, spotted me reclining on the roof across the way.

One of the tubby boys in a striped shirt, hollered, "Hey! You got a name?"

"Poppy," I said. "Poppy Wainwright."

The other twin in the same striped shirt called out, "Is she holding you prisoner up in there?"

"Naw," I answered back.

Unconvinced, he replied, "My pa is a really good lawyer, so if you need him, he and the sheriff can come fetch you."

"Naw. I'm fine, but I appreciate the consideration."

The boy holding the rake scratched his fat head and called back, "Why ain't you in school? Are you slow or something?"

I giggled to myself and replied, "No, my aunt Sookie thinks it's best for me to stay put for now. But she says, I'll be enrolled by next September."

"Golly, you're a lucky duck," he hollered back. "My homeroom teacher is Mrs. Stutzman. She's a real ball buster. She's got her a wooden paddle that stings like a son of bitch."

The matching McAllister, knee-deep in a pile of freshly mowed summer's grass, yelled, "I'm stuck with Mrs. Graf. She's so old, she farts dust."

I reckon my mysterious presence inside Aunt Sook's place had gotten all the neighbor ladies buzzing like busy bees. I overheard a collection of local women chatting as they strolled up and down the sidewalk. One short, squatty woman pointed at the house and whispered, "That child needs her a proper momma."

Another lady with teased hair the color of cotton candy re-marked, "I've heard it said, the little girl is sleeping in a box, and she's fed on the floor alongside that nasty goat."

The following week, when Sookie and I were shopping at the Piggly Wiggly, a big lady with ratty mauve hair and a big black mole on the tip of her nose leaned close to a skinny elderly woman working behind the register and remarked, "That spiteful woman shouldn't be raisin' no children!"

One afternoon, sitting behind Sook and me at the Saturday picture show, I overheard two women chatting up a storm during the matinee.

One of the ladies commented low in the dark, "It's an absolute shame what that wicked woman is doin' with that sweet little girl. Keeping her imprisoned like some jail bird."

The other woman responded in a whisper, "I heard that poor child isn't even receiving a proper education. Dixie McAllister told me just yesterday that she's gonna report old Sook Wainwright to the school board."

Fed up, Aunt Sook stood up from her seat and directed her comment to the crowd in the darkened Avon Theater. "Stella Nance, if you don't shut your gawd-damned pie hole, I'm gonna come find you and beat you with this stick." My aunt waved her walking cane high in the air. "And Mildred, just keep up your gabbing, and you'll get what's comin' to you." Sook's silhouette projected onto the movie screen as she wildly swung her walking cane.

No matter the gossip of my imprisonment, Sook remained stubborn as a mule and would not be moved. Even with my constant nagging and pleading for my freedom to venture out beyond the front gate, Sook would not budge.

"You're a different sort, Miss Poppy Wainwright," she explained. "You'll remain inside the perimeter of these walls until I believe no harm can come."

"But, Sook, ain't nobody gonna hurt me. I'll be fine."

"No, I was speaking of my concern for the citizens of Savannah. Not you. I ain't sure Georgia is ready for all of this." She pointed at me with her walking stick. "Missy, your oddity will provoke folks."

It was only later, while Sook and I were sitting on the front porch, that I first detected cracks in her obstinate constitution.

"Child, Savannah may be a bigger, more metropolitan city than Mountain Home, but people are every bit as small minded," she remarked. "You understand me?"

"Yessum. But Sookie, even in Mountain Home, Grandma Lainey permitted me to ride my bike into town."

The always-quaking old woman rocked in her chair and answered back with a stubborn silence.

"I promise to venture only as far as the park. Not an inch further."

Sook pointed to the front hedge along the perimeter of the house. "Poppy, when you're tall enough to see over that there hedge, then you're free to go scouting up and down Digby Street. Until then, you are to stay within these grounds. Understand me?"

"Yes, ma'am." I couldn't conceal my beaming grin.

So, I waited. For weeks, I waited, watching the growing hedge. It took no time to reason that the front myrtle hedge was sprouting at a faster pace than my bones could ever muster. So I took myself into the house, hunting for Sook.

I came stomping into the sitting room, where she was consumed with her soap opera.

"Sook, this just ain't fair!" I sighed.

Her eyes didn't turn from the television.

"Sookie, are you listenin' to me?"

I walked up to the set and turned the knob. The tube went black.

"Child, I don't want to miss my story. You turn my set back on right this minute!"

"No, ma'am, I won't. Not until we've come to a clear understanding."

She drew in a deep breath. "Speak your piece."

"Sook, that hedge will be sky high by spring, and I ain't never gonna be free." I held her stare.

"So, it's freedom that you're after?" she asked. "I don't suspect you're gonna give me a moment's peace until this issue is put to rest."

"No, ma'am. I won't."

"Well then, next week, I'll take you into town, and we'll get you a bicycle, on one condition. You don't take the bike anywhere but up and down Digby. You understand me?"

"Yes, ma'am!"

CHAPTER 4

MY REAL MOMMA IS MISS Loretta Jo Nell Wainwright—a terrible tangle of a mess.

Miss Loretta never planted herself in one place for a sufficient length of time to cultivate deep roots. Tortured and always slightly tipsy, she only came poking around Grandma Lainey's place when she needed a soft pillow to lay her weary head or when she felt compelled to behave like my proper momma for a short spell.

Miss Loretta always arrived in a fitful storm. When she approached, hound dogs would begin howling, and livestock would look to the sky with worry. Heavy, dark clouds would quilt the sky on a perfectly fine day, and then there she'd be. Miss Loretta Wainwright would come strutting up the road.

It was difficult to rile my patient Grandma Lainey, but her only offspring, Loretta, was well practiced at ruffling her tail feathers. She was always off gallivanting from state to state, sniffing around for trouble. Picture postcards arrived at Mountain Home, postmarked for me from Biloxi to Bakersfield.

I hadn't set eyes on Loretta for more than a year. I wasn't even sure if she got word that Grandma Lainey, her own momma, had gone off and died.

I recall one afternoon, while coming home from church service, Lainey explained to me, "Child, your momma is like the old yellow alley cat under the front porch, who keeps pushing out litters of kittens but won't stick around long enough to let them taste the milk from her teats."

It was true enough. Miss Loretta had birthed enough children to keep the Mountain Home County Social Services busy from daylight to dusk. Like the old stray cat, Loretta had herself a mound of mangy, matted yellow hair piled atop her head and two big 'ole hard boobies, swollen high up on her chest, appearing to be in need of a good milking.

When she sobered up, Loretta would find her way back to Mountain Home and show up at Grandma Lainey's place, poking around the house and crying a river of crocodile tears.

"I'm so sorry, baby," she'd repent, wiping her sloppy nose with her forearm. "I've been a bad momma. But I swear on my heart, I'm gonna get myself clean. And I won't never touch the stuff again." She'd squeeze me tight in her arms.

"Loretta, you listen good." I squared her shoulders with mine and looked at her direct. "When I'm of legal age, I'll come find you and take care of you. You just gotta hold on until then."

She sniffled, batted her wet false eyelashes, and asked, "You promise me, Poppy?"

"Yes, Loretta, I swear. I'll be of legal age in seven years. You gotta hang on until then."

But her visits to Mountain Home never lasted long. It wouldn't take any time at all before the devil would arrive, whispering in her ear, calling for her to come follow him. Her wicked cravings would return, and after only a few days with us, Miss Loretta would start itching and scratching. I'd watch as she frantically paced the floorboards with yearnings. Her eyes would no longer meet mine. Money would go missing from Grandma Lainey's pocket book, and Miss Loretta would be off wandering the streets, hunting her some dope or some booze or another mean, redneck beau.

For the longest time, I held to the belief that a train only moved forward on its tracks, never to return from where it departed. Folks would board and take a seat, and the whistle would sound. The steel wheels would start turning, and the train would pull away from the station. I had the notion that the leaving train was long gone, never to be seen again. I also believed the same to be true when my momma got into the backseat of a yellow cab or if I saw a Greyhound traveling down a lonely stretch of interstate. Over the years, watching the comings and goings of Miss Loretta had taught me a fine lesson: if folks had a hankering to return, they could walk themselves up to a ticket counter, purchase a ticket back home, and return to whomever they long for and what was remembered. I determined it was those of us left waiting who must believe with all of our might that the same chugging train was somewhere on its rusty rails bringing them home. And so, with head bowed and palms pressed, I learned to pray to the Lord for my momma's deliverance.

But with each visit, it seemed she was only sinking deeper in despair. Poor Grandma Lainey wore her footprints into the floorboards, fretting about her wayward daughter. On the very night before Grandma Lainey passed away, Grandma beckoned me up to her room, and together we planted our knees on the carpet next to her bed. With heads bowed and hands clasped, we prayed for the Lord's mercy. We prayed that he might deliver Loretta from Satan's wickedness. We asked Jesus to guide her to a clear path to higher ground. Grandma Lainey was well familiar with the ways of the Almighty, so I rested safe in knowing the Lord had heard our earnest prayers.

CHAPTER 5

———◆———

BY THE TIME I WAS eight years old, I had determined that I was at my most appealing wearing pastel yellow. The sunny hue shone on my face and brightened my drab brown eyes. A frilly, yellow frock brightened my muddy complexion and lifted my skin with light.

On one of Loretta's visits to Mountain Home, she told me, "Yellah is a color only a few select young ladies can pull off." She dusted my cheeks with a powder blush. "Not every girl can wear yellah, but you're special, Poppy. Sunny yellah suits you."

Miss Loretta was a true beauty and knew about such things, so I placed her compliment in my small purse like a treasured gift.

But I wasn't a "looker" like my momma. Not a single boy had ever promised his affections or whistled as I strolled along the sidewalk. I reckon, I understood at an early age, that I was one of the unlucky girls whose reflections betrayed them. I recognized the ugly truth when I faced the mean mirror. But being homely ain't so bad. Pestering boys steered clear, and I would never be bothered with diamond tiaras, silk sashes, and such frivolous nonsense.

Ordinary girls like me understood when Pretty walked into a room; everyone stood up. We learned to clear a wide path when Pretty arrived, because Pretty owned the center of every room. Us homely girls recognized the admiration in the eyes of the circle of ancient, silver ladies who watched on in fond remembrance when Pretty was anywhere near. Menfolk gazed longingly, unable to pull their eyes away from Pretty. Even the gray, stodgy old men smoking cigars like chimney stacks lusted for Pretty, wondering if they stood a chance to still win her affections. Rooms seemed to brighten, and days seemed warmer anytime Pretty smiled. Those of us with unremarkable faces and clumsy, bumpy bodies recognized our imperfections when Pretty made an appearance. All of us girls who would never be the sweet pea in the garden or the ripest peach on the tree just stood back in awe when Pretty entered.

Constance White was painfully pretty. She had long, luxurious hair the color of corn silk. Her braided ponytail was like a long yellow rope that traveled down her back. I imagined Constance was the loveliest thirteen-year-old girl in all of Chatham County. Every morning from my hedge, I spied Constance and the other girls playing hopscotch along the sidewalk, waiting for the school bus. As she skipped down Digby, her yellow ponytail reflected in the sunlight. When she smiled, admiring boys flushed red. From my hiding spot, there were plenty of little girls who seemed sweet, kind, and clever. But Constance White was gifted with pretty, so Constance won before any game began. Her teeth were impossibly white, and her skin was as smooth and pink as one of Grandma Lainey's porcelain dolls.

The loitering boys stood up straight with stiff backs and puffed chests anytime Constance strolled up the sidewalk carrying her school pack. If Constance was anywhere in sight, the denim roughens scrambled, adjusting their baseball caps and tucking in their unpressed shirts. From my hiding hedge, I learned when Pretty strolled by; boys looked right past the ordinary to catch a glimpse.

After Aunt Sook and I completed my daily studies, I kept a watchful eye on the hands of the clock over the fridge. At half past two, I'd hurry back to my hiding spot in the myrtle and hunch low out of sight. Peeking through the pickets, I'd wait for the rumble of the dusty yellow bus down Digby, returning all the children back home. The line of boys and girls would file out of the bus onto the sidewalk. When Constance White emerged, she'd wave to the departing bus, and she and the other girls would giggle as they ran off for home. Every boy turned to watch Pretty skip by as she disappeared down Digby Street.

———————◆———————

From atop the shingled roof on a fine Sunday morning, Savannah looked like some lovely imaginary land. I'd climb through my open window and scale the steep pitch to take my spot. On some mornings, the early light painted the town like a watercolor souvenir. It seemed to me, out past the hedge, Savannah was a wondrous place.

Rising high above the green canopies of the magnolias, clanging bells chimed from the brick steeples. The glimmering, gold dome of city hall rose taller than the tallest tree, and the turrets and cupolas of the old Victorians reached into the bluest sky. Below me through the magnolias, I watched the families dressed in their Sunday best on the way to church services. The distinguished men politely tipped their brimmed hats to their neighbors. The lovely ladies of Digby wore the finest fashions of the day. They donned white lace gloves and clutched their purses on their forearms. As the neighbors strolled to their chosen churches, Sook's rows of happy sun flowers peeked over the picket fence, heavy headed, nodding in the breeze to all who passed. From my perch, Digby Street appeared to be a mighty fine place, indeed.

On one particular Sunday, Annabelle was below, grazing in the front yard. When she spotted me high above, she tilted her head to the sky and began a whining cry, calling up to join me. She released a long, aching wail like the loneliest train whistle. I shushed her, but Annabelle's persistent bawling was beginning to work on Sookie's already-frayed nerves.

From inside the house, Sook hollered, "Shut up, you gawd-damned goat!"

But Annabelle's cries continued.

I called down to her, "Hush up, or you're gonna get yourself beat."

But a determined goat wants what she wants, and there was no silencing her. She hopped atop an abandoned tire in the yard; her grief-stricken wails only grew louder.

Sook's voice threatened from behind the screen, "I'm giving you fair warning. If I have to come out there, there's gonna be a heavy price to pay."

But Annabelle paid Sookie's threats no mind. The passing neighbors eyed the wailing goat suspiciously over the fence as they walked along the sidewalk on their way to Sunday service.

Finally, Sookie busted through the screen door, brandishing a broom. "OK, you gawd-damned goat! It's a fine day for dyin'." Sook took full wide swings at Annabelle, frightening the weeping goat off into the back yard.

I hollered down, "Sook, you sure are mighty spry when you need to be."

The old woman searched about the yard.

"Up here!" I called, waving my arms. "I'm up here!"

She followed my voice to the top of the shingles. "What in tarnation are you doin' up there? You're likely gonna fall and break your neck." Her quivering hand sheltered her eyes from the morning sun.

"I'm just doin' some thinkin'."

"Is that so?"

"Yessum. I've decided when I get my bicycle, I'm gonna scout out the local Savannah Baptist church."

I waited for any response.

"Sookie, I know you ain't got the slightest inclination, but I'm gonna take myself to the church next Sunday on my new bike."

The old woman stood below, scrutinizing me. "Is that so?"

"Yessum."

"I thought we had ourselves an agreement and determined that you'd stay put on Digby?"

"Yes, ma'am," I answered. "The Baptist church is six blocks on the left." I pointed to the modest stone steeple down the road a way.

Sook mumbled low to herself and shook her head. "I ain't too crazy 'bout you running loose in town, but I reckon I can't stand between a soul and its salvation."

"I'm planning on going to service next Sunday morning."

She hollered back, "Fine, but you gotta ride directly there and straight back. No detours! And remember to latch the front gate when you come and go. And never bring around any missionaries sniffing for money. I won't abide charlatans under my roof."

"Yes, ma'am."

She continued, "And you'll travel directly to the church and directly back here?"

I laughed. "Yessum."

"Well, praise the Lord!" Sook started shuffling back to the porch. "Sister Wainwright, if you're wantin' breakfast, you know how to heat up your own skillet. But you best hurry before the almighty raptures your ass right off my rooftop," she added. "And why don't you clean those gutters, while you're up there?"

Sook went back into the house, singing a gospel hymn,

> *"There ain't no grave that can hold my body down.*
> *There ain't no grave*
> *Can hold my body down."*

I laughed, calling out to her, "Sookie, you're a blasphemous creature."

From inside the house, she bellowed,

> *"When I hear that trumpet sound,*
> *I'm gonna rise right out of the ground*
> *Ain't no grave*
> *Can hold my body down."*

I sat on the roof's peak and suspiciously eyed the big, blue sky, watching for any sign of my savior's return.

———◆———

Dixie McAllister's noggin was created for displaying a proper hat. Her bony skull was miniature and compact, and her sculpted, platinum hair was teased high to the heavens, perfectly formed to display a brimmed pillbox or bonnet. Her two miniscule ears sat unusually low on the side of her head, and her long, elegant neck carried her skull with a graceful composure.

"For the likes of me, I ain't sure how Dixie can hear from them little ears of hers," Sookie commented. "They look like two teeny-tiny corn dodgers."

Come Sunday mornings, Mrs. McAllister showcased another new, exquisite headpiece from her vast collection. As she, Carl, and the twins strolled to church service, I waited on the front porch, eager to see the newest creation adorning her head. The vast array of hats sparkled with gems and sequins, piled with lace and netting, silk flowers, ferns, and feathers.

Sookie complained, "Those McAllister's could feed two more sets of fat-headed twins with the money Dixie spends on such wanton luxury."

I replied, "I think Mrs. McAllister looks absolutely divine."

In the late evenings, we'd hear Carl scolding his wife from their open kitchen window: "Woman, you're going to land us in the poor house with all your frivolous spending."

Dixie countered, "Carl, I have my position in the community to uphold. Do you want me to go strolling down Broughton Street in a cotton picker's frock?"

Every week, we overheard the same bickering from their window. Nonetheless, with giddy anticipation, I anxiously awaited Dixie's newest extravagant purchase every Sunday.

All the fine ladies of Digby Street arrived on their front porches, dressed to the nines, leaving for church services. Like on some Paris runway, the elegant women promenaded along the sidewalk in their finery, under the shade of the magnolia trees. I watched in awe from our porch swing while Sook concentrated on her crossword puzzles.

I gushed, "Isabelle Atkinson looks simply stunning today." Admiring Mrs. Birchard's new fur stole, I commented, "Sook, Betsy's chinchilla wrap is absolutely dreamy."

Sook griped, "If I had my druthers, I grab me a lawn hose and spray them all down. I cannot abide such garish pretension."

On the morning of Old Man Curtis Cleveland's funeral, Dixie arrived on her front porch wearing a marvelously massive black headpiece with satin bows and a pile of purple mesh. Tall, lavish, purple plumes of feathers rose from the center of her creation, like some dark crow's nest on a pirate ship.

Sitting on our front porch, Sookie muttered under her breath, "Dixie looks like a gawd-damned fool."

As for me, I thought Mrs. McAllister looked splendid.

She strolled onto her porch and down her front stoop, balancing the glorious vessel atop her tiny skull. Dixie bent low, ever careful that the extravagant dark plumes missed the porch's gutter.

Carl nervously guided his wife to the car and assisted Dixie into the passenger seat of their Cadillac—cautious not to disturb a single feather—and off they went to Old Man Cleveland's funeral service.

Sookie commented, "If poor old Curtis ain't dead yet, the horrific sight of Dixie's gawd-damned hat will certainly finish him off."

It had been just days earlier when Sook actually had predicted old man Cleveland's passing. It seemed as if my aunt Sook could see clean through the walls. She sensed something was gonna happen well before it came to pass. On the clearest day, she'd stand on the front stoop, sniffing the air like a hunting hound, and then declare, "It's fixin' to rain." Within the hour, a perfectly fine blue sky would turn black as night, open wide, and pour water from the heavens.

Sook remarked the week before our postman, Wilmer Crane, had croaked, "Poor Wilmer don't got long on this earth."

On the following Tuesday, sure enough, the news arrived that Mr. Crane had gotten run over by a horse-and-buggy tour on Market Street.

Sitting at the supper table one evening, I asked Sook if she could foretell what the future held for me. She instructed me to switch off all the lights and pull the window blinds closed. Sookie shut her eyes tight and rested her open palms on the kitchen table. I sat near her side, on the edge of the seat. She remained silent for the longest while until a low rumble started rolling in her throat.

Her mouth went slack, and her head dropped back, then violently jerked forward.

I nearly jumped from my skin and reached for her hand. "Sook, are you OK?"

She rocked back and forth in the wooden chair. A low, mournful sound repeated in a rhythmic pattern, like an Indian's beating drum. Finally, she lurched toward me with her eyes still squeezed shut and spoke out loud, "I can see it all as clear as day."

Her eyeballs moved about below her closed lids.

I gulped. "What is it, Sook? What can you see?"

She spoke, "It's all comin' to me."

"What?"

Suddenly, she jumped, frantically reaching into the air in front of her, like she was searching for something lost in the dark. "Yessum, I can see danger."

"Danger?" I asked. A lump lodged in my throat.

"Yessum, I see terrible danger."

"What is it, Sook?" I swallowed hard. "You can tell me. What can you see?"

She mumbled some gibberish and then replied, "Missy, I can see, if you dare pedal your bike anywhere other than Digby Street, you're gonna be in awful danger." Sook opened her eyes and took a casual sip of her coffee.

I shook my head and cracked a grin. "Sook, I ain't never witnessed such cruelty."

———————

I reckon I had imagined that my aunt was going to drive me down to Sears and let me choose my own bike from rows of brand-new shiny bicycles. Instead, I found a rusted-out Schwinn on the front porch one morning. I washed it down with a lawn hose, greased its joints, and changed the two rubber tires.

Sookie walked from the screen door and announced, "I'm plumb tuckered out. I believe I'm gonna sit for a spell."

"Thank you kindly for my bicycle, Sook."

She backed her rump into the rocker. "You ain't wasting no time. You gonna hit the pavement?"

"Yessum." I fought with the rusted chain. "I'm thinkin' now that I got wheels, it's time I start venturing out past the gate."

She grumbled low, like she was arguing with herself.

"I'm thirteen—old enough to go out by myself."

"Poppy, folks out past our gate aren't as kind and gentle as me." I grinned.

"They're spiteful by nature. They'll cut ya rather than look at ya."

"Sookie," I replied, "that ain't true."

"It is, I tell you." She wrang her quaking hands. "Just where are you proposing to go? Remember our agreement?"

"Yessum. I think it's time that I spread my wings."

"Spread your wings? Pffft! Missy, you can spread your wings as far as Digby Street. But if I catch you wanderin' off any further, I'll clip them wings, and you'll be grounded."

"Yes, ma'am." I tried to disguise my beaming grin.

Sook offered a final warning, "If you end up behind bars, I ain't posting your bail."

"OK. It's a deal!"

CHAPTER 6

———◆———

IT DON'T MAKE A LICK of difference where a dusty Greyhound bus
dumps you; all Baptist folk are cut from the same sacred cloth.

Sitting on the wooden pew in the back row of the Savannah
First Baptist Church, I watched the congregation receive their
anointed dosage of God's holy tonic. Except for their fine, tailored
threads, this congregation didn't look no different from the God-
fearing Baptists back in Mountain Home. It seemed to me that it
don't make a lick of difference which pastor preached behind the
pulpit. Their sermons were all the same: the Almighty was returning from heaven, and he was none too pleased with folks' sinful
ways.

The red-faced preacher raised his arms high into the air,
reaching to the heavens, warning that the Lord's rapture was soon
at hand. From his heaving, anguished mouth, tiny spits of saliva
doused the praising congregation sitting along the front pew.

His voice lifted into the rafters. "Brothers and sisters, hold tight
to your babies! Bring them close to your breast—hold them tight!"
Wiping slopping sweat from his forehead with a handkerchief, he
turned up the burners with blazing fire and brimstone.

The Holy Ghost simmered inside the small church. Seasoning
his sermon with alternating hallelujahs and amens, the minister

reminded us, "There is no greater measure of a community's compassion than how they nurture their youngins! To all the fathers in our blessed congregation, the most noble gift you can give your children is to love and respect their mommas! And mothers, heed my words; it's far easier to raise a child strong in faith rather than repair a broken man and woman in the eleventh hour!"

The ladies of the choir waved their hankies in praise.

"Prepare yourselves!" The plump preacher warned the hushed congregation. "Our Lord Savior is returning for his faithful flock. His chariot is quickly approaching." Clutching to both sides of his pulpit, he asked, "Are you ready for our Lord's return? Have you laid a solid foundation for your children?" He pounded a clinched fist, causing the grand old ladies of the congregation to jump from their powdered skin. "Judgement day is growing near." He shouted out into the hushed sanctuary, "Will you be ready to answer our Savior's call?"

The saved among us all rose up rejoicing, "Halleluiah!"

The silent sinners shrunk small in the rows of pews, nervously studying the floor.

The collection plate was passed down the rows of pews, and the ladies choir led us in *What a Friend We Have in Jesus*.

The bouffant beauties fanned themselves with folded papers, while folks sufficiently moved by the spirit blabbered in an unrecognizable tongue. A few seniors who had the good fortune of bad hearing decreased the volume of their hearing aids and napped soundly until the pastor's closing prayer.

The only other soul sitting with me in the back pew was a young lady with pretty brunette pin curls arranged along her forehead. When our eyes met, I returned her nod with a smile.

She was a wisp of a woman with pretty, delicate hands that gripped tightly to her small leather-bound Bible, like it was the last buttered biscuit in the skillet.

After service, as the congregation emptied the pews, she walked up to me.

"Good mornin', young lady. I'm Donita Pendergast," she said. "Are you new to our little congregation?"

"Yes, ma'am. I'm Poppy. Poppy Wainwright."

"It's a pleasure to make your acquaintance, Poppy. Welcome to our church. Did you enjoy Pastor Nance's sermon?"

"Yessum. He don't sweat as much as the preacher back at Mountain Home, but he gets himself just as worked up."

She cracked a grin, and laughed. "Yes, he certainly does."

"I do believe you have the prettiest pin curls I've ever seen," I told her. She touched them nervously like no one had ever complimented her before. "They are splendid." I moved in closer to examine the perfectly placed ringlets. "My wretched hair won't hold a curl. It's straight as straw."

"I think your hair is just lovely," she commented. "Where is Mountain Home? Are you new to Savannah?"

"Yes, ma'am. My grandma recently passed over the river Jordan. I've moved from Arkansas to come stay with my aunt Sookie."

We walked out from the church doors together into the Savannah sun.

"Of course, Miss Sookie Wainwright on Digby." She smiled. "Well, you tell your aunt that Donita Pendergast says hello. Tell her that I owe her a peach pie for her donation to the church bake sale."

"Donation? Ma'am, I'm guessin' you got the wrong Sook Wainwright," I replied.

Donita winked. "There's only one Sookie in Savannah."

I fought my kickstand and mounted my bicycle. "Mrs. Pendergast, it's been a pleasure to make your acquaintance."

"Yes, Poppy Wainwright." She smiled. "I'm certain we will meet again."

"Have yourself a fine day."

I pedaled myself back home and found Sook working a crossword puzzle on the front porch while Annabelle grazed on the grass sprouting in between the cracks of the cobblestone. I wrestled with the front gate latch and pushed my bike up the path.

"Well, look who's returned. I'd assumed the Lord had whisked you away to heaven."

"Church was lovely. Why don't you join me come next Sunday?"

Sook snorted, "No, no! Christians are sneaky, self-righteous bastards. They'll smile at your face, and when your back is turned, they'll plant a stiletto right between your shoulder blades."

"Ain't true, Sook."

"It is, too."

"No, it ain't." I shook my head and linked the lock and chain around the front wheel of my bike. "I met a nice lady named Donita Pendergast at church service today. She sends her regards."

Sook mumbled to herself and then asked, "Donita didn't threaten to bring around any of her dreadful pies, did she? She's always threatening me with those gawd-damned pies of hers."

"Donita seems awful sweet to me," I said and walked up the steps of the porch. I took a seat on the arm of Sookie's chair and considered her crossword puzzle from over her shoulder. "Mrs. Pendergast was much obliged for your donation to the church."

"That's fine," Sook replied, and with the tip of her eraser, she rubbed out a few letters from the squares. "I need a seven-letter word, and the clue is another word for *mucus*." With her quaking hand, Sookie penciled letters into the tiny boxes, S N O U G H T.

"Sookie, *snot* ain't spelled that way, and I don't reckon that's the correct answer—no how."

She cursed to herself and started erasing the letters. "Donita Pendergast is married to one of the Pendergast boys—Rodney.

You'd best stay well clear of him. You won't find a sweeter soul than Donita, but she married herself a lawless hooligan. He's rattlesnake mean. Rosemary and Charles spared the rod with their boys, and now not a one of them is worth a lick. They're all easy on the eyes, but any gal who tied her hopes to one of those ruthless Pendergast boys can expect to be tangled up in misfortune, heartache, and misery."

I asked, "Why do you suppose Donita would marry a man like that?"

"Don't have no clue. It's never made a lick of sense to me. Like your foolish Grandma Lainey, some women yearn for the finest-strutting rooster in the pen, and then one morning, they're gob smacked when they roll over and find a worthless cock under their bed covers." Sookie shook her head.

"That's a cryin' shame," I said. "Donita seems charming. She offered her gratitude and mentioned she's gonna be bringing you a peach pie."

"No, no, no!" Sookie protested, shaking her head. "You tell Donita Pendergast I don't want none of her peach pies." She twisted her nose like she'd detected the sulfur scent of a skunk. "Her pie crusts are as dry as dirt, and the fillings are sickly sweet."

———

The repeating thumping of bouncing, coiled springs on the pavement announced a young visitor's arrival. Before I'd even spotted her noggin bobbing above the top of the front hedge, it was the approaching pogo stick striking against the sidewalk that sounded her entrance.

I was sitting on the porch, perusing the glossy pictures of my *Teen Beat* magazine when I first glimpsed a messy mop of fiery-red curls. Two wide, green eyes appeared over the hedge and then disappeared just as quickly. With another pogo bounce, a round, freckled face with a pug nose arrived back above the hedge, then dropped out of sight again. Her wild head of frizzy, crimson ringlets moved like something untamed and free. Her bouncing course propelled her past our front yard and around the corner, where she vanished out of sight. Within a moment, the thumping of the rusted pogo springs returned for another pass by.

When she was back in front of our gate, she maintained her bouncing and hollered over, "Name's Pearl!"

I stood up on the front stoop. "I'm Poppy. Poppy Wainwright."

She sprang in place for the longest while, surveying Sook's house. Finally, Pearl's bobbing ceased, and she waved me over. Breathless, she pointed to the ramshackle of a house. "They say this here is a haunted house."

"Naw, it ain't haunted, but it's dirty as a grave."

"How many rooms does it have?"

"Not sure. Never counted, but plenty of 'em."

She asked, "You ever played hide-and-seek in there? Must be a million places to hide."

"Nope. Never. My old aunt can barely make it up the stoop, let alone go chasing me through the rooms."

"The McAllister boys sure did a mighty fine job papering this place," Pearl replied.

We both stood admiring the strands of sunbaked tissue.

"Not since the twins toilet-papered the old Methodist Church in Telfair Square last year have I seen such a sight. Timmy and Tommy are infamous around these parts for their handiwork. When they papered the Methodist church, it made the front page of the morning edition," she said. "Why ain't your aunt cleaned up all this tissue paper?

"Aww. She's just bein' spiteful. My aunt has got a nasty mean streak."

"The Methodists had their mess of toilet paper tidied up lickety-split."

"Well, maybe the Methodist congregation aren't as spiteful and stubborn as my old aunt Sook."

Pearl scratched her forehead. "I ain't sure about that. Have you ever met a Methodist?"

I asked, "Wanna come inside?"

Pearl hesitated, considering my invitation. "Sure. I guess so." She dropped her rusted transport on the sidewalk. "They say the old woman who lives here is crazy as a loon."

"Aunt Sookie? I suppose. That could be a true conclusion, but not the kind of crazy that howls at the moon or eats children for supper. Come on in." I grabbed hold of Pearl's hand and pulled her up the porch. "There ain't nothin' to be scared of."

As we walked through the carved front door, Pearl's head tilted up to the humongous bronze-and-crystal chandelier, suspended above the mahogany staircase. "Holy moly!"

"It has three hundred and eighty-eight crystals," I boasted. "One afternoon, I counted each and every one of them."

Pearl cleared her throat. "My mom says that you ain't getting proper schooling, cuz you spend your days practicing voodoo up in here."

"Naw. Aunt Sookie don't believe in such nonsense, be it voodoo or the Pentecost."

Pearl said, "My momma told me your people are old money."

From the top of the banister, Sookie snorted, "Well, your momma is half-right. We're old, dusty money." Sook started her long journey down the staircase. "Now, what's all this ruckus?" Sook hollered.

"Nothin', Sook."

Pearl stepped back, pushing her spine straight against the front door.

I said, "I'm just showing a friend the house."

"This is not some hippie commune where people come and go at their whimsy." My aunt eyed Pearl suspiciously. "Who the hell are you?"

"I'm Pearl Tucker, ma'am."

"Pearl Tucker?" Sookie made it to the bottom of the stairs and shuffled her feet up close to Pearl. Sook took a sniff near to Pearl's head, like a hound dog sniffing the air for a coon. "Are you a communist?"

Pearl stuttered, "Ain't sure, ma'am." She nervously looked to me, frightened that she had the wrong answers to my aunt's inquisition. "I believe my momma will cast her ballot for Mr. Hubert Humphrey."

"Yes! Just as I suspected, a yellah-bellied communist." Sookie pointed her quaking finger directly at Pearl's nose. "Do you smoke the marijuana?"

"No, ma'am."

"I've yet to meet a redhead worth their salt," Sook declared. "It's been my experience that they are intrinsically dishonest creatures. I ain't got no time for a red-haired communist." Sookie dismissed us with a wave of her hand and hobbled on past into the sitting parlor. "Poppy, you're welcome to show her about, but don't let her anywhere near my silver." Sookie adjusted her lumbar pillow and turned on the TV set.

"Take no notice of her," I whispered. "She's so full of bull crap, her eyes are shit brown."

"Hello, Missy, you do understand that I can hear you?" Sook shouted over the volume of *The Guiding Light*. "I'm old, but I ain't deaf."

Pearl asked in a hushed voice, "How old is your aunt?"

Sook hollered out, "Child, I'm so old that when I was in school there weren't no history classes!"

"Come on." I said, pulling Pearl up the stairs to my room. "She's been in a foul mood all mornin'. Leave her be."

At first glance, there wasn't much remarkable about Miss Pearl Tucker—nothing notable nor a hint of special significance. I reckon most folks walk right on by a buried treasure and never think to go digging any deeper. But Pearl Tucker was a red-haired, green-eyed, seventh-grade firecracker. She carried her stout, compact frame like the tiniest bulldozer, and she spoke with an absolute certainty on all matters. She laughed from her belly, and it seemed to me, even on an overcast day, she carried sunshine stuffed in her back pocket.

Pearl lived on the ragged edge of town, out near the paper mills. She, her momma and older sister Nedra Sue resided in a modest place with scarcely enough elbow room to turn about. Mrs. Tucker scratched out a lean living waiting tables at Delia's Diner. Nedra Sue was in her last year of high school and was idolized by her younger sis.

Pearl confided to me that her pa had taken off with an exotic, raven-haired lady who wore plumes of feathers about her neck and swung on a swing, high above a stage, shaking her boobies for men who should've been raised better.

"Before my pop left, Mom would stand at the sink washing dishes, singing like the prettiest songbird," Pearl confessed. "Before dad followed that lady's tail feathers out of town, our house was a mighty fine place."

Pearl told me it didn't matter one wit about her pa's leaving, but she couldn't fool me. I knew that it mattered—it meant the world.

She said her momma had soured like milk in the afternoon sun ever since her pop had ditched them.

"Momma ain't never been the same," Pearl admitted. "She don't wash dishes no more because she don't cook, and I reckon it's been years since I've heard her sing any songs. After Pop left, we had to move from our fine house in town. Bad luck followed us." Pearl confessed, "Good luck don't travel to our place, out past the train tracks."

With just the mention of her momma's name, Pearl's eyes turned to the ground, and she'd go searching for any reason to forget what waited for her back home. But when Pearl spoke of her pop, a smile returned to her freckled face, and a spark would reignite in her wide, green eyes.

Sitting on my bed, Pearl confessed, "Before the feathered chickadee took Pa from us, he would sit me high atop his shoulders and parade me around the house, like I was something that belonged to the sky."

I confessed, "I ain't never had a pa."

"How can that be?"

"Ain't sure. My momma told me that her dancing card was full on the night I was conceived," I said, "I reckon she was too busy dancin' to ever get my pop's name."

"Where's your momma at now?"

"Dunno. The last card was postmarked from Oklahoma City."

Pearl looked at me strangely.

"I was raised by my grandma in Mountain Home, Arkansas. She passed on a few months back."

"Is that how you came to live here with your aunt?" She asked.

"Yessum."

"Did you leave a beau back in Mountain Home?"

"Nope, never had me no boyfriend." I shook my head. "You?"

"No, but I'm hunting me one. My older sister, Nedra Sue, has plenty of boyfriends, one for every night of the week. And I'm fixin' to grab me one of my own." Pearl smiled like she was conjuring up mischief. "Nedra has a head for knowing, and she says finding a beau ain't hard, but the secret is you can't never let him know that you're out lookin'. Nedra says it's just like fishing for a trout. You bait your hook and throw out your line; then you wait and go about your business like you ain't the slightest concerned. Be real patient and still. Then, when that slippery trout starts swimmin' near your bait, you tease him, tempting it, with a slight tug of your line. And just when he takes that first bite, you pull your line as hard as you can muster. The sharp hook pierces the soft under of the trout's lip, and the deed is done!" Pearl grinned. "My sister Nedra says even if he wants to run off into the deep, it don't matter, because he's all yours—hook, line and sinker!" Pearl fell back onto my bed, chuckling. "Poppy, you wanna go do some fishing for a beau with me sometime?" She flashed a wide, toothy grin.

I shrugged my shoulders up to my ears. "I reckon so."

Hopping up from my bed, Pearl giggled, "Well, I know the best watering hole. The boys hang out in Calhoun Square after school! Let's go fishing sometime."

"It's a deal!"

"Well, I gotta run, or my momma's gonna break a broom over my backside. My sis is picking me up." Like a red-haired bullet, Pearl shot out of the room, ricocheted down the stairs, and darted out the front door. From my window, I watched her bounce out of view.

My grandma Lainey once said that God's gifts don't always arrive in boxes wrapped in pretty foiled paper or tied up with ribbons and bows. Grandma told me, "Some of the Lord's finest gifts appear when you're not even looking for them. Sometimes, God's gifts are as quiet as a whisper and arrive on gossamer wings."

The Lord delivered Miss Pearl Tucker too me on a rusted pogo stick.

———◆———

CHAPTER 7

Port Wentworth, Georgia

A HOUSE KNOWS WELL BEFORE it's gonna come crashing to the ground. Its footings quake, and all the walls lean and sway. The ceiling plaster cracks and crumbles, breaking loose and falling to the carpets. The rafters moan low and begin to buckle. Wood planks begin to splinter, and the glass in the windowpanes crack and shatter. The rusty nails bend and snap, and the roof gives way.

Donita Pendergast had seen all the signs. She had felt the rumblings below her feet and heard the quaking of its footings.

When Rodney had bought her the modest little place, out past the dairy on a dead-end gravel road, the meager cottage was supposed to have sheltered the couple from any approaching storm.

The small home had been purchased to be a proper home for Donita and their babies, who were to follow. But Rodney and she had been married for some six years, and each precious baby had been born cold and still. All the while, she had sensed the house's foundations were crumbling. Brick by brick, the newlywed's little house was falling down all around her.

During their first years, Donita confessed, Rodney and she had found happiness inside its rooms. She cooked Rodney's meals in the little kitchen. They watched television together side by side on the sofa in the sitting room, and at the end of the night, Rodney sweetly kissed Donita in their tiny bedroom.

With the help of his father, Rodney opened an auto paint shop on Duffy Street and was off every morning attempting to drum up business. Donita stayed at home and hung sky-blue curtains in the windows and planted marigolds around the mailbox. She played music on the radio and kept a tidy house, growing a fine garden out back. But *happy* never took root in the Pendergast household. No matter how sunny she painted the walls or how appetizing her home cooking was, Donita could hear the awful aching sounds of a house collapsing.

Rodney Pendergast had been a local high school legend: a Friday-night football star. Savannah cheered the hunky quarterback on from the wooden bleachers, watching a favorite Georgian son lead them to the state championship for three years. He was destined to be drafted for Georgia State and pursued by a pro team. But the college-football scouts never appeared, and soon after graduation, Rodney inherited his pop's thirst for gin and willing Southern blondes. The homegrown golden boy lost his shine. The auto-paint shop was failing fast, and when no one was watching, Rodney took to sniffing paint cans in the back of his shop. The aerosol fumes wrecked his noggin and ignited his quick temper. He'd return home jacked up, stumbling through the back-screen door higher than a kite in a March wind and itching for a fight. It was around that time when Donita first felt the trembling of her little house.

Like any self-respecting Southern bride, she told herself that her husband deserved peace and quiet after a hard day's work. A cold beer and a hot supper waited for Rodney every evening. She learned to only speak when spoken to and kept her eyes turned to the floorboards when he was in one of his foul moods.

The first time Rodney slapped her with his open hand, he swore to his trembling bride with tears streaming down his handsome face that it would never happen again. On bended knee, he begged Donita for forgiveness. The second time he landed a punch to her cheek, Donita told herself that she'd never tolerate such cruelty from any man. She packed her case and moved out to her folk's place for two weeks.

It was after their third round, when he left Donita with a black-and-blue face and a bruised ribcage, both she and Rodney understood without a single spoken word passing between them that their little house was built on faulty foundations. It was destined to come tumbling down.

With his high school glory days disappearing in his rearview mirror, Rodney found a dead end around every bend. Although he saw the same devilishly handsome man reflected in the mirror as he shaved his black scruff every morning, Rodney knew he was running out of time. Fate had gifted him with striking dark features and an athletic prowess on the football field. But now, Rodney hadn't the patience or the decency of character to strive for anything that didn't come easy.

On the evening when Sheriff Delany phoned Donita, informing her that Rodney and his bud had been arrested for stealing cars from a competing auto shop and then driving them into Atlanta to sell them, Donita could hear over her head the sound of splintering trusses.

On the phone, the sheriff informed her that her husband was sitting in a jail cell, charged with grand theft auto. As Sheriff Delany spoke, Donita sobbed while gripping the receiver with one hand and balancing herself by holding a kitchen chair with the other—all the walls were swaying, and the mortar was crumbling from the joints of the red bricks.

His folks put up the bail money, and Rodney was released on bond to fight the charges in court. After the sheriff's call that evening, Donita cowered in the corner of her bedroom, clinging to her Bible. The wood beams above her were buckling, and the window glass was shattering. She frantically scoured the pages of her Bible, searching for any single scripture that could save her from a house collapsing down around her.

CHAPTER 8

———◆———

AFTER SEVERAL WEEKS IN SAVANNAH, I knew with absolute certainty that life was going to be different than during my years at Mountain Home. Her manicured gardens and lush city squares were unlike anything I'd ever known. The cobblestone lanes and intricate, scrolling ironwork were like pictures from a storybook.

Mountain Home, Arkansas, was like some penniless relation when compared to Savannah. For years, Grandma had told me stories of my kin in Georgia. I imagined Savannah was like some distant, wealthy relative, who arrived in her fine, tailored clothes and coiffed hair, tied in pretty silk ribbons. Savannah was a cousin brought up in the best schools, with a keen knowledge of proper manners and social graces. She smelled of sweet perfume and blushed pink when told an off-color joke. She curtseyed and said *thank you* and *no thank you*. But Arkansas hadn't the time for such niceties. Arkansas labored long, hard hours and sweat clear through his undershirt. He didn't tip a hat as you strolled by. Instead, he begrudgingly grunted with a slight nod as you passed. Mountain Home was a second cousin once removed, with rusty elbows, who wore frayed overalls and cursed aloud at the supper table. Arkansas was poor country-grown kin, who arrived uninvited and whose ja-lopy leaked motor oil on the front drive. Georgia smiled coyly and batted her long lashes. Arkansas farted and blamed the sleeping mutt.

The single familiarity in Savannah to my life back at Mountain Home was the chiming melody of the local ice cream truck as it paraded through the neighborhoods. The same music-box melody played from its speakers as it approached Digby. But the familiarity to Mountain Home stopped there. Savannah's ice cream truck was painted the bright colors of the rainbow. Back in Arkansas, the rusted jalopy stopped and stalled along the street, but Savannah's ice cream cruiser arrived with foil streamers whipping in the breeze, shiny hubcaps, and polished chrome bumpers.

At the first ringing of its chimes outside the window, Sookie yelled, "Poppy, go fetch me my change purse. Here comes Daryl Turnball, Savannah's most flamboyant sodomite!"

Giddy with excitement, Sookie would wrestle herself out of her rocker when she heard the music-box serenade. Grabbing her walking stick, she would shuffle out to the porch, down the stoop, and toward the front gate.

Mr. Turnball was Savannah's ice cream man. A slight fellow, thin as a rail and no taller than Sook but standing high behind his counter, Mr. Turnball appeared more substantial than his diminished frame would indicate.

After maneuvering the singing truck up to the curb beneath the shade of the magnolias, Daryl would holler out, waving to all the children on Digby Street. Kids came scurrying out from behind screen doors, descending from tree houses, and scampering from back alleys. Excited and with their weekly allowances stuffed deep in their pockets, they perused the sweets from Daryl's metal racks and iced coolers. Like some pied piper, Mr. Turnball teased each child, knowing by heart each kid's favorite fancy. From inside the open window, Daryl displayed a vast assortment of hard candies, suckers, chocolate bars, caramel apples, and puffs of cotton candy. The Piggly Wiggly couldn't compete with Mr. Turnball's selection of sugary delights.

Daryl Turnball was Savannah's mayor of everything sweet and good and yummy. Long whips of red licorice hung from the truck's ceiling, and glossy candy apples sat in perfect rows along his Formica counter. Deep in his aluminum freezers, Daryl stocked icy bullets, rainbow pops, ice cream sandwiches, and fruit-flavored popsicles.

He wore a constant grin at the corners of his mouth, and his blond hair was greased with a razor-clean part. Although he wildly waved to all the ladies of Digby, it seemed to me Sookie was Daryl's favorite curbside customer.

"Good afternoon, Sookie," he called from his ice cream truck. "My gawd, you look particularly beastly in that old terry cloth robe this morning. Jesus, Sook, can't you kill that haggard rag and put it out of its misery?"

The children gathered near his truck, sucked on their Popsicles, and giggled at the twosome's constant bickering.

"Daryl, if you'll hold your acid tongue long enough, I'd like to introduce you to my niece. This here is Poppy."

"Well hello, Miss Poppy." Mr. Turnball, bending low over the counter, smiled. Shaking my hand, he said, "Aren't you a precious little thing. Welcome to Savannah!"

"Thank you, sir."

"Poppy has come to stay with me for a spell." Sook rolled her eyes.

"Well, isn't that special." Daryl patted the top of my head. "You poor child, havin' to live with this ghastly woman. You're fortunate your old aunt has one foot in the grave." He winked and whispered to me over the register, "You won't have to deal with her belly achin' for very long. She's as close to a corpse as you'll ever see stalking the cobblestone streets of Savannah. Perhaps if you stick around long enough after she finally keels over and croaks, you can inherit her piles of money. She's as rich as Midas, ya know?"

"Poppy, don't pay no mind to this Mary's foolish babblings," Sook quipped. "He's as dandy as Disneyland."

"Sookie!" I scolded. "You're terrible!"

"I'm just saying, the man is as fruity as Dixie McAllister's boysenberry jam."

Mr. Turnball dismissed Sook with a wave of his hand. "What can I get you today, Poppy?"

I surveyed his vast selection of sweets.

"This man's prices are downright criminal," Sook warned. "He charges double the Piggly Wiggly's prices. Turnball should be arrested and hauled off to jail."

"I'll take a rainbow snow cone, sir."

"A rainbow snow cone, it is!" The friendly man went about preparing my colored ice.

"And here you go, Poppy."

"Sook, do you want your regular?"

My old Aunt answered with a fart in the affirmative.

Mr. Turnball fanned his hand in front of his nose. "Good Lord, Sook! You are foul. What has crawled up inside your innards and died?"

Sook snickered.

Daryl yelled to all the laughing kids gathered around his truck, "Run, children! Run for your lives. Go seek shelter under your school desks!"

All us kids laughed.

While I suspected Sook enjoyed passing gas in public, it was less a pastime and more of a social experiment, a tactic. My old aunt had a keen sense of the affect her wretched social habits had on the fine, upstanding citizens of Savannah. But Sook was of the belief that if an individual was easily offended by her belching, burping, and backend blasts, then those were the precise individuals whom she'd choose to avoid at all cost.

"The denial of nature is plain foolishness," Sookie stated as a matter-of-fact. "I will not abide those insufferable simpletons."

Aunt Sook utilized her digestion test to gauge the worthiness of a person's character. Most folks failed her test. Thereby, she believed, most were not worthy of her friendship.

"A fart," Sookie declared, "is merely a hiccup in reverse. And I don't see folks getting all bent out of shape when they encounter a blessed hiccup."

Mr. Daryl Turnball was one of the select few who had passed my aunt Sookie's test. The ever-smiling man searched deep into his metal cooler and pulled out a bottle-rocket Popsicle. "Here's your regular, Sook." He handed her the slender frozen treat on a stick.

Mr. Turnball watched on as Sookie tore the Popsicle's paper wrapper like some excited school girl. "Sookie, I must say you're looking especially grotesque today. That hair of yours is a fright."

The old woman ignored the insult, concentrating on sucking the tip of her pop with ferocious intensity.

"Poppy, you understand, your aunt is considered a crazed lunatic around these parts?"

Sook spoke, "Don't listen to a single word he says. He's a grown man who waltzes about town dressed up like Nurse Nightingale."

"Young lady, I'm not sure how you can live with this nasty jackal," Daryl remarked. "Remember to bolt your bedroom door at night, and keep a dagger buried beneath your pillow. She turns into a hairy beast at the stroke of midnight and stalks the streets of Savannah." He grinned broadly and handed me a hard candy. "Now, here's a peppermint stick. Any child who lives with sour Sookie Wainwright deserves a big helping of sweetness."

Anyone could certainly see Sook delighted in Mr. Turnball's quick quips and sassy mouth. Twice a week, she anxiously awaited the chimes of Daryl's approach. After all the neighbor kids had chosen their sweets and disappeared back into their homes, the pair exchanged the tantalizing gossip of the week. They snickered over Dixie's most recent ridiculous hat or Stella Atkinson's most recent lover. Mr. Turnball kept Aunt Sookie abreast on all of Savannah's latest scandals. Long after her Popsicle had been licked down to its bare stick, Sook and Mr. Turnball would still be devouring the most recent tasty morsels of rumor and lurid speculation.

Mr. Turnball leaned out his window, closer to Sookie's listening ear. "Twyla Dandridge went and got herself knocked up by the Patterson boy," Daryl whispered.

Sook gasped, "That child is only sixteen years of age!"

"Yessum. And did you hear, Mr. Rodney Pendergast has been messing around with Debbie Davenport?"

"No!"

"Yes, indeedie." Sook sidled up closer to the truck. Mr. Turnball continued, "I was told by a most reliable source. Rodney was changing the oil on Debbie's Caprice, and then one thing led to another, and he ended up lubricating her right there in her backseat."

"Scandalous! That man has no shame," Sookie exclaimed. "He's an absolute scoundrel."

Mr. Turnball swooned, "But a criminally handsome scoundrel."

"I'm not one to gossip," Sook confided, "but have you heard, Sissy Marston was allegedly carrying the Hudson boy's bastard child?" She glanced in both directions down Digby. "That brazen hussy thought she had finally gone and trapped herself a young man of substantial means."

"No!" Daryl shuddered.

"Yessum. Poor Beatrice Hudson was so brokenhearted about her boy. She was absolutely beside herself in the Piggly Wiggly on Saturday," Sook said. "Beatrice told me she just couldn't bear the thought of that social-climbing Sissy Marston marrying her boy and someday inheriting all Beatrice's late mother's fine china. So, do you know what Beatrice did?"

"No!" Daryl listened on intensely, chewing on a piece of red licorice.

"Poor ole Beatrice was so distraught by the mere thought of that wanton, raven-haired hussy sipping from one of her late momma's tea cups that she took all of that beautiful, delicate china and shattered it right on her kitchen floor. One teacup at a time. Poof! The entire set of china was obliterated, left in tiny pieces on her linoleum!"

"Oh, my! You mean to tell me that lovely serving set with the pink rose buds and gold detailing from Paris has been destroyed?" Daryl grimaced in pain at the mere thought. "Every piece, shattered?"

"Yes, sirree. The entire serving set." Sook nodded her head up and down. "Two days later, it turned out that Sissy wasn't never carrying the boy's child! That silly girl was just bloated up like a summer squash because she'd had too many shakes of salt on her buttered popcorn at the Saturday matinee."

The ice cream man gasped. "No!"

"Yessum. And to make matters even worse, poor ole Beatrice went and sliced her toe on a sliver of one of them broken tea cups. Now Beatrice is laid out in the hospital with three stitches, a nasty infection, and her piggy toe swollen up the size of a walnut—all because Sissy Marston had an extra-large bucket of popcorn during the matinee showing of *Chitty Chitty Bang Bang*."

I suspected Daryl was my aunt Sook's best and only close friend in Savannah. The two laughed the hours away standing on the curb.

One afternoon, as his ice cream truck exited from Digby, I asked Sookie, "Why don't you ever invite Mr. Turnball over for a spot of afternoon tea or for a nice hot supper?"

Sook clutched her chest like she was having a heart palpitation. "Goodness no, child! That man is the most flamboyant homosexual in all of Georgia! How could I seat him at my supper table? What would people think?"

But, I knew that was just old Sookie spouting off. It was crystal clear to anyone who observed the two giggling near his truck that Aunt Sook was mighty fond of Mr. Turnball.

Forecasting what any particular day will bring is just plain foolishness. There ain't no reasoning with fate. Pearl and I were piecing together a jigsaw puzzle on the front porch on a fine afternoon when a coughing yellow taxi pulled up to the curb.

A messy broad in dark sunglasses struggled to exit the back seat. She fought with her purse strap and tripped on the sidewalk. The cab driver, in a dirty T-shirt, hoisted two scuffed pieces of luggage from the trunk. The woman went searching through her leopard-skin pocketbook for loose change. The driver tipped his hat and pulled away from the curb. The lady wrestled with our front gate latch, cursing, "Gawd-damn it!"

I hollered, "You gotta wiggle the thingamajig."

Finally, freeing the latch, she gave it a good hard kick, and the wooden gate swung wide open and came back around, striking her square in the shins. "Mother fucker, you son of a bitch!"

With her oversized black sunglasses and teased bubble of yellow hair, she resembled a bulging-eyed, buzzing bumblebee. Seemingly unbalanced on her scuffed red pumps, she stumbled a crooked line all the way up the cobblestone path to the house. When her heel caught on the front stoop, she was sent tumbling to the ground. She fought back to her feet and cursed again, "Mother fucker, gawd-damned, son of a bitch!" Adjusting her ridiculous corkscrew hat, she grabbed her dented Samsonites. Looking weary, wrinkled, and disheveled, she attempted to regain her composure by tugging at her short, frayed skirt and adjusting her skimpy halter top, which scarcely contained her massive set of knockers.

I said, "Howdy."

"Poppy, wherezourAunSookat?" Her words slurred together like she had a mouth full of cotton. "I need to speak to Sookie." She walked right past Pearl and me, slamming the screen door behind her.

"Holy moly!" Pearl turned to me with wide eyes. "Who is that?

"That's Loretta Jo Nell Wainwright," I replied. "That would be my momma."

"Holy moly! She's got herself some whooper titties."

"Yessum."

"And did you see those high-heeled shoes? How can she walk about in those stilts?"

"Dunno. Miss Loretta says high heels accentuate her long, luxurious legs. Ever since I can recall, she's worn 'em high."

Loretta bellowed from inside the house, "Soooookie! You up there?"

Pearl inquired, "Is your momma OK? Is she gonna be all right?"

"Yup. But I reckon she's already three sheets to the wind."

Pearl asked, "Already drunk on a Saturday morning? Holy moly."

"Pay her no never mind. From all my reading, I've gathered that Miss Loretta stays inebriated to cope with her disillusionment."

"Disillusionment?" Pearl crinkled her pugged nose.

"Yessum, disillusionment. After studying on it, I gather Miss Loretta suffers from disillusionment caused by her abusive pa, my grandfather. He was mean as spit, and my grandma Lainey, her momma, never did nothin' to put a stop to all of his cruelty."

Pearl wore a puzzled expression.

"Yessum. I've read up on it in her AA pamphlets," I said. "Loretta medicates her disillusionment with dope and booze. And she always keeps the company of distasteful men because she ain't got no self-respect."

Bewildered, Pearl shook her head.

"The AA literature says she could eventually come 'round, but she's gotta fall hard first. She's gotta hit bottom. But I figure, as long as there are barstools, Miss Loretta's always got her some seat cushion to catch her fall. I don't suspect she'll ever find her bottom."

Pearl shook her head and said, "That sounds like a big heap of trouble."

"Yessum."

"I'm sure sorry, Poppy, 'bout your momma's ailing condition."

"It ain't nothin'," I replied. "Back in Mountain Home, there was a lady on the front page of the newspaper who went bat-shit crazy. On a cold winter's night, she grabbed her two babies and tossed them into a burning fireplace."

Pearl's mouth went slightly agape.

"Yessum. The woman pitched her precious bawling babies in the fire like a cord of cedar."

"Why'd she go off and do that?"

"Dunno. But when the town officials arrived, she was sipping herself a cup of hibiscus tea and stoking the blazing fire. I reckon it was then I decided to stop my griping about Miss Loretta."

From inside the house, Loretta hollered, "There's a gawd-damned goat drinkin' from the toilet bowl!"

I turned to Pearl. "Well, I'd best get goin'."

Loretta's room was the third door on the left. I followed her as she dragged her cases up the stairs and down the long hall. She pulled back the lace curtains and fought open the window, allowing the slightest breeze to filter in. I lay across her bed with my elbows bent and my chin resting in the palms of my hands.

I asked, "Where ya been off to, Miss Loretta?"

"Oh, baby, where hasn't your momma been? Let me see. I was in Memphis for a spell and then Tulsa." She unfastened her scuffed pumps and kicked each one free from her feet. "I met a lovely boy in Atlanta and spent a few months in Richmond." Unbuttoning her dress, Loretta let it drop to a puddle on the floor at her feet. She walked about the room in her lace bra and panties. "Richmond has flies the size of gawd-damned para-keets." Blotting her face with a moist cloth, she complained, "Sweet Jesus, I don't believe Savannah could be any more gawd-damned hot." She wiped a damp cloth under her pits and below each boob, complaining, "It's like you're swimmin' in a gawd-damned swamp."

Miss Loretta went about unpacking her cases, taking each garment from the Samsonites and placing them inside the bureau drawers. Arranging her brushes, powders, creams, lotions, and potions on the side table, she lined them up like the makeup counter at Levy's. She placed her raggedy hats atop the four posters of the carved bed and hung her stockings over the footboard.

I asked, "What about your fella in Houston?"

"That cowboy was the kind of stupid that hurts. He couldn't pour piss from his boot without instructions written on its heel." Crossing the room, Loretta caught a glimpse of her rump's reflection in the mirror. Inspecting her image, she sighed, "Oh, Lordy, look at me, I've blown up like a fat tick on a hound dog." She adjusted her bra strap. "I look like a big tub of lard."

"Ain't true, Loretta," I said. "You look plenty fine to me."

Anytime Miss Loretta was doing the dope, she'd come back home just a walking skeleton, nothing but skin and bones. I was always relieved to see her arrive carrying a few extra pounds, a sure sign she was winning her battle with the dope. I'd exhale and thank the good Lord if I detected ten extra pounds on her frame, like my life depended on it.

"You're so sweet, baby doll, but the mirror don't lie." She moved in for a closer examination. "And look at these dark rings under my eyes. It looks like I got sucker punched by a prized fighter. And this awful ratted hair of mine resembles a tumblin' tumbleweed."

Reaching for her teasing comb, she stuck the end of it into her pile of sprayed, ratted hair, trying to lift it. "Good Lord! It's all catawampus!" She said. With both hands, she carefully went about shifting the mass of frozen hair like she was trying to balance a bowling ball on the head of a pin. "Well, shit! I give up."

Inside Loretta's forearms were bruises lined with healing needle pricks the size of skeeter bites. Her rusty elbows and knees were in need of a good scrubbing. Her bare feet appeared as if she'd been walking a long dirt road.

"Never grow old, Poppy. You hear what I'm sayin'?" She turned to me with weary eyes. "Never grow old."

"Yes, ma'am."

"Stay young and lovely as long as you can." Miss Loretta took a seat by me on the edge of the bed. "Beauty is the single thing we gals have that sets us apart." She peered deep into my eyes, like she was sharing the only truth she knew. "Men have power and money and pride. But us Southern women gotta hold tight to our beauty and our figures, or life will slip through our fingers like the tiniest grains of sand. You wake up one morning, and you got bags under your eyes, and your knockers have slipped deeper south." She grinned and shimmied her big titties. Laughing, she fell back onto the bed, beside me. "Men age like a fine red wine, but we women age like buttermilk left in the afternoon sun."

For as long as I could recall, men were hypnotized by Miss Loretta's bountiful bosoms. Passing fellas gazed longingly at her knockers like they were the first set they'd ever seen. Her massive pair were prized and praised among the admiring men back in Mountain Home. She bathed, moisturized, powdered, and polished her two bulbous trophies every day before venturing out into the public. Obliging local fellas would accommodate her every request—a complimentary oil change, a free tire rotation, or unlimited soda pops at the picture show. Even my late Grandma Lainey admitted she'd consider getting herself a pair of knockers if it got her a discount with Kirby, our local plumber.

"Has your Aunt Sookie been good to you?"

"Yes, ma'am."

"Very good. Well, you make sure to listen to her, and remember your manners. Say *thank you* and *no thank you*."

I said, "I miss my Lainey."

"Aww, baby." Loretta took my hand and kissed it, then held it to her cheek like something cherished. "I bet you do. Your grandma is in a far better place. Lord knows that old woman has been knocking on heaven's door for a long, long time. She always had one foot in the grave. The Almighty must have finally said *fuck it* and let her stroll through the pearly gates. She's probably up there right this very minute, instructing the good Lord how to best arrange the sun, the moon, and the stars."

"Loretta, I found her sittin' upright in her rocker on the front porch."

"What, child?"

"Grandma Lainey was sittin' upright with her eyes open wide, lookin' out to the yard, like she was enjoyin' the fine day parading right before her."

"I'm so sorry, baby." Loretta gently ran her fingertips along my forearm.

"No, Miss Loretta. I sat right at her side for the longest while."

"Aww, that's so sweet."

"No. I sat there and talked to grandma for the better part of an hour without the slightest knowin' that she'd passed over to the other side."

Loretta tilted her head slightly and thought on it. "Oh, I see. Well, Poppy, I ain't a bit surprised. Frankly, it's understandable. Your grandma was always a bit of a bore. God bless her soul. She was a woman of few words, and most of them words could put a hummingbird sound to sleep."

"I felt awful. It wasn't until a house fly buzzed directly into grandma's open mouth did I realize she had passed on to glory."

Loretta cleared her throat. "I see." She ran her hand over the floral quilted bedspread. "Poppy, when I was your age, your Grandma Lainey sent me up here from Mountain Home to visit Sookie. I don't think a single thing has change. Just look at these awful bed linens and those pitiful paper flowers. And is that old woman still wearing that gawd-damned bed robe?"

I giggled, "Yessum."

"Well, that's disgustin'. I'm certain critters are burrowing deep inside her pockets. I think we should take ourselves to Montgomery Wards and buy her a new one. What do you say?"

"Absolutely not!" Sook objected, standing in the open doorway. "I see no good reason for lavish spending. Why squander a hard-earned dollar when this dressing robe is perfectly adequate?" She pulled the terrycloth sash, cinching it a bit tighter around her bloated belly.

Loretta laughed, "Sookie, that ragged thang is thread bare, and you look like you've just battled a muddy hurricane. It's well past time that it's tossed in the bin."

"Nonsense." She dismissed Loretta's suggestion with a wave of her hand. "So, is it your intention to stay for a spell?"

Loretta nodded her head. "Just for the shortest spell, Sook, until I can get my feet under me."

Sook remarked, "Poppy, looking at Miss Loretta standing here with her udders exposed to all of Savannah reminds me that the ice cream truck should be comin' along anytime now. Go fetch me my change purse."

"No ma'am," I protested, remaining on the bed, planted next to Miss Loretta.

Sook looked at me hard. "That wasn't a question, child."

Loretta gave my arm a push. "Run along, Poppy, like your Aunt Sook says."

I walked from the room but stopped short in the hall and listened on.

"Loretta, I won't have you startin' no trouble here." Sook's tone took a harsh turn. "This ain't Mountain Home, and I don't have a soft underside like that fool-hearted Lainey. The first time I start missing money from my change purse or any of my silver goes missing, you'll be booted out on the street so fast you won't know what happened. You understand me?"

The room went quiet. I pressed my ear closer to the door and could hear Loretta's soft sniffles.

"Sook, I need a break. I need to find my footing. It's been so hard for so long. I promise I'll be as quiet as a church mouse. You won't even know I'm here."

"Loretta, you've never done right by that child, and I won't have you comin' into town messing with a young soul who's already battling such peculiarities. I just won't have it!"

"Sook, all I need is a single chance to prove I'm on the straight and narrow. I swear, I'm clean as a whistle." She held her forearms out in front of Sook, "Look, I'm on the mend. Three full weeks, clean as a whistle. Please, just one blessed chance."

"Sookie, I say, we give her a chance." I poked my head inside the open door. "I promise I'll keep a watchful eye on her." I walked over and sat down at Loretta's side. "If she steps out of line, Sook, I'll come running. You'll be the first to know."

Arms crossed tight, Sook grumbled low.

Miss Loretta pulled me into her chest, my nose planted directly in between her two heaving bosoms. They smelled like sweat and the sweetest perfume.

"Loretta, you can't come spinnin' into Savannah like a tornado and think I'll permit your foolishness."

"Sookie, please," I said. "Pretty please."

Loretta searched Sook's eyes for a teaspoon of compassion. "I'm beggin' you, Sook." She pulled me even closer and pleaded, "Savannah was the only place I knew to run. I just had to come find my precious little baby boy." Loretta squeezed me tighter. "Sookie, please, don't keep me away from my baby boy."

CHAPTER 9

———————

THERE AIN'T NO USE EXPLAINING something that don't make a lick of sense: a soul being birthed into a world without the knowing of where it belongs. I suppose it will remain a mystery and lost to me for all of my days—a reckoning that lies just out of my understanding, like a hushed whisper too quiet to be heard.

Grandma Lainey loved me in her way—as much as a person can love my sort. Being a God-fearing Christian, Grandma did her damnedest to grasp a hold of my predicament. Gripping my hand, she kept me near her side, protecting me from any mean-spirited folks back at Mountain Home.

Delivering me to the front steps of our Baptist Church, she requested for our preacher to exorcise my perversion. Old Pastor Barnett kneeled at my side and placed his palms over my eyes. He prayed with a vengeance for my soul's salvation, reaching for the sky, like Jesus was handing him down my redemption from the heavens. Suddenly, the pastor's raging fire burned down to a silent ember. He mournfully mumbled through a long prayer while my grandma Lainey stood by, bawling sorrowful tears. The preacher cupped my chin in his hand, bringing my eyes to his, and asked, "Samuel, are you are healed? Are you redeemed in the blood of our Lord savior?"

Being reared to be a respectful, considerate, and polite young boy, I nodded my head up and down.

He shouted out, "Hallelujah!" like the final number on his bingo card had been announced over the loud speaker.

Later, driving back to the house, Grandma Lainey adjusted her rear mirror to view me, sitting in the back seat. With concerned eyes, she asked, "Samuel, do you think it stuck? Do you think you're healed?"

I shook my head in the negative. "Nope. I'm suspecting Pastor Barnett didn't pray on me with enough conviction to fix my broken parts."

It wasn't long after our pastor's failed attempt on a sweltering Sunday afternoon in a room behind the pulpit that Grandma Lainey asked the church ladies to pray for the healing of my abomination. The women gathered around, shedding anointed tears, and laid their hands on me. With their arms stretched high to the heavens, they praised Jesus and called on the Almighty to cast out my dress demon. I sat small on the folding chair while the church ladies whipped themselves into a fitful fury. Even though the summer sun was sizzling and the Holy Ghost was cooking inside the little back room, I reckon my pie was done baked. While the ladies were praying, I was itching to change from my britches and into my cool, cotton summer dress waiting for me back at home.

After Jesus couldn't unravel my messy, tangled affair, a worried Grandma Lainey whisked me away to Little Rock to visit with a fine fella once a week.

Doctor Penn wore black-rimmed glasses and a pinstriped suit. He sat across from me, behind a big oak desk, and scribbled serious notes on a pad of paper.

During those weekly sittings, I sat directly in front of the fellow while he gazed into my eyes like he was looking for a speck that he couldn't find. For a solid hour, the nice man asked me a string of questions.

"Samuel, can you tell me why you feel it necessary to wear these particular clothes?"

I shrugged my shoulders up to my ears. "Dunno."

"Son, can you expand on this matter any further?"

"Ain't sure I understand what you're askin'." I surveyed his office, with its cherry-paneled walls and rows and rows of thick books.

He cleared his throat. "Samuel, you've chosen to come here to meet me today in a girl's dress. Most young boys wouldn't desire to wear such attire. I'm sure you are aware that your grandmother is very concerned about this peculiar predicament."

"Yessum," I answered. "She's none too pleased. I don't think she's slept a wink in a month of Sundays."

"Do you think wearing this pink dress is the appropriate attire?"

"No, sir. I wanted to wear my yellow one for you, but it was in the dirty-clothes hamper."

The dark-haired man bit down on the end of his pencil, chewing it like he'd skipped lunch.

"The yellow dress is my favorite," I confessed. "It has delicate white lace around the collar and small pearl buttons all the way down the back. If you'd like I can wear it for you next week."

His face turned the color of a ripe pomegranate. "That won't be necessary, but thank you." He gathered himself. "Did your grandmother purchase you the pretty yellow dress?"

"Oh, no. She'd never do that. Miss Loretta bought them all for me. When she comes to town she'll take me shopping. But, Grandma Lainey always hides my clothes. Twice, I found them buried in the bottom of the garbage bin out back."

"I see." The doctor raised his eyebrow as if he'd discovered the missing word from a crossword puzzle.

"When was the first time you decided you looked best in girls' clothing?" He asked.

"I was two months from turning eight years old. Loretta had come home to me. Her beau from Porterville had promised to marry her, but he got cold feet and ended up leavin' Loretta in a motel outside of Fresno. She was mighty upset and got herself awfully messed up." I added, "Doctor Penn, you'd best know my momma is a dope fiend."

He nodded his head. "Yes, Samuel. I understand that is the case."

"The best I can recall, Grandma Lainey sent Miss Loretta enough money for a bus ticket back to Mountain Home. And one afternoon, me and Loretta were in her bedroom. She was getting all gussied up to go out to the honkytonks for the night. We were laughing and carrying on. Just playing dress up. Bein' silly. She pulled me over to her side, lined my lips with her colored stick, and then powdered my cheeks with a brush. In the mirror she fixed my hair with a lavender ribbon, pulled one of her blouses over my head, and slipped a pair of her cha-cha heels on my feet. Then Loretta took me down the stairs and paraded me in front of Grandma Lainey. Poor ole Lainey pitched a fit and demanded, 'Loretta, you take that boy upstairs and wash that makeup off his face, right this very moment!'

"Miss Loretta laughed at Grandma, like she always does, and paid her no never mind.

"Lainey grabbed me by the arm and with a washcloth scrubbed my face clean. But it was too late. It could never really be washed off," I said. "After that day, I just knew."

"You knew what, Samuel?" He inquired.

"I dunno, sir. I just knew that it felt right," I replied. "The same way I feel when Grandma plays a hymn on her upright piano or the way the sun shines warm on my face. I understood that it was as it should be."

"Was it during this same period of time when you decided to let your hair grow out?"

"Yes, sir," I answered. "And that didn't sit well with my grandma Lainey. I woke one night to find her tiptoein' into my room, like a cat burglar with a pair of her scissors."

"I told her, there in the dark, 'Grandma, you can shave my head smooth as a bowling ball, but you can't cut the girl from me.'"

"And how did she respond? Samuel, what did your grandma Lainey say?"

"Nothin' at all. Grandma just stood there for the longest while, quiet as a ghost. And then, she left and closed the door behind her. After that night, I slept with a stocking cap."

"Are you frightened of being discovered by other folks? Or other little children?"

"Doc, after those older boys busted me up, Lainey pulled me from school. Taught me from books, sitting at our kitchen table. I've always been a runt, so most folks have never known no better."

"Are you fine with being mistaken for a little girl?"

I looked at him straight. "Doctor Penn, I *am* a little girl."

After my visits with the kindly doctor in the pinstriped suit, Grandma Lainey would treat me to a corn dog and a root beer at the A&W. When we had gobbled up our lunch, before we'd leave Little Rock for Mountain Home, Lainey and I would stroll, hand in hand, along the shops on Main Street in Little Rock.

One afternoon, Grandma asked, "Samuel, did you learn anything from Doctor Penn today?"

"Yes, ma'am."

"And what did you learn?"

"Doc Penn is also mighty partial to yellow."

Grandma Lainey went pale and hurriedly pulled me along the sidewalk. "It's time we get on back to Mountain Home," she replied.

"I'm gonna wear my yellow dress next week for the doc. I'd hate to disappoint him."

"Heavens to Betsy, child, these times are vexing enough without you flaunting such blatant sin right out in public."

"I'm sorry, Grandma."

It was a fine sunny day as we made our way back to Grandma's Ford. The sun reflected in the glass of all the shops along Main Street. In the brightest pink letters, above the tall glass windows of one of the fashionable boutiques, a sign read: The Poppy Seed. Through the window glass, I could see all the racks of pretty skirts, blouses, and dresses displayed in the store front.

"Grandma?"

"Yes, Samuel."

"I ain't Samuel no more," I announced. "My name is Poppy. Poppy Wainwright."

"Goodness gracious. Don't be ridiculous, child." Tugging my arm down Main Street, Grandma insisted. "Your name is Samuel Lee. You are named after your late grandpa, God rest his soul."

"No, ma'am, it ain't."

"Yes, it is."

"No, it ain't. It's Poppy."

Lainey huffed and puffed, pulling me down the sidewalk.

"Grandma?"

She sighed, "Yes, child."

"Next week, can we go shopping in that store?" I pointed behind me to The Poppy Seed.

"Absolutely not!" She snapped." We won't never be returning to Little Rock ever again!"

Grandma once told me that redemption was only a single, solitary prayer away. She said, "The black, burnt souls of the unforgiven can be made light when redeemed in his blood."

I reckon my grandma Lainey believed my soul was polished as black as my Sunday church shoes. No matter—she loved me just the same.

CHAPTER 10

———◆———

WALKING A STRAIGHT LINE WAS a trying task for old Sookie. The tremors that had wrecked her bones caused her unsteady feet to shuffle on a wayward path. Sook advanced at a snail's pace. A simple stroll down Digby was an arduous expedition.

The short walk to the Piggly Wiggly would begin at the front gate, but our journey inevitably included visits to both sides of the street. With her eyes fixed to the ground, Sookie watched the passing pavement and paid no never mind to her forward trajectory. She kept her pace up, but her shuffling always veered to the right and then back to the left, heading far off course until she'd realize that we had drifted, Sook would then overcorrect, and off we'd go zigzagging in the other direction. Relying on her walking stick, she'd grab a firm hold of my arm when necessary.

Behind the steering wheel of Sook's big maroon Buick was an entirely different matter. Aunt Sook drove right down the dead center of any street. It seemed to me that she was of the belief that all roads, bi-ways, and boulevards of Savannah were paved solely for her alone. No painted centerline could fence in Sook and her big Buick. Instead, she opted to cruise down the middle of any street. I'd grip to the side panel with white knuckles, silently praying for God's safe passage through Savannah. All the while, ignoring the honking and cursing from the passing cars, Sookie concentrated on the task at hand.

When Sook agreed to deliver me to Pearl's place near Dixie's Sugar Mill, I was over the moon. I couldn't contain the sheer joy of being released out into the big wide world.

Surviving the harrowing journey in her Buick, God delivered me safely to the curb outside of Pearl's place.

"Child, I ain't sure about this." She nervously surveyed the meager house with a barking yellow dog behind the chain link fence. "I don't know nothin' about these folks. Don't look like they got a pot to piss in. Could be cold-blooded killers for all we know. And if they discover your peculiarities, there could be a heap of trouble."

"No need to fret, Sook. It's just Pearl."

"Exactly!" Sook hollered over the spitting exhaust of the Buick's engine. "Redheads are the bane of civilization. Every calamity and catastrophe throughout history can be traced back to a deviant redhead."

"Oh, Sookie, that's foolishness!" I slammed the car's door shut and waved to her disappearing taillights.

Pearl greeted me at the door with a toothy grin. Inside, the little house was sparsely furnished with a dingy upholstered couch and recliner. Paper blinds hung from the windows. When Pearl introduced me to her momma, Mrs. Tucker was wiping off the kitchen counter and didn't take the time to lift her eyes to greet me. She was a thin, haggard woman with pockmarked skin and gray hairs weaving through her lopsided, black bouffant. It seemed to me that Mrs. Tucker must have woken on the wrong side of the bed and then resolved from that day on to greet every day with a scowl.

"You children don't make a mess in this house. I've been cleaning all afternoon," she chided Pearl. "I swear, you and your sister are filthy pigs. You weren't raised in a barn. I better not come home from work and have to do it all again."

"We won't, Momma. I promise," Pearl replied. "Poppy and I are heading out. Nedra is drivin' us to the park."

Mrs. Tucker shrugged her slight shoulders and walked from the kitchen.

When we entered Pearl's older sister's room, the record player wailed Jefferson Airplane through its speakers. Concert posters were taped to every wall. The Grateful Dead, Joan Baez, The Who, Arlo Guthrie, and Janis Joplin papered every inch of her small chamber. Incense burned, creating a thin, dancing trail of blue smoke that dissipated into the ceiling. An assortment of candles was lit on her dresser, next to mason jars full of seashells.

Sitting on her bed, Miss Nedra Sue Tucker was a wondrous sight, almost seventeen years old, with a crop of freckles that covered her face and bare shoulders. Crowned with the same mass of glorious red mop top as Pearl's, Nedra braided several strands about her face and adorned them with strings of random wood and plastic beads. When Nedra shook her head, the braids rattled like a baby's toy. She wore an oversized tie-dye T-shirt, and frayed jeans hugged her hips and were patched at the knees. Her dirty bare feet had toes painted the glossy color of a candy apple, and each one of her fingers were stacked with an assortment of rings, bejeweled with glass rubies, plastic opals, and rhinestone diamonds. Nedra's skinny frame appeared to be existing on the nourishment of the single cigarette that dangled dangerously loose from her lips.

When we walked into the room, Pearl jumped on the bed next to her older sister. Hollering over the music, Pearl called out, "Nedra Sue, this here is my friend, Poppy."

With her eyes shut tight, Nedra was lost in her music. She rocked her head to the pulsing rhythm, and with her hands, she kept time, beating invisible drums with imaginary drumsticks. I glanced over at Pearl, who shrugged her shoulders up to her ears. When the singer bellowed his final note, Nedra arched her back, tilted her head, and wailed along with the singer. She then raised her hands high into the air like the pastor when the spirit moved deep in his soul.

Pearl waved her arms in attempt to bring her older sister back from her trance. She hollered again, "Nedra, this here is Poppy."

Nedra Sue grinned and flashed me a peace sign.

"Howdy. I'm Poppy. Poppy Wainwright."

The lanky teen sat cross-legged on the bed. Her sleepy almond-shaped eyes had long black lashes resembling spider's legs. She took a deep drag off her ciggy and blew a great plume of gray smoke into the air.

"My sis believes music can heal the world," Pearl announced. "Nedra believes in free love and the power of the people."

"What people?" I asked.

"Don't know." Pearl shrugged her shoulders again.

Nedra shut off her phonograph. "Hey, squirt. So, I'm chauffeuring you two numbskulls to Calhoun Square?

"Yessum," Pearl replied.

"Cool." Nedra slid the record into the paper sleeve.

"Are you a hippy?" I asked.

"Kid, I don't believe in labels," she replied. "When common folks are scared and ain't willing to look any deeper, they'll stick a label on it."

I looked back over to Pearl, who again shrugged her shoulders up to her ears.

"There is a revolution comin' soon," Nedra Sue announced. "When the bureaucracy is overthrown, we won't put labels on what we are frightened of. I'm heading to San Francisco to join the uprising and fight *the man.*"

I hadn't a single clue what she was speaking of, but I knew with absolute certainty, I wanted to join any alliance in which Miss Nedra Sue Tucker was a member.

Pearl added, "My sister is a flower child, and she believes you gotta let your freak flag fly."

"Right on, little sis. Spoken like a true revolutionary!" Nedra slapped the open palm of her little sister's small hand. "Squirt, when you're old enough, I want you to ditch this lame town and hop on the first Greyhound to come join me, fighting for the cause in California."

Pearl had already confided that her older sister was just biding her time in Savannah, staying locked behind her bedroom door until the day she would pack up her Volkswagen bug and escape to Northern California.

Pearl reported that the louder Mrs. Tucker hollered from the other side of Nedra's locked door, the higher the volume was turned up on Nedra's phonograph player. Jimmy Hendrix's guitar wailed well above Mrs. Tucker's rage. Free-spirited Nedra would drown out her momma's fury and paid her no never mind.

"Pearl, haul your tail in here right this minute!" Mrs. Tucker yelled from the kitchen.

"Comin', Momma." Pearl ran from the room. "I'm comin'."

Nedra and I could hear Mrs. Tucker's rant in the kitchen.

"Pearl, look what came in the post. Did you see this? Can you explain your report card? Your math teacher says you're failing your class."

"It's so hard, Momma. It don't make a lick of sense to me."

"You're as stupid as your father. He was as dumb as a pile of rocks, and look where that got him. I won't have it! You hear me?"

"Yes, ma'am."

"If these grades aren't improved, you'll get your ass whipped until it bleeds. You understand me?" Mrs. Tucker threatened.

"Yes, ma'am," she cowered.

"Pearl Tucker, you're a complete embarrassment. You're as worthless as your daddy."

The sound of soft sniffles filtered from the kitchen.

Nedra called out, "Momma, lay off!"

"Young lady, shut your gawd-damned mouth!" Mrs. Tucker hollered back. "You ain't too big for me to come in there and slap your mouth!"

Nedra Sue hopped from her bed, dropped her ciggy to the wood floor, and squished it under the sole of her leather sandal. She grabbed her purse from the dresser and motioned for me to follow her. We walked down the narrow hall and into the kitchen.

Pearl stood with her back against the fridge. Her little shoulders shook uncontrollably as she tried to restrain a sobbing fit. Her red eyes met mine and then quickly turned to the ground.

"Hey squirt, let's get outta here." Nedra reached for her little sister, but Mrs. Tucker pulled her youngest back over to her side.

"And where do you think you're goin'?"

"I'm takin' the girls to the park."

Pearl kept her eyes fixed to the floor.

"The hell you are. This child is failing her math class." Mrs. Tucker jerked at the sleeve of Pearl's cotton dress.

"I'm taking her and Poppy to Calhoun Square."

"You ain't doin' no such thing." Mrs. Tucker slapped her hand onto the counter, and Pearl winced like a dog that's always waiting for a hard kick from a familiar boot. "This is my gawd-damned house, and only I say who goes where and when."

Nedra rolled her eyes. "Leave her be. You ain't gotta be such a bitch."

Mrs. Tucker gasped, "Just who do you think you're talking to with that gutter mouth?"

The two stood, nose to nose, playing a dangerous game of chicken.

I remained motionless, holding my breath behind the kitchen table as they fought a battle without saying so much as a single word. Mrs. Tucker held Nedra's unflinching stare for the longest while, until, with one blink, Mrs. Tucker seemed to concede victory in the test of wills with her oldest daughter.

"Come on, Pearl. Let's get outta here," Nedra said, never breaking away from her mother's hard gaze.

Pearl stood still as a stone, uncertain if she should walk or remain at her momma's side.

"Let's go, squirt."

When Pearl took the first step toward Nedra, I exhaled.

"Come on," Nedra called. "Poppy, go get in the car."

Mrs. Tucker warned, "Nedra Sue, if you think this matter is put to rest, I promise you, this discussion will continue on later this evening."

Nedra snickered, shaking her head. She flashed her mother a peace sign. "Later."

Pearl muttered not a word and walked to the refrigerator, opening the door and pulling out a brown paper bag.

"What the hell is that?" Mrs. Tucker asked.

"It's a sack lunch for Poppy and me."

"I don't work my ass off all week to feed every hungry orphan in Georgia."

"No, ma'am," Pearl said and nodded.

"Oh, Momma, give it a rest." Nedra pulled Pearl to her side and ushered her through the screen door.

We sped away from the little house, Mrs. Tucker barking at the car from behind the chain link fence, like their old yellow dog.

Little Pearl remained quiet all the way to the park, while Nedra's orange Volkswagen Beetle buzzed along Taylor Street. I sat in the back seat, admiring the two sisters' unruly mass of ginger locks. Strings of beads hung from the rearview mirror, and the radio played the Mamas and the Papas. The car's vinyl seats had been painted with stripes of lavender and pink, and the back windshield was plastered with bumper stickers. I was worried sick about silent Pearl in the front seat. She sat solemn, shoulders dropped low.

When Nedra pulled up to the curb on Abercorn Street in front of the park, she turned down the volume of her radio and placed her hand on her younger sister's knee. "Are you gonna be OK, squirt?"

Pearl kept her watery eyes fixed, looking down at the floorboard.

"Momma's just messed up. Don't you pay her no mind." Nedra lit herself a cigarette. "You see, Mom has fallen victim to society's definition of a woman. It's all bogus propaganda that tells us women that we gotta keep a tidy house and cook a fine supper for our man, or we ain't a *real* woman." Nedra's cigarette smoke clouded the interiors of the small Volkswagen. "Squirt, until Mom frees herself from the archaic indoctrination that's keeping her chained to her stove, she's always gonna be bummed out. You dig? She's just a cog in *the man's* wheel."

I listened on, awestruck, hanging to Nedra's every word.

"You understand me, Pearl?" Nedra brushed a single stray hair from her little sister's wet eyes.

"Yessum," Pearl sniffled. "I understand."

Smothering in her haze of cigarette smoke, I swatted the plumes of gray, trying to clear the polluted air from the back seat, and remained spell bound by the wisdom from Nedra's lips. I didn't want to miss a single syllable of Nedra Sue's insight. I hadn't the slightest notion what system she spoke of, but I gathered a rebellion was heading to Savannah, and I needed to arm myself.

I asked her, "In this revolution, will we need guns and grenades and such?"

"Poppy, we will take up arms, but peace will be our rifles, and love will be our bullets." Nedra assured her little sister, "After the revolution, you won't have to live under the tyranny of Momma's backward, Republican hierarchy. You dig?"

Pearl mustered a grin. "Yessum."

"Groovy." Nedra rubbed the top of Pearl's head. "I'll pick you two up in a couple hours."

Persuaded by Nedra's conviction, I made a vow, right there in her Beetle's backseat, to free myself from the chains that apparently were holding me captive and to join Nedra's fight against the oppression.

Pearl and I climbed from the car and started into the park. We walked, shoulder to shoulder, along the cobblestone pathway.

"Your momma was really mad."

"Aww, she's just belly achin'," Pearl replied.

But it seemed to me Mrs. Tucker was intent on dousing the bright spark that reflected in Pearl's eyes. "It don't seem right," I said. "Your momma ought not be so hateful to her own offspring."

Pearl stopped on a dime and pivoted. "If Pop hadn't gone and left, I reckon Momma wouldn't have such vile poison runnin' through her veins. Poppy, she ain't got nobody. And ain't no stranger gonna stand around and listen to all her fussin'." Pearl kneeled and tied the laces of one of her sneakers. "She ain't always been like this. We once were a happy lot - - Momma, Pops, Nedra and me. He was always up to mischief. Pop came home from work one evenin' and there, peekin' from his shirt sleeve was just a hint of a lavender handkerchief. When momma gave the hanky a tug, out from his cuff came a long line of silk handkerchiefs, one after the next - - pink, purple, gold and scarlet red, like they was hangin' on a clothes line. They were so pretty, Poppy." Pearl smiled. "He surprised momma one night by pulling a long-stem velvety rose out from his shirt sleeve. Mom blushed redder than the rosebud. At the supper table, Pop waved his hands and said, 'Abracadabra', and made a white-winged dove appear from inside his work hat." Looking up to me, Pearl sheltered her eyes from the sun with her hand. "Poppy, I just know that one fine mornin' I'm gonna wake up and my momma will believe in magic again. But for now, she's got some heavy burdens, and I got me some big shoulders. I will carry 'em for her." Pearl grinned and pointed to the swing sets off in the distance. "I'll beat ya to the swings!"

We darted across the September's yellowing grass.

In the park, a circle of boys hunched low, shooting a game of marbles, while some older boys sat shirtless atop the monkey bars, smoking ciggies. Sitting in the shade of an oak tree, I recognized several girls from the bus stop. Pretty Constance White sat in the center, circled by her giggling friends.

As Pearl and I approached, the boys' heads turned from their marble match. They eyed me up and down. Two girls already on the swings skid their sandals in the dirt, bringing their swings to a stop.

"Hey, Tallulah." Pearl waved.

"Mornin', Pearl." A skinny blonde with knobby knees and cat-eyed spectacles that magnified her eyeballs to the size of two silver dollars called out, frantically waving her tiny hands. "Come on over here, Pearl. Swing by me."

Pearl took a swing next to the awkward little one. "Tallulah, I sure like your dress."

"Thank you kindly, Pearl." Little Tallulah opened a small yellow note pad and rapidly scribbled something in its pages.

Pearl inquired, "How's your allergies and asthma spells?"

"My doctor says I'll be just fine," the pasty-white girl replied. She opened her pad and seemed to be reading from a list. "The doctor suggests that I don't run about too much or walk great distances. It's best I don't jump rope or play hopscotch or dance about. He insists I steer clear of all dairy products, beef, bread, and honey bees. I can't venture near citrus orchards or bodies of water with mosquito infestations. And no sniffin' bloomin' flowers or stink weeds."

"Holy moly!" Pearl shook her head. "Should you be swingin'?"

"Sure. Swingin' is fine!" Tiny Tallulah replied. "Just not too fast, for too long, or too high."

Constance and her girls made the stroll over to greet us. Their long manes of shiny hair were perfectly coiffed, and their cotton dresses were pleated and pressed.

Pearl took a running start. Her momentum took the swing high into the air. She kicked her legs, lifting her even higher. "This here is Poppy. She's new to town."

All the girls greeted me with friendly smiles. Constance White took the empty swing next to mine and said, "Welcome to Savannah, Poppy." She grinned. "Are you starting school?"

"No, not until next year," I replied.

With a push, Constance started swinging. "That's a real pity. We could've been best friends."

Working up the nerve, I said, "Constance, I do believe you have the prettiest hair I've ever seen."

She tossed her locks over one shoulder. "I brush it three times a day and wash it in lemon water."

"It's lovely," I said.

"Yessum." She nodded in total agreement. "My momma says a girl's hair is her crowning achievement."

I suspected Constance White had a grander opinion of her beauty than any mirror could ever reflect.

The group of boys had abandoned their marbles and moseyed over nearer to us.

"Hey, ain't you the orphan livin' across the street?" one of the tubby McAllister twins asked.

I recognized the rolls of fat on the back of his shaved head. "Yessum," I answered.

"I've seen you sittin' on Sook's roof top."

All the boys inspected me, like I was the newest Schwinn model in Sears & Roebuck's window front.

The second McAllister boy, in a matching T-shirt, confirmed his brother's suspicions. "Yup, she's the orphan livin' at crazy old Sook's place."

"I ain't no orphan," I said. "I'm staying with my aunt for a spell."

Another fella piped in, "Your Aunt Sook is a mean ol' biddy. Just the summer before last, she shot me with her pellet gun." He raised his shirtsleeve, revealing a tiny round scar on his left shoulder. "She's got good aim for an old geezer."

I replied, "Well, I ain't never seen no BB gun around Sook's place."

"Oh, keep lookin'," another boy, who had a crazy eye, added. "It's there. One afternoon, I was riding my bike home, and she nailed me 'tween the eyes." He leaned in close and pointed to a pea-sized pellet scar in the center of his brows.

"Are you sure it was my old Aunt Sook?"

"Is a frog's ass water tight?" The kid rubbed his forehead like the wound still stung.

Another freckle-faced boy, with an impressive scab on his chin, asked me, "Does she beat you?"

"Nope," I answered. "Not as of yet."

"Well, it's just a matter of time," he said. "She's gonna. It's in her nature."

"Sook's got the shakes real bad," I replied. "She has a devil of a time even gettin' round. I'm thinkin' I could out run her in a foot race."

"Ain't your momma a junkie?" a handsome, blue-jeaned boy with a blond head full of cowlicks inquired.

Pearl snapped, "Jackson Taylor, you ain't got no manners."

"No," I corrected the handsome kid. "My momma is a drunk. She used to be a junkie, but she's healed herself of dope. Now she drinks to quiet her cravings."

A little girl, even smaller than me, in a pink-and-yellow polka-dot dress, asked in a voice no more than a whisper, "I heard you're from Oklahoma?"

An older shirtless kid wearing overalls and whose front teeth had gone missing called out, "Nuttin' worse than a dirty damn Okie!"

The good-looking boy with hair the color of wheat directed his comment to the shirtless kid, "Lest you've forgotten, Bradford, I'm an Okie. You got a problem with that?"

The shirtless kid hesitated and then stuttered, "Nope, I got no issue with you, Jackson."

I replied, "I'm not from Oklahoma. I'm from Mountain Home, Arkansas."

"Ain't no real difference that I can tell," Jackson said with a grin. "Folks from Arkansas are just Okies with a respectable pair of Sunday shoes."

Constance White laughed, "Jackson Taylor, you're no more of an Okie than I am." As she swayed on the swing, her long hair caught the wind and shimmered like strands of floating gold.

"Ain't true, Constance. My pop is from Chickasaw, Oklahoma," Jackson replied. "I got Okie blood running through my veins."

Little Tallulah spoke up, "Pearl, if Poppy has a mind to, she's welcome to come to my party on Saturday."

"That's mighty cordial of you, Tallulah," Pearl replied.

I gestured to the little one with a nod of gratitude. She pushed her spectacles further up on her button nose and again made a few mysterious notes in her private pad.

One of the McAllister boys announced, "My momma says that Sook Wainwright don't enroll you in school because you're retarded."

"Timmy McAllister, you're as dumb as a pile of rocks," Pearl hollered from her soaring swing. "If you spent more time searchin' your books for learnin' and less time mining your nose for a nugget of gold, you'd be a heap smarter."

All the kids laughed.

"Shut your mouth, Pearl! Ain't no one talkin' to you."

"Just try and make me," Pearl countered. "You don't have any proper manners."

Timmy kicked the dirt at his feet. "Pearl Tucker, you're so ugly, even the tide on Tybee Island won't take you out."

Some of the older boys chuckled, but Pearl kept up her swinging. Her cheeks flushed red. "Tim, you're aching for a knuckle sandwich."

Jackson piped in, "McAllister, not all of us have our mommas buyin' us fancy matching britches, so we can run around town lookin' like twiddle dee and twiddle dumb."

Again, all of the kids broke out into laughter, and the McAllister boy stuck his hands deep in his pockets like he was digging for a clever word.

Pearl's worn sneakers slid into the dirt, bringing her swing to an abrupt halt. "Come on, Poppy. Let's get goin'." She took my hand and led me from the swings. "These boys ain't got a lick of sense."

We left the other kids and walked across the park into the shade of a hackle berry tree.

From behind us, Jackson Taylor hollered, "I'll see you around, Poppy Wainwright." When I turned, he flashed a smile in my direction, and I felt warmth from the back of my neck race clear down my spine to the tips of my toes.

There was no denying that Jackson Taylor was dreamy. He was three inches taller than the nearest boy and had wide, hunky shoulders. The rips in his frayed jeans had been patched at the knees, and he neatly rolled his pant legs to rest atop his sneakers. Jackson had two dimples that mysteriously appeared like a magic trick when he grinned, and his eyes reflected the palest green in the Savannah sun. When the wind caught his shirt collar, he resembled the James Dean poster at the matinee. The other boys had red-spotted skin, but Jackson Taylor's face was smooth, without a single blemish. His attempt at growing two side burns looked promising, and his eyes were clear and green as Dixie McAllister's rye lawn. It was hard for me to set my eyes on Jackson for any longer than a moment without my face flushing red. I feared my telling eyes would hint that I was crushing.

Pearl and I found a clearing away from the others. From a brown paper bag, she delivered two pickle-and-cheese sandwiches wrapped in cellophane. Her curly mass of hair burned red and gold in the sunlight. Freckles spotted her sunburned cheeks, dotting up and over the bridge of her button nose. I thought Pearl was a marvelous creature. Unlike the other girls at Colonial Park, who were all sugar syrup and honey, Pearl was spiked with a tablespoon of vinegar: tart to the taste, compared to the sickly sweet of the sugar pies gathered over near the swing set.

I asked, "What does little Tallulah write in her note pad?"

"Beats me. Don't have no clue. Tallulah Banks is always scribbling in that pad of hers. Some of the kids say she keeps lists of magical spells or mystic potions. Her parents are Lutherans, so I suspect black magic could be involved."

"What grade is that Jackson in?" I asked.

"Jackson Taylor is in eighth grade."

"Is he courting Constance?"

"Naw. Constance has herself a boyfriend, Derek, over at the high school. He drives a sweet, cherry-red Ford. Constance has her pick of beaus." Pearl took a drink from her thermos and then wiped her mouth with the back of her hand. "Girls like us, Poppy, we gotta go lookin' for a passin' compliment, but Constance White is so easy on the eyes that flattery is rolled out at her feet, like some plush red carpet. I suppose it's just the nature of things. Praise comes easy for Constance, while the rest of us gotta go searchin' for a flattering word, like a needle in a bale of hay."

Pearl and I had a laugh under a fine Savannah sun.

"Does Jackson have a girlfriend?"

"Poppy Wainwright, do you fancy Jackson Taylor?" Pearl quizzed.

"Nope."

Pearl moved in closer to inspect my expression, her freckled nose almost touching mine.

Flashing a wide grin, she announced, "You sure do, Poppy. You fancy Jackson Taylor!"

"I do not."

"Do too!"

"Do not!" I laughed, covering my telling eyes with the palms of my hands.

"Well, you'd best get in line. Jackson has a string of girls who follow him around like love-struck puppy dogs. If you're lookin' to snag Jackson, you gotta play it smart. You can't be too obvious." Pearl lay back in the cool grass and crossed her legs at her socked ankles.

"A boy like Jackson is never gonna give a girl like me a second look," I said.

"Ain't true," Pearl replied. "Nedra Sue says that guys may get all hot and bothered over a pretty face, but fellas will always fall for a girl's true essence."

I asked, "What's that?"

"Ain't sure. But if you wanna snag a big fish like Jackson, we gotta get you some essence."

A September breeze blew through the trees and cooled the afternoon sun. Swallows swirled above us, scavenging for any crumbs. They fluttered low, in and out of the treetops. Pearl signaled to me when a curious squirrel moved in closer to her untied sneakers. She peeled some bread crust from her sandwich and tossed it near the critter. The two of us remained silent. He chattered at us like he had a story to tell and then scampered about, investigating the promising morsel at her feet. Always keeping a watchful eye on us, the squirrel sniffed at the breadcrumb. Pearl's slight giggle sent the furry varmint across the grass and up into an oak.

CHAPTER 11

———

IT SEEMED TO ME DONITA Pendergast's faith was carved from the softest balsam wood. On Sunday mornings, she'd find me among the congregation and scoot her way down the pew, taking a seat at my side. Even before the pastor had begun, Mrs. Pendergast was sobbing a storm of tears. While the choir sang the final hymn and continuing through the preacher's closing benediction, waves of sorrow washed over Donita, like the repeating tide on the shores of Tybee Island. I watched her as she prayed from the corner of my eye. Hands clasped tight, she prayed with such conviction it seemed she was reading from a grocery list of wants, wishes, and worries. By the time the tithing basket made its round, Donita was a puddle in the backrow pew.

My grandma Lainey once said a believer's faith should be as strong as a mighty oak, not weepy like a willow. It seemed Donita's faith wasn't grounded by any firm deep roots and could be toppled over by the slightest breeze. After the service, she would gather herself and powder her red nose, placing a friendly smile back on her face, like she'd stored it in her purse during the pastor's sermon.

One Sunday afternoon, following church, I accepted her invitation for lunch. We loaded my bike in her trunk and drove to her small place, out past the train tracks.

The phone on the wall was ringing as Donita scrambled with the lock on the back door.

"Hello." Out of breath, she answered, "Hi, Momma."

I trailed behind her into the tiny kitchen.

"Yes, I've just returned home from church," she reported. "It was a lovely service." Donita covered the phone's receiver with the palm of her hand and whispered to me, "Poppy, please, excuse me. I need to take this call. My daddy has been feeling poorly." And she walked around the corner out of sight.

"Everything is fine, Momma," I overheard. "Yes, I know. Money is just tight. The mechanic shop is slow, and with Rodney's lawyer's cost, it's hard to make ends meet."

I meandered into the little sitting room and observed the collection of photographs of Donita and Rodney hanging on the walls. I admired her perfect pin curls in each framed image. The pair brightly smiled and made a handsome couple. His dark eyes and chiseled features resembled a matinee idol on the marquee posters at the theater. Her thin frame and lined eyes looked like those of a young movie starlet.

The modest sitting room was painted a pale yellow and had simple hand-stitched curtains draped over the windows. Atop the wooden fireplace mantle, several football trophies and plaques were proudly displayed, engraved with Rodney's name. Alongside his awards were blue ribbons from the local county and state fairs. Each pretty ribbon was marked with Donita's name, printed in golden letters: Chatham County Fair 1966, Best Apple Pie; Georgia State Fair 1967, Best Peach Cobbler; First Place Recognition to Mrs. Donita Pendergast for her Plum Preserves, Savannah Baptist Church Bake Sale; First Place Prize, awarded to Donita Pendergast for her Red Velvet Cake.

"Momma, Rodney's under a lot of pressure." Her voice filtered from the hallway. "Yes, I understand. But don't you fret. We will be just fine. Send Daddy all my love."

A glass vase with a few modest carnations sat on a lace doily on the coffee table, next to a leather-bound family Bible.

Donita entered the room. "I'm sorry, Poppy. That was my sweet momma, long distance. My folks live in Richmond."

"I've never been there," I replied. "But my momma has spent some time there."

"It's a lovely place," Donita said. "My poor daddy was stricken by a stroke last spring, and now Mom must tend to him night and day." She disappeared into the kitchen. "I've made us some finger sandwiches. What do you say we take them out on to the porch and enjoy this lovely afternoon?"

She dressed a small wicker table on the porch with a checkered tablecloth, delicate china, and silverware. We sat and nibbled tiny cucumber sandwiches and sipped iced tea.

"These are absolutely yummy," I licked my fingertips clean. "Sook can't cook at all, and Loretta eats plenty of groceries, but she'd need a map to find her way around a kitchen."

"Is Miss Loretta your momma?"

"Yessum," I answered. "She was a dope fiend, but she's been healed."

"Halleluiah." Donita slightly raised one hand into the air. "That's just wonderful, Poppy. Did the Lord heal her?"

"No, ma'am. As far as I can reason, she did it all on her own. I don't believe Miss Loretta and the Lord have met. If they have, they ain't on a first-name basis."

"Oh, I see." Donita smiled and disappeared back into the kitchen.

I called to her through the screen, "Miss Loretta battles a fist-ful of demons."

"I understand," Donita answered back. "Maybe you can bring her to church. It sounds like your momma just needs to find her way to the Lord."

"With all due respect, Miss Donita. Loretta ain't too keen on the Almighty. She says faith in the Lord requires a lot of heavy lifting. And she says she's gotta travel light. I reckon my momma wants a heaven that don't weigh so much."

Mrs. Pendergast reappeared, holding two slices of chocolate cake with fresh strawberries and cream. "Maybe our pastor could say a prayer over your momma and help her with her demons."

"Miss Loretta has a taste for trouble, liquor, and mean men. And she entertains all three on most Saturday nights. She's tuckered out come Sunday mornings."

Donita giggled.

"I pity the preacher assigned the chore of casting out Miss Loretta's demons. Her own momma, my grandma Lainey, tried to bring Loretta to know Jesus, but she wasn't having none of it."

"Some folks have to find their own way to salvation. The clear path can be right in front of them, but they'll ignore the signs and forge their own way to find Jesus," Donita said.

I commented, "You have a lovely home, Mrs. Pendergast."

"Thank you. I just love it out here. It's so peaceful and quiet. When the day is done and I'm alone, I feel so tranquil and close to the Lord."

Donita and I chatted until the sun was setting low in the pasture across the way. When she saw the jet-black pickup rumbling down the gravel road, Donita hastily began clearing the plates and silverware. "That will be my Rodney coming," she announced.

"He's been playing football with the boys, and he always comes home hungry."

The pickup pulled up the driveway with shiny chrome wheels and bumpers. When Rodney Pendergast came up the porch steps, he was more handsome covered in dirt and sweat than he was all spit-polished from the framed photographs hanging on the walls inside. He wore frayed, patched jeans and a T-shirt with the sleeves cut off. A soiled baseball cap rested backward atop his head, and greased black hair peeked from beneath the bill. He had broad shoulders, and his two big-barreled arms were tanned and had wisps of dark hair down his forearms.

The striking fella sauntered up the stoop. "So, we have company?" He eyed me.

"Rodney, this is Poppy," Donita introduced us. "Remember, I mentioned I'd met Poppy a few weeks back at church. She's new to Savannah. She's come to live with her aunt, Sookie Wainwright over on Digby. Poppy, this is my husband, Rodney."

"So, you're old Sookie's kin?" His dark eyes were as black as coffee grinds. He wore a half smile, but I still felt uneasy with Rodney's direct stare on me. His teeth were perfectly straight and pearly white, and his handsome face was covered in scruff.

"Yes. Sookie is my grandma's sister."

"Welcome to Savannah." Rodney passed on by, disappearing into the house. "Is my supper ready?"

"Baby, I'm going to deliver Poppy home, and then I'll be right back."

He called from the other side of the screen door, "Jesus Christ. Supper ain't ready? I'm starvin'."

"There's a pot roast in the oven." Donita attempted to pacify him. "By the time you shower up, I'll be back home."

He reappeared at the screen door. "So I'm gonna go hungry cuz you two women have wasted the day away having a gawd-damned tea party?"

His words hung like a heavy smoke on the air.

Rodney set an angry stare on his young wife. She turned her eyes down to the ground. He exhaled and returned inside.

"Honey, please, mind your language. We have company. I'll be right back," she called. "Black-eyed peas, your favorite, are simmering on the burner."

She leaned in closer to me and whispered, "Rodney always returns home hungry, growling like an old grizzly bear. Why don't I run you on home now?"

On the drive back into town, Donita told me that she'd met Rodney during their last year in high school. She had attended Franklin, while he was enrolled at Savannah High.

"Everyone in these parts knows of Rodney Pendergast," she boasted. "Rodney could've had any of the prettiest girls in Savannah. All those snooty debutants had set their sights on him. One Friday night, at a school dance, I was standing with some of my girlfriends, and the band was playing the Everly Brothers. Rodney came strutting right up to me, took my hand, and led me on to the dance floor. I just about fainted. He comes from a well-established family here in Savannah. He is his momma's pride and joy, and she wasn't none too pleased when Rodney chose me over all those syrupy Southern belles. The day he marched up to his momma at the Fourth of July picnic at the courthouse and announced, 'Donita is gonna be my wife, so you'd best get used to it,' I thought I was just gonna die. I don't mind telling you that Mrs. Pendergast was ready to pitch a fit. The fireworks flew. Lordy, you should've seen his momma's face." Donita giggled. "Rodney has got two older brothers, but he's the jewel in his father's crown. My poor folks can't find two nickels to rub together, but Rodney's kin come from old Savannah money. Of course, my Rodney is too proud to accept a dime from his father."

"He's a mighty handsome fella," I said. "He's got the deepest, darkest blue eyes I've ever seen."

"Yessum." Donita smiled. "He's a looker, all right. I know the local gossip. Folks believe Rodney married below his pedigree. They're spiteful and eaten up with envy because he's all mine."

I sensed Donita was pleased as punch that Rodney had chosen her from the line of eager Southern sweethearts.

She confessed that in their early years it was enough for her just to walk by his side.

"When he wrapped his arm about my waist and we strolled along the sidewalks downtown, I could feel the admiring eyes following us. Sure, we've fallen on hard times," she admitted. "Rodney and his buddy have gotten into some difficulty with the law, but with the Lord's help we'll get through this troublesome time."

I said, "Tonight I'll say a prayer on it."

"I begged Rodney not to keep the company of those rotten boys down at the pool hall, but he doesn't listen to no one. I swear, he's as stubborn as a mule. I'm not sure what I'm gonna do with him." Donita's voice broke. "With God's grace, I'm sure he will see the error of his ways. Every night, I pray that Rodney will come to know the Lord." There was an uncertainty in her voice, as if she didn't believe her own words.

As she spoke, it dawned on me that perhaps Donita Pendergast dared not ask for anything more than dime-store cut carnations, because she didn't believe she was worthy of a dozen long-stem, velvety roses.

"Sure, my Rodney wrestles with his demons," she admitted. "I imagine every hard-workin' Southern man does. But down deep in those places where folks can't see, in those places where only the Lord and me know of, he's a good, decent man."

We followed the gravel road until it turned into pavement and back into town. She pulled to the curb and honked at Sook, who was rocking on the front porch.

"Howdy, Mrs. Wainwright!" Donita waved. "I hope you're enjoying this lovely evening."

Sook acknowledged Donita with the slightest nod.

"How's your phlebitis?"

"Aww, fair to middlin'," she answered back. "I reckon it'll be the death of me."

Donita grinned. "Well, I've got just the cure for what ails you. How about one of my coconut-cream pies?"

From her rocker, Sook hollered, "I ain't interested in none of your gawd-damned pies!"

"Pay her no mind," I said. "My aunt is at the advanced age when her mouth and her heart ain't hard-wired to the same outlet."

Sookie shouted, "I can hear you, Missy!"

"Thank you so much for spending the afternoon with me, Poppy," Donita said. "I truly love my little house, but it can be a lonesome place."

"Thank you kindly for your hospitality, Mrs. Pendergast."

I took my bike from Donita's trunk and waved her off as her Galaxie pulled away.

Grandma Lainey once said to me, "The Lord waits at the end of every road. You must have an abiding faith and know deep in your heart that he is always there, just patiently waiting."

I thought about Mrs. Pendergast for the remainder of the day.

It seemed to me that she was heading for a dead-end and didn't know that Jesus was waiting for her around the next blind corner.

CHAPTER 12

———◆———

A YELLOWING PHOTOGRAPH OF MISS Loretta with some mystery fella sat next to my bed on my nightstand. The framed image was my favorite of my momma. She was young and as pretty as a peach. She sat on the hood of an automobile. The fellow stood near her side. He leaned against the polished Chevy with his arm wrapped around Momma's slender waist. In sienna shades of light, the two posed for the camera. Miss Loretta's head was slightly tilted. Her smoky eyes smoldered, but she shared not a hint of a smile. Posing for the camera's lens, she gazed expressionless. The young boy's hand rested on her hip. Between his fingers was a lit cigarette.

For as long as I could recall, Loretta's smoldering eyes in the framed photograph had bewitched me. I knew without a word that those haunting eyes captured in the black-and-white photo knew more about this old world than I would ever understand. Her eyes had already seen more than mine would ever behold. I'm certain Miss Loretta was already giving poor Grandma Lainey plenty of grief during the time of the old photograph.

The young fella's face in the image had been scratched clear from the glossy paper. Someone had taken an ink pen and scribbled until his face was torn from the paper. I hadn't a clue who'd done the damage—maybe Grandma Lainey. Maybe Loretta. Maybe me. Sometimes I imagined the faceless admirer was my pops.

In the dark of my room, lying in bed, I believed if I stared at Miss Loretta's photograph for a spell, I swore I could bend her solemn expression into a smile. If I gazed at Loretta's picture long enough, I believed with absolute certainty that I could make my momma happy.

It wasn't no time after her arrival in Savannah that Miss Loretta was up to her mischief. On her fifth night at Sook's, after supper, she disappeared upstairs to her room. Within an hour, she descended back down and hollered, "I'm heading out for a bit. I'm gonna go plain stir crazy in this house."

Sook and I were watching *The Lawrence Welk Show* when Miss Loretta sauntered into the sitting parlor. She had lined her lips the color of licorice and ratted her yellow hair to heavenly heights.

Adjusting her two bosoms, which were wrestling to make a surprise appearance from the top of her cinched dress, she asked, "How do I look?" With a satisfied smile, she modeled her scandalous red dress in the middle of the room. Every curve of her voluptuous body seemed to be busting the seams of her skimpy frock.

Sookie glanced above her bifocals. "Missy, that dress is so tight, I can see your religion."

"Don't pay her no never mind, Loretta," I said. "You're pretty as a picture."

Sook remarked, "You look like a wanton jezebel."

"Thank the Lord. That's the look I was going for." She admired herself in the mirror over the credenza, running her hand along her hips and bosom.

Miss Loretta was, indeed, all woman. Mother Nature and a sturdy girdle from a Sears Roebuck's catalogue had perfectly positioned all her curves and feminine assets exactly where the Almighty had intended.

Sook remarked, "Loretta, dressing immodestly is like wallowing around in mud. You'll certainly get noticed, but most likely from pigs."

"Hush up, Sook. I've met me a new beau. A burly hunk of a man," Loretta squealed. "A real cowboy. He's got himself a big, long, shiny Cadillac with polished chrome hub caps and a set of bull horns mounted right there on the front grill. He says I'm his sweet cowgirl."

"Bullshit, Loretta. Do you know what a cow pie and a cowgirl have in common? The older they get, the easier they are to pick up."

Loretta attempted a pleasant expression, but her eyes reflected a flint of hurt. "Sook, go ahead and make fun, but he's got real potential."

"Miss Loretta, don't ya listen to her," I said. "I think you'd look mighty smart in a cowgirl's hat."

"My new beau is gonna take me on a picnic over at Lake Mayer and gonna teach me to shoot a rifle."

"Good Lord," Sookie sighed. "Heaven help us all."

I asked, "Sookie, did you know that the kids over at the park suspect that you go around shootin' them with a BB gun just for sport?"

"That ain't true. It's a lie!" Seemingly incensed, Sook vehemently denied the accusation. "That's a bold-faced lie. What kind of hideous creature would aim a loaded gun at an innocent child? Mind you, some of them varmints are deserving of a hard paddling, but it's a vicious rumor that I would go shootin' at little ones." She held out her quaking hand, "Lookie, my bones are wrecked from the shakes. I certainly can't aim no pistol!"

Loretta searched her purse for a ciggy. "For the likes of me, I just don't see how you two can sit here, night after night, staring at that dreadful TV set. I'm goin' out to see the sights of Savannah."

I asked, "Can I go?"

"Absolutely not!" Sook interrupted.

Miss Loretta wrapped herself in a ratty fur stole and checked her reflection one last time in the mirror of her powder compact. "You ladies enjoy your evening."

"Missy, the front door will be locked and bolted by ten o' clock sharp," Sookie announced. "If you're not home by then, you'd best locate yourself another mattress for the night."

Miss Loretta checked her wristwatch. "I'm just going for a stroll. I'll be home with plenty of time to spare." She placed her purse strap over her shoulder and took her leave.

Aunt Sook glanced over in my direction, rolled her eyes, and then turned her attention back to the set.

I said, "Miss Loretta told me a woman's appearance is all she has that sets her apart."

"Is that what that silly woman believes?" Sook sipped her coffee from a mug, never lifting her eyes from the television. "I reckon a sinking woman can commit no bigger blunder than believing her beauty is a life preserver."

"I don't understand, Sook."

"Missy, no matter how dolled up she may be, a drowned woman never floats to the water's surface lookin' pretty."

I said, "I suppose it's good that Loretta is being social."

"Child, common sense is like deodorant. The folks who need it most are the same folks who won't use it." Sook shook her head. "That foolish woman is gonna plop her ample rump on some barstool downtown and guzzle gin fizzes like she's siphoning diesel fuel from a John Deere tractor."

"We can't be sure of that, Sookie," I replied, not fully believing my own optimism. "Maybe she's not up to any mischief. Maybe Miss Loretta is just hankering to see the sights of Savannah."

"I'll bet my last silver dollar that she's out sniffin' for trouble." Sook turned her attention back to the television.

"Grandma Lainey always said that Loretta was thirsting for love, but until she plugs up the big old hole inside her spirit, she'll always be left empty."

"Your grandma was a foolish woman, but on this particular matter, she was right as rain."

Come early the next morning, before the crack of dawn, I woke to the ear-aching shrieks of Annabelle's crying. I snuck a peek from the crack in my window blinds to find the violet-and-blue glow of the lifting horizon. I rubbed my eyes clean of sleep and tried to focus. Following Annabelle's cries, I trudged down the stairs and onto the front porch. The anxious goat stood on the stoop, wailing up a storm. Attempting to hush her whining, I scratched her hide, but Annabelle continued her weeping in the direction of Sook's vegetable garden.

When I first saw the body, it was laid out flat in the garden bed. A pair of long, muddy bare legs were sprawled among the corn stalks, and two twisted arms were entwined among the creeping squash.

I swallowed hard and attempted a yell for Sookie, but only air escaped.

Her head was face down in the row of turnips. The familiar red dress was soiled and hiked up well above her hips, and Loretta's bare white ass was blooming white in the early morning light.

I nervously approached the chicken wire and whispered, "Miss Loretta? Are you dead?"

Her heap of tangled yellow hair was caked in mud, and leaves and twigs had collected among the mangled mass like some great bird's nest. Her left boob had slipped free from her dress and lay in the dirt beside her, like some ripe fleshy melon.

She snoozed soundly.

"Miss Loretta, are you dead?" I asked again.

Nothing.

I cleared the knot in my throat. "Loretta, if you ain't dead, Sook is gonna kill you for trifling about in her garden."

Her false eyelashes fluttered once and then again. Her eyes opened wide to the sky. She mumbled incoherently to herself and patted the earth to determine where she'd landed from the night before. Her head slowly lifted from above the radishes, and she looked in both directions.

"Are you OK, Miss Loretta?"

"I ain't sure, just yet." She slowly rolled over on to her muddy hands and knees and began rummaging about, her bare ass still exposed to all of Savannah.

Cursing, she quipped, "I can't find my gawd-damned pumps. They're my favorite."

"Over here," I called. "They're on the stoop."

After a few failed attempts, she stood upright among the vines of squash and staggered over Sook's prized tomato bushes. Loretta fought her way through the corn stalks, out from the chicken-wire enclosure, and then trudged across the muddy lawn.

I helped her up the front steps.

"Are you OK?"

Miss Loretta appeared lost. "I'm fine, honey." She spat a chunk of mulch from her mouth.

"What were you doin' in there?" I asked.

She picked straw from her hair. "I ain't sure, Poppy. Maybe I was huntin' me a midnight carrot." She grinned.

I wiped the caked mud from the side of her face and placed her traveling tittie back in its proper place. I corralled the strands of her wild hair, picking manure bits from her lashes. "Sook is gonna to pitch a fit when she sees the sorry state of her garden."

Loretta scratched her forehead. "Best I can recall, I came home, and Sook had bolted me out of the house."

"Well, you've gone and done it now. Sookie will be loaded for bear when she wakes and notices the calamity in her corn crop."

Under the smeared mud on her forearms, I tried to spot if any new needle pricks were evident but was relieved to find only a ripe bruise on her wrist.

"Loretta?" I asked. "What is this? It looks like you found yourself on the wrong side of a cat fight."

She examined the bruise like it belonged to someone else. Shrugging her shoulders, she replied, "Ain't nothing that time won't heal."

"Let's get you up to your room before Sook rises."

I walked her up the stairs and down the hall to the bath. She undressed and stood naked as a jaybird on the cold tile floor. Running her a bath, I helped momma into the cast-iron tub. She slid in to the steaming water, and I sat cross-legged on the floor beside her.

With a wet cloth, she scrubbed the mud from her elbows, arms, and knees. She lathered her hair and blew bubbles from her palm in my direction.

I confessed, "You really scared me, Miss Loretta."

"I'm sorry, baby." She reached to me and ran her slender fingers along my jaw. "I'm so sorry. Your momma is always making a mess of things."

"It ain't nothin'," I replied. "Miss Loretta, I'm thinkin' if your pops wouldn't have gone and died, he could've taught you right from wrong."

She smiled. "Is that what you think?"

"Yessum. Maybe you wouldn't have struggled so."

"My pa was an awfully hateful man," she said. "He was a low-down scoundrel."

Cupping warm water in the palms of her hands, she brought it to her face. It spilled from her palms, soaking her muddy cheeks, nose, and chin.

"Grandma Lainey told me Grandpa was a fine, upstanding man. She said that you were like a restless wild pony, born with an untamed spirit."

"Your Grandma Lainey was a foolish woman, and I was a pitiful excuse for a daughter." She turned to me. "But baby, there ain't no good reason for a drunk daddy to ever touch his little girl." She shook her head. "Ain't no words for a daddy whose hands go travelin' where they ought not."

"Miss Loretta, what did he..."

She interrupted me, "Those days are long gone. I suspect I've traveled a million backroads since Mountain Home. I've two-stepped in every honkytonk this side of the Mississippi," she said. "My daddy's long dead and buried. If I'm dancing in a circle, goin' nowhere, I gotta own my missteps."

My grandma Lainey told me never to carry hate in my heart, but I despised the grandpa I never knew. I hated him for touching my momma's warm and soft places, turning her cold and hard as she fought to forget.

"Your Aunt Sook is gonna cook my goose, isn't she?"

"I'll handle Sookie. It won't take me no time to repair any damage done, but you gotta be careful, Loretta."

"Baby, the moon could turn blue from cold before I could fix all the damage I've done." Her weary, almond eyes turned up to the plaster ceiling.

"I'll go put on a pot of black coffee, but you gotta swear that you won't pull another stunt like this again."

"I promise you, baby." Her cheeks were streaked with trails of black mascara. "I promise you." Loretta closed her eyes for the longest while.

I sat silent near the tub and watched on.

It seemed I'd lost her to some distant thoughts. She ran the soap along her healing arms and over her chest and to the back of her neck.

I believed my momma was one of God's most lovely creatures. She brought more palms of water to her face, spilling from her hands like a warm rain upon her ivory skin. Beads of water fell from her brows and from her lashes like tiny, translucent pearls. She rested her head against the tub's edge, closing her eyes. My momma was, all at once, beautiful.

CHAPTER 13

FROM MY ROOFTOP, I SPOTTED Jackson Taylor at our front gate, his hands buried deep in his pockets. Back and forth, he paced the sidewalk and then turned about and traveled the same path again. I watched for the longest while until he spotted me high above on the shingles.

"Hey, Poppy!" he hollered, wildly waving his arms. "I'm down here!"

"Hi, Jackson!"

"Come on down."

I climbed into my open window and darted down the stairs. I checked my reflection twice in the foyer mirror and headed out the front door.

He called to me from the gate, "Poppy, come on, let's take us an evening stroll."

"I gotta ask Aunt Sook for her permission," I said.

I stuck my head back in the door and hollered, "I'm heading out!"

"What? Where?" Sookie called. "But it's nearing my supper time!"

I slammed the door shut and dashed up the front path.

"I'm deducting this from your weekly allowance!" Sook threatened through the screen door. "Remember to take a sweater!"

At the gate, Jackson waited with a wide grin and a box of chocolates. His hair had a razor-sharp part, and his white T-shirt was tucked into his belted jeans. He opened the gate for me and gestured with his arm, inviting me through, bowing his head low like he was greeting royalty. An easy smile seemed to always play at the corner of Jackson's mouth.

I laughed. "Stop it. You're being retarded."

Together, we walked along the sidewalk. Jackson smelled like an older man's cologne.

He gestured back to the house. "Folks say Sook's old place is haunted. They say they've seen ghosts stalkin' her yard at night. I even heard 'em once, when I was walking by." He then made a low grumbling in his throat that quickly rose to a high-pitched screech. "It sounded just like that." He cracked a smiled.

"That's no ghost. I suspect it was Annabelle."

"Is Annabelle some tortured kid your aunt has locked up in her attic?" he asked.

"No, Jackson," I giggled. "Annabelle is Sook's goat."

Laughter erupted between us.

He bent down, lowering his head and scratching the ground with his sneaker, readying to charge me like some barnyard animal.

"You're a fool, Jackson Taylor."

"I heard your momma has come for a visit."

"Yessum, for a spell," I confessed. "My momma is half-crazy."

He waited a moment before answering, "I'm real sorry 'bout that, Poppy."

We strolled further along the sidewalk, smiling at nothing in particular.

He inquired, "Do you have a special beau back at Mountain Home?"

I recalled Pearl's strict guidance on such matters. "Yessum," I lied.

"Oh." Jackson's broad shoulders seemed to slump low, and he buried his hands deeper in his jean pockets.

"My boyfriend is a pitcher at Mountain Home High School." I watered the little lie, hoping it would grow into something that would make Jackson green with jealousy.

"I'm on the baseball county league," he boasted. "I'm the first-string catcher. It ain't nothin' to throw a ball. Any fool can pitch, but to catch a sizzling cut fastball from behind the plate, now that's a different matter altogether," Jackson continued on with his sales pitch. "Pitchers are pussies."

Hunkering down low on the pavement, knees bent, he pounded his fist into his imaginary glove. "Us catchers gotta be courageous to stare down a hardball as it's flying right between our eyes." He repeated, "Yes sirree Bob, all pitchers are pussies."

"Well, since leaving Mountain Home, my boyfriend and I have grown apart," I remarked. "I broke the news to him over the telephone that we had to split the blanket 'cuz of the distance between us. He took the split hard, but I suspect he'll heal from the heartbreak."

Jackson seemed to have a sudden bounce back in his step. His face smiled in all the right places. Pulling three green apples from Mildred Atkinson's tree, he began showing off by walking backward in front of me and juggling the fruit in the air. "Can the punk back in Mountain Home, do this?" He grinned broadly as he tossed the apples high over his head.

Mildred's voice hollered from behind her screen door, "Jackson Taylor, you leave my apples alone!"

"Sorry, Mrs. Atkinson."

"Them apples aren't ripe, and they're gonna sour in your belly," she warned. "Boy, you'll have the squirts if you eat 'em!"

"Yes, ma'am," he answered back.

She continued yelling through the screen, "Just because you see a thing don't make it yours to take!"

He called, "My sincerest apologies."

Mrs. Atkinson finally appeared out from her front door. She was a big bull of a woman, the size of Sookie's upright piano. She came shuffling onto the porch stoop. "Jackson Taylor, you best remember, your pretty young friend ain't gonna be impressed by no stolen green apples. It's a man with integrity and proper social graces who will always catch a young lady's fancy, not some fool juggling stolen green apples."

"Yes, Mrs. Atkinson." Jackson took my hand and pulled me along the sidewalk. His palm was warm against mine. Our fingers entwined. We escaped down 52nd Street, laughing from our bellies.

Jackson spoke about the newest single by Ricky Nelson and how the fading sky was the most brilliant color—part lavender and part violet. Brittle leaves scattered at our feet, and the empty street was completely ours.

By the time the sun was setting, folks with any good sense had already gathered around their crackling fireplaces. It was the kind of chilly evening that gave October a bad name, but Jackson and I didn't care one wit. We laughed at the cold. His hand warmed mine as we walked side by side.

At Frances Watson's place, we stopped to admire the changing colors of her elms. The top of her blue bouffant bobbed from above her garbage can as she attempted to hide empty whiskey bottles nearer to the bottom.

She spotted us, rapidly closing the bin's lid. "Good evening, young Mr. Taylor."

"Good evenin', Mrs. Watson."

She asked, "It's a bit late in the evening for a stroll, don't you reckon?"

"No, ma'am. I think it's a perfectly fine night," he replied.

"You know, son, a proper gentleman always walks on the street side of his lady friend."

"Yes, of course, Mrs. Watson."

Jackson stopped on the sidewalk, tipped an imaginary hat, let me pass by, and then gallivanted up to my other side. His *Teen Beat* dimples made an appearance every time he laughed.

Our shoulders rubbed as we walked along the cobblestone sidewalk, and the street lamps sputtered on.

"Have yourself a lovely evening, Mrs. Watson."

She waved. "Tell your momma I'll be sending over some blueberry cobbler for the bake sale."

"Yes, ma'am. I will."

We walked on to West Jones.

Jackson told me that after he graduated, he was going to become an astronaut or a cruise ship captain. He chuckled when I told him that I'd never once boarded a ship or ever been to the moon.

"I'll take you there, Poppy," he said.

Stopping along the sidewalk, Jackson knelt on one knee and tied my shoestrings into a bow of one of my untied sneakers.

On his knee in front of me, he looked up to the lonely moon. "Poppy, in a just few weeks Apollo 8 will blast our boys clear up there. They'll be the first astronauts to ever leave earth's orbit and circle around the moon. We're gonna kick those commies' butts. The Russians can't beat us at nothin'."

Jackson looked at the stars the way I wished he'd look at me. I wanted to confess that I'd follow his green eyes all the way to the moon and back, but I remained hushed.

He was articulate in ways that other boys his age weren't. He confessed to me that his pa drank too many bottles of Pabst at the end of a long workweek. Jackson said that's why he would hate Fridays forever.

"On my eighteenth birthday, I'm gonna hitchhike all the way to the Oregon coast," he said. "If you've ever had a hankering to see that corner of the world, you could travel along with me."

I smiled but said nothing. Pearl's advice repeated in my head—a proper girl can never seem too eager about such matters. So, I casually nodded at his passing invitation, remaining closed-mouthed and not daring to confess that I wanted more than anything to see the Oregon coast with him.

By the time we'd made it back to 22 South Digby, the lights in the windows of the old house glowed gold behind the curtains. Sookie was bickering at Loretta about something or other.

Jackson said his good-night and swung the gate wide open for me. As I walked up the front path, I suddenly felt warm and uneasy.

"Child, where'd you run off to at this ungodly hour?" Aunt Sookie stood waiting behind the screen door, her arms folded and with a furiously tapping foot. "Who in the hell is that boy?"

"Jackson," I answered. "We went for an evening stroll, Sookie."

"What's wrong with you?" She asked, looking at me with equal parts anger and concern. "You're white as a ghost, child. Are you chilling?"

"I ain't sure, Sook," I panted. "I'm feeling a bit dizzy."

"Serves you right! It's too damned cold to be roaming the streets of Savannah at night."

A weight was seemingly pushing down heavily on my chest. I complained, "I can't catch my breath, Sook."

"Are you choking, child? Did you swallow something wrong?"

"Naw. I just can't breathe," I repeated. Feeling flush, I inhaled and pushed a rush of air from my lungs.

"Are you chilling?" She placed her palm on my forehead.

"No, ma'am. I'm burnin' hot."

Sook took my shoulders and squared them with hers. Searching my eyes, she leaned in closer and spoke loudly. "Should I call for a doctor? Are you gonna be OK?"

Clutching to my chest, I felt dizzy. My knees grew weak.

"I'll be fine, Sookie." I took a seat on the bottom step of the staircase.

"Well, I ain't payin' for no doctor's house call unless you're lyin' flat on your death bed. They're all crooks, ya know? Doctors and lawyers are all crooks."

"Sookie, he gave me these." I held out the box of chocolates with the red bow.

"Who?" She asked. "What's this?" Sook tore at the wrapping and examined the box of chocolates. "Did someone poison them their peanut clusters?"

"No." I attempted at another deep breath. "Jackson brung me the box of chocolates."

"Who? That bean-pole of a boy?"

"Yessum, Jackson Taylor."

Miss Loretta came rushing into the foyer. "What's wrong, baby? Are you OK?" She, too, pressed her palm against my forehead. "Child, you're warm. Can I get you a cold soda pop?"

Disgusted, Sook placed her hands onto her hips. "You mean to tell me you're all flustered over Charlotte and Cecil's youngest?

Jackson Lloyd Taylor?" She tapped her agitated bare foot on the wood floor. "Is that what all this tomfoolery is about? You're all twisted over some hairy-legged boy?"

Loretta appeared more confused than usual. "Could someone please explain?"

I felt my pulse beginning to ease.

Sookie scoffed, "I ain't never heard such foolishness in all my days. You're gettin' all hot and bothered over the Taylor boy? For Christ's sakes, the Taylors are from Oklahoma! You're gettin' heart palpations over a damned Okie?"

Loretta's worry melted into a wide smile. "Aww. That's so sweet. My little baby girl is growin' up."

I swallowed a lump lodged deep in my throat and started to breathe with ease.

"Hush up, Loretta," Sook insisted. "I've known that boy since he was no taller than a stump. I believe he's grown a foot in the last six months. It's certainly not on account of Charlotte's cookin'." Sook crinkled her nose in disgust. "I ain't got no time for the folly of affairs of the heart. If you're sweet on that boy, please don't bring it inside my house. Take it outside, on the far side of my front gate. Even the hint of sappy, unrequited love makes me nauseous. I don't want that nonsense to stench up my home. Your momma is already tramping around here like an alley cat in heat!"

"Oh, Sookie, you're heartless," Miss Loretta whined. "Leave the young lovebirds alone."

"Shove it up your keister, Loretta! What happens when this boy finds out what's goin' on below this child's gingham skirt? What then? I happen to know that his pa, Cecil Taylor, is a crack shot with a pistol." She shook her head. "Gimme those peanut clusters!" Sookie snatched the box from my hands and shuffled toward the sitting room. "Now run along. It's time for *Peyton Place* on the telly. Keep all the noise down."

I climbed the stairs and slipped out my window. Sitting on my housetop perch, I rested my back against the roof shingles and smiled under Jackson's moon.

CHAPTER 14

———◆———

A WHITE, LACEY CRY RAG was an absolute necessity for any respectable Baptist woman. Every God-fearing female who was easily moved by the Holy Spirit always kept buried in the deepest abyss of her purse a delicate, monogrammed hanky to mop her anointed tears. Never in my days had I known a devout woman who didn't keep her handkerchief within reach. At the choir's first note of "How Great Thou Art," my late Grandma Lainey started slobbering and went digging in her purse for her embroidered hanky. I reckon God created the weeping rag to save the many frilly Sunday frocks from being soaked and soiled beyond repair by the salty tears of the believers.

Donita carried a wadded tissue deep in the bottom of her pocket book. Every Sunday, during the pastor's welcoming prayer, she would pull from her purse a fresh Kleenex and blot away a few tears from her powdered cheeks. Later during the preacher's sermon, as fire and brimstone burned inside the little church, Donita, overcome with grief, would use her little tissue to dam her streaming river of tears and blow her running nose. By closing prayers, she was sniffling and snorting, her wadded tissue reduced to a wad of soggy pulp in her palm.

After service, Donita and I would step from the little chapel's front doors out into the clear light of day and join the congregation among the shade trees. On a row of folding tables spread before us was a potluck of fried delicacies. A spread of chicken, ribs, casseroles, catfish, and cream puffs was offered to the Lord's faithful flock. Famished children and thick, hungry church women wrestled for their place in line while their husbands stood off near the gravel parking lot, smoking unfiltered Camels and pitched horseshoes.

The ravenous Christian women crowded in front of the Tupperware smorgasbord, bumping shoulders, nudging elbows, pushing children aside, and fighting to position themselves for the feeding. Donita's strawberry-and-chocolate cream pies were their rewards, waiting on crystal platters at the finish line of the buffet.

Donita Pendergast's baking skills were widely admired in all of Chatham County. Her secret recipes were prized possessions, and her intricate pastries and desserts were considered some of the finest among the culinary elite of Savannah.

"Rodney has been just an angel," Donita gushed as we waited our turn in line. "I'm not sure what has come over him lately, but he brought me home a pendant necklace and the sweetest card." She opened her blouse slightly and proudly flashed her shiny gold necklace with a delicate rose pendant. "I really think all my prayers have finally been answered."

"That's just swell, Donita," I commented, examining the rose pendant in the palm of my hand. "It's lovely."

"It's a genuine diamond in the center," she gushed. "I told Rodney that he shouldn't have. We don't have the money for such luxuries. But he said, 'Darling, only the best for my sweet girl.' Poppy, I really do believe that the good Lord has seen us through these troublesome times. I'm certain if we can get past the dust up with the law that things are going to get better." Donita squeezed her eyes shut tight, like she was wishing or praying. "I just know the good Lord has finally answered our prayers!"

———

Aunt Sookie reclined back in her rocker, snickering as she perused the obituaries in the Sunday edition of the *Savannah Morning Daily*. On the porch steps, Miss Loretta ran a brush through my hair while I sat planted between her legs, snapping string beans into a plastic Tupperware bowl.

I reported, "At church service today, Donita told me that her Rodney has changed his ways."

Sook lifted her left hip and farted a reply.

"Sookie, you're just awful," I remarked. "Rodney even called her *darling* and bought her a real pretty diamond necklace."

"That's really sweet, baby doll," Loretta commented as she brushed my hair.

"I wish I could have pin curls in my hair just like Donita's."

"Sugar, I love your long hair," Loretta replied. "You've inherited your luxurious chestnut mane and your small stature and your devout faith from your grandma." She gathered my locks into a rubber band.

I complained, "Loretta, there ain't nothin' luxurious 'bout my hair."

"Thank the Lord!" Sookie exclaimed. "Bitsie Booth kicked the bucket! She was a gawd-damned, dim-witted busy body. Good riddance!"

Loretta ignored Sook's celebratory rantings and continued, "I think your hair is beautiful. I suspect you inherited your stubborn disposition from your grandpa."

"Hot damn!" Sookie snorted. "Jim Douglas croaked! Yessum! Hell has claimed another rat bastard!"

Loretta glanced over at Sook and sighed. But Sookie remained engrossed in the list of the daily dead.

I asked, "What did I inherit from you, Miss Loretta?"

"Your lovely bone structure. You've gotten your delicate fine features from me." She smiled. "Look at those high cheek bones— just like mine."

Sook remarked, "I suspect you got your sassy mouth from your momma."

"Miss Loretta," I asked, "what did I get from my daddy?"

She leaned in close over my shoulder and whispered in my ear, "Your pecker." She giggled.

Sook glanced from her paper, shaking her head in disbelief. I blushed a tomato red.

Miss Loretta stood from the stoop and announced, "Well, excuse me, ladies, but I have me a date. I met me a real gentleman. And he's taking me out to the picture show tonight."

Sook snickered aloud.

"Go ahead and roll your eyes, Sookie, but this one has got real potential. He tips his hat and opens the car door for me, like a proper gentleman."

"Pfft!" Sook sounded off. "And what does this new fella do for a vocation?"

"He sells ladies' shoes at Levy's Department Store," she gushed. "He's got a real sense of style. He smells like jasmine and always wears a yellow rose in his jacket lapel."

Sookie spouted off, "This man sounds like a raving poofer! Are you sure you ain't dating a Savannah sodomite? Maybe you can introduce him to Daryl? That pickle kisser needs himself a date more than you do."

"You're just awful, Sook," Loretta replied. "He's got real panache."

"Hot damn, that old Jew Norman Schneiderman died!" My old aunt was downright gleeful. "That stingy son of a bitch has taken his last dollar from me down at the bank!"

We ignored her.

"Loretta, why ain't you never been courted by a Jew?" Sook inquired. "Lord knows they got all the money, and they could keep you in fine furs rather than that ratty road kill hide you strut around in."

"Oh, Sookie." She blushed.

"No, no, missy. Don't be so cavalier when dismissing my suggestion," Sook insisted. "I'm only looking out for your best interest. I'll ask around town and see if there's any eligible Jews who are huntin' to court the *old hooker* type."

"Thank you, Sook. That's mighty kind of you."

"Sookie, why haven't you never made any mention of having yourself a beau?" I asked. "Grandma Lainey told me that you once had yourself a boyfriend. Is he one of the fellas in the pictures up in the attic?"

Sook waited the longest while before replying, "Child, if I believed that it was any of your concern, I'd take it up with you."

I commented, "Pearl Tucker believes there's a strong likelihood that you fancy womenfolk. A lesbian."

"She did, eh?" Sook looked over to me. "A lesbian?"

"Yessum."

"Well, you can assure little Miss Tucker there is only one other loathsome creature who sounds less appealing to lay with than a hairy-legged old man, and that would be a back-biting, yappin' female," Sook replied. "Besides, Digby already has old Alice Faye a few doors down. Savannah only permits one lesbian per every other block. I suspect it's a city ordinance."

Loretta slightly squeezed my shoulder and smiled. "Sookie, you should go and find yourself a man. Your plumbing must be as rusty as an old drain pipe."

"Hush up! And not that it's any of your beeswax," Sook added, before returning back to her newspaper. "But some fingers aren't meant to wear a wedding band."

Down the street a way, we spied the cluster of well-dressed ladies. The Society for the Beautification of Savannah was walking the street, previewing the homes of Digby. It seemed, on that fine afternoon, the members were making plans for the annual spring walking-garden tour.

The prominent, dignified ladies seemed to glide along the cobblestone sidewalk. I watched from the other side of the hedge as the gracious flock seemingly floated like swans, elegant and proud, led by Dixie McAllister, who wore a delicate headpiece with bright, happy sunflowers sprouting from its brim.

Dressed in their finest threads, white-laced cotton gloves, and wide-brimmed hats, the ladies followed the proposed path of the upcoming spring garden tour. After visiting each home to be featured on the season's tour, the ladies cloistered, discussing every minute detail.

Dixie conducted the meeting with an iron fist, taking meticulous notes in her binder as the ladies walked from house to house.

Every year the Savannah garden extravaganza commenced at Alice Faye Nance's, where guests nibbled on some Southern delicacy while enjoying Alice's trellises of Wisteria and Confederate Jasmine vines. Then the guests moved farther down the street to the next manicured garden.

It was determined the upcoming tour would include a peek at Mabel Gladden's formal hedges, and then the tour would proceed to Bertie Lloyd's to enjoy her baskets spilling with azaleas and

English ivy hanging along her expansive front porch. The tour would then move on to the Wilkes's place, to view Loma Wilkes's flowering rose trees.

From our front stoop, I spied the ladies standing at Minnie Pott's front yard and gushing over her line of sculpted topiaries adorned with white ribbons.

"Sookie, it looks like the ladies are heading this way," I replied.

"Yippee!" she squealed sarcastically.

The refined ladies made a final stop at the McAllister's house to admire Dixie's prize-winning white Princess Anne rose bushes.

When the glamorous gals exited the McAllister garden, they strolled up the sidewalk with Dixie in lead. As the ladies neared Sook's dump, all their giggles fell to silence. Their gaits slowed, more closely resembling a solemn funeral procession. They peered past the hedge at the shocking state of Sookie's place. Shaking their heads disapprovingly, they whispered in one another's ears.

Sook hurriedly struggled to stand from her rocker. "Dixie McAllister!" she hollered, shuffling to the front stoop. "I need to speak with you right this instant!"

"Good evening, Sookie. I hope you're having a lovely day." Dixie wore an expression of loathing, gussied up with a saccharine-sweet smile.

Sook hollered, "I've told you before, and I'm now telling you for the last time. That there magnolia is encroaching over my garden!" Sook pointed to the single branch of one of the majestic trees extending into the yard, casting its wide shadow directly over her prized garden bed.

Dixie attempted to sprinkle some sugar on her response. "Now, now, Sook. These magnolias are a miraculous marvel. They are a living testament to God's glorious handy work. They are cherished and protected in section two hundred and fourteen, article sixty-nine, in the handbook of the Society for the Beautification of Savannah."

"Stop with all your bullshit, Dixie! The township has been notified. I swear, I'm gonna take matters into my own hands if someone don't tend to this gawd-damned tree!"

Dixie blurted out, "Oh, poppycock!"

Our porch went dead silent.

Loretta looked over to me. I turned to Sook.

"Pardon me, Dixie?" My aunt held her quaking hand near to her ear. "I didn't catch that?"

"You heard me. That's all poppycock!"

Miss Loretta snickered, but smothered her mouth with her palm.

Sookie slapped her knee. "Did you hear that ladies?" She gestured to me and Loretta. "Dixie thinks it's all poppycock!"

I blushed red. Miss Loretta was bent over fighting a giggle fit.

Gathered in a tight circle, all the ladies yakked among themselves, formulating a unified response.

Dixie cleared her throat and called back over the fence, "Sookie, you know these magnolias are the pride of Savannah. It's a punishable crime to ever touch 'em."

"Hogwash! Savannah was spared the devastation of Sherman's march to the sea, but I ain't sure she'll withstand you bunch of bureaucratic bouffants!" Sook planted her shaking hands on her broad hips. "I've given all the authorities fair warnin' 'bout this dadgum magnolia!" Pointing to the invading tree's branch overhead with her walking stick, she warned, "I ain't messing with you fools no more."

The nervous flock of Savannah socialites clucked among themselves.

"I don't care how highfalutin you believe yourselves to be," Sook yelled. "All y'all can dress yourselves up in strands of perfect pearls and the finest petticoats, but y'all shit squattin' over a hole, just like the rest of us!"

Indignant and utterly offended, the society ladies huffed and puffed.

"Sookie Wainwright!" Dixie called back over the hedge, "You'd best not touch a single stem on that tree, or the law will be breathing down the back of your neck!"

Sook countered, "I'm at my wit's end! My garden cannot thrive without proper sunshine. That there tree is intruding on my rightful piece of the sky!"

I whispered, "Sookie, now don't go getting yourself all worked up. Let's head inside and have some supper."

But my wiry aunt advanced closer to the porch's edge, her eyes fixed on the ladies.

The insulted women conversed behind their white-laced gloves.

Loretta gave the high-society ladies a slight wave of her hand. "Y'all have a lovely evening." And muttering from the corner of her mouth, she said, "Sookie, you need to calm yourself."

But Sookie stood firm.

All of Digby Street went quiet but for the thumping of the end of old Sook's walking stick on a wood plank.

Thump. Thump. Thump.

From the other side of the picket fence, Dixie and her squad straightened their spines and, in an act of solidarity, staked a firm position on the sidewalk. Arms crossed tight, a battle line drawn. Both sides had taken their stand.

Thump. Thump. Thump.

All was quiet, but the rhythmic pounding of Sookie's cane sounded like a call to war. Even the birds in the treetops seemed to cease their singing.

Thump. Thump. Thump.

"Sookie, come on now. Let's go have supper," I said.

Miss Loretta and I walked to her side and gingerly attempted to escort Sook to the door, but the cantankerous old woman protested, twisting about and breaking loose from our hold.

"Sookie, you're gonna overheat," I said, "and blow a gasket."

Flailing her arms, she hollered to the ladies, "You're a bunch of girdle-wearin', gawd-damned, bubble-headed buffoons!"

"Good night, ladies!" Loretta interrupted Sook's rant in the nick of time. "Have yourselves a glorious evening! Toodle-loo!" She waved.

We lifted Sook's flailing feet off the porch, carrying the fussing senior by the forearms back inside the house.

The posse of upper-crust prima donnas marched in lock step down the street.

Back in the kitchen, we sat Sook at the table. Miss Loretta poured her a shot glass of whiskey.

"What the hell has gotten into you?" Loretta asked. "They'll have you locked up in the loony bin if you continue to carry on like this."

"I won't have that gander of loose-lipped geese tell me nothin'."

I slid a plate of fried chicken and corn bread in front of her. "You need to calm yourself, Sookie, and eat some supper."

She guzzled the shot of whiskey and poured herself another. "My nerves are shot," she sighed. "As God is my witness, that magnolia is comin' down."

"Sook, have some chicken, and settle yourself." Loretta lingered near the stove top, sniffing under the pot lids simmering on the burners.

Sook and I watched on as she nibbled from the skillets of fried potatoes and okra.

"Loretta, sit yourself down and have a proper supper," Sook remarked. "Poppy has cooked us this fine meal."

"I just can't," she whined. "I'm getting as big as a barn, and all this greasy fried food is causing havoc on my waistline."

I asked, "Where are you off to tonight, Miss Loretta?"

"It just so happens my beau is taking me to see a movie at the drive-in!" Her eyes lit up. "He has a convertible with plush, sky-blue interiors. It's dreamy." She dipped a spoon into the sizzling skillet of gravy and licked it clean.

"What picture are you two seeing?"

"Miss Audrey Hepburn is starring in *My Fair Lady*." She swooned and sampled more fried potatoes from another skillet. "He loves the theater. He's mad over musicals. He's cultured and refined."

"A raving queer, no doubt," Sookie muttered under her breath.

Loretta baptized a buttered biscuit in the brown gravy.

"Would you please just sit down and eat sumpthin', Loretta," Sook insisted. "You're working my last nerve."

Finally, Miss Loretta reached in the cupboard and grabbed herself a dish. "On second thought, I'll help myself to the tiniest portion."

She went about filling her plate with abundant piles of pot roast, okra, fried taters, and collard greens. "I just won't eat anything at the picture show," she told herself. "Poppy, if you want to keep a man, never ever let him see you eat. Always remember to peck like the tiniest bird when you're on a date."

"Yes, Poppy," Sook piped in. "Don't ever let a man know that your body requires nourishment."

Loretta spooned a generous helping of gravy, smothering her entree. She carried her plate to the table. As she bent to take a seat, the unmistakable sound of ripping seams and tearing fabric could be heard from beneath her substantial rump.

Sook and I both looked over to Miss Loretta.

Adjusting her buttocks in the wooden chair, she blushed. "Oh Lordy. I believe I've gone and busted my back seams wide open." With her confession, Loretta placed a cloth napkin on her lap and began her feeding frenzy.

Sookie remarked, "That's what you get when you stuff fifty-five pounds of ass in a five-pound sack."

Loretta giggled, "Well, Sookie, I'll have you know that my new man enjoys my feminine curves."

"When can we meet this new suitor, Miss Loretta?" I asked. "He seems to be becoming your steady."

Sook abruptly stood from the table. "Well, before Miss Loretta descends into one more of her vulgar tales of her tawdry romantic pursuits, I'm gonna head upstairs and go use the commode."

With her pronouncement, Sook started shuffling from the room.

"Sookie, you know what your trouble is?" Loretta declared. "You don't believe in true romance. You don't believe in passion or desire or love at first sight."

My aunt began her long journey up the staircase, and hollered, "Missy, I'll tell you what I do believe in. If I don't make it to the toilet in a timely fashion, I'm gonna shit a pile in my bloomers."

It was later that night when Miss Loretta arrived back home. Sook had gone off to bed, and Annabelle slept soundly in the sitting parlor. The house was quiet, and I lay in bed, waiting for the sound of Momma's cab pulling up to the front curb, bringing her home to me—assurance that it was safe to sleep.

Returning from her nightly adventure, Loretta gingerly moved about downstairs. Dizzy from drinking, she bumped about in the dark, smacking into walls and tripping over carpets. From my bed, buried under quilts, I listened on as she clumsily maneuvered up the stairs. Stumbling down the corridor, she cursed aloud when she entered the wrong door.

"Where's my gawd-damned room?"

From the dimmed light of a hallway sconce beneath my door, I saw her feet just outside.

She repeated, "Where's my gawd-damned room?"

I held my breath, hoping she wouldn't stagger in, but with the turn of my knob, I pulled the covers over my head and peeked through the edge of my blanket. The light from the hallway cut through my room, and Miss Loretta came trespassing in. Closing the door behind her, my room was once again dark, except for a spying moon through my open window. Loretta's silhouette tiptoed toward my bed. Attempting in vain to be quiet, she tripped on shadows.

She mumbled, "Poppy? Are you awake?"

I didn't dare answer.

"Poppy?"

I knew with certainty that she was drunker than a skunk. Tripping on a lamp cord, she stumbled, knocking a picture of her and me off the wall. I watched on from beneath my covers as she went about the room blindly reaching, grabbing at nothing. I lay still as the dead while she felt about my room—the dresser, a chair, the floor lamp.

When she found the edge of the bed, I felt her touch on my toes.

Mumbling incoherently, she cursed aloud, "I ain't sure why everyone has gotta be so gawd-damned quiet."

Finding a folded patchwork blanket, she tossed it on the ground next to my bed and arranged the quilt with her bare feet, sculpting it on the hardwood planks. She lay herself down on the floor at my bedside.

I could hear her wrestling and restless breathing.

I whispered, "Miss Loretta you can come on up. There ain't no need for you to sleep on the hard wood floor."

Without a word, she came slipping beneath the covers, nestling behind me. She smelled of cigarette smoke and sweet perfume. Her knees bent with mine. My head fit into the nape of her neck, like the last piece of a puzzle.

She asked, "You awake, baby?"

Her breath was sour.

"Yessum."

Lifting her head from the pillow, she spoke in the dark, "Poppy, don't you listen to old Sook. If a sweet boy offers you a box of chocolates and a cordial smile, you accept them. You hear?"

"Yessum."

"Baby, life is a hard, mean thing. When happy comes a knockin', you open your door wide and invite it inside. Do you understand me?"

"Yes, Momma."

I turned on the pillow to face her. She smiled with tired eyes, heavy with the wanting for sleep.

I asked, "Momma, when you're gone, do you ever think about me?"

She snuggled nearer, her nose almost touching mine. "Yes, baby. Not a day passes..." She pulled the white cotton linens up to her chin.

I watched in the dark as sleep overtook my drunk momma - - her loose lashes fluttered, a slight yawn, a breathy sigh.

I inhaled her stale breath like it was my own. She was, indeed, a marvelously messy creature.

I watched over her slumber for the longest spell. With my momma resting near me, safe under the covers, a bedtime prayer seemed like folly.

Outside the window, the magnolias rustled in an autumn breeze. The house was quiet except for the sound of hoofs roaming the corridors.

In the moment before I surrendered to sleep, I leaned in close to my momma's ear and whispered, "Stay."

When I woke the next morning with the new light of dawn, Miss Loretta had snuck from the room. The blanket was neatly folded and laid across the foot of the bed. The lamp was sitting upright, and my dolls were all precisely lined along my window seat, their stitched grins smiling back at me. The black-and-white photograph of Loretta and me was placed back on the wall, and all of my allowance money was emptied from my piggy bank.

CHAPTER 15

Port Wentworth, Georgia

WHEN NO ONE WAS LISTENING, Rodney Pendergast professed his undying love and devotion to his wife. When he'd caress her with his calloused fingertips, goosebumps traveled up her spine. If he had consumed a few beers, Rodney would whisper softly, "Baby, to the moon and back. That's how much I love you. To the moon and back."

Donita would tell her mom on the phone, "He wasn't always a scoundrel. For a time, Rodney was a good, sweet man. It's all the drugs that has turned him hard and mean."

There was the smallest part of Donita that wanted to believe Rodney was still a kind, decent fella. The pages of photographs in their picture albums were a testament that at one time the newlyweds smiled at the sun and walked hand in hand. There were soft moments when Rodney's hands folded over hers, and she felt his warm breath on her neck. It was during those times that Donita would convince herself that their mess of a marriage could be untangled. Those shining days when she could breathe fully—when he came home happy, with clear eyes and an obliging smile—were few and far between.

His strong hands that had thrown a football for Savannah High were now the same fists stained with motor oil and black grime that beat her down. Rodney was no longer the high school golden boy. He was no longer the young man she'd fallen in love with while slow dancing to the Everly Brothers.

Like her recipe cards that she carefully stored in a small three-by-five tin box, Donita had begun collecting a record of his wrongs. She dated every incident and scribbled a note on pieces of paper:

October 28, 1965—Rodney punched me in the mouth; April 7, 1966—Rodney came home drunk. Threw a working boot and struck me in the head. June 17, 1967—Rodney slapped me; July 8, 1967—Rodney came home high, busted a chair, and broke my arm after a scuffle; November 2, 1967—Slugged my right cheek.

Donita kept the small folded pieces of paper in a little tin box high in the cupboard, above the fridge and behind her mason jars. She never could square why she treasured the records of Rodney's brutality. In some peculiar way, the box even brought her an odd comfort. Maybe, the small tin box was a constant reminder, like little paper souvenirs, of where Donita had been and what she had survived. Maybe, she believed, with her eventual passing, Rodney Pendergast would be made to pay his debt for all the damage done.

When Rodney was out causing a ruckus with his buds, Donita fetched her stepping stool, pulled the metal box down from above the fridge, and sat on the porch alone.

She'd revisit each folded remembrance. Like traveling through the pages of her yellowing photographs in one of her picture albums, Donita sat with a glass of sweet tea and celebrated her survival of another passing season, another passing year. The bruises had healed, cuts had scarred over, and broken bones had mended. Donita was still alive.

At the end of another evening, Donita closed the small tin box and celebrated another passing day, another passing hour. She was proud to have weathered the pounding storms. Her little house out past the railroad tracks was still standing.

One afternoon at a Sunday social, over at the Veteran's Park, she overheard her mother-in-law whisper to her son, "Rodney, something just ain't right in that girl's head. I swear to God, I believe Donita is losing her mind faster than she loses those precious babies."

Rodney rebuked his mother, "That ain't fair, Mom. That's a hateful thing to say."

"Son, I'm only truth telling. I ain't sure Donita cared one wit about those sweet babies. I've never seen her shed a single tear."

Donita never blamed the Pendergast matriarch for such unkind words. She couldn't even bring herself to fault her mother-in-law for rearing a rotten, cruel man. It seemed Donita was too busy blaming herself for all the world's woes.

She bore the blame for Rodney's auto shop failure and for him stealing those cars in the dead of night. She found reason to blame herself for his brutal beatings and for their babies she couldn't carry to term. Donita Pendergast blamed herself for cloudy days and falling stars.

However, Donita did take exception with her mother-in-law's insertion that she hadn't mourned her babies. The senior Mrs. Pendergast was sadly mistaken—wrong as rain.

In Donita's quiet moments, she grieved each one of her lost babies. With a sorrow that spilled from her eyes like stinging turpentine, Donita mourned every child. Whether it was sitting in the last row pew on Sundays, or standing alone in her kitchen at the Formica counter, or working at her sewing machine, the babies were always with her. As she kneaded the dough, forming the precise ruffle of a pie crust, Donita wept for the baby girl she'd lost on a clear April morning. Icing a red velvet cake, she cried for the little boy who arrived too early on a cold October day. While tending to her garden, she sang along to the radio, propped in the open window, and serenaded the memory of the tiny infant that she'd cradled in her arms just long enough to never forget the scent of her powdered skin.

Her grief remained in a sacred place where her abiding faith could not heal, somewhere in a silence that was too quiet for her mother-in-law to hear and too loud for Donita to bear.

CHAPTER 16

———

"A FINE MORNING TO YOU," I greeted Mrs. Tucker with a broad smile. "How are you on this lovely day?"

Pearl's momma shrugged her slight shoulders and muttered something. Turning from the door, she yelled, "Pearl, you got company!"

"Thank you, ma'am."

Pearl hollered, "Poppy, come on back. I'm back in Nedra Sue's room."

I followed her voice down the narrow hall.

Mrs. Tucker reminded us from the kitchen, "There will be holy hell to pay if you kids make a mess in this house."

"OK, Momma," Pearl replied.

Inside the tiny bedroom, Nedra Sue sat crossed-legged on the floor. Janis Joplin blared through the speakers. Thousands of colorful tiny beads were scattered about Nedra on a patchwork blanket. Nedra was focused on stringing the plastic beads on a long strand of twine.

"Hey, Poppy," Pearl grinned. "Nedra is making her some jewelry to sell at the street fair."

Nedra Sue glanced up just long enough to flash a wide smile. "What are you two chicks up to this afternoon?"

"Poppy fancies her a beau, and we're fixin' to catch him."

Nedra scrunched up her nose like she was downwind of one of old Sook's farts. "Why in tarnation do you want a boyfriend?"

"Nedra is a feminist," Pearl stated. "She believes in the women's liberation movement."

"Menfolk have held us women down since time began," Nedra explained, "We girls have to stand up, unified against our subjugation. Poppy, take as many beaus as you want, but only on your own terms." She continued threading the tiny beads onto the twine.

"Poppy fancies Jackson Taylor," Pearl remarked. "And it looks promising, cuz Jackson bought her a box of milk-chocolate peanut clusters."

"I suppose the Taylor kid is a nice enough boy. Easy on the eyes." She winked my direction. "But Poppy, don't you ever kowtow to no man. They ain't worth it. It always starts with a box of chocolates from the Piggly Wiggly and a bouquet of some silly wildflowers, and then, they got you! You're locked up in chains. Men think we're their rightful property, like livestock or a favorite baseball cap."

Confused, I looked over to Pearl. "Uh?"

"Nedra Sue says that men believe the Holy Bible gives 'em the notion that us girls are theirs for the taking."

"Yessum," Nedra agreed. "It started as far back as Adam and Eve. Bible scripture perpetuates this great injustice."

I asked, "You don't believe in the Bible?"

Nedra shrugged her slight shoulders, concentrating on her beads.

"But how about the Father, the Son, and the Holy Ghost?"

Nedra Sue declared, "Poppy, they ain't real. Those are only hallucinations conjured up by men to keep us women in shackles. God don't exist."

"Ain't true," I said. "He does, too."

"No, Poppy. God's an illusion created by man to subjugate women."

"That ain't true, Nedra. My grandma Lainey spoke to the Holy Ghost every single night," I insisted. "When she was stricken with a deadly bout of pneumonia, my grandma swore the Lord Jesus himself came right into her room and took him a seat on the edge of her deathbed. The Lord sat near her side and sang my grandma to sleep. Grandma Lainey told me Jesus had long, silky white hair and the bluest, clearest eyes, but she confessed the almighty couldn't sing to save his own life," I said. "But he sure saved my grandma Lainey's life that night."

Puzzled, Pearl asked me. "Really? The Lord can't sing?"

"Nope. Grandma told me that he can't carry a tune in a bucket."

Pearl scratched her mass of ringlets. "Huh. I would've imagined that the Almighty had a real pretty singing voice."

"Are you two numbskulls even listenin' to me?" Nedra Sue remarked. "Jesus of Nazareth wasn't no savior. He's bein' used as part of the conspiracy to keep us gals barefoot and pregnant. Now, I'm not suggestin' that Jesus wasn't a fine man. A real cool cat, maybe, the very first hippy ever. If he were alive today, I suspect he'd be on the front lines with Hoffman, Ginsberg and the minister from Montgomery, Martin Luther King. Yessum, Jesus was a cool cat, but no savior. The church has twisted his words to keep us women all in a straight line." Nedra looked at both of us sitting at her bare feet. "Do you understand?"

"Yessum," Pearl replied. "But I would've thought that Jesus had himself a real purdy singing voice. Like one of them singing parakeets."

Exasperated, Nedra Sue threw up her arms, sending the hundreds of tiny beads scattering around her like psychedelic confetti. "I give up!"

Pearl and I went about gathering up her colorful beads. "Nedra, can you help Poppy snag Jackson?"

"So, you really want the Jackson kid?" She asked me. "It's easy as pie."

Pearl and I both leaned in.

"Well, menfolk are simpletons," Nedra said. "They're easily pleased. You gotta act coy and sugary sweet. Boys like *the chase*. They fancy mousy, soft-spoken Barbie-doll types. You gotta swoon at their muscles and agree with all their foolishness. Converse in words with no more than two syllables. Don't trip 'em up. Keep it simple with words like *honey, baby, darling*, and *yummy*. Menfolk like a woman to have supple curves and giggle at their corny jokes."

"Like these?"

Pearl had taken two wads of Nedra's socks and stuck them down the front of her blouse. She smiled seductively and blinked her lashes.

Modeling her new enhanced figure, Pearl strolled in front of Nedra and me, rubbing her hands up along her hips and her enhanced chest. "Poppy, you need to get yourself a pair of these!" Pearl's eyes reflected mischief, and she moved in to stuff a pair of socks down the front of my dress.

"No, no. I'll do it!" I insisted. "Let me do it myself." I disappeared into the small closet and positioned the padding inside my trainer.

"Hurry up, slow poke!" Pearl called to me.

"I'm comin'. Hold your horses."

"Let's see!"

"OK. Here I come."

I walked from the closet, and Nedra and Pearl burst into laughter.

"Oh, my Lord, they're way too high," Nedra Sue advised. "We gotta shift those titties." She went about rearranging my stuffing.

"Look at me," Pearl chuckled. "I'm Marilyn Monroe." She had wrapped a blanket around her shoulders like a fur coat and struck a silly pose. "Poppy, you look just like Miss Loretta!" Pearl fell onto the bed, chortling, rolling, and holding her tummy.

"There ya go, Poppy!" Nedra stepped back with a satisfied smile.

I stood admiring my new curves in the mirror's reflection. "Golly, I just don't know. Don't feel right, advertising merchandise that ain't mine to sell."

"Aww. Ever since time began, folks have been lyin' to get what they desire," Nedra Sue replied. "Now, you straighten your spine, walk proud, and go get yourself Mr. Jackson Taylor."

"My aunt Sook says that menfolk are nursed from their mommas' teats every day, and later they spend every waking hour searching out another obliging pair."

Pearl grabbed a pink pillow from Nedra's bed, smothering her giggles.

I considered my padded profile "I just ain't sure it's right."

"Just consider them a little upholstery work," Nedra Sue replied. "You're the sofa, and we're complimenting you with a couple soft, fluffy pillows for Jackson to rest his head."

I walked an imaginary runway, hands on my hips, strutting like a Paris model, showing off my new curves. "Pearl, do I look like the chickadee who your pa ran off with?"

"What in tarnation is all of this?" Mrs. Tucker barged through the door.

Our laughter fell to silence.

"What the hell is goin' on here?"

"Nothin', momma. The girls are just playin' dress up."

Pearl frantically scrambled, pulling the socks from beneath her blouse.

"What are saying about your pa?" Mrs. Tucker grabbed a tight hold of Pearl's forearm. "What have I told you? You shut your ungrateful gawd-damned mouth about your daddy!" She raised a single hand ready to strike.

Pearl swallowed hard. "I swear, I didn't say nothin' about Pops!"

"I'll slap you up the side of your ignorant head if you go spea- kin' about that son of a bitch!" Mrs. Tucker's angry eyes burned a hole clean through little Pearl. "I swear to God, I'll beat your ass if you're talkin' to folks about that worthless bastard!"

"Momma, stop it!" Nedra shouted. "Stop it!"

"Mind your own business, Nedra Sue," she warned. "This ain't your concern."

"The hell it's not! Let squirt go."

"If this child has been told once, she's been told a million times to keep her gawd-damned mouth shut about her pa. And the same goes for you!"

"They were just having some fun," Nedra stated. "She ain't said nothin' about Daddy."

Mrs. Tucker's eyes remained locked on Pearl. "You'd best keep it that way."

"Momma, I ain't mentioned Daddy," Pearl sniffled. "I promise."

"Mom, they're just playin'." Nedra pulled Pearl to her side, wrapping her arm around her little sister's shoulder. "Dad is gone! It don't make no difference who knows the truth. All your lies are gonna catch up with you. They're all gonna come tumbling down. You hear me?" Nedra Sue held her mother's stare. "All your lies are gonna come crashing in on you, and I ain't gonna let it bury me and squirt. Do you hear me? Aren't you tired, momma?" Nedra Sue's voice broke. She swallowed hard and wiped a runaway tear with her forearm. "Aren't you tired of all the lies? They're gonna bury us, Momma."

Mrs. Tucker studied her eldest daughter's eyes and then turned to Pearl. She crossed her arms tight across her sunken chest. For the slightest moment, I thought Mrs. Tucker was conjuring up a kind, forgiving word, but then she demanded, "Pearl, you got chores to do. They ain't gonna get done by themselves."

Mrs. Tucker's hand gripped the top of my shoulder as she led me directly to the front door, disposing of me on the welcome mat. "You run along home now."

Pearl cried out from her bedroom, "Momma, Poppy can't ride her bike home. Nedra Sue has gotta take her home. It's too far for Poppy to pedal all the way to town!"

"I'll be just fine, Pearl," I called to her. "Don't fret!"

With a stern nod, Mrs. Tucker slammed the front door in my face.

I mounted my bicycle and started off down the gravel road toward town.

A watercolor Savannah sky was fading behind a field of green and gold. Pedaling toward Digby, it occurred to me that this old world wasn't made for the likes of little girls like Pearl. It's a mean, unforgiving place that is hard as stone—ain't no proper place for fragile, tender things. I reckon that's why the Lord don't let us remain youngins for too awfully long.

I bicycled past acres of cotton fields. A crooked wire fence followed alongside the lonely stretch of road. Dogwoods shaded some grazing cattle that watched me with lonesome eyes. A family of sparrows rode on the wind beside me, fluttering low before lifting on the air and flew from sight.

The day was dimming when I heard the rumbling of a truck's engine approaching from behind me. I slowed my pedaling and stuck to the shoulder as it sped on past, turning up dust. I recognized Rodney Pendergast's jet-black polished pickup as it rumbled by. The truck followed the gravel road up further ahead, and before it disappeared into a grove of live oaks, it slowed with the red glow of its brake lights.

The truck reversed its course and slowly began backing up the twenty yards toward me. When the Ford moved alongside my bike, the passenger's window cranked down. Smoke and loud music escaped from the pickup's cab.

"Well, little lady, good afternoon." The passenger greeted me.

He was a gnarly fella, bare chested, with hair the color of muddy straw. His green eyes reflected in the setting sun. His teeth were crooked and stained with coffee and chewing tobacco. He leaned out the window, closer to me. "What do we have here? What's a pretty young thing like you doin' out in the middle of nowhere, all alone?" He smiled like he was conjuring up trouble. I could see black grinds of tobacco pinched between his bottom lip and teeth. There was nothing hospitable in his grin. He gazed at my padded blouse.

I felt conscience of his inspecting eyes.

"I'm just riding my bike home," I replied. I saw Rodney sitting behind the wheel of the idling truck, staring through the front glass. "Good afternoon, Mr. Pendergast. I'm Poppy. Poppy Wainwright. I'm Donita's friend from church."

He acknowledged me only with the slightest nod.

His grimy bud leaned even further out the window, like he was ordering something from a drive-thru. From the short distance, I could smell his foul breath. "Well hello, Miss Poppy Wainwright," he snickered. "You're a pretty young thang, aren't you?"

Rodney sat silent, his wrist rested on the top of the steering wheel, looking up the long road ahead of him.

The shirtless man asked, "Why don't you let me and Rodney load your bike in the tail bed of this truck? We can go for a little joyride."

Mr. Pendergast finally glanced across the cab, calling through the open window, "Aren't you Sook's kin?"

I smiled. "Yessum."

But Rodney was wild-eyed. His handsome face was gaunt and pale. His watery eyes nervously blinked, and he repeatedly wet his parched lips with a nervous tongue. His hand trembled when he ran his fingers through his greasy, black hair.

The shirtless man spoke again, "Sweetie, you shouldn't be out here."

"I'm just out for a ride on my bike."

"What do you say?" His bud repeated the suspicious offer. "You can hop in the truck with us, and we can go over yonder in the trees and have ourselves a soda pop." The fella gestured to a grove of oaks and then laughed out loud like he had said something funny. "Why don't you let us show you a good time?"

"No, thank you, sir," I answered. "That's awfully kind of you."

The straw-haired man leaned in to Rodney, whispering something out of my hearing. He turned back, giving his door panel a hard push. It swung open toward me. "A pretty little thing like you shouldn't be out here in the boondocks all by yourself. Who knows what could happen? Some unsavory characters could drive up on you."

A few of the cows off grazing in the meadow trailed over slowly to the barbed-wire fence along the gravel road, pushing their heads through the gaps in the wire. Their low, aching moos called to me. Their lonesome eyes watched on.

"What do you say?" He patted the truck seat. "Hop on in here, and we'll make sure that you get home. And, maybe we can have ourselves some fun on our way back into town."

"No, thank you." I started to push my bike further down the road, but he swung his door open wider.

"You're not being too neighborly, are you, little one?"

"I just want to go home."

"I ain't sure I can let you do that, missy."

The corralled cattle cried a low mournful sound. I looked to Rodney, but his eyes were fixed on the dirt road before him.

"It's a lovely evening," I said. "I was enjoying my ride."

Again, I tried to push my bike, but the man reached out and with one hand, gripped my handlebars. "I can't with a clear conscience leave a pretty, helpless little thing out here in the middle of nowhere. It wouldn't be gentlemanly." His half grin chilled me.

From the corner of my eye I scouted a possible escape route - - under the barbed wire, dashing across the meadow and trying to lose the men in the grove of oaks.

"Little lady, you're gonna climb up in this here truck and go for a ride with Rodney and me." His tone was no longer accommodating nor hospitable.

"Let it be," Rodney muttered. His eyes still fixed on the winding road ahead.

His bud looked over his shoulder, back to Mr. Pendergast.

"Just let it be."

The shirtless fella deliberated for a minute. He eyed me once again but this time without the grin. Spitting a mouthful of tobacco on the ground near my sneakers, he snickered, "You'd best be careful, little lady. The next time, maybe it won't be two proper gentlemen like Rodney and me who come up on you on a lonely backroad."

He climbed back inside the cab, slamming the door. The jet-black truck accelerated, kicking up dust and gravel, and sped on up the road.

I slowly started pedaling back toward town. The sun was setting, casting long shadows reaching from the groves of live oaks into fields of meadow grass. The bending horizon burned orange like a raging fire as the sun slipped from sight.

This old world ain't made for little girls, I thought to myself. It's a mean, barren place—too hard for anything tender to thrive and flourish.

CHAPTER 17

SOOK WAS FIT TO BE tied when she beckoned me into her sitting parlor. With a crooked finger, she summoned me to the side of her rocker.

Having stewed in a foul mood all through supper, Loretta and I knew the old wiry woman was not to be trifled with. When I walked into her chamber, the television sat dark, and she was rocking at a determined pace.

"Missy, we need to have us a conversation about the tomfoolery with you and the Taylor boy. You two dunces have all of Savannah talkin'."

"I don't understand, Sookie."

"Today at the Piggly Wiggly, Loma Skousen was flapping her gums about this nonsense. I will not be made the fool!"

"We ain't done nothin' improper," I said. "Jackson is a fine, decent fella."

Miss Loretta called from the foyer. "Oh, Sookie. They're just kids. Let them be." Momma stood at the foyer mirror, chomping on a mouthful of chewing gum, primping herself for a night out. "I think they're adorable," she smacked.

"Shut up, Loretta. It's bad enough that you're out every evening, walkin' Savannah's streets like some floosy. This child needs a good talking to, and you certainly don't behave like any self-respectin' momma that I've ever seen."

Seemingly unaffected, Miss Loretta continued to rat her bleached follicles with a teasing comb to an unearthly height. She exhaled, "Oh, stop it, Sookie. You're gonna bust a blood vessel."

"Tend to your own affairs. This child must learn what it means to be an appropriate young woman."

"Sookie Wainwright, you'd cut a fart at a funeral if the spirit moved you," Loretta quipped, smacking her wad of Bazooka. "You lecturing my sweet Poppy on proper etiquette just don't seem right."

"Poppy, your momma ain't got the sense of a dim-witted goose."

In the foyer mirror's reflection, Miss Loretta lined her lips and powdered her cheeks with peach blush, appearing to ignore Sook's harsh words.

"Missy, you must quell this sordid affair with the Taylor boy immediately!" My aunt demanded. "Lord help us all if he discovers that pecker under your lace panties."

I stood at the arm of her chair as she wagged a strict finger in my face.

"What did we do, Sook?" I asked. "What have we done wrong?"

"Missy, you're wrong as rain. It's disgustin'—a child of your age runnin' around town with that boy, like two love-struck fools. I won't have it! I won't be made the laughing stock of Savannah because you two are carrying on like an Okie variety of Romeo and Juliet."

"When I arrived to Savannah, Sook, it was the first time folks saw me for who I really am. I wasn't the misfit from Mountain Home no more. Everyone back home in Arkansas looked at me like I was a sideshow at the Baxter County carnival. But when I got off the bus at the depot, I was just a girl. Sure, I was an orphaned, homeless girl, but I was finally just a girl."

Sook snickered, "You look as ridiculous as your momma!"

Turning from her reflection, Miss Loretta stomped a direct line into the sitting parlor. She arrived in the room, boiling mad, seething in anger. Pointing the sharp end of her teasing comb at old Sook, she shouted, "Go ahead and throw your stones at me, Sookie! I'm easy pickings for your spiteful nature! You can take me out to the barn for a whippin' as often as you'd like. I reckon I got the licks comin'. But you be sweet to my Poppy! You hear me?"

My old aunt stood from her chair, readying to speak her piece, but Miss Loretta wasn't quite finished.

Such an ire was roused inside my momma that her nostrils flared, and her eyes went red. "I was raised by a hateful daddy and a momma whose neglectful eyes were always turned to heaven. But a little bit of kindness can be a soothing, healing balm." Loretta moved in even closer. "Sookie, love don't always have to be about right or wrong. And love don't have to sting like a leather strap. You remember that, old woman!" The two stood nose-to-nose. "Be good to my precious little girl. I know I ain't got no room to speak on such matters. I know I'm a tangle of a mess, but you'd best love her strong. You hear me? I've made a vocation out of failing all my blessed babies. Don't you fail my Poppy!"

Sook was stunned by the scolding. She returned ever so slowly back into her seat.

"Now, I've said my peace." With that, Miss Loretta adjusted her bra strap and blew an enormous pink bubble with her gum.

The balloon of Bazooka burst, covering her nose, mouth, and chin. She giggled like a giddy school girl and went about clearing the sticky goop from her face with her fingertips, "Now, excuse me, ladies. I'm goin' into town and having myself a night cap with a fine gentleman who I met at the lounge. I believe he's got real potential."

Sook sat quietly as Momma shimmied from the room. Draping her fur stole around her bare shoulders, Miss Loretta winked and blew me a kiss from the foyer. "Sleep tight, baby girl."

With the slamming of the front door, Sook and I were left listening to the clicking of Loretta's heels as she trotted down the path and out the gate. Silence filled the sitting parlor. The two of us sat facing each other. I couldn't recall a time when my aunt missed an opportunity to fill an empty silence with her opinion on one subject or the other.

I waited for old Sook to bridge the hush.

Finally, standing upright, bones stiff from the sitting, she announced, "Well, I'm off to bed."

"Night, Sook," I said. "I'll shut off the lights."

As she waddled from the room, she grumbled, "The day that Miss Loretta Jo Nell Wainwright is the voice of reason, I figure the entire gawd-damned world must be going to hell in a hand basket."

I went about closing shades and turning off lamps. I scratched Annabelle's ears as she followed along my side.

From the balcony, Sook hollered, "Poppy, perhaps you should invite the Taylor boy over for supper."

I grinned. "OK, Sookie. I suspect Jackson would be mighty pleased with your invitation."

———◆———

A trespasser had crept into Sook's yard.

Ignoring the *Keep Out* signs posted along the rickety picket fence, the unwelcome intruder, slowly and deliberately skulked into her lawn, casting a wide shadow over Sook's prized tomatoes, her crop of collard greens, and rows of carrots. The shady, uninvited guest sent Sook's squash vines crawling from beneath its shadow overhead, searching for any sunlight. Over the years, the mighty magnolia's branch had extended well into her yard. Its silhouette shaded the patch of earth occupied by Sook's prized garden below. This particular magnolia had invaded what Sookie believed was her rightful slice of the sky. The tree's canopy had interrupted the sun's rays, denying her sweet peas and celery the sun's glorious warmth. Nearly every day, while tending to her rows of vegetables, Sook shook her fist to the sky, cursing the encroaching bough.

She'd complained to anyone who'd listen, but the officials swatted her away like a pestering fly. She attended the monthly council meetings at the Township of Savannah and outlined her grievances, but her repeated requests for action were denied.

"Poppy, wake up!" Aunt Sookie whispered in the dark. The blunt end of her walking cane jabbed into my side. "Get yourself up!" Her shadowy silhouette stood over me.

"What's the matter, Sook?"

"Get yourself out of bed right now," she demanded.

"What?" I rubbed my eyes trying to focus. "What time is it?"

"Hop up. I need you downstairs, lickety-split! Get yourself dressed, and hurry it up. Don't dally, times a wasting'."

"I'm comin', Sookie. I'm comin'."

I trudged down the stairs to find Loretta waiting in the dark foyer, her face smeared in white cold cream. She stood at the front door, wrapped in a pink terry cloth robe and a pair of pink, fuzzy slippers. Annoyed, she had her hands hoisted high on her hips.

"Hurry yourself up!" Sook called.

"Miss Loretta?" I asked. "What in the cat hair is goin' on?"

She shrugged her shoulders and rolled her eyes. "Don't ask, Poppy. Your aunt has gone and lost her marbles. She's as crazy as a loon." Loretta's head was covered with a scarf. Her scalp was populated with dozens of tiny plastic pink curlers.

"Shush up, you two." Waiting at the front door, Sookie held a flashlight in one hand and gripped a rusted saw in the other.

"Sookie, what are you up to?" I asked again.

"Shh! Quiet yourselves!"

I remarked to Loretta, "This ain't gonna end any which way but badly."

"Hush up!" Sook inched opened the front door, and we three crept onto the porch and into the waiting night. Following the dim beam of Sook's flashlight, we made our way down the path, to the front gate, and out to the sidewalk.

Sookie peeked her head out to the street. Looking both directions up Digby, she announced, "Coast is clear."

The three of tip-toed along the picket fence. When a pair of headlights crossed, we ducked low and waited until the car had passed on by.

Standing at the mammoth trunk of the invading magnolia, the three of us surveyed the sprawling canopy of twisted, gnarly branches.

Sookie pointed the beam of light up to the trespassing bough. "That's it! That's the son of a bitch! It's gotta go." She snickered with giddy delight.

"Sook, there ain't no possible way I can climb up there," I insisted. "Ain't no way."

"Nonsense! If I was to tell you that hairy-legged Mr. Jackson Taylor was up in that tree, you'd be up there lickety-split! Me and Loretta are gonna hoist you up, and then she'll follow behind."

"The fuck I am!" Loretta protested. "There ain't no way in hell I'm goin' up that tree."

"Oh, yes you are, Missy." Sook gave Loretta a hard look. "You've been eating all my groceries from the cupboards for months now. I swear to God, you've been packin' sufficient food to hibernate for the winter. It's the least you can do." Sook turned her flashlight back to me. "Poppy, once you get on up there, then I'll hand Loretta this here saw. She'll deliver it on up to you."

Miss Loretta complained, "Sookie, I can't hoist these big titties up in that dadgum tree!"

"Hush up." Sookie put her finger in front of Loretta's pouting mouth. "You can, and you will."

Sook barked out directions, and Loretta reluctantly bent low on her knees. Sookie helped me on to her back. I steadied myself and reached for the lowest branch. Loretta grimaced, trying to carry my weight. I grabbed for the next hold, pulling myself up into the twisted canopy.

"I've made it!" I whispered in the dark. "I'm up!"

"Good. Now keep on climbin' higher." Sookie directed me with the beam of yellow light. "OK, Loretta, it's your turn."

Loretta cursed and began stripping. Her pink terry cloth robe dropped to the ground.

Sookie asked. "What on earth are you doin'?"

Below, I could see momma almost stark naked, standing in one of her skimpiest pink negligees.

"You ain't expectin' me to climb up that tree in a heavy robe, are you?" She kicked off her fuzzy pink bed slippers.

Sookie sighed, "Oh, sweet Lord!"

I called down, "It's a fine time for you to find religion, Sook."

The beam of light captured me like a trapped raccoon. "Hush up! Or everyone on Digby Street will hear your yapping."

Loretta placed one foot into the old woman's cupped hands and hoisted herself and her tits up into the tree. She struggled to find a place to secure a grip. Her sizable bare ass was exposed to all of Savannah.

Sook stood below, shaking her head in disbelief. "Well, lookie here, we've got ourselves a full moon over Georgia tonight." She projected the flashlight's beam directly on Loretta's exposed white ass.

"Shut your mouth, old woman," Loretta grumbled as she shimmied further up. "When I get down from this dadgum tree, I'm gonna beat you until you're dead!"

"Just keep climbin'," Sook ordered.

Suspended high above the sidewalk, Loretta's arms clung on tight. Her painted finger nails gripped to the bark, and her thick legs wrapped about the branch, her bare feet crossed at the ankles. She cursed, "Sookie, I'm gonna fall and bust my ass on the sidewalk."

"Yeah, yeah. Shut your trap and keep climbing."

After Loretta found a crevice with ample space for her to plant her rear, Sookie handed her the rusty saw. Scaling up further to the intruding bough, I watched and waited while Sook passed the tool to Loretta, and she stretched to deliver the tool up to me.

"Poppy, now you've gotta get firm footing," Sookie directed. "Don't fall and crush my tomato bushes."

"OK, Sook." I positioned myself and the saw and took aim at the overreaching branch.

"Well, what the hell are you waiting for?" Sook cursed from below. "That damn branch ain't gonna saw it self. Get to cuttin' the son of a bitch!"

The first swipe of the rusted metal teeth only skimmed the thick, twisted branch. I bore down, attempting another pass.

Sookie complained, "For God's sake! There must still be some part of a strapping, able boy living beneath your frilly night gown. Get to sawing!"

Loretta and Sook anxiously watched on through the leaves. With a third try, the rusted blade kinked and stuttered.

"Slow and steady," she said. "Poppy, slow and steady."

I stroked back and forth as the teeth tore into the meat of the branch. I continued my sawing until my arm began to tire, but Sook encouraged me on from below.

With each pass, the blade tore deeper.

Annabelle arrived at the fence, whining at us. Her aching cries cut through the night.

"Be quiet, you stupid old goat." Sook picked up one of Miss Loretta's fuzzy bed slippers and chucked it at Annabelle. "Stop your gawd-damned bawling."

Annabelle picked up the slipper and returned to the porch for a midnight snack.

I was in midstroke when I heard the sound of splitting wood. I peered below at Sook, whose wide-eyed gaze stared back up at me. Then came the sound of ripping and tearing—the heavy branch began to give way.

"Glory be to God! It's comin' down!" Sookie shouted. "Get your asses from that tree quick!"

In my panic, I yelled into the night, "Timbeeeerrr!"

The old heavy branch came crashing to the ground.

With my legs wrapped about the tree, I scurried past Miss Loretta on her way down.

"Hurry up, Momma!" I hollered. "Hurry up!"

Loretta was bawling as she scrambled from the tree. Sookie was off, hobbling to the porch for cover.

The extending bough collapsed to the earth with a thud, obliterating a long section of Sook's picket fence and landing squarely on her prized garden. It ripped the gutter off the porch fascia and flattened the ornate iron historical street marker on the corner of Digby and West Jones Street.

Miss Loretta, having finally made her way down, sprinted at a record pace, squealing like a tortured pig, leaving behind a trail of pink plastic curlers up the sidewalk.

As the lights in the windows along Digby switched on, I was attempting to corral Annabelle into the house.

Sookie called, "Come on, you fool, quickly, quickly!"

Suddenly, the porch lights along Digby burned brightly, and folks dressed in their pajamas peeked from the corners of their window blinds and began filtering out through their screen doors. They hollered to one other from their front porches.

By the time the McAllisters and the rest of the neighbors had progressed down the sidewalk, gathering at the base of the hacked magnolia, Loretta, Sook and I were hiding, bent low, peeking through the front-window curtains.

A cluster of concerned neighbors collected outside. All the men stood in flannel robes, arms crossed, grimacing and examining the scalped tree, while the women clucked incessantly like chickens, surveying the destruction. Dixie held court in the center of the yapping females. She pointed her rigid finger at the pruned branch, then back over to our sleeping house.

Sookie scoffed in the dark, "Those ignorant, damned fools can't pin this on me."

Miss Loretta whispered, "Sook, have you gone and blown a gasket? Of course they know it was you."

About that time, Dixie McAllister started a direct tract over to the house. She traveled through the remnants of the picket fence, stomping her way through the flattened garden and up the steps of our front porch, clutching in her tight grip what appeared to be a sack or a piece of fabric.

"Sookie! Sookie Wainwright! I know you're in there!" Dixie's knuckles rapped on the front door. "Open up! You're gonna pay dearly for this!"

Sookie snickered.

Dixie pounded her clinched fist on the door. "First thing in the mornin', the sheriff will be paying you a visit." She yelled into the narrow crevice of our bolted door. "Perhaps you can explain to him how this trashy pink robe ended up at the base of the tree's trunk."

Loretta gulped hard.

Sookie went pale.

The knocking of Sheriff Delany on our front door woke me up early the following morning. I answered and greeted the sheriff, who wore a serious, furrowed brow. Dixie and a few of the ladies had already reconvened outside our front gate, arms crossed, chatting among themselves.

"Good morning, young lady." The portly uniformed officer tipped his hat. "May I speak with your aunt Sook?"

"Yes, sir." I invited the officer in. He removed his hat and appeared mighty anxious as he fiddled with his buttoned collar.

"Sookie!" I called up the stairs. "You've got company!" I turned to him. "Sheriff, you're welcome to come wait in the parlor."

"Well, good mornin', Bernard." Sook appeared at the top of the stairs. She carefully maneuvered each tread. Holding tight to the banister and using her walking stick. She smiled broadly as she made her way down the mahogany staircase, like Dolly Levi herself. "What a delightful surprise," she greeted him. "What brings you out on such a fine morning?" Aunt Sook's voice was syrupy sweet. "How is your Annie and those precious babies?"

"Just fine, Miss Wainwright. They're all growin' like bean sprouts."

"I bet they are. You come on inside and have a seat with me in the parlor." She led the officer into her sitting room. "Poppy, go fetch the sheriff some coffee or sweet tea and a piece of pie."

"Ain't necessary, Sook," he replied. "My Annie says if I don't cut back on the sweets, I'm going to bust the seams of my trousers." He rubbed his belted paunch. "Sook, this morning, I received a call from some of your concerned neighbors about the tree out yonder. One of its branches appears to have met a tragic ending."

"I know, Sheriff. Tsk, tsk. Isn't it a terrible tragedy?" My aunt solemnly shook her head. "Bernard, come on in, and have yourself a seat."

The big man sat awkwardly in the tiny upholstered chair, looking about the room, nervously. "Now, about the tree..."

"Yessum, it's truly a tragedy. I've been asking for your boys to patrol Digby for years, and now, look what has transpired. This neighborhood has been on the decline for decades. Just yesterday, I saw one of Dixie McAllister's fat-headed boys masturbatin' right in broad daylight. The boy was standing in their front yard, yanking his pecker for the whole world to see. Perhaps you could speak to Carl and Dixie. I've got a young, impressionable little girl livin' here." Sook pulled me to her side and gently caressed the top of my head. "This unspoiled, innocent child shouldn't be witnessing such foul obscenities. Ain't that right, Poppy?" Sook held me in her arms like I was her prized possession. "Ain't that right?" I felt her sharp elbow poking into my side. "Ain't that, right?"

"Yes, ma'am," I answered begrudgingly.

"Sheriff, this angelic child shouldn't have to view some juvenile delinquent flogging his manhood right out in public. She has never even seen a boy's unmentionable, but now, Poppy will have to live with that repugnant memory burned into her brain like a red-hot poker. It's a crying' shame what has happened to this neighborhood."

"OK, Sook. I'll speak to Carl and Dixie about their boys."

"Thank you kindly," she replied. "If you arrest both those boys and need for me to come down to the jailhouse for a line up, just let me know. The two fat bastards may be a mirror's image, but I'll recognize the little pervert's pecker from a country mile."

Sheriff Delany cleared his throat. "Speaking of the McAllister boys, Carl made mention that he believes someone is using his boys as target practice with a pellet gun out yonder. You wouldn't know nothin' about that, would ya, Sook?"

"Oh, my Lord!" She gasped, "What is happening to this neighborhood? A lone gunman?" Sook held out her quaking hands. "These shakes have crippled me so. I can hardly feed myself. I fear I'm gonna wither away."

I rolled my eyes out of the sheriff's view.

Sheriff Delany opened his small notepad. "OK, Sookie, now, about the magnolia..."

"Bernie?" Loretta's voice called out from the foyer. "Bernie, baby, is that really you? I knew I recognized your voice, honey!" Miss Loretta came bouncing into the parlor, dressed in a skin-tight halter and the skimpiest shorts. "Bernie baby! It *is* you!" She squealed and plopped herself in his lap, smothering the sheriff with kisses. "I can't believe you've come to visit me, baby. Who told you where I lived?"

The god-smacked sheriff was left with her lipstick all about his face. His eyes darted about the room, and his cheeks turned red as a beat. He squirmed to free himself from Loretta's grasp. Giving her a slight push, he sent Miss Loretta's ass to the hard wood floor.

Dejected, she whined, "Beerrnniiee?"

"Sheriff, it seems you're already acquainted with my sweet niece?" Sookie grinned, with the devil in her eye. "She's been staying with me for a spell."

"Why, yes," the sheriff stammered, tripping on his tongue. "I do believe we've been acquainted. Yessum, I've had the pleasure of meeting Miss Loretta briefly at Charlie's Tavern."

"Baby?" Loretta frowned.

Tiny beads of perspiration formed along the sheriff's top lip. He wiped his sweaty forehead with his forearm.

Pulling Momma from the room, I said, "Miss Loretta, could you come help me pour some tea?"

She whined low, "Bernie, baby?"

Outside the parlor, Loretta and I straightened our backs against the paneled wall, listening on.

"Sheriff, my sweet niece is known throughout all of the South for her obliging disposition," Sookie remarked. "Loretta is so hospitable that she finds herself a plethora of gentlemen acquaintances in every town she visits."

"Yes, ma'am," he stuttered. "I really must head out to the precinct."

"Now, sheriff, the moment you leave, I'm gonna phone up your Annie and invite you both over for a fine supper with me and Poppy and Miss Loretta."

He cleared a lump lodged in his throat. "I'm sorry, ma'am. Annie has been under the weather as of recent," the flustered sheriff answered. "She's caught herself a nasty bug."

"Well, bless her sweet heart," Sook declared. "Now, Bernie, what exactly did you need to know about the old magnolia?" Sookie leaned in closer to him. "I have my suspicions that one of Dixie McAllister's little monsters had a hand in this destruction. If those boys aren't masturbatin' in broad daylight, they're out terrorizing the neighborhood or defacing one of Savannah's many monuments or historical treasures."

The sheriff stuttered, "I'll take note of that, Miss Wainwright." He scribbled a note in his small pad while struggling to regain a semblance of composure.

"Thank you so much, Sheriff Delany." Aunt Sookie advanced closer to the nervous officer. "On second thought, I won't bother sweet Annie with any dinner invite, if you can assure me this dust up with the magnolia is put to bed."

The sheriff politely tipped his hat. "Yes, ma'am."

Sookie walked out on to the porch, arm in arm with Sheriff Delany. Speaking loudly enough for Dixie and the other ladies loitering at the front gate to hear, "Thank you so much, Bernard. I'm, simply, heartsick about that magnolia. They are one of God's most miraculous marvels." Waving him a farewell, she added, "And could you please send around your boys from the sanitation department to clean up this ugly mess. I am also expectin' full compensation for my picket fence from the City's coffers. The hooligans who committed this utter act of vandalism will surely get what's coming to them."

The red-faced sheriff turned and walked a quick pace down the path to the front gate. He frantically fussed with the tricky latch.

I hollered, "Sheriff, you gotta wiggle the doohickey!"

"Toodle-loo!" Sookie called. "Bernie, baby, make sure to tell sweet Annie to get plenty of rest. She's in my prayers." My aunt shut the front door and slapped her knee. Cackling, she snorted, "Did you see that? Old Sheriff Delany folded like a lawn chair."

Loretta swooned, "My Bernie baby is an absolute Southern gentleman. He always opens the door for me. Last Friday night, he even paid for an upgraded room at the Motel 6 with a vibrating mattress and ordered me a rib-eye steak dinner from the room-service menu."

"He sounds like a real Ashley Wilkes," Sook hooted. "I figured the only thing hardening on old Bernard Delany these days were his arteries!"

Miss Loretta announced, "Bernie confessed his undying love for me."

"Missy, that man has himself a wife, five youngins, an old yellah hound, he's partial to poppin' a cork, and is the deacon over at the Assembly of God Church!"

CHAPTER 18

———

PEARL TUCKER CAME SKIPPING UP the sidewalk. Arriving at our gate, she suspiciously eyed the flattened fence and inspected all the splintered wood pickets lying about and the massive magnolia branch stretching out across our yard.

Pointing to the calamity, she asked, "What in tarnation happened here?" She gestured to the magnolia.

I shrugged my shoulders. "It was nothin'. We're thinkin' a lightning bolt struck it last night. Sookie!" I hollered. "Pearl and I are headin' out to Tallulah's party."

"Good riddance!" she called from inside.

I shrugged my shoulders at Pearl, and the two of us took off up Digby.

As we were turning on to 52nd Street, a flatbed truck carrying a bed full of young migrant cotton pickers whistled in our direction. As the Ford traveled past, Pearl blew them kisses, and the eager boys stood up in the bed, whistling and waving their arms at us.

I remarked, "Miss Loretta believes that we girls hypnotize men with our feminine charms. She claims men just can't help themselves. It's like a moth to a flame."

Pearl kicked a tin can along the sidewalk up 52nd Street. As we strolled under the rows of sprawling oaks, nets of sunlight and shadows cast on her mass of glorious red curls.

I said. "Loretta says we women are like drippin' honey to a mean grizzly bear."

Pearl booted the can further up the sidewalk. "Well, my momma says if it weren't for women needing assistance with jumper cables, all men should be shot with a revolver in between the temples." She gave the cola can one final kick and hollered, "Step on a crack, and you'll break your momma's back!"

Together, we hopped along the pavement, avoiding the veins in the concrete.

The entry to Victory Drive Estates was protected by two tall, grand gates. The sturdy ornate iron stood opened wide for everyone, but regular folks like Pearl and me felt grateful to be granted entry. Inside the stone wall, rows of mansions sat side by side like stodgy, old gray men, each one more ancient and stately than the next. Pearl's mouth went slack-jawed as she gazed on the magnificent houses. The square was lined with sprawling oaks that dripped with Spanish moss. The lush park in the center was manicured like a plush carpet, and planting beds bloomed with geraniums and pansies. Each mansion had its own expanse of green grass. Perfect rosebuds bloomed red, yellow, and white.

Rows of parked polished automobiles lined the curb in front of the Banks's grand estate. Children dressed in their finest ran up the steps and into the massive walnut front doors. Bundles of balloons were tied to the necks of two granite lions that reclined on pedestals flanking both sides of the entry.

We stood small at the steps of Tallulah's house.

Pearl gasped, "Holy moly."

"Yessum," I replied. "Tallulah's folks must be loaded."

As we entered the house, the birthday festivities were in full swing. Smartly dressed children ran in and out of the elegant rooms and up and down the carved mahogany staircase. Like attacking "injuns," boys chased girls through the marble hallways. Pink, yellow, and purple balloons were tied to the carved banister, and strands of crepe paper draped like garlands along the upper balconies, reaching into the center of the grand foyer, tied into big bows on the crystal chandelier. The polished floors reflected like glass. I couldn't detect a speck of dust or any signs of roaming goats or grazing livestock. Girls dressed to the nines in ruffles and ribbons sipped fruit punch from cut-crystal glasses.

Little Tallulah stood in the front entry, greeting each arriving party guest. Fastened to the side of her head was an enormous pink satin bow, the sheer weight of which seemed to cause Tallulah's tiny head to dip slightly to the left. "Good afternoon, Pearl! Poppy!"

"Happy birthday," Pearl declared. "Tallulah, you're awfully quiet for a kid who was borned into such loud money. If I lived in such grandeur, I'd be braggin' to anyone within an ear shot."

Tallulah smiled and curtseyed. "Poppy, I'm so pleased you could attend."

"Thank you kindly for the invitation." I handed Tallulah a small wrapped box with a tortoise ink pen for her journal.

"Thank you so much," She cordially accepted my gift with a gracious nod to the left, struggling a bit to lift her adorned noggin. "There's chocolate cake and fruit punch in the dining room."

I spotted Jackson Taylor in an adjacent room. He was surrounded by a bunch of other kids. I nudged Pearl, and we casually moseyed over in his direction.

The room had crimson velvet drapes cascading from the beamed ceiling. Jackson stood in the center of the laughing partygoers, doing his spot-on imitation of Dixie McAllister. He'd placed a lace doily atop his head and walked about the room with a snooty air of pretention. He held a punch glass with his pinky stuck high into the air, like a high-society teetotaler.

Peering down his nose at the howling boys, he mocked, "Jeffrey Marshall, didn't your momma ever tell you not to chew with your mouth open? You're disgustin'!" Jackson reprimanded each boy, speaking in a strict, syrupy drawl. "Jimmy Atkinson, I swear, if you don't start learnin' to say *thank you* and *no, thank you*, I'm gonna call your momma to complain."

All the boys cackled wildly.

Grabbing a feather duster, Jackson scolded another boy, "Jessie Lee, you need your filthy mouth washed out with a bar of soap."

When Jackson saw Pearl and me, he winked and continued with his Dixie impression. "Christopher Isaac, you're an absolute scoundrel. It's high time you learn to behave like a proper gentleman." Jackson tickled the boy's nose with a swipe of the feather duster.

Two girls, whom I recognized from the bus stop, walked past Pearl and me with turned-up noses, snickering at Pearl's modest dress.

Pearl growled low, and the prissy pair quickened their pace from the room.

Constance White sat in the center of a circle of chatting, pretty girls, while some older, menacing boys encircled them, all vying for Constance's attention.

"I'll never understand boys," Pearl declared. "They are dirty, squirrely critters who don't use the good sense God gave 'em." She pulled me from one opulent room to the next. "I haven't met one who is worth his weight in salt."

I agreed with Pearl's sentiment, but I always kept a watchful eye for any sight of Jackson Taylor.

"I reckon we need boys for some things, like diggin' dirt and pumpin' petrol," Pearl remarked. "But for the likes of me, I can't see much more value."

A few boys with plastic squirt guns dashed through the sitting parlor, chasing two screaming girls.

"Buses," I replied.

"What?"

"Drivin' buses. We need menfolk to drive buses. I'm certainly not boardin' no bus with a woman sitting' behind the wheel."

Pearl laughed out loud, "Me neither! Can you just imagine?"

We made our way into a tall, serious room with leather tufted chairs and walls papered with tiny roses. There were shelves of old books and stacks of even more thick texts on the desk and tables. Alabaster sconces lit the room, and a stuffed and mounted peacock stood in the corner with its long tail of sapphire and purple feathers. Some older kids played records on a phonograph and paid us no never mind. The same two snotty girls who had crossed our paths earlier entered the room, but this time they flashed Pearl forced smiles.

"Howdy, Pearl." One of the stuffy girls slightly curtseyed.

Pearl returned a practiced smile. "Hi, Lisa. Hi, Tara. Lisa Horan, I do believe that's the prettiest dress I've ever laid my eyes on."

"Well, thank you, Pearl."

The two kept walking.

Whispering from the corner of her mouth, Pearl muttered, "I believe that's the ugliest frock I ever did see." She rolled her eyes and stuck her index finger down her throat.

From behind, a pair of hands reached around my face, covering my eyes. "Guess who!"

"Hmm." I grinned in the dark. "Can you give me a hint?"

Jackson lowered his voice an octave and chuckled, "A hint, eh? Well, let me see. I'm the closest thing to a livin', breathin' Superman in all of Savannah, Georgia."

"Superman?" I wondered. When I blinked, I could feel my lashes against Jackson's cupped palms. "Hmmm? Bobby Fredericks?" I guessed.

Jackson's hands were warm on my face. He smelled of cologne.

"Not even close!" He laughed. "Guess again!"

"Well, if it's not Bobby, it must be Mr. Jackson Taylor."

He shouted, "Bullseye!"

I reached up and pulled his hands from my eyes but would've preferred for them to have remained longer.

Jackson flashed a dreamy grin and quipped, "I reckon I gotta be content with second-place prize, behind the illustrious Mr. Daniels."

Pearl piped in, "Jackson Taylor, you're no more Superman than I'm Brigitte Bardot!"

He pulled the sleeve of his cotton T-shirt up to his shoulder, flexing his modest muscle. "Come on, Pearl, you can touch it," Jackson teased her and then offered his flexed bicep to me. "Come on, Poppy. You know you wanna touch it."

"Jackson Taylor, you're a dang fool," Pearl dismissed him. "Let's go, Poppy. Let's leave these hooligans and go find some more civilized conversation."

Pearl pulled me in to the next room, leaving Jackson and his buds behind.

"Where are we goin'?" I asked.

"Let's let Jackson stew on it for a while," she whispered.

"Stew on what?"

"Nedra Sue says that ladies shouldn't go round town giving free milk to a hungry cow."

I considered her theory. "Huh? Is Jackson the cow?"

"Yes. Menfolk are the hungry cows."

I asked, "Do cows even drink milk?"

Pearl sighed, "Just never mind!" She pulled me along.

I hadn't the vaguest notion what Pearl meant, but I rarely questioned any of her older sister's wise counsel.

"Jackson is sweet on you. Poppy, you've snagged yourself the bull in the farmyard. He's hungry for some Poppy Wainwright, and if he stews on it for a spell, he'll appreciate the meal even that much more!" Because Pearl so fervently believed in the opinion she was sharing, I nodded my head in total agreement.

Jackson and his boys trailed behind us into the library and out to the back terrace. Pearl tugged me through yet another door and into an expansive grand room as wide as Sook's entire yard, with inlayed rosewood and marble floors. When we heard the following boys' laugher, we ducked back into the main hallway and escaped down to the foyer.

"You can try, Poppy Wainwright," Jackson called, "but you won't never get away from me." Some of the other girls gasped and whispered in one another's ears.

My face went pomegranate red.

"Jackson Taylor!" Pearl hollered back. "Your momma didn't raise you right."

She pulled me up the carved, curved staircase, leaving the boys at the bottom of the banister. We escaped to an upstairs sitting parlor with overstuffed chairs and satin drapes the color of Jackson's eyes.

With the boys now out of sight, Pearl panted, "Now that you got Jackson swimmin' near your bait, you gotta hook him!"

CHAPTER 19

———◆———

I INCHED OPENED MISS LORETTA'S door and snuck a peek into her darkened room. Her window blind was pulled closed; only the thinnest sliver of morning filtered in. Her clothing from the night before was strewn about, and the air smelled of cigarette smoke and sickly, sweet perfume. Her mangy fur stole rested at the foot of her bed like a sleeping stray cat. A single red pump sat on her nightstand. Its companion had journeyed to the far side of the room, teetering on the top of a haphazard lampshade.

"Miss Loretta," I whispered, "you awake?" Poking my head inside her chamber, I spied her lying unconscious, buried beneath piles of white cotton sheets and patchwork quilts, snoring like a sawmill. I treaded lightly across the littered floor. A brassiere hung from the alabaster chandelier, and her stockings were tossed across the foot board. A half-eaten slice of apple pie sat on a dish and was adorned with a dozen extinguished cigarette butts.

When I pulled the cord to her window blind, the shade retracted, rapidly sending white sunlight pouring into the room. Miss Loretta popped up from the tangle of blankets and bed sheets. Sitting upright, she sheltered her eyes with the palm of her hand, cursing, "Oh, Lordy. Are you tryin' to kill your momma? Baby, please, close that gawd-damned window shade. My head is splittin' right in two."

Blinded by the daylight, she fell back into her pillows and pulled the covers back over her head. "Now, be a doll, and go fetch your momma an aspirin and a glass of freshly squeezed juice."

"No, Poppy. She can get her ass out of bed and go squeeze her own blessed orange juice." Sookie came shuffling into the room. "If Miss Loretta wants breakfast in bed, she can sleep in the kitchen. It's approachin' midday. Only gluttons and ladies of the night sleep until this advanced hour. Loretta, are you either one of those two dubious deviants?" With her walking stick, Sook poked the mound of blankets quilted over Miss Loretta. "This ain't some motel where you can stay out until an ungodly hour and then sleep in till dusk."

Loretta mumbled something foul from under her smothering pillows.

"Miss Loretta, we need to have ourselves a talk."

"Please, not now, Sook," Loretta pleaded. "Not now."

"Get yourself out of this bed."

Loretta huffed and asked, "Baby girl, will you hand your momma her robe over yonder?"

I picked the robe off the wooden floor and offered it to her. As she reached for the frilly pink wrap, her bare forearm was exposed. Dotting inside her arm were two tiny red pin-holes where a needle had recently punctured the skin.

I wasn't sure who saw the wounds first, Sook or I, but Momma went quiet and quickly withdrew back under the covers. Sookie looked over to me and with a wave of her hand gestured for my leave. "Poppy, Miss Loretta and I need to have ourselves a talk. Go on downstairs."

I walked from the room, closing the door behind me.

"Loretta, a piece of my silver serving set and my sweet momma's diamond-rose pendant have gone missing. I have my suspicions who took 'em."

"Ain't true, Sookie. I swear to God, it ain't true."

"Don't make me do this, Loretta. Floyd down at the pawn shop has already phoned me. No need to further the lie. And I have a hunch I know exactly what you've done with the money."

"Don't dare accuse me of nothin', Sook."

"Loretta, you've been warned. I will not tolerate this under my own roof. Perhaps it's best you start makin' your plans to leave this house."

Loretta deliberated for a moment, seemingly to determine just how deep of a hole she'd dug for herself. "I slipped up, Sook. I got messed up with the wrong fella. I've already sent him on his way."

"Missy, it seems to me that you've made a vocation of messin' with the wrong fellas. Don't be the tragic sort of woman who needs a man. Be a woman who a man needs." The room went quiet for a spell until Sookie spoke, "I believe you're nearing the end of your stay in Savannah."

I wanted to bust through the door and save Momma from Sook—save her from herself. But I steered clear. My back remained stiff against the wall, while the war waged on inside her room.

"Loretta, who's gonna clean up the mess when you leave? Who's gonna pick that child off the floor after you've gone?"

Momma spoke in a whisper, "I'm so lost."

I didn't recognize the weary voice on the other side of the panel.

"It's been so hard for so long," Loretta admitted. "I can't see no way to save me or save Poppy from all this darkness."

"Miss Loretta, I ain't never had no youngins of my own," Sook replied. "But it seems to me that a child can endure darkness. I've seen 'em survive mighty heavy dark days as black as night. But they just need to know there's a glimmer of light waitin' for them some-where on the horizon. Loretta, you gotta let that precious child downstairs know that one fine morning she'll rise and find her momma with honest eyes and a healed heart. Give Poppy a flicker of light to hang her hopes on."

I recalled years earlier, after Miss Loretta's last stay in a hospital. Grandma Lainey and I made the drive to Little Rock to visit her for a spell. It was a Saturday, visitor's day, and we found Momma under a lonely sycamore, sitting at a picnic table. She waved wildly in the air when she spotted us coming through the chain link gate. Momma's eyes were clear as the clearest water, and when she smiled, I knew with absolute certainty that she truly saw me.

We sat and gobbled up Grandma's egg-salad sandwiches and laughed until the afternoon turned to shadows. For most of the day, Miss Loretta held Grandma Lainey's hand like a good daughter would. Before we had to depart, before the nurses ran us off, Loretta searched about in her mound of teased yellow hair and pulled a single bobby pin. With the metal end, she scratched into the wooden picnic table her and my name in the center of an etched heart. She carefully engraved *Loretta loves Samuel* into the pine table.

On the long drive back to Mountain Home, Grandma Lainey told me that the heart is a fragile thing. "It breaks easily, like one of my delicate porcelain dolls on the foyer credenza," she said. "A heart needs to be held gently in your hands and treated with care like something cherished." Lainey reached over and rested her palm on my knee. "Do you understand, Samuel?"

"Yes, ma'am."

I reckoned it wasn't much later when I understood that a heart didn't ever truly break. It pulls and stretches like Silly Putty. In warm palms, it can be shaped and molded by whomever you let play with it. But in neglectful hands a heart can be toyed with, and if left unattended, it hardens like a clod abandoned in an unforgiving sun.

———◆———

Pearl and I walked side by side down Gaston Street into Forsyth Square. When I first saw him, Jackson was sitting cross-legged in the park with the other guys. His head was tilted back, laughing at the blue sky. Timmy and Tommy McAllister, dressed in matching striped T-shirts, were squatting on their knees in the dirt with some other fellas, shooting a game of marbles.

Pearl jabbed her pointy elbow into my side. "Stop staring at Jackson! A lady has gotta play hard to get. No boy wants a girl who's an eager beaver."

I sighed, "OK, OK."

We found Constance, Tallulah, and some of the other girls resting in the shade with their backs leaning against a singular giant oak that canopied over most of the park. Pearl and the girls started gabbing about school gossip, ornery, older boys, and the upcoming Halloween festivities. I feigned interest, always keeping the corner of my eye turned to track Jackson Taylor's whereabouts.

The giddy girls' continual giggling lured the boys' attention away from their marbles.

One of the no-neck McAllisters hollered over, "You girls sound like a bunch of clucking chickens."

Us girls huddled together and made the joint decision that no response to Timmy's pestering would be our best approach. Instead, we carried on, laughing even louder, testing the patience of the always-watching boys.

"Poppy!" Jackson called to me, waving his arms. "Over here. I'm over here!"

"Poppy, ignore him," Pearl spoke low. "Just ignore him."

Constance advised in a hushed whisper, "You make Mr. Jackson Taylor come on over here and address you like a proper gentleman should. No boy should call to you like you're some loyal hound dog."

Finally, all the boys stood up from the grass, dusted off their backsides, and moseyed on over to us.

"Hey, Poppy Wainwright, do have a bucket of wax in your ears?" Jackson asked, and all the other boys snickered.

"You're disgustin', Jackson," Constance replied.

The other girls agreed in unison, "Yeah, Jackson. You're disgustin'!"

I answered, "My ears are very much clean. Thank you very much. But they only listen when there's something worth hearing."

"Glad to hear it." He shrugged his shoulders and gave a puzzled expression over his shoulder to his buddies.

All us girls remained silent, shaming the boys with our disinterest.

Tommy McAllister stepped up, announcing, "I do believe you girls are the most unfriendly bunch of stuffy know-it-alls I've ever laid my eyes on."

We girls sat expressionless.

Constance White flipped her luxurious locks of yellow hair over one shoulder and remarked, "Tommy McAllister, why don't you walk yourself back over yonder to the other side of the park? And take these hoodlums with you."

"Hoodlums? Hoodlums?" Jackson piped up, "Oh, great, Tommy. Now I'm in the doghouse for sumpthin' that don't concern me no how."

Pearl quipped, "You fools don't know the first thing about courting a gal."

Timmy McAllister stepped up to take his swing at bat. "Maybe if y'all were more kindly, we fellas would be more obliging. Besides, you gals need to learn a thing or two 'bout pleasing a man. My momma says it's easier to tempt a growling grizzly with a pot of honey than a jug of vinegar."

Little Tallulah worked up the courage to speak her piece. "Tommy, I mean no disrespect to your momma, but that's hogwash." She adjusted her spectacles on her nose. "Why would any proper girl want to attract a mean grizzly bear anyhow?"

"Tallulah, I don't think Tommy here meant no disrespect." Jackson tried to run interference. "Us menfolk would be wholly lost without you lovely ladies strolling around town on our arms. Womenfolk are sweet and simple. They're everything we men aren't," Jackson explained. "Us guys...we're coarse and sweaty and disgustin' beasts. It don't take nothin' to keep you ladies happy." Jackson turned to the other boys, who were listening on as though he were preaching from the holy gospels. "I consider myself an aficionado of sorts on women folk. You gotta learn to play 'em right."

Pearl hoisted her hands on her hips. "What exactly do you mean, 'you gotta play 'em right'?"

"Yeah, Jackson," I repeated. "What do you mean?"

The other girls leaned in with listening ears.

Jackson scratched his cowlick. "Now, wait a cotton-pickin' minute! You gals don't go get all twisted," he stuttered. "All I'm suggestin' is you ladies are susceptible to pitchin' fits and gettin' worked up over the smallest of nothing. My pa says we men have to keep the engines runnin' smooth and life's roads flat without any bumps or potholes so the truck don't bounce about too much. Because women don't take kindly to a rough rocky road."

"That's a pile of steamin' horse shit," Pearl snapped. "My momma's driving the roughest roads in all of Savannah. Not a single solitary man is driving it for her. My momma is on that long road all on her own."

Jackson went silent.

After Pearl finished, I jumped into the wrangle. "The only rides Miss Loretta ever gets are from some worthless men at Claude's Tavern, asking to take her back to their place. I promise you, Jackson Taylor, those Southern gentlemen aren't offering her a safe ride home!"

Constance spoke, "Jackson, what you don't know about women folk could fill all the shelves of the Live Oak Library."

"Ain't true," he said. Sufficiently shamed, Jackson shoved his hands deep into his pockets as though he were digging a hole to make a clean escape from Forsyth Square. "Poppy, I wasn't sayin'…"

Constance interrupted, "Jackson, you've said quite enough."

Looking defeated and dejected, he shook his head and signaled with his shoulder for the other fellas to follow him over to the tether ball poles.

Timmy declared, "Well, that went over like a fart during church service."

As Jackson walked from us, slumping his shoulders and kicking dirt with his untied sneakers, he turned back to my direction. "Dadgummit!" he griped with a pathetically sad expression. "So, are you gals still gonna join us on Halloween night? We can all go huntin' for spooks."

Giddy with excitement, I wanted to accept his invitation on the spot, but Constance hushed me and took the lead. "Jackson, we'll consider your invitation, but you leave us be for now while we ponder your deficiencies as a potential beau."

———

CHAPTER 20

Johnny Harris Supper Club

AN INTRICATE, SCALLOPED LACE DETAIL adorned Donita's dress's collar. A pale-blue satin sash cinched her slender waist and was tied into a lovely full bow at the curvature of her lower back. She had sewn the dress from a paper pattern. The instructions had called for the same lovely white lace to be stitched along the hem of both sleeves, but the fabric store hadn't the sufficient yardage, so Donita substituted delicate antique buttons on each cuff. She paired the new dress with pearl-colored pumps and a matching purse and the diamond rose pendant that Rodney had gifted her was strung about her throat. She had sprayed Rodney's favorite perfume on her neck and décolletage.

It was a rare night out for the couple. Donita had been jittery all afternoon, allowing herself to be excited about their date. But sitting across from Rodney at Delia's, she now felt uneasy and would've preferred to be at home. A single compliment in the car on the drive over about her dress or the scent of her perfume would have eased her anxiety, but Rodney had long since stopped offering such niceties.

The two sat quiet at the table. Any futile conversation was only meant to bridge the uncomfortable silence. Donita graciously smiled over at a couple at another table whom she recognized from church.

Rodney announced, "I saw Craig Murdy and Skipper Doyle in the lounge when we walked in. I'm goin' over to say *howdy*. I'll bring you back a glass of wine." He walked into the adjacent bar and shook the hands of a few of his hell-raising buds from his high school days.

Donita was left sitting alone at their table for two. She took the opportunity to check her reflection in a powder compact. Donita had believed herself to be sufficiently attractive, but only in the way that any slender Savannah girl with straight teeth and clear skin was pretty. She understood that she was no debutant. She wasn't of the proper pedigree or lineage. Her poppa had been a poor farmer and her momma had sewn dresses for the same school girls who had snickered at Donita's simple frayed frocks.

Donita believed her eyes to be nothing special—they were dull and flat and seemed to carry no light. She wished her auburn hair could hold a curl without having to be lacquered with an aerosol spray. Tonight, she worried that her dress appeared to be crudely home-made. She examined the slightly crooked stitch on her left cuff and took notice of a pulled loose thread in another seam. Donita hated that she wasn't a more skilled seamstress. She hated that her eyes were brown as mud and hated that her smile wasn't pearly white.

Inspecting her reflection in the compact's mirror, Donita was relieved to find on that particular night, her appearance was acceptable; she was almost pleasantly pleased with her long hair. She exhaled. The club's dim lighting and the penciled black liner along her lashes made her eyes appear smoky, almost alluring. Her powdered skin looked smooth and supple. Her gathered hair had held tight to a soft curl that cascaded about her shoulders.

She closed the round compact and waited alone at their table while Rodney laughed with his boys in the restaurant's lounge.

Donita recalled a time when Rodney wouldn't ever leave her sitting alone. He shadowed her about town. The mere thought of another man admiring his bride would set Rodney off. Now the idea of Donita sitting alone at home or at nice supper club never crossed his mind. If Donita stayed up through the night waiting on his return, it wasn't his concern.

Donita recalled how she had romanticized Rodney's jealous-fueled rages. Years earlier, at the picture show, when they crossed paths with one of her old high school sweethearts, an incensed Rodney burned hot with jealousy, punching his balled-up fist right through a wall, breaking a wooden chair, and putting her old flame in a hospital bed. There was a time when Rodney's possessiveness made her blush, when she felt flattered by his rage.

Some seven years later, Donita understood that she was a painfully silly, stupid woman. She was sickened by the scent of his aftershave, repulsed by the sound of his breathing as he slept on the pillow beside her. On a few occasions, she had conjured a few new recipes of Rodney's favorite entrees, seasoned with arsenic. On this night, she hated herself for never having served Rodney his last supper.

Listening to Rodney's boisterous laughter filtering in from the lounge, Donita felt herself growing uneasy, slightly nauseous. She sipped from the glass of ice water and blotted perspiration from above her lip with a cloth napkin. She'd been with Rodney long enough to detect by the tenor of his laughter what mischief he was up to. From his obscene cackling, she knew with absolute certainty that Rodney and the other men in the bar were speaking of something crude and tawdry—boasting on some sexual conquest or some drug-fueled escapade.

Donita wondered if the other diners looked on her with pity and sympathy as she sat alone. She wanted to slide beneath their table for two. Adjusting the napkin on her lap, she quietly cursed for not having the sufficient lace to stitch to the hems of her cuffs. She grew furious that she'd lost herself in a marriage of shame.

When Rodney returned to the table with a drink in his hand, having forgotten her glass of Chardonnay, Donita said nothing.

When the blond waitress in a tight blouse arrived to take their order, Rodney and she held a glance a moment too long. But Donita remained quiet.

It was after her husband's eyes followed the waitress's shapely backside all the way to the kitchen that Donita said in a hushed whisper, "Rodney, you're embarrassing me."

"Oh, baby. She ain't nothin' but some damn waitress." He dismissed his wife. "Don't go get all pissy."

"It's just not appropriate, honey," she said.

Like the many times before, Donita worried about a potential public scene. She slightly smiled, "Behave yourself, baby."

"You do this every gawd-damned time we go out." He took a drink of his scotch, and the table went quiet.

The curvy waitress returned to their table with his soup and Donita's salad. As the server placed the dish in front of Rodney, their hands brushed ever so slightly. Rodney and she then exchanged private smiles. The blond waitress's false lashes fluttered, and she blushed red.

Donita had witnessed it all. She wanted to disappear—shrink into her chair into the smallest of nothing. But Donita swallowed hard and turned her eyes to the table.

Unaware or unconcerned, Rodney stuffed his cloth napkin down the front of his shirt and began slurping his soup. He tore pieces of warm sourdough bread, sopping it about the bowl of bisque.

Before their main course had even arrived, Donita had lost her appetite. Her salad sat undisturbed in front of her.

"Why are you with me?" she asked.

"What?"

With pleading eyes, Donita asked him again, "Why so, Rodney? Why are you with me?"

"Oh, Christ." He shook his head. "Are you gonna go crazy on me tonight? Can't we just have one gawd-damned night without you goin' bat-shit crazy? She's a silly fucking waitress," he chuckled. "If I wanted to get the third degree tonight, I would've walked my-self into the prosecutor's office. Don't make a gawd-damned scene over nothin'."

"It's not about her," she replied. "It's true, I'm humiliated by your behavior, but it's not about all the other women, Rodney."

"Bullshit!" His volume raised to an uncivilized level. "With you it's always about one thing or the other." He finished his drink with one gulp.

Hoping to prevent a public spectacle, she repeated in her li-brary voice, "It's not about all the women."

Rodney leaned in close, still gripping his empty scotch glass. "If you were a better wife, there wouldn't be a need for other women."

Donita dabbed the corners of her mouth with her cloth napkin. "I'm afraid I'm feeling sickly. I must be comin' down with the flu bug that's goin' around." She rose from the table and smoothed her skirt with the palms of her hands.

Their nearest neighbors, Fred and Charlotte Wilkes, were din-ing in a corner booth and called to Donita, but she kept walking in a straight line, leaving her purse and knit sweater. After dropping a ten-dollar bill on the table, Rodney gathered Donita's belongings and followed behind her out to the parking lot.

They remained silent in the car all the way back to their little house out past the train tracks.

Donita sat numb, and Rodney was seething.

Back inside the privacy of their small place, Rodney beat her with his bare hands until Donita lost consciousness on the kitchen linoleum.

CHAPTER 21

MISS LORETTA ARRIVED, SKIPPING INTO the kitchen through the back-screen door. Clutching a bouquet of wild flowers, she exclaimed, "It's finally happened! I do believe it has finally happened!"

I was making buttermilk biscuits at the counter. "What's happened, Loretta?"

Downright giddy with glee, she held the bouquet under my nose for a sniff. "Today, I met the man of my dreams. A true gentleman!"

Sook was cracking pecans into a bucket. She rolled her eyes behind her low-riding spectacles.

I said, "That's terrific, Miss Loretta!"

She found a vase in a cupboard and went about arranging the flowers.

"Oh, Poppy," she gushed. "He's the most handsome man I've ever laid my eyes on. Dark, mysterious features and smooth skin, the color of caramel. His name is Senor Juan Gabriel Medina." She pronounced his full name out loud like he had the winning raffle ticket. "Juan Gabriel was tending to the front yard of the yellah house four doors down. He waved me over—*Senorita! Senorita!*—and handed me these lovely, happy flowers over their picket fence. I don't want to jinx it, Poppy, but I do believe it was love at first sight!"

Sookie separated the hard shell from the meat of the nut. "Loretta, do you mean to tell me that you've fallen in love with the Mexican help over yonder at Clyde and Gladys Culpepper's place?"

Miss Loretta replied, "Love is colorblind, Sook."

My ancient aunt thought on it. "So, on the sidewalk this Juan Carlos confessed his undying love?"

"Gabriel," Loretta corrected her. "His name is Juan Gabriel."

Exasperated, Sookie squeezed her nutcracker. "Sweet mother of Andrew Jackson! So, this Juan Gabriel confessed his undying love for you?"

"There ain't no boundaries or borders that a true heart can't climb over," Miss Loretta explained. "Our love can rise above the chain link fences keeping us apart."

"I don't care if the man is a Mexican or a Methodist. That don't make a lick of sense." Sookie shook her head. "Other than this fella giving you a handful of Gladys Culpepper's stinkweeds, how did you determine that you and Senior Juan Jose were a match? What exactly did he say?"

"It's Juan Gabriel."

"Holy mother of Jefferson Davis! What did this Juan Gabriel say?"

"Say?" Miss Loretta looked puzzled.

I spoke up, "Yes, Momma. Did Juan whisper romantic sweet nothings into your ear?"

She licked her slippery lips. "Oh, no, no. Senor Juan Gabriel Medina can't speak a syllable of English," she declared. "I just knew it was our destiny when our eyes first met. We knew instantly that we were made for each other." She gazed starry-eyed up to the ceiling.

"Knew what?" I asked.

"We knew that we were a perfect match! Like you know when you find the ideal handbag or when you slip into a comfortable bra with adequate underwire support at the department store."

"I give up!" Sookie replied. "This is one nut I ain't never gonna crack!"

———

Donita Pendergast and Miss Loretta weren't never gonna be friendly.

I suspected they tolerated each other on my account. The two women were cut from different cloths. Donita was proper and polished with her perfect, pious, pin curls. Miss Loretta was tawdry and tarnished.

If they passed on the sidewalk, they walked a wide path around each other. When Donita came by for a glass of sweet tea with Sookie and me, the two only exchanged stiff niceties, and then Miss Loretta would find reason to leave the house or head up to her room.

As for Donita, she was cordial enough to Loretta, but Momma made it crystal clear at every turn that she believed the *Pendergast woman* was the prissy sort and carried herself with an heir of superiority.

"Ain't true," I said. "Donita is real good people."

"Poppy, those buttoned-up, holy-roller types ain't got the time of day for the likes of me," she replied. "Her snotty sort turns up their snooty noses in judgement at the mere scent of my perfume."

"It just ain't true," I repeated. "I don't believe I've ever heard a mean-spirited word pass from Donita's lips."

Loretta remarked, "She may not come right out and say it, but I promise in her mind, she's already got me burnin' in the fiery pits of damnation."

When Donita dropped me off after a church social, she would amiably smile and nod to Loretta from her car's window.

Reclining on the front porch, dressed in a blouse exposing a healthy helping of her ample bosoms, Loretta begrudgingly offered Donita a half-hearted howdy.

From her automobile, Donita waved. "It's a mighty fine afternoon, Loretta."

Reading from her Hollywood gossip magazine in the shade of the porch, Loretta responded back, "This ungodly humidity flattens my hair and makes my tits sweat."

Donita blushed a deep shade of crimson and hurriedly cranked up her window. "Bye, Poppy. I'll see you at next Sunday's service."

"Thank you kindly, Donita, for the ride home."

I sauntered up the front stoop. "Miss Loretta, you're just awful."

"I'm only truth telling." Adjusting herself, she quipped, "That woman wouldn't take a whiz on me if I was on fire."

I supposed it was true—the two women were different sorts. Loretta was running fast and wild. She'd never be a Savannah socialite, accepted among the proper social circles. Miss Loretta was a moonlight lady, courted only in shadows and loved one night at a time. Donita Pendergast had chosen for herself a strikingly handsome man but painfully cruel. She willingly accepted the two-dollar cut carnations from the Piggly Wiggly and never ever thought to ask for a dozen long-stemmed roses from the elegant florist shop on Pennsylvania Avenue. However, if both of the ladies' cards were spread out across the table and they saw the hands each were dealt, the pair could've clearly understood they weren't so dissimilar.

Both women were playing a losing game with the deck stacked against them. Both desperate, both lonely. Donita grieved at night for the love she had lost, while Loretta grieved for the love she'd never found.

Michael Scott Garvin

I reckoned sometimes it was too easy for womenfolk to judge one another by the shade of red lining their lips or the length of a skirt's hem instead of investigating any closer.

Aunt Sook said Miss Loretta and Donita Pendergast weren't so very different. "Until they understand they're *enough*, those two women won't never sleep a restful night," Sookie told me. "Since time began, womenfolk go about sniffin' around for some man to tell them they are treasured. No fella can make them believe somethin' they don't already know." Sookie peered over the top of her bifocals. "Poppy, promise your old aunt Sook that you won't wallow in such foolishness." She held her quaking finger to her chest. "Always know you're worthy. Always know you're deserving of more."

"I will, Sook," I said. "I promise."

"Until Donita and Miss Loretta fix the broken pieces, they're just damaged goods waitin' for the next scoundrel to break them again and again."

I had my suspicions that Momma was pea green with envy when it came to Mrs. Pendergast. One afternoon at the Piggly Wiggly, as Loretta pushed our buggy up the aisle, I spotted Donita coming toward us in the produce section.

Mrs. Pendergast wheeled her grocery cart up to ours, greeting us with a pleasant smile. "Afternoon, ladies."

Miss Loretta offered an uninspired howdy.

Spotting the bag of Tootsie Pops in our cart, Donita remarked, "Poppy, I can see that you and Miss Loretta are stocking up on Halloween treats."

"Yes, ma'am."

"I believe this will be the first time I can recall Sook's front porch light will be burnin' bright on Halloween. Usually your aunt darkens her doorway and runs any trick-or-treaters clear off her porch. I'm here to pick up some Granny Smiths. I'm making caramel apples for the children at the church."

I commented, "Loretta, Mrs. Pendergast is a fine cook. I suspect she can bake up anything. I swear her kitchen cupboards are stocked with every spice and seasoning. It's somethin' to behold!"

"Oh now, Poppy. You're sweet, but I think you're bragging on me."

"No, it's true," I said. "It's a marvel what you can cook up."

"Stop it." She blushed.

Admiring a bag of plump, ripe peaches in Donita's buggy, I commented, "Oh my, those peaches look lovely."

"Yessum. It appears it's a fine season for Georgia peaches."

"I hate peaches," Loretta announced with a scowl. "They're soft and mushy. Too sickly sweet for my taste."

With a puzzled expression, I turned to Loretta. She expounded, "I love cantaloupes, and I'm fond of watermelons. I love me some pears and pineapple and persimmons."

Perplexed, Donita attempted an awkward smile.

Miss Loretta showed no sign of stopping. "I'm partial to blackberries and boysenberries. On occasion, I enjoy kiwis and kumquats. But I detest prissy, pious peaches!"

Donita and I stood silent, uncertain of an appropriate response. "Well, Miss Loretta, I have a scrumptious recipe for kumquat jam. I'll send a jar home with Poppy come next Sunday after church."

Miss Loretta declared, "I hate jam."

Donita gave me a baffled expression.

The two ladies stood facing each other until Donita graciously nodded to Loretta. "Have a lovely afternoon, ladies."

She sped her grocery buggy clean out of sight.

———◆———

CHAPTER 22

SAVANNAH BELONGED TO HER GHOSTS.

In the clear light of day, tourists would take to the streets, snapping cameras and strolling along the cobblestone sidewalks, buying up T-shirts, coffee mugs, and postcards. All the locals would go about their business on Bull Street, and the shops and boutiques would bustle with the fashionably fine ladies of the South. During the daily hours, folks carried on as though the sun had risen just to hear them crow, but during the bewitching hours of night, Savannah belonged to its ghosts.

Stalking the alleys and haunting the cemeteries, the spirits lurked about like black cats. In the gloomy shadows of moonlight, they danced about on the granite gravestones. The whispers of the dead called from the darkened doorways of the family tombs and mausoleums. The vacant town squares became their midnight playgrounds.

The locals knew it was wise to bolt up their doors and keep garlic cloves near their beds before drifting to sleep. The superstitious ancient ladies poured a thin trail of table salt every night along their doors' thresholds to keep a haunting spirit at bay, or they hid an image of our Lord Jesus under a box spring to stop an angry apparition dead in his tracks.

Buried deep under the old Colonial Park Cemetery lay the unmarked graves of tens of thousands of forgotten lost souls, yet no more than a thousand grave markers stood within the iron gates. Over the decades, Savannah's graveyards had been covered, and more corpses were stacked atop them. It was said that Savannah slept on these forgotten mass graves.

Aunt Sookie told me that at the stroke of midnight, if you put your ear near to the ground, you could hear the anguished cries of the fallen souls stirring just below the muddy earth.

Folks round here believed the willful desecration of all of Savannah's burial grounds kept the ghosts from their rightful, eternal sleep.

Halloween arrived in Savannah with sidewalks bustling with ghouls, ghosts, and goblins. Under the golden glow of street lamps, the children of Digby rang doorbells and snatched up candy from Tupperware bowls. Dixie McAllister poured a spooky witch's brew punch in Styrofoam cups from her porch, while Carl, dressed as Frankenstein, hid low in their hydrangea bushes, scaring the tar out of the young trick-or-treaters.

From as early as the cradle, Savannah's youngest citizens were told the story of the orphan Rene Asche Rondolier, a young adolescent whose face was so disfigured, he was feared by many in town. It was said that the lonely, destitute boy called Colonial Park Cemetery his home in the early 1800s, the graveyard where young Rene slept among the cold, hard gravestones.

Rene's tale was retold through the ages. One evening he was caught in Colonial Park Cemetery, accused of murdering two young innocent school girls. Throughout the night, a vengeful mob searched the city for Rene, believing he had committed the heinous and brutal killings. With torches and lanterns in hand, the citizens scoured every nook and cranny of Savannah. After young Rene was cornered in the cemetery, the angry crowd strung the boy up and hung him by his neck.

Soon after that night, locals reported, a shadowy figure haunted the grounds of Colonial Park, Rene's only home.

In the days following his lynching, more murdered bodies of innocent little girls turned up in Colonial Park, and the townspeople blamed the ghost of young Rene.

Jackson told me he'd spotted Rene's spirit walking aimlessly through the cemetery on one cold, blistery evening. Tommy McAllister reported he had seen Rene's corpse hanging from the Hanging Tree in the back of Colonial Park. All us kids referred to Colonial Park as "Rene's Playground." Not a single one of us would be caught dead anywhere near the hanging tree after nightfall.

Sookie's take on the old Savannah ghost story was direct and unsympathetic: "I suspect those snotty little girls had it comin'."

"Sook," I said, "you can't mean what you're sayin'?"

"I sure as hell do! If I ever met this Rene out stalking Digby Street at night, I'd congratulate him and point him directly to those McAllister boys' open window."

I laughed, "Sook, you're just messin' with me."

"The hell I am! I'd let him borrow my ladder in the back of the shed, so he could reach the McAllister's second-story window."

On Halloween night, all of Digby Street was abuzz. Children, costumed in their most ghoulish, ran shrieking from house to house. Glowing pumpkin jack-o-lanterns burned with fiery eyes and angry mouths. Plastic witches rode broomsticks, and bedsheet ghosts were strung from the magnolias.

Miss Loretta came tripping down the stairs. "Poppy, I've gotta run! I've got me a date. I'm off to a fancy costume party at the Johnny Harris's Dining Room." She strutted in the middle of the foyer and slowly spun about, showcasing the same skin-tight red satin dress I'd seen a dozen or more times. Her mangy fur stole was wrapped about her bare shoulders. "So, what do you think?" she asked and then slowly and seductively spun about.

I shrugged my shoulders. "Who are ya supposed to be, Miss Loretta?"

"You silly. Can't you see? I am a lady of the night!"

"But Loretta, that's your same old Saturday-night frock."

"No, it ain't." She smiled wickedly and struck a suggestive pose. Ever so seductively, she began hiking up her dress high above her thigh, exposing two lace garter belts with silk black stockings.

I giggled. "I swear, Loretta, you ain't got no sense at all. Are you goin' to this party with Sheriff Delany? Juan Gabriel?"

"Goodness, no!" She scowled. "I've got me a new beau. He's got real potential. A real gentleman." She adjusted my tipsy tiara. "Poppy, you look just precious."

I announced, "I'm a princess."

"Baby girl, you've blossomed into the most beautiful princess I've ever set my eyes on."

"I hope Jackson will approve."

"Oh, he will. He'd have to be blind as a bat to not see how lovely you are." Loretta winked and went about fiddling with my hair with her fingers. "There ya go." She smiled like a proud momma. "You're pretty as a picture."

"Are you gonna be careful tonight, Miss Loretta?"

"Yessum. Your momma is gonna behave herself. I promise." She held her hand over her heart.

I called up the balcony, "Sookie! Hurry on down."

Loretta and I stood at the bottom of the staircase, waiting for the sound of Sook's shuffling.

"Sookie, are you awake?" I called again. "It's not like her to go to bed this early. I'm worried about old Sook," I confessed. "Have you noticed how she's been dozing off in the middle of the day during her soap opera?"

"Child, that's just what happens with old folks. It's the nature of things." Miss Loretta sounded absolutely convinced of her theory. "Old folks start sleeping more and more, and then one morning they're dead."

"That ain't true," I said.

"Is too," she insisted. "Old folks start winding down like a tired clock. It begins when they start gettin' lazy. The next thing ya know, the geezers start goin' to bed before sunset and sleep well past breakfast. And then, lo and behold, one day you find them cold and stiff in their beds, deader than old man Barney."

"Loretta, have you already been stealing sips of Sook's hooch this evening?"

"Nope. I'm just truth telling. Aunt Sook could be up there right now as stiff as your grandma Lainey."

"I ain't dead!" Sookie hollered, making her appearance up on the catwalk. "Lucifer will have to wait another day to collect my soul, and Poppy will have to wait a spell to collect my fortune!"

Sookie was a spectacle to behold. Balanced atop her head was one of the outrageous feathered hats from up in the dusty attic. She'd adorned the hat with several additional peacock feathers to appear even more ridiculous. The lavish purple and violet plumes nearly reached the dusty chandelier as she descended. Wrapped about her shoulders was a full-length white fur coat that I recognized from the stacks of boxes in the dark, dank basement. Sookie wobbled her way down the staircase, carefully maneuvering each step.

As she approached, it was clear Miss Loretta was the culprit who had lined Sook's lips in a scandalous red, applied false eyelashes to her upper and lower lids, and blushed Sookie's cheeks with pink powder.

I laughed from my belly and hollered up, "Who are ya supposed to be?"

"You gotta guess," she smiled coyly.

I asked, "Maybe some high-society lady?"

"You're gettin' close," she hinted.

"I ain't sure, Sook." I covered my mouth with both hands, giggling. "You're painted up like some circus clown with a silly hat! You look absolutely preposterous!"

"That's it! You've guessed right!" She exclaimed, "I'm Dixie McAllister!"

"Oh, Sook. You're just mean to the bone."

Outside one could hear the racket of all the approaching gang rushing up the path to the house. I greeted them at the front door.

Pearl had corralled her mass of red frizz into a cowgirl hat. "I'm Annie Oakley!" she declared and then drew a plastic pistol from her holster. She pulled the toy gun's trigger and then blew the imaginary smoke from the end of its barrel.

Constance and Tallulah were dressed as cheerleaders for Savannah High, complete with pleated skirts, monogrammed sweaters, and pompoms. Timmy and Tommy's faces were covered by plastic masks held in place by elastic strings that stretched behind their ears and all around their fat heads.

Timmy held the flat palm of his hand up in the air and spoke in a low octave, "Me, Tonto." His voice escaped through the small breathing hole in the lips of the plastic Indian mask. "Me want to smoke a peace pipe."

Tommy hollered, "I'm the Lone Ranger!" He spun a long rope high above his head and lassoed poor little Tallulah, whose panicked expression led me to believe she actually was fretting about the possibility of being scalped right there on Sook's front porch.

Jackson's blond hair was combed wet with a sharp, clean part. He wore a suit jacket over a crisp, white button-up. His recent growth spurt had stretched his long arms well past the cuffs of his shirt sleeves. His black slacks were pressed, but I guess the pants must've belonged to his pops because the slacks were cinched like a ruffle at his waist with a black belt. He wore a pair of black reading spectacles with both glass lenses missing and a pencil slid above his right ear. Scrubbed clean and polished up, Jackson shined like a new dime, but he moved about in the suit like some stiff storefront window mannequin.

"Jackson, who are you supposed to be?" I asked.

He fidgeted with his buttoned collar. "I'm Clark Kent, of course!" He flexed and flashed me a grin, then leaned in close and gave me a slight peek of the superhero T-shirt beneath his white button-up shirt.

I giggled, "Of course you are!"

Jackson blushed tomato red. He was lanky and awkward and perfectly dreamy.

Aunt Sookie came out strutting onto the front porch like a crippled cockatoo with her ivory fur wrap and plumes of feathers nesting high on her head. She took a seat in her rocker and gripped to the bowl of Tootsie Pops treats in her lap.

Nervous that old Sook was sitting at only an arm's length distance, the McAllister twins retreated a few steps back further into the grass lawn.

From her rocker, Sookie slightly raised her right hip, releasing a sour, off-pitched note. Like some squealing fiddle strung well out of tune, her fart cut through the chilly Savannah night.

Constance grimaced, and little Tallulah squeezed the tip of her nose.

Jackson asked, "Did your Aunt Sookie just rip one?"

"Yessum. My sincere apologies," I said. "Pay her no never mind. She's like a jukebox that keeps playing a stinky song, whether you've fed her a nickel or not. Her smelly tunes just keep comin'."

"All y'all clear out! How many times do I have to flush to get rid of y'all?" Sookie waved us away. "I hate children in packs." Pointing her quivering walking stick directly over to the masked McAllisters, Sookie threatened, "And don't think I don't know who you two little fat bastards are."

The Lone Ranger and his trusty sidekick straightened their spines at attention.

Sookie offer up the Tupperware bowl to the trembling twins. "In this bowl of treats, I gots me two special chocolate bars with hidden razor blades with your names on 'em!"

The boys withdrew even farther back into the lawn.

"Now, all you brats, skedaddle!" she shooed us away.

We joined the other casts of characters on the sidewalks, running wild through the streets of Savannah. We bumped shoulders in the dark, laughing as we walked past the gates of the National Cemetery.

"I dare you to go in," Tonto challenged the Lone Ranger.

"No way!" Tommy declined from behind his plastic disguise.

"I double dare ya!" Timmy egged him on. "You chicken shit?"

"Shut up! I ain't no chicken." Tommy slugged his brother's shoulder.

Tonto grabbed the Lone Ranger by his holster. The two brothers started scuffling on the pavement.

Jackson stepped up. "I'll go in. I ain't no scaredy-cat!" He took a deep breath and walked up to the bolted iron gates of the cemetery. Maneuvering through an opening between two twisted iron posts, he made his way to the other side.

The rest of us, still stalling on the sidewalk, eyeballed one another and then filed in behind him, one after the next, except for little Tallulah, who adamantly refused, clutching to her pompoms.

"I'm staying put," she declared. "There ain't nothin' behind those gates that the good Lord wants me to see at this ungodly hour." She stood in place near the tall iron fence.

The graveyard was dead quiet except for wild cats, who stalked about in autumn's leaves and crops of gravestones.

"Did y'all hear that?" Jackson questioned.

The McAllister boys both snickered.

Pearl replied, "I didn't hear nothin'."

Constance death gripped my arm. "I wanna go home," she whined. "Let's get outta here."

We walked the cobbled streets of granite markers, through row after row of the forgotten dead. A curtain of fog drifted off the water and lingered around us, moving about the crypts and ivy-choked vaults like some invading smoke.

Suddenly, Jackson and the twins scattered, giving us the slip. We heard them sneaking low among the granite tombs.

Pearl called out, "Jackson, we know what y'all are up to. We're not scared."

In an attempt to frighten us girls, the hiding boys hooted like owls and squeaked like scampering mice.

I huddled in close to Pearl and demanded, "You boys stop it! Stop it right now!"

A low-hanging tree branch bristled in an October breeze, causing us girls to jump from our skin. Constance let out a high-pitched scream that pierced through the night.

The voice of one of the McAllisters called out from behind a stone crypt. "Constance, zip it! The caretaker is gonna boot us outta here if you don't shut up!"

I pleaded, "Jackson, come on out."

Only silence answered back.

The flailing of a raven's wings caused another screaming frenzy from Constance.

Unnerved, Pearl rolled her eyes and whispered to me, "I swear, the first open grave we come across, Constance White is goin' in head first."

Finally, we spotted Jackson posing atop the tallest family mausoleum. He stood high above us; his suit jacket and white button-up shirt were discarded. There was no sign of his black-rimmed glasses. He flexed his modest biceps, modeling the T-shirt with Superman's S proudly displayed on his chest. His pop's oversized slacks were still cinched around his waist.

"Did someone call for a superhero? May I assist you lovely ladies?" He grinned from atop his stone pillar. "Howdy, fair ladies. Superman has come to your rescue!"

Constance dismissed Jackson with a snarl. I couldn't help but silently swoon.

He extended his hand to me from high above. "Is that my sweet Lois Lane that I see?

Constance muttered, "I believe I'm gonna throw up."

Pearl shook her head. "Jackson Taylor, I swear you're retarded." She drew her plastic pistol from her holster, took aim, and shot him.

Jackson dramatically clutched his chest. "I'm shot!" he moaned in pain. "You got me!" He took a theatrical fall off the top of the mausoleum and into a pile of October leaves.

I applauded his performance.

Constance complained, "I'm gettin' the hell out of this god-forsaken place. It gives me the creeps."

We made our way back onto the street to find tiny Tallulah still waiting patiently under the streetlamp, shivering in the cold. Her blue lips quivered, "What was all that ruckus?"

Constance shook her head. "Annie Oakley killed Superman."

Little Tallulah looked baffled.

"The boys were just bein' fools," Pearl answered.

Timmy ran ahead of us, shouting, "There's a haunted house over at the high school! Let's go!"

Breathless, we sprinted to Savannah High, little Tallulah lagging far behind. She came trailing up the sidewalk, gasping for air and gripping tight to her pompoms. She dug in the pockets of her cheerleader's pleated skirt for her plastic asthmatic breather.

I asked, "Are you gonna be OK, Tallulah?"

She nodded in the affirmative as her white lips sucked on the plastic inhaler.

We paid our admission at the ticket booth and waited in a long line of screaming girls and mischievous boys.

When we entered the first pitch-black chamber, the door slammed shut behind us. We waited silently in the dark. When a rubber spider landed on her shoulder, Constance screamed, piercing our eardrums. She stumbled in the black, collecting strings of cobwebs in her hair. Pumped-in smoke lingered like the spreading fog back at the cemetery. Wicked laughter came through a loud speaker, and flashes of white light illuminated the tiny room for the briefest moments. A plastic witch with blinking green eyes cackled high above us.

The pitch-black room was filled with our faceless, laughing voices. My hands reached blindly in front of me. Pearl walked, face first, into a wall. A dull thump in the black was followed by Pearl erupting into uncontrollable laughter. Jackson was doing his best Count Dracula "I vant to suck your blood" while Constance and Tallulah were insisting that the lights be switched on immediately.

I reached blindly, careful not to stumble. My fingers read the braille night. All at once, Jackson was at my side. His hands were on my shoulder. Under my fingertips, I felt his skin; I touched his eyes, lips, nose, and hair. I read his laughing mouth.

Placing both his palms on my face, cupping my cheeks, he asked me, "Are you frightened, Poppy?" His breath was warm and smelled like hard candy.

I admitted, "Yes. I'm scared."

Holding me in his awkward arms, he whispered in the dark, "Don't be afraid. Don't ever be afraid. I'll protect you." And he kissed my mouth.

Tommy yelled out, "He's got a knife! He's got a knife!"

Little Tallulah screamed, tripping on a Styrofoam headstone. She hit the floor with a thud. Her pompoms flew into the air, landing directly on Constance's head, who believed them to be yet another giant spider's web. We all screamed and laughed, then screamed again. But Jackson stayed near my side. In between our shrieks and squeals, he kissed me again.

Pearl called out, "Tallulah, are you OK?"

"Uh, I think so," she replied with a whimper.

A hidden door opened wide, and we all rushed into another black chamber. Jackson held my hand tightly. When the door behind us slammed shut, Constance let out another ear-deafening shriek.

Pearl's voice threatened, "I'm gonna strangle your neck, Constance, if you don't shut up your screaming."

The McAllister twins laughed riotously; their Lone Ranger and Tonto masks glowed in the dark. When a zombie appeared, gripping a chain saw, high above his head, I moved even nearer to Jackson.

I reckon I understood in that moment that if I let Jackson kiss me again that he'd be tangled up in my mess. No more would it be just me lying to all the fine folks of Savannah, but Jackson could be branded with a red-hot poker as the blue-jeaned local boy who was duped by some fella gussied up as a girl. Standing in the haunted house at the Savannah High gymnasium, I knew full well that if I let Jackson kiss me again, he could be hurt bad by my masquerade.

He whispered low, "Poppy, I suspect I'm fallin' for ya."

Between the terrified screams and the laughter of caged teenagers, I made the selfish choice. I let Jackson Taylor kiss me again.

"Do ya think you'd ever consider bein' my girl?" His warm breath was on my neck.

I was six months and eight days shy of turning fourteen. Life had been a hard, burdensome thing, more sour than sweet. And so, there in the dark, I gripped to Jackson's hand and held tight to my first-ever chance at happy.

A white light flashed like a bolt of lightning, and everyone could see one another for the briefest second.

Timmy sang out, "Two little lovers sitting in a tree...K-I-S-S-I-N-G."

But Jackson didn't care one wit. He held me tighter in his arms.

"First comes love, then comes marriage, then comes Jackson with a baby carriage!" Timmy chuckled.

Pearl hollered, "McAllister, you're so immature!" She fumbled in the black, making her way over to Timmy's glowing disguise, and whacked him with her bag of treats.

We all giggled and pushed toward the exit.

Jackson grabbed my hand and pulled me from the haunted house.

We escaped, running like howling banshees up Drayton Street. Delirious and out of breath, we fell on the wet grass in the park under a bloated, full moon, Jackson still holding tightly to my hand. Lying on our backs, we examined the night sky, pocked with a million stars.

Pearl inventoried her bag of candy while Constance fussed with her hair, untangling the strings of spider webs. Our asthmatic little cheerleader siphoned oxygen from her inhaler and wrote in her notepad under a streetlamp. The McAllister boys had squared off and were engaging in a round of fisticuffs about nothing in particular. We were young, and the moon and stars were ours.

Jackson asked if he could walk me back home. We said good-bye to the rest of the gang. The streets had gone quiet, except for some older boys dressed as pillaging pirates. The buccaneers went about looting in silence, from porch to porch. They busted up carved pumpkins on the street pavement.

One of the sword-toting pirates, wearing a patch over his left eye and a stuffed parrot riding on his shoulder, called from across the street, "Hey, Taylor. How's it goin' tonight?"

"Fine, Jimmy."

The plundering swashbuckler raised his blade high into the night air and viciously impaled the skull of the pumpkin with his sword. "I'll see ya at practice on Tuesday! Make sure to say howdy to your momma and pop."

"Sure, Jimmy!"

The pirates ran off, rollicking into the disappearing night.

Jackson shoved his hands deep into the pockets of his trousers. "Poppy, I reckon, I owe you an apology for stealing a kiss in the cover of dark. It wasn't proper of me."

"I suspect not," I said.

He stopped on the sidewalk and took a deep breath of the cold October night. "It wasn't the gentlemanly thing to do. I'm down-right ashamed of my scandalous behavior."

I replied, "If I let you kiss me in the sunlight, would you it put your shame to rest?"

Jackson's wide grin shown in the pale moonlight.

As we strolled, he explained to me that he believed God created a perfect match for every living soul.

"Poppy, some poor saps have to go searchin' to the far ends of the earth," he said. "Aren't we so lucky that we found each other now?"

At the front gate, Jackson brushed a stray strand of hair from my face and thanked me for a lovely evening.

"Good night, Poppy Wainwright."

I liked the way my name sounded coming from his mouth.

"Jackson, get yourself home safe, before you get caught in the rain."

He pounded on his chest with a closed fist. "Shucks, I ain't afraid of a little drizzle. I'm Superman!" Saluting me, he took off sprinting up Digby.

I sauntered down the path, grinning like some dreamy, star-crossed fool.

"Poppy Wainwright!" Jackson called from the dark in a faraway voice.

I stood on my tippy-toes on the front porch, searching the lonely lane for any sight of him.

His voice echoed in the night. "Poppy Wainwright! You've got my head spinning!"

I looked for Jackson, but only a glowing streetlamp stood solemn along Digby. Blushing, I turned from the watching moon.

His voice hollered out again, "I've never known such a night!"

Running back to the gate, I called, "Good night, Jackson. Good night!"

Exuberant and breathless, I laughed out loud. My cheeks ached from an insuppressible grin. It was such a hollow kind of lonesome, believing affections bestowed on other girls wouldn't ever be offered up to me, but on that chilly autumn night, I knew with certainty Mr. Jackson Taylor was mine, and I was his.

I crept into a sleeping house. Annabelle rested in the foyer, feeding on the spilled bowl of Halloween sweets. Sookie had never made it upstairs. She snored on the couch in the sitting parlor still wrapped in her fur. Her television was gray, sizzling with static. Miss Loretta was still out, trying to cling on to what remained of the night. I closed my bedroom door behind me and took myself up to the rooftop.

The moon over Savannah was a lovely sight, suspended from the stars. It hung low and lonely, casting a golden glow over Georgia. A November rain was coming on out over the ocean. I sat on the shingles and listened to a whisper on the breeze. I wondered if Jackson could hear the words.

Below me, shadows moved about the yard like ghosts hiding from a fading night. Did Jackson make it home safely? Was he somewhere searching the same night sky for any hint of me? I asked the bloated moon, but it turned away shyly.

With the first droplets of rainfall, I climbed in from the roof and back into my window. I slipped into my nightgown and snuggled beneath my bed covers. Holding tight to my pillow, I dreamed a lovely dream that only lucky girls like Constance White and me could dream.

"Poppy, wake up!" I was startled from sleep to find a breathless Loretta hovering over me. "We gotta go! Hurry up, baby!"

"What?" Rubbing my eyes, I tried to focus. "What's wrong, Miss Loretta?"

"Just get up, baby." She smelled of cigarettes, and her voice was panicked.

"What's wrong?"

Her lipstick was smudged violently across her anguished face. Her mangled, mangy mess of yellow hair was knotted and unruly. Still dressed in her same red frock from her night out on the town, but her new black nylon stockings were snagged and torn.

She tugged at my covers.

"What time is it, Momma?"

"We gotta run."

"Why? What's goin' on?"

Loretta fought with my blanket, pulling my covers to the floor. "There's no time, baby! We gotta go. They're coming for us." Pulling at me, she strained my wrists.

I cried out, "Momma, you're hurting me!"

"We ain't got no time." She was spooked, like a wild animal. Streams of mascara stained her cheeks.

With a tight grip of my arm, she yanked me from my bed, off the mattress, pulling me across the wood floor into the hallway. I stood myself up, but she had me again, leading me down the darkened staircase and out the front door, into the night.

"You're hurtin' me, Momma," I whimpered. "Please, stop. You're hurtin' me bad." Fighting to release her tight hold, I reached, peeling back each one of her gripping fingers until she finally released her clutch.

"Poppy, you've got to come with me!"

Out on the front porch, she stopped for a moment, manically peering into the dark.

"You're scaring me," I cried.

Stumbling off the stoop, momma darted barefoot, out across the lawn, still soaked from a midnight rain.

"Come on, baby!" Motioning for me, she panted, "Hurry!"

I followed her around to the back of the house, through the wet grass. The night was cold. I passed Sook's garden and tripped through the rusted metal box springs from a soggy, discarded mattress. Somewhere in the back yard, I lost her, calling out, "Miss Loretta, where'd ya go?"

I noticed the open, darkened door to Sook's shed.

From inside came a rustling, like a stray cat who was sniffing for shelter from the passing storm. I walked closer to the door, whispering into the black, "Loretta, are you in there?"

She hissed, "Hurry, Poppy! Hurry!" Her arm extended from the shadow, snatching me and pulling me inside. She slammed the door shut behind us.

I asked, "What's wrong?"

But she ignored me.

Inside the old shed, the walls were lined with rows of rakes, hoes, and clippers. Sook's jalopy sat idle, covered in a quilt of dust. Loretta scampered about, peeking through gaps in the wood siding. Squatting low to the ground, she gasped as if all the air was escaping the room. She ducked, peering through the thin sliver.

"Loretta? Are you OK?"

A slice of moonlight filtered in through the louvers of the old window shutters, illuminating only a corner of the dank, dingy quarters. The two of us remained silent for the longest while, hunched low, waiting.

"Loretta, I'm scared."

"Shh!" She smothered my mouth with her sweaty palm. Her rapid breaths were short and shallow. She frantically warned, "Keep still, or they'll find us."

I fought her fingers from my mouth.

"Loretta, you're strung out."

Her head darted about, distraught and wild eyed. "Shh! Baby, we gotta hide. Just hunker low until they've gone."

Squatting on the cold concrete floor in my dressing gown, I heard Sook beckoning to us from the porch. "Poppy! Loretta! Where have you run off to?"

"I'm cold," I whined. "And it's starting' to rain again."

"Stay with me, baby, just a little longer, until they've gone."

"Who, Loretta?"

The tapping of falling rain slapped on the tin roof, and her panting was the only sound inside the tight room.

"Are you're drunk? Are you strung out?" I asked. "No one is comin' for us."

She turned to me, lost in her madness, searching my eyes for any comfort.

"No one's comin' for you, Momma. I swear."

"Baby, you're as wrong as wrong can be. They're all around us. Just listen. You can hear them coming." She waited, listening for an indication of an invading intruder. "They're after us."

In the moon's half-light, I saw Loretta had come undone. She was as pale as a ghost with haunted, glassy eyes nervously darting about, looking at everything but seeing nothing.

"Poppy, I'm gonna get us out of here. We'll leave town at the first hint of sunrise."

"No, Momma. I don't wanna go nowhere." I rubbed my aching wrists, her fingertips still imprinted on my skin.

"But baby, it'll be better if we get outta this town."

"No, Momma."

Mumbling in a whisper, she asked of no one, "Why do you come 'round here?"

I glanced over, but Loretta was lost to me. The sliver of moon-light shone on her crazed eyes.

She repeated, "Why you gotta come 'round here?" Asking questions of ghosts, she mumbled more nonsense that I couldn't make any sense of. Loretta rattled off gibberish to the night, like my grandma Lainey speaking with an anointed tongue during church service. I shivered from the cold and from fright, listening to the rants of a mad woman.

"Please, I'm beggin' you, Momma. I'm scared."

She looked around the small shed as if she was cornered by angry shadows. "Leave me be," she asked of the night. "Leave me be." Staring blindly into the darkness, she whispered again, "Please, just leave me be."

I grabbed her, shaking her shoulders. "Momma, you're scaring me! You're actin' crazy. Stop it now!" I took her hands in my own, gently squeezing, until I saw a hint of recognition in her eyes. "Loretta?" Seemingly, she was back with me again, hunched low in the dank shed.

Inspecting my wrists, she cried, "Baby, have I hurt you? Did I hurt you, Poppy?"

I attempted to calm her. "It's OK, Loretta. I'm fine. It's just sore."

"No, no, no!" she cried. Her panic spiked again. "I told myself I'd never leave another mark on you. I said, Loretta Wainwright, if you ever touch Samuel again in anger, you gotta take yourself down to the river and bury yourself deep beneath the water. Now, look what I've gone and done."

She grabbed my hands, kissing them over and over.

"No, Momma, they're just tender. It's nothing a little ice won't fix. I'll be good as new."

She brought my hands in front of her mouth as though attempting to hush her own words. "Baby, if I could make it stop. If I could just stop this freight train from runnin' through my head."

"Momma, we can get you help. Remember? You had a good spell after your time in Little Rock."

"Poppy, I've made such a mess of things. Surely there must be a particular place in hell for the kind of momma who puts her baby in a hospital bed." She turned, focusing her sights on me. "It's an unforgivable thing. No proper mother would ever put her sweet baby boy into a hospital bed." Her voice failed her. She seemed to be breaking into a million pieces.

Outside the door, Sook continued to call for us in the night.

"Miss Loretta, you need to gather yourself. The rain is coming down. We need to get ourselves to the house."

"I'm so sorry. I'm a bad momma." Her eyes welled until a single sloppy tear fell on her cheek. "I gotta go someplace far, far away, where my hurt doesn't fall on you."

"Momma, come to church with me next Sunday. The pastor will lay his hands on you and say a prayer."

Loretta tried to muster a smile. Reaching over, she cautiously touched my arm as if she didn't have the right.

For the briefest moment, I glanced down, finding new puncture marks to her skin. She quickly crossed her arms tight to her chest to cover the tracks.

"Poppy, ain't no God gonna save me."

"That ain't true," I said. "He's partial to sinners."

"I gotta leave, baby, before I hurt you again." She winced as though she had witnessed an awful sight in the black night.

Aunt Sook called out again from the porch.

"Momma, it won't be no better any other place. If you can't get ahold of this, it will follow you no matter where you run."

She took a deep breath, trying to steady herself. Loretta seemed to think on my words. "No, I suspect not." With her fingertips, she brushed my cheek. "Poppy, things weren't supposed to turn out like this."

"I know, but until you get yourself clean, it ain't never gonna be no different." I brushed the streaming tears from her anguished face. "Now, let's get ourselves inside. Sookie must be worried sick."

Momma mumbled incoherently and then nodded, seeming to answer her own question.

"Are you gonna be OK?"

Studying my face, Loretta looked puzzled, as though it were the first time she'd ever laid eyes on me.

I asked, "Can we go back to the house now?"

"Yessum," she conceded. "Poppy, I'm gonna get myself clean. I promise, I ain't ever gonna touch the stuff again."

"I know, Momma. I know." Standing, I took her hand, leading her to the door.

Before I could turn the knob, she took a hold of my forearm. "Baby, you listen." Her weary eyes searched mine. "When you've had enough...when you've finally given up on your momma...you keep it to yourself. Do you hear me?" She turned away, seeming to whisper to the night. "When you're finished with me, when you've had enough of your messy momma, don't you speak a single, solitary word. When you're done, just carry on. Because it's gonna break my heart in two." She squeezed my hand.

"Loretta, I'll never—"

She blunted me, "Poppy, you have to promise."

"OK. I promise."

She wrapped her arms around me, squeezing the breath from my chest. My momma wept softly, holding me there in the dark, until the quiet of the night was louder than our breathing.

The two of us stepped from the old shed into the October rain and made our way across the yard to a waiting Sook.

CHAPTER 23

Port Wentworth, Georgia

PERHAPS IT WAS ALL THE scandalous stories circulating about Rodney's cruelty or their pending legal woes, but Donita sensed how the congregation of Savannah Baptist Church would step a wide path around her like she was the broken step on the stoop as they entered church.

Always cordial in the Southern way, they greeted her with smiling faces and a slight hug about the neck. They chatted briefly on the weather and then moved along. Every Sunday, Donita took her seat in the last pew of the sanctuary and remained quiet, waiting for the opening hymn. She had become a stranger among the same folks she'd known since childhood. She reckoned that's what happens when a local gal's life becomes too uncivilized in a town where its citizens expect a lady to mind her p's and q's. A proper wife was expected to cook a respectable supper and corral even the most wild and unruly man with a gracious smile and a pleasant disposition. Folks don't like mess in a tidy town.

Perhaps it was Donita who had withdrawn from sight, embarrassed by her failings as a wife and a mother. She had retreated to her little house out past the railroad tracks.

Until the arrival of the little one from Arkansas, there wasn't a single soul who beckoned her to join them in a pew closer to the pulpit. Until that Sunday when Poppy came in and found a seat next to Donita in the last-row pew, it was only the pudgy pastor who openly embraced Donita for longer than a moment. With compassionate, graying eyes, he'd listen to her for longer than just a passing *howdy*.

On a few occasions after church service, the pastor would lead Donita off under the shade of a dogwood, where the two would speak for a spell in soft hushed tones on matters that only Donita, the minister, and God could hear.

Now, Miss Poppy Wainwright had become her confidante. Sometimes Donita fretted that it was unseemly for her to be so friendly with such a youngster, that she ought not burden a thirteen-year-old girl with her struggles. She worried that she shouldn't confess her secrets to an impressionable Poppy. But the girl from Mountain Home seemed to understand that the world was a heavy place—she seemed to possess a gentle old soul. The two had become fast friends. In unspoken words, the pair of Savannah misfits had become allies.

Every passing day with Rodney at the helm, Donita was sailing out further into troublesome waters without a compass or any sign of land. In a muted cry, she was sinking fast and calling out for help. It seemed the congregation of Savannah Baptist Church couldn't hear or wasn't listening to her desperate cries.

Sometimes Donita believed that it was plain foolishness to tether her hopes to a precocious youngster, but Poppy Wainwright was buoyed with a strength that Donita Pendergast did not possess.

———

CHAPTER 24

Daryl Turnball resided in an apartment at the top of the stairs above the bakery on Broughton Street. I spied his comings and goings from a side door, off the alley.

After my school lessons and after Sookie disappeared into the sitting room to watch her story, I'd pedal myself up to the bakery and park my bike across the street from Mr. Turnball's place.

Each Tuesday, while the other kids were still in class, before Mr. Turnball made his late-afternoon ice cream run through the neighborhoods, I trailed behind him, acting out my most convincing private-eye routine, as Daryl went about his mornings. Peddling just out of view, I watched Mr. Turnball saunter along State Street and browse the boutiques and shops. He always chatted up two men who operated the flower shop on Congress Street, and on some days, he sipped tea with three posh ladies on Drayton.

On Tuesday afternoons at twelve-thirty sharp, Daryl lunched with another debonair fella in a cafe on the corner of East Broad Street. The two dapper men laughed as they dined on the bistro's patio. Dressed in tailored jackets and pressed slacks, the stylish pair sipped iced tea and enjoyed their afternoons together. At the end of their lunch, the two friendly fellas always embraced and walked down the sidewalks in opposite directions.

One afternoon, as Mr. Turnball returned to his apartment above the bakery, he glimpsed me sitting on my bike across the way.

Waving in my direction, he sauntered across the street. "Good afternoon, Miss Poppy Wainwright. What brings you over to my side of the tracks?"

"Afternoon, Mr. Turnball. It seemed like a lovely day for a ride on my bike."

"Yes, indeed, it is a glorious day. Let's sit for a spell."

He and I found a park bench and sat side by side in the afternoon sun.

"Mr. Turnball, my aunt says that you're a dandy."

"She did, eh?" He grinned broadly. "Well, your old aunt Sook is of the belief that being different is *all* that I am. It's just the nature of some folks. You see, if I was a fella who tended to the sickly and dying in New York City, your aunt would only see me as a Yankee. If I was some negro man who repaired her leaking water tap, I'd be the darkie with a pipe wrench."

I asked, "That man who you lunch with…is he your fella?"

"Who?"

"I've seen you enjoying lunch on Tuesdays with a fair-haired man. Is he your special beau?"

Daryl flashed a quizzical smile. "Oh, Monroe? Well, maybe. One day." He winked.

"He seems like a fine choice to me," I commented. "If he *was* your beau, how would you go about courting a fella without all the townsfolk pitchin' a hissy fit?"

"Miss Wainwright, I suspect most folks in Savannah will never believe that love isn't always comprised of a blushing bride in white lace and a stiff groom in a top hat and tails. My sort has to go about searching for love in places where proper social circles don't approve of. But, my child, make no mistake, it's still love." He patted my knee. "Poppy, whether you're a sweet little girl in Savannah or a precious little boy living in Mountain Home, you're always deserving of love. You understand me?"

"Yes, sir." My cheeks blushed red as two cherry tomatoes. I realized my aunt and Mr. Turnball's afternoons spent exchanging gossip had also included my predicament.

The always-smiling man wrapped his arm around my shoulder. "You and I, Poppy, we are worthy of respect, happiness, and love."

I wanted remain there on the bench with Mr. Daryl Turnball at my side. His embrace felt warm and familiar.

"Thank you," I said.

"It's been my pleasure, Poppy," he replied. "Let's make a pact. If you're ever in need of anything at all, you come find your old friend Mr. Daryl Turnball. Deal?"

"It's a deal!" I said.

"Come next Tuesday, if you happen to find yourself in my neck of the woods again, why don't you come by and join Monroe and me for a bite of lunch?"

"I look forward to it."

"Run along home, and tell your old aunt Sook that Mr. Daryl Turnball has a frozen rainbow bullet in his freezer with her name written on it."

"Yes sir."

"And would you, please, tell that old woman to brush those grimy teeth of hers. I don't believe they've felt a bristle in a month of Sundays."

"You bet! I'll tell her!"

I pedaled up Broughton wearing a smile as big as the Georgia sky.

On my way home from Mr. Turnball's, I caught my passing reflection in the tall storefront glass. The windows of the boutiques mirrored me as I rode in a February breeze. I saw little Samuel there, looking back over at me in his cut-off jeans, white T-shirt, and untied sneakers. With a pitiful, lonely gaze, Samuel rode along my side in the reflection. Perhaps he was on his way back to Grandma Lainey as he was on the summer afternoon when the local boys caught up with him.

I maneuvered in and out of the strolling tourists and the locals lunching at Logan's, moving through the busy Savannah streets. I recalled that hot afternoon. The rowdy boys' bikes were faster; their thick, powerful legs were stronger. The Arkansas rough necks had been waiting for a good spell to pounce.

I pedaled along the shops—the little one remained right beside me. He struggled to keep up. I remembered his panic as he tried to flee from the redneck boys. Turning off Broughton, I sped down Clayton Street, trying to outrun little Samuel's frightened eyes in the glass, but in the windows of Woolworths and Levy's Department Stores, he struggled to keep pace. I accelerated faster, pumping my Schwinn through Savannah's busy streets.

On that fateful day, Samuel had mistakenly taken the shortcut through the abandoned dairy down Parker's Path. But the determined older boys pursued him with their spiteful words, baseball bats, and angry, hard fists. When his single, stray shoelace caught in the rusty bike's gears, twisting like a string on a spool, the deed was done.

Peddling as swiftly as I could, I tried to escape the memory of that sweltering afternoon back at Mountain Home. I was breathless by the time I turned on to Digby, my heart pounding like a drum inside my chest. All at once, the sun was at my back, and I was relieved to discover that my shadow on the pavement was the silhouette of a perfect little girl.

Before the day when those Arkansas rough necks beat me down, leaving me black and blue, I believed I was protected by the Holy Ghost. The scriptures in Grandma Lainey's Bible said it was so.

"If the Lord's eye is on the smallest sparrow," Grandma told me, "you can be certain his eye is on you."

She assured me that the Lord's love was like a great suit of armor. I trusted that I was sheltered by the Almighty's love like one of the silver shields worn by the superheroes in my comic books. Until that hot August afternoon, I was certain of God's always-watching eyes. But I was a stupid kid and foolishly believed that I could walk about Mountain Home in my yellow cotton sundress and my favorite hair barrettes.

After the beating, Grandma remained vigilant at my bedside, nursing all my broken parts. From morning to night, she read from her old Bible with pages as fragile as tissue paper. But I suspect Grandma already knew, as did I, that Lainey's Lord hadn't the time for my sort. His protection was reserved for the lucky ones, those youngins who were born into this world fitting together perfectly, like a puzzle that arrives with its pieces already in place.

I reckoned I had to leave little Samuel behind to fend for himself. I had no choice—my life depended on it.

———◆———

Pieces of a blue sky floated between the branches of the magnolias. I was flat on my back in the yard, my head propped on a spare tire, listening as Sookie encouraged her tomatoes. On her knees, she worked the soil and removed any sprouting weeds.

Lying on the grass, I listened to the sounds of Digby. Annabelle's tin bell clanked about her neck as she ate books in the study. A few pretty girls played hopscotch on the sidewalk. Further down the street, some boys dribbled a ball and shot hoops on their paved drive. The McAllister twins had been fussing all morning, until finally they'd squared off in the front lawn with clenched fists, readying to exchange blows. Miss Loretta was sleeping off a bender from the night before. Sookie had finished admiring her tomatoes. Moving her affections on to the row of radishes, she serenaded the saplings and paid no never mind to passing neighbors.

"Good afternoon, Miss Wainwright." Mr. Calvert tipped his hat as he sauntered by, but Sook's regard remained fixed on her gardening.

Mr. Calvert gave neighborly hospitality another attempt. "Those are some fine cherry tomato bushes. In fact, I believe they are the prettiest I've seen this season."

In between the rows of radishes, on all fours, Sookie returned his gracious compliment with a thunderous fart. The propulsion of her flatulence sounded like a horn's blast from her bloomers.

The passing man took a second glance over at Sook's bent backside and quickened his pace. Mr. Calvert escaped down the lane.

Across the way, Dixie came out charging from her screen door, swinging her fly swatter, sending Timmy and Tommy running off down Digby.

"You get back here right this instant!" she demanded. "I'm gonna skin you two alive!" But the two boys paid her no never mind, disappearing down West Jones Street.

Standing at her front gate, Dixie took notice of Sook and me. Sniffing into the air like some hound dog, she seemed to be detecting on the breeze if it was an opportune time for a visit.

I always felt an ache of sympathy anytime Dixie came calling. She just couldn't help herself. Tangling with Aunt Sook was a rough, rocky road she'd traveled many times, always ending up at a pitiful dead end. Like a moth to the flame, Dixie got burned every dadgum time.

With each visit, Mrs. McAllister seemed to have some new facial tic or nervous twitch, as if the mere proximity to old Sook made Dixie's entire body convulse and revolt.

On the occasions of her visits, I'd watch as Dixie positioned herself on the sidewalk outside our front gate, conjuring up the courage to come up our cobblestone path. She seemed to debate her entry, as if she was returning to a hornet's nest for another round of poisonous stings. It was only when she felt the Holy Ghost move inside her did she have the righteous fortitude to come marching up to our porch and, again, battle wits with old Sook.

This particular day, Dixie seemed uncertain of her crusade. Hesitantly and ever so slowly, Mrs. McAllister meandered a casual track across the street and up to our gate.

"Yoohoo. Mornin', Sook," she called. "Mornin', Poppy."

"Howdy, Mrs. McAllister," I replied. "It's a fine day."

Sookie ignored all the niceties and continued to weed in and around her bell peppers.

"What brings you across the street, Dixie?" Sook inquired without lifting her eyes from the precise rows of vegetables.

"Sookie, it dawned on me this morning, I haven't come over and formally introduced myself to your visiting niece." Dixie's left eyelid involuntarily twitched. "Is it Loretta?"

I offered up, "Miss Loretta is my momma, Mrs. McAllister."

Dixie feigned a sympathetic sigh, "Well, sugar, bless your heart. Is she now? I'm ashamed of myself for not coming by sooner and bringing over one of my coconut cream pies."

"Don't want none of your pies, Dixie," Sook muttered. "Your last pie gave me the squirts."

Dixie attempted to rise above Sook's vulgarity. "This mornin' I said to myself, Dixie McAllister, you've waited entirely too long to stop by and say howdy to Sook's house guest! I'm just an awful neighbor for not being more hospitable."

Aunt Sookie hollered up to the open second floor window, "Loretta, you got a visitor!"

"Sookie, there's no need to disturb your kin, if she's currently occupied with pressing matters." Dixie's left eye uncontrollably blinked in rapid succession.

"No, she ain't occupied." Sookie called out again, "Loretta, you got company! Get your fat, lazy ass outta bed!"

"Oh my." Dixie blushed red, as if her miniscule ears hadn't ever been polluted by a curse word.

Sook remarked, "Dixie, what the hell is wrong with your eye? You look like a gawd-damned buffoon."

"It's just a silly spasm. Pay it no mind."

From the open window, Loretta's voice complained, "Shut up all that gawd-damned racket. Can't a gal get some sleep around here?"

Sookie shouted, "Miss Loretta, someone has come calling for you!"

"Who?"

Sook answered, "Dixie."

Loretta's voice bellowed from the open window. "Ain't acquainted with no Dixie! Leave me be! A woman needs her beauty sleep."

"Loretta, you'd need to snooze for a decade to ever appear presentable!" Sook yelled. "It ain't polite keeping your guest waiting."

From her open window, we could hear the sounds of Loretta tripping over chairs, stumbling on suitcases and cursing up a storm.

She arrived to her window butt naked. Her pile of ratted yellow hair appeared to have been whipped in a coastal hurricane. Her eyes were smudged with teal makeup, and her two mighty jugs were exposed to all of Georgia.

Sheltering her eyes from the Savannah sun, Loretta grumbled, "Whadayawant?"

Dixie gasped at the obscene sight of Loretta and her pendulous knockers. Mrs. McAllister took a deep step backward. "Good morning, Miss Loretta," she stuttered through a nervous greeting, "I wanted to stop by and welcome you to our fair city."

Sook remarked, "Dixie here is the welcoming committee of Savannah. She's the ambassador of all things good and righteous and holy."

Miss Loretta leaned out the open window. Her pendulous heavy breasts dropped a considerable distance past the window trim, as if they were racing each other to the ground below. "Well, ain't this down-right neighborly of you? That's mighty hospitable." Loretta grinned and scratched beneath her left tit. "Now, please, excuse me, ladies. I gotta whizz like a derby race horse."

"Oh my." Dixie swallowed hard. "Of course, Miss Loretta. Have yourself a lovely day."

Mrs. McAllister attempted to gain some pittance of her composure and took herself back across the street.

◆

Standing at her kitchen counter, Donita went about icing the red velvet cake. With her knife, she smoothed the buttercream icing, coating the sides and spreading over the top of the freshly baked crimson dessert.

I watched on as she meticulously covered the fluffy white topping evenly about the round layers. She applied the icing until it sat perfectly pretty on a cut-crystal glass stand.

Donita offered me the knife, and I licked the utensil clean. She filled her piping bag with a sugary scarlet red frosting. She began forming perfect tiny rose buds around the cake's perimeter.

"It's Rodney's favorite," Donita said as she went about decorating the red velvet dessert. "Rodney deserves a cake. Life has been so tough. The prosecutors aren't cutting him any slack."

I asked, "What will happen if Mr. Pendergast has to go away for a spell? What will you do?"

"I'm fixin' to get me a job," she answered with a sense of pride. "I've never been scared of hard work. My family has struggled all our lives. I've had to labor for everything I've got."

"What kind of job, Donita?"

"I've been talkin' to Principal Ginn over at Savannah High. I may be hired on at the cafeteria or try waitressing at Delia's. A few local restaurants mentioned that they'd buy my cakes and pies. My Rodney absolutely despises the idea of me workin', but it's something I have to do. We can't borrow no more money from my folks. They can't even make their own ends meet."

"Ain't Mr. Pendergast's folks wealthy?"

She shook her head while she concentrated on the intricate sugary buds. "Rodney's too proud."

"Sookie says a man's pride is his undoing."

"Poppy, your aunt Sookie is correct. Pride can make a kind man callous." She wiped her hands on the front of her apron, then asked with a satisfied smile, "Well, what do you think?"

"It's lovely. It looks scrumptious."

"I hope it makes my Rodney happy."

I asked, "Mrs. Pendergast, does your Rodney ever hit you?"

Donita responded without taking a breath, "No, never. Why would you ask such a thing?"

I instantly knew I'd treaded down a perilous path Donita wasn't willing to walk. "Just wondering," I said. "Sometimes I've seen you wearin' some awful bruises."

"Oh, never mind those. I'm just a terrible klutz. Rodney says I can't walk a straight line without trippin' over something or the other."

Avoiding my eyes, she walked across the kitchen and busied herself at the sink. The room suddenly felt small and awkward.

"Donita, my apologies, if I stuck my nose someplace where I ought not."

"Goodness, no." Her back was turned to me as she went about washing the dishes. "Besides, no self-respectin' man would ever strike a lady. And no self-respectin' woman would ever stand for it."

———◆———

Stumbling through the back door in the wee hours of the morning, Loretta was greeted by a waiting Sook. Their irate exchange echoed in the foyer and down the long corridors.

"Loretta, what the hell are you doin' out at these ungodly hours of the night?"

"Leave me be, Sook."

"Just take a look at yourself. You're a walkin' skeleton," Aunt Sook remarked. "You need to eat yourself a proper meal and get a good night's rest."

"Sookie, I'll have you know I was out with a respectable gentleman."

"Horseshit! A true gentleman wouldn't never keep a lady out until dawn. Child, that's the kind of filth you can't never wash off. One of these nights you're gonna find yourself in the company of a very bad man. I heard all about your night in Tulsa a few years back. Missy, you're gonna end up dead in a dirty motel room."

"You're cruel, Sookie."

"Call me what you will, but this reckless behavior must stop," Sook hollered. "You ain't pulling the wool over this old sheep's eyes. You're injecting' your body with poison and carryin' on with men who'd rather see you on your back than look in the whites of your eyes."

"Ain't true!" Loretta yelled. "You're a vicious, nasty old woman!"

"Missy, you'd best start thinking about packing your belongings and heading out."

"Fine! It just so happens that there's a certain fella who wants me to move with him to Fort Worth," Loretta announced. "He's got a big spread, over a thousand acres."

"Aw, that's a barrel full of bullshit!" Sookie remarked. "Let's see if your cowboy takes you as far as the gas station."

"Fuck you, Sook. Fuck you!"

The sound of Miss Loretta stomping up the stairs was followed by the slamming of the door to her room.

Sook hollered, "I'm at my wits end!"

The house went quiet.

I laid in my bed, waiting, until I heard the shuffle of my aunt's journey up the stairs, followed by the closing of her bedroom door.

It seemed to me Loretta believed she had to go searching to the far ends of God's green earth to find herself some love. She'd worn off the rubber soles from her red pumps walking dirty sidewalks, hunting for a man's affection. I didn't suspect there wasn't a nook and cranny where she hadn't gone poking her nose in her search. Like some fairy tale or a great love affair in a picture show, Loretta believed she'd find love in a pair of longing eyes, and all the world would be gentle and kind.

Bowing my head, hands clasped, I prayed to the Lord to guide Miss Loretta to love before the search would kill her. I prayed for the forgiveness of all her sins and that the Almighty might see fit to quiet her cravings.

Outside my room, the sound of her bedroom door slowly opening stopped me mid prayer. I listened on. Loretta tip-toed in stocking feet in the hall and down the steps, careful not to make a squeak. In the foyer, she cautiously opened the front door, and once she was outside, I heard the clicking of her heels on the sidewalk, disappearing into the unforgiving night.

CHAPTER 25

———◆———

IF DONITA HAD THE GUMPTION, she'd run.

If she was the courageous kind, she would've packed up her belongings and left Rodney in the dead of night. If Donita Pendergast could have seen any clear path leading from Rodney to a place where she could breathe freely, surely, she would've followed it out from the dark and into the light. But Donita Pendergast was caught. She was cornered, and all paths seemed to lead right back to the crumbling little house, out past the railroad tracks.

It was December in Savannah, but instead of Christmas cards arriving to the Pendergast's postbox, only more past-due bills and late notices were delivered. The judge had set Rodney's trial date for August. His attorney begged his stubborn client to accept the prosecutor's plea deal. Rodney's folks asked for leniency from old Judge Cleveland—but the judge wasn't hearing none of it.

One Sunday after church, Donita confessed to Sookie and me that she was weary from the constant struggle. "Rodney's father is certain Rodney won't see any jail time," she confided. "I'm certain if we can just get past Rodney's legal troubles, and if the auto shop starts turning a profit, we can make it."

Sook replied, "Donita, no arrest or no meager bank balance is reason for a man to raise his hands in anger."

"Rodney is just under so much stress," she said. The lace collar of her cotton dress effectively covered the bruises about her neck, but she still clinched it closed with her left hand. "He came home last night wanting to make amends. He brought me the prettiest bouquet of happy yellow flowers. He has sworn off the bottle and promised to get himself clean."

"Child, you'd best gather your strength, and leave that house of shame." Sook shook her head. "When a desperate man's lips are flappin', he's usually lyin'."

"No, I believe him *this* time." Donita's weary eyes turned to the ground. She sniffled and wiped her forearm across her red nose."

Sook reached for Donita's blouse, slightly opening the collar, exposing the bruises. "What kind of man loves like this?" With her index finger, Sookie lifted Donita's sunken chin and met her gaze. "Child, you'd best remember who you are. Don't you ever let a man make you feel unworthy."

"Yes, ma'am."

I spoke up, "Donita, why don't you stay here with us for a spell."

"No, Poppy, I can't do that." She attempted a smile.

Sookie pushed a sealed envelope across the table to Donita. "Take this, and pay your bills. Stock your cupboards with groceries."

Donita stared at the envelope like it held some forbidden secret. "I just can't."

"Missy, there won't be any further discussion."

She fought back welling tears. "It's all gone so wrong. I don't recognize my life." Hesitant, she reached for the money. "I can't thank you enough. Of course, I'll pay you back every dime. I'll pawn my wedding band and pay you back every last dime."

Sook shook her head. "My late mother used to say that there are three *rings* in marriage: the engagement *ring*, the wedding *ring*, and suffe*ring*."

Donita almost cracked a grin. "Well, ladies, I must go. He'll be hunting him some supper." She stood from the table. Gripping the envelope, she mouthed a silent *thank you* to Sookie. Gathering her purse and sweater, Donita turned to us. "We were happy for a time, Rodney and me." She was seemingly attempting to convince Sook and me of something she couldn't believe herself. "He wasn't always like this. Rodney was a sweet boy. When we first met in school, Rodney was a real sweet boy."

"Some beautiful boys never out grow their glory days," Sookie replied. "Charles Pendergast should have used a leather strap on all three of his boys."

Donita wished us a fine afternoon and left for home.

Sook poured herself a cup of black coffee. "Trouble is gonna find that woman."

I said, "For the likes of me, I can't understand why Donita frets so for a man who don't seem to hold no affections for her."

She sipped from a chipped cup. "From the cradle to the grave, Southern women are schooled in the proper social graces. They are judged solely on their pie crusts and the heights of their ratted hair. They go about town batting their eyelashes and shaking their pretty tail feathers. They say *bless you* when they mean *fuck you*. They say *yes* to a tablespoon of poison just to avoid a spat. And they blame a sleeping dog when they fart in public." Sook sat her cup in the saucer. "Shame on the woman who lets a man ever raise a fist to her in anger. Poppy, don't you ever be a consolation prize."

CHAPTER 26

———◆———

CHRISTMAS ARRIVED IN SAVANNAH WITH all the pageantry of a formal cotillion. The grand homes along Digby were dressed in their finest. Twinkling lights were strung along the eaves of the elegant estates, their front doors adorned with spruce wreaths. All the street lamps along Digby were decorated with red bows and plastic candy canes. Majestic Christmas trees, draped in silver and gold garlands, stood in every front window.

Aunt Sook permitted Jackson and me to go select a silver spruce from the corner tree stand.

Jackson stood at the base of the stairs, waiting on me. "Hurry up, Poppy! The tree lot is gonna close."

"I'm comin'. I'm comin'."

"I'll never understand why you gals have to be late every dadgum time."

"Hold your horses! Miss Loretta says it's better for a lady to arrive late, rather than show up timely but ugly."

I deliberated up and down the rows of pines while Jackson stood by.

He complained, "Poppy, we'll be ringing in nineteen sixty-nine before you pick a dadgum tree. Do you suppose you could hurry it up?"

I paid the man four dollars for an eight-foot-tall pine, and Jackson carried it all the way back home on his broad shoulders.

When no one was watching, he kissed me softly under a holly sprig over Sook's front door.

Miss Loretta went missing for the holiday. Out late on most of those December nights, she'd disappear into her room during the daylight hours. I slid platters of warm vittles outside her door, only to find them still untouched the next morning.

I watched as my momma withered away to nothing and bone. With each surrendered pound from her frame, my hopes for her diminished like those many times before. The smack stole my momma from me one pound at a time.

One afternoon I tempted her to join me out Christmas shopping along Broughton. Momma stared dumbly through the storefront windows as we strolled along the sidewalk. Her clammy hand trembled in my palms. I squeezed, flashing her a smile, but she was lost to me. Her eyes were glassy, and her greasy unkempt blond hair showed dark black roots, as if her follicles were leaking motor oil.

Loretta examined the heavy gray sky above us, as if she was certain it would fall.

"Miss Loretta, are you gonna be OK?"

"Yessum, baby girl," she lied. "Your momma is gonna be just fine."

Pearl tagged along with Donita and me on Sunday nights as we caroled with the church choir. Dressed like Charles Dickens' characters, we strolled through Chatham Square, serenading tourists and locals alike.

Constance White and her high school beau, Derek, were crowned Christmas Royalty at the Chatham County Christmas Festival. She was lovely, standing on the stage with her golden hair intricately piled on her head like one of Donita's meringue cakes.

In Colombia Square near the Wormsloe Fountain, Constance permitted Pearl, Tallulah, and me to take turns wearing her be-jeweled tiara. I draped her royal red velvet cape over my shoulders and walked in a straight line, attempting to balance the glittering crown on my head. The other girls cheered me on. When it was Tallulah's turn to wear the tiara, she waved her tiny hand from side to side, like she was riding atop a flowered float in the New Year parade.

Anxious for the return of her shimmering crown to its rightful noggin, Constance snatched it off Pearl's head. "OK, that's quite enough!" She snapped. "As the reigning Chatham County Christmas Queen, I mustn't let the tiara venture too far from my rightful royal head."

Mr. Turnball's ice cream truck continued to make a pass down our street but only once a week. With plastic reindeer riding on his chrome bumper, he offered up hot chocolate in Styrofoam cups and freshly baked Christmas cookies from his open window. Daryl wore a fuzzy elf's hat and a red rubber ball pinched to his nose as he greeted us.

Sookie remarked, "You look like a gawd-damned fool, Turnball. As if this damned holiday ain't gay enough, now you're trotting up Digby in leotards and a hat like one of Santa's queerest helpers!"

"Hush up your mouth, Sookie Wainwright. I swear, you're Savannah's own Scrooge," he replied with his bulbous red nose. "I hope one of these giant magnolias tumbles over and crushes your bones."

Sook snickered.

Admiring our Christmas tree in the front window, the green garland trimming the porch and a wreath adorning our front door,

Mr. Turnball quipped, "Sook, have you gone and found Jesus? Are you born again?"

She grunted her displeasure.

Turnball grinned. "This year old Sookie Wainwright has herself a Christmas tree. Come next year, you'll have your very own nativity scene right dab in the middle of your front yard."

"Never!" She protested. "Besides, Jesus could never be born in Savannah. You can't find a single virgin or three wise men in all of Chatham County!"

"You're a blasphemous creature." Daryl poured Sook a cup of steaming hot cocoa. "Poppy, what do you say we try and fit your old aunt Sookie in a chimney?"

I laughed, "Yessum. She could slide right down like old Saint Nick."

"No, no," he answered. "I was thinking we'd just stuff her decaying carcass in a chimney stack and concrete her corpse in there for good."

Sookie went to chuckle but swallowed wrong, and hot cocoa came squirting from her nostrils like the gushing water fountain over in Ellis Square. "Daryl Turnball, you're good people, despite you bein' a homosexual and all."

The smiling ice cream man leaned over his counter. "Sookie Wainwright, you're a real hoot, despite you being a royal pain in my arse!"

One chilly December night, the McAllister boys and their buds snuck out from their bedroom window and went about stealing all the plastic baby Jesuses from the mangers of Savannah's many nativity displays.

The ornery boys then proceeded to string up the dozens of baby dolls by their plastic necks on the flagpole over at the high school. After the principal discovered who the culprits were, Carl McAllister summoned the unrepentant boys to his study, where he proceeded to beat the two within an inch of their lives with a leather belt.

For Christmas, Dixie bought the rowdy boys boxes upon boxes filled with matching shirts, britches, belts, and bowties. The twins were paraded to the Christmas Eve Sunday service in identical, horrendous, red knit sweaters, with the baby Jesus's nativity scene meticulously stitched in every minute detail—grazing camels, donkeys, the three wise men, Joseph, Mother Mary, and her baby Messiah were all woven with picture-perfect detail. In fine script across the back of the boy's silly seasonal sweaters was embroidered "We Live for Jesus."

Refusing to step out onto their porch, an embarrassed Timmy and Tommy wanted to boycott Sunday service. When Aunt Sookie spotted the humiliated boys outfitted in their holiday sweaters, she was so gloriously gleeful, she cobbled her way across Digby, calling to me, "Poppy, grab my camera!"

The boys adamantly refused, but Sook insisted that the shamed twins pose with her for a holiday memento.

The wiry old woman stood grinning like a giddy possum who had just eaten a sweet potato, the frowning boys flanking her sides.

I aimed the camera lens at a joyous Sookie with the humiliated twins.

My aunt gushed, "Come next year, I believe I'll use this precious photo for my annual Christmas card!"

Dixie piped in, "Sookie you ain't never sent out Christmas cards in your entire life."

"I'll start!" she quipped. "Say *cheese*, children!"

For my Christmas present, Jackson gifted me a gold bracelet with tiny ivory pearls. As he clasped the link around my wrist, he proudly announced, "These are guaranteed, authentic, ocean-grown, bona fide pearls. They're the real deal, Poppy! My mom helped me pick it out at Levy's. There was another bracelet under the glass counter that caught my eye 'cuz it sparkled just like diamonds, but my momma explained, 'Proper girls prefer real pearls over imitation rhinestones because it's not about cheap glitter.' She said it's about the fella knowing that his gal is deserving of something real. I told Momma, 'My Poppy deserves genuine pearls, not second-rate cut glass.'"

"Thank you," I said. "I do believe it's the most beautiful thing I've ever seen."

Jackson's cheeks blushed red.

CHAPTER 27

———◆———

DAYS TURNED LIKE SO MANY fluttering pages, and winter gave way to March. The azaleas were in full bloom—red, orange, and yellow. I'd never witnessed such a wondrous, radiant sight. Spring arrived to Savannah with a lovely breeze blowing off the ocean, hinting of warmer, longer days.

Jackson and I flew his kite off the shores of Tybee Island. The skies were clear, and tourists arrived on the cobblestone sidewalks in droves, strolling in Bermuda shorts and posing for snapshots in front of the live oaks dripping with hanging moss.

Pearl and I were like peas and carrots. After school, she'd come by the house, and off we'd go exploring Savannah. Under warming skies, we canvased Cumberland Island, rummaging through the ruins of the old Carnegie Mansion. Wild horses grazed on the grasses, and we ran like bandits through the trees. Picnicking on the salty flats of Skidway, we collected minnows inside mason jars.

An old rubber tire was strung up by a long, frayed rope, suspended from an oak's bough in the back pasture of mean Widow Walker's place. When the old goat was off to a church social, Pearl and I would sneak about and take turns swinging.

I'd push while little Pearl held tight, soaring out of over the reservoir. Back and forth, the swinging tractor tire would take her soaring out over the blue. As Pearl swung, the exposed backs of her bare legs showed signs of raised, red welts from a hard strapping by her momma's belt, but little Pearl never made mention of the beatings.

The tight, twisted rope strained under the weight as she flew through the air. I suspected our knowing that the weathered rope was bound to snap only caused us to squeal louder. The wild wind streaming through Pearl's mess of red hair was a wondrous sight, but I worried Pearl's momma would one day come completely unraveled, finally breaking, sending her little one flying with no one to catch her fall.

Spring came skipping in with colorful bonnets and bright bouquets of April's colors on Digby.

Aunt Sookie once told me that Mother Nature doesn't favor any one youngster over the other. "Before blossoming into a lovely flower," she said, "every child must dig their way up through the muddy dirt."

Apparently, this was true for even Miss Constance White. It seemed she, too, was susceptible to the cruel march of Mother Nature. Puberty arrived that spring to a particularly pretty thirteen-year old with hair the color of corn silk.

One Saturday, Pearl and I took ourselves to Franklin Square. We pedaled our bikes under the shade of the oaks, where the cluster of girls had encircled a weeping Constance. She sat on a patchwork blanket in April's rye grass. As Pearl and I approached, we noticed the murmuring girls were tending to a bawling Miss White.

Pearl asked, "What's wrong?"

"Is she OK?" I wondered.

The others made room for us on the blanket, where Constance had completely covered her face with the palms of her hands, crying an uncontrollable jag.

"I'm gonna die. I swear, I'm just gonna die," she sobbed. Her slight shoulders shook violently with each sniffle and snort. "I just wanna crawl into a deep, black hole and let the earth swallow me up!"

"Calm yourself, Constance," Tallulah said. "It ain't that bad."

Slowly, she withdrew her hands from her face.

Tallulah winced, but with a forced smile, replied, "There, there. You're crying over a few silly spots of imperfections."

When I first laid eyes on the crop of pus-filled pimples populating Constance's face, I lost my breath. Gone was her perfect complexion. Gone was her supple skin, smooth as one of Lainey's porcelain dolls.

"Holy moly!" Pearl's gasped from over my shoulder.

Another girl attempted a compliment, "Constance, you're still pretty as a picture. Ain't no blemish gonna ever change that."

The milky-topped boils seemed to be on the march, traveling from her left cheek, up over her perfectly pugged nose, and invading her opposite cheek.

Pearl asked, "Has a doctor seen them there zits?"

"Shuddup, Pearl!" Constance snapped.

A concerned girl with straight brunette bangs that covered her eyes, remarked, "Try a tablespoon of lemon juice with a pinch of oatmeal. That will take care of them lickety-split."

Little Tallulah wasted no time, rapidly scribbling the recipe for the oatmeal concoction in her private pad. The rest of us girls gazed on in disgust—but also with a teaspoon of glee at the sight of the blooming bumps ravaging Constance's once-pristine complexion.

"They're just zits," Pearl declared. "My older sister, Nedra Sue, had plenty of pimples. They were gone in no time at all."

"Really?" Through tear-filled eyes, Constance turned to Pearl with the slightest glimmer of hope. "Pearl, did Nedra's complexion ever clear up?"

"It sure did!" Pearl encouraged her. "You've seen Nedra Sue. Her skin is as clear and smooth as a baby's butt."

"How long did it take?" Constance asked. "When did her pimples clear up?"

"It took no time at all. It was a breeze." Pearl smiled assuredly. "It was the better part of a year."

"A year? A year? An entire blessed year?" She began bawling once again. Her sniffling nose was as red as the pimples, populating her face.

All of us tried to settle her.

Tallulah confided to the gaggle of us girls, "This morning, Constance heard that Derek ain't gonna escort her to the Savannah High Formal because of her skin's ailment. Derek is gonna take Brittany Cleveland instead of Constance."

"That's a lie!" Constance shouted. "Derek is not taking Brittany to the formal! That's a bold-faced lie!"

Tallulah spoke in almost a whisper, "It's true. My brother, Brody, is on the junior varsity football team with Gordy Mull. His momma works at Levy's. She was behind the register in the young ladies' fashion department when Brittany was trying on dresses. Mrs. Mull said Brittany was admiring herself in a full-length mirror, and confessed, 'I'm buyin' me a dress for the May Formal. I'll be escorted by Mister Derek Bledsoe.'"

"Shut up!" Constance countered. "That ain't true."

Tiny Tallulah pushed her spectacles up further onto her nose. "Constance, I wouldn't lie about such a thing. Brody said Derek fancies Brittany 'cuz she has sprouted herself a respectable pair of breasts, and her pa has a really keen fishing boat."

Indignant, Constance clinched her perfect fists. "Well, let Brittany have him. Good riddance! My momma always taught me to give my used toys to the less fortunate! Brittany Cleveland can have my leftovers!"

———————

It was the first week of April when news came from Memphis that the Reverend Martin Luther King was killed, shot down in cold blood. Townsfolk walked the sidewalks with lowered heads and solemn brows. There was a heaviness hanging in the air. Even the visiting tourists riding in the horse-drawn carriages and strolling through the squares seemed to wear uneasy expressions.

Nedra Sue said that the killing of the minister from Montgomery was all part of a dastardly conspiracy. "There's no stopping them killers. Those men who done this to Mr. King ain't gonna stop until they've gunned down every last colored man who is courageous enough to speak up."

"Why so?" Pearl asked. "What business does anyone have bringin' harm to a man of God?"

"The bigots, racists and bureaucrats are scared of any negra man who is smart enough to see clear through all of their intolerance and ignorance."

I never spoke a word to Sookie or Miss Loretta, but the gunshots over in Memphis left me frightened and running for cover. Always watching and waiting, I looked over my shoulder when I passed a pair of suspicious eyes on the sidewalk or if a pickup full of riled up rednecks drove by.

One afternoon standing near his ice cream truck, I asked Daryl about the loss of Mr. King. "These are vexing times, child. It seems it used to be that decent folks could be quiet and go about their own business," he replied, "but nowadays if common folk remain silent on such issues, they are as guilty as the loudest among us who are spewin' such vile hatred."

Pearl and the other kids were dismissed from school the first week of May for summer vacation. We celebrated by sneaking out a pack of Nedra Sue's cigarettes and a mason jar of Sook's moonshine.

In an abandoned boxcar, me, Jackson, Pearl, Tallulah, the McAllisters, and Constance got liquored up and puffed on ciggies.

Little Tallulah sniffed the jar's contents and then put the hooch up to her lips with one hand and pinched her nose closed with the other. She took a single sip and then covered her face with both hands. "I'm drunk!" She declared and fell to the floor.

Pearl shook her head. "Tallulah, you just drank it. Get up. The liquor takes some time before it can work its magic."

She stood up, dusted herself off, and walked to the corner of the train car. She took a seat and began scribbling in her journal.

Pearl guzzled the clear alcohol like it was sweet tea and then wiped her mouth with a swipe of her forearm. She handed the jar to a leery Constance, who tried a taste, then grimaced. "It's disgustin'! It's like drinkin' petrol from the pump."

Already drunker than a skunk, Tommy McAllister serenaded all of us with a swollen tongue,

> *"Row, row, row your boat,*
> *Gently down the stream…"*

Pearl climbed from the train car and waltzed about, all by herself, in the field of summer grass along the tracks. She whirled and pranced about like an inebriated ballerina. Falling onto her back, she disappeared in the meadow grass and watched the spinning world.

"Merrily, merrily, merrily, merrily…
Life is but a dream."

Tanked up and tender, a sappy Jackson confessed the depths of his love. "Deeper than the ocean," he whispered to me. "Poppy, my affections run deeper than the ocean." A breeze off the water blew stray strands of his yellow hair into his green eyes.

A few of us formed a line in the deserted train car and Constance tried to teach us the steps to "Do the Choo Choo" by Archie Bell and the Drells, but we weren't attentive students—Tommy McAllister tripped over his big feet, Tim was mining for gold with his index finger, and Jackson and I weren't paying attention to our dance instructor.

Finally, Constance, frustrated with our shenanigans, threw her hands in the air. "I give up! You're all hopeless cases! You're never gonna be permitted into the circles of the hipper kids at Savannah High!"

Little Tallulah, who kept returning for another sample of moonshine, gripped the empty mason jar in one hand and a ciggy in the other and announced, "I'm an alcoholic."

"No, you're not, Tallulah," I said. "It takes more than a single sip."

"Well, I'm either drunk or it's hotter than Hades in here," she complained. Her cheeks were flushed red. "Poppy, I can't see clearly. The world is all catawampus." Drunk and dizzy, Tallulah stumbled about the abandoned train car. Attempting to focus her magnified eyeballs, she declared, "I reckon I always knew that one day I'd turn to a life of fast livin' and drinking Satan's moonshine." She staggered about until she fell on a few abandoned gunny sacks of cotton in the corner. She plopped on the stuffed cargo and passed out. Her little notebook slipped from her loose grip, dropping to the planked car floor, its pages left exposed.

The McAllister boys looked over the open notepad. One of the twins moved in closer to investigate. Constance, too, lingered near Tallulah's binder. Jackson looked over to me for any hint in my expression.

Pearl arrived back to the train car. Blades of yellow straw had collected in her wild frizz. "What the heck has happened to Tallulah?"

"She's passed out cold," Timmy replied and then signaled with a nod to young Miss Banks's open notepad.

Pearl turned to me. I shrugged my shoulders up to my ears.

Tommy gave her journal a slight kick with his sneaker.

"Don't you dare touch it, McAllister, or I'll kick your ass all the way into next week!" Pearl threatened. "It's none of our business! I'm certain that diary contains all of Tallulah's most intimate secrets and darkest desires. She may be small in stature, but I reckon she's a mountain of wisdom behind those round wire spectacles."

We all gazed upon little Tallulah, who slept soundly on the bed of cotton sacks. A steady stream of syrupy drool leaked from the corner of her lips, down her chin, and drizzled onto her blouse.

"She's a deep thinker," Pearl added.

"Dunno. I've always suspected that she's a secret agent for the FBI," Tommy declared. "She's got those magnified shifty eyes. I've never trusted her no how."

Timothy replied, "Yessum. She's certainly involved in some kind of espionage. Maybe a communist? Those coke-bottle glasses and her meek and mousey disposition are just a disguise to throw us off her path. I have a hunch she's got the nuclear codes scrawled on its pages."

"No way," Jackson replied. "I'm certain that it's Tallulah's private journal. I bet she composes beautiful sonnets and lovely poems. I reckon that there book is filled with some of the most profound and tender words ever written on pulp."

"Naw. I've always suspected that Tallulah is an artist," Constance surmised. "I bet she draws the most beautiful pictures on its pages. I see her sketching in it all the time. I just know Tallulah is itchin' to ask me to pose for one of her portraits." With one flip Constance corralled her golden locks over one shoulder. "Sketching someone of my beauty would be a thrill and honor for an aspiring artist like Tallulah."

Pearl took possession of the mystery notebook. "It's none of our dad-gum business!" she replied. "Until she sobers up, it's in my safekeeping."

Little Tallulah snuggled in deeper into the sacks of hay and slept the summer afternoon away.

CHAPTER 28

———

AUGUST ARRIVED TO SAVANNAH, OPPRESSIVE and unforgiving.

Aunt Sook said August in Savannah is like a fat Southern woman—they could never get comfortable and were impossible to get around.

Folks ran for cover from the oppressive sun and swarming mosquitos. The most you could hope for was a whimper of a breeze off the shore. The afternoon heat hung heavy in the air, like the moss dripping from the oaks. The ancient ladies moved their rockers nearer to the oscillating fans, and the lazy hounds hunted for sympathetic shade trees.

Jackson and I lost afternoons on Tybee Island. The sweltering days passed like rioting sparrows, always flying just ahead of us. They moved in a flurry, staying just out of our reach. After our chores were done, the gang would meet up on Broughton Street at Leopold's for a cone of tutti-frutti ice cream. In a vinyl booth, we conspired, pooling our money. We bought Tallulah a single ticket over at Avon's Theater for the afternoon matinee. Terrified by the prospects of incarceration, little Tallulah stood nervously at the ticket window and purchased her single ticket. Once safely inside, she snuck about, letting the rest of us kids slip in through the back door off the alleyway.

Jackson and I sat watching Mr. Charlton Hesston in *Planet of the Apes* in the darkened theater, sharing a popcorn and an orange soda pop. He'd steal a kiss when no one was looking. All the gang emptied out onto the street, and the McAllister boys went about grunting and beating their chests like angry gorillas and terrorized little Tallulah and Constance by picking at their scalps like feeding chimpanzees.

Those warm afternoons with Jackson, Pearl, and the other kids allowed me to forget all the fighting and fussing going on back home. My momma wasted away her days with me, squandering them with mean men, moonshine, and more poison.

Earlier that spring, Mr. King was shot dead. In June, the young Mr. Kennedy's life was taken. Silenced with a single bullet. Like his brother before him, the young fella was slaughtered like some hunted animal.

Watching the news reports on television, old Sook shook her head. "Poppy, there's a fire comin' on," she said with absolutely certainty, like she was forecasting the coming week's weather. "The assassins who took the life of the minister from Montgomery and now murdered young Mr. Kennedy from Massachusetts, have started a mighty fire."

I asked her, "You mean like the forest fire near Moody's swamp?"

"No, child," she replied. "A fire is comin' to our city streets. I suspect the blaze will burn so red hot that folks in this country won't recognize themselves in the ash and destruction."

Just a few weeks later, Sook's premonition came true. The Democrat's rally over in Chicago burned like a blazing bonfire. Jackson and I sat cross-legged in front of Sook's TV, watching the reports from the Democratic convention.

Jackson turned to my aunt with a hint of fear in his green eyes. "Mrs. Wainwright, do you suspect downtown Savannah will be torched?"

"Ain't no tellin', son," she answered. "But the smothering smoke from these fires will cover this entire country like a blanket of shame for decades to come."

It was a long, hard summer on Digby. Miss Loretta had come unhinged. She no longer attempted to camouflage the tiny puncture wounds dotting up and down her forearms with a lace shawl or wrap. Momma had come clear off the rails. Like a runaway wheel on a track, she was spinning further away from me and her sanity.

With skin as pale as a ghost and with weary, hollowed-out eyes, she roamed the rooms of Sook's place, stumbling about, talking nonsense to no one. When I'd call to her, she'd turn with a lost expression. On some nights, she'd study my face and refer to me by the name of one her other youngins, who were spread out like seeds all over the South.

Sook and Miss Loretta battled around the clock. A war was being waged on 22 South Digby Street. Angry, hateful words were thrown across the rooms like shattering plates. Shards of cutting words left Miss Loretta bawling and old Sook weary from the fight.

As for me, I tried my damnedest to steer clear of the flying debris. Miss Loretta made hard promises in the sober light of morning and broke them all by nightfall. She'd go missing along with another piece of Sook's jewelry or another dish from the family silver. She'd return home at night wearing someone else's smile, laughing too loud, dancing about the house like some lunatic. Wanting to hide from all the quarrelling, I'd ascend the staircase to my room after supper and use a pillow to smother out the sounds of my family tree tumbling to the ground.

From my room, I could hear Miss Loretta tearing about the house deep into the night. When only Savannah's ghosts lurked about, Momma still haunted the rooms below, knocking over vases and tiffany lamps. She sang along to the records on Sook's phonographs in the sitting parlor. Finding her way into the attic, she rummaged through the old dusty boxes and danced like some drugged debutante in the yellowing lace wedding dress. I secretly spied her from behind the stacks of boxes as she deliriously waltzed, a lost bride betrothed to Satan's serum.

On a few nights, I cracked open the door to my room to find Aunt Sook standing just inside her own bedroom door at the far end of the hall, listening to the rants and ravings of a mad woman below. Sookie would acknowledge me with the slightest nod of her head, silently pressing her index finger to her mouth, shushing me, and then slowly shutting her door. Latching her lock, Sook would surrender her home to the dope fiend downstairs.

In a blink of an eye, Momma would go from being frantically high, tripping through the house, laughing like some crazed woman, and then suddenly, she would trudge from room to room, as solemn as a funeral procession. Miss Loretta would plod about with shoulders slumped low, back bent, like she was hauling some cumbersome load. The weight of her wicked ways was a heavy burden to carry for her diminishing frame. I wished my momma knew that truth was as light as a sparrow's feather.

Frightened by momma's ever-changing moods, I took to hiding on the rooftop or behind the heavy curtains with Annabelle in the dining room. Quiet as a mouse, we waited for Loretta's crazed parties of one to end or for her fitful furies to pass.

Early one morning, Carl McAllister discovered Miss Loretta passed out in their lawn after Sook had locked her from the house the night before. Curled up like a weary stray, she slumbered in the McAllister's azalea beds.

Dixie provided Loretta with a cup of black coffee and a fresh Danish roll, and then Carl walked my momma back across the street before sunrise, delivering her to our front-porch swing.

The next morning, I caught old Sook cobbling back across the street after delivering a basket of her most pristine vegetables to the McAllister's front stoop.

One afternoon, while rocking in her rocker, Sookie called up to me as I sat on my roof perch. "Child, you understand, your momma is knee deep in the weeds?"

"Yessum," I answered back. "She'll come around, Sook."

"I suspect the time has come for me to request Miss Loretta to move on."

My aunt's cumbersome words were too heavy to truly be heard high atop my shingled roof.

"Just give her more time, Sookie," I pleaded. "Please, just give her a little more time." But, I knew my aunt had endured Momma's outlandish behavior far longer on my account.

Early one morning before sunrise, when the sheriff escorted Miss Loretta home in the back of his flashing patrol car, he and Sook spoke in hushed tones out by the front gate, while Miss Loretta sat locked in his backseat. She hollered from behind the glass, crazed and cursing. All the neighbors watched on from their porches. Sookie stood on the pavement in her slippers and terry cloth robe, thanking Bernard.

I peeked from behind the curtains as Sheriff Delany opened the door to his patrol car, and Miss Loretta fell like a gunny sack to the hard asphalt. Sookie rushed about, trying to help her up onto her feet, but Momma tumbled into the myrtle hedge, heaving and vomiting up her last meager meal.

I reckon, the good Lord might never forgive me for my selfishness on that particular morning. As Miss Loretta lay in her own sick, my prayers weren't for her soul's salvation. Not once did I ask the Almighty for her restoration. Her redemption never even crossed my mind. The single silent prayer I repeated from behind the draperies was for the sheriff's flashing red and gold lights atop his patrol cars to go dark. Carl, Dixie, the McAlister boys, the Atkinsons, the Hudsons, and the Calverts, all in their flannels and dressing gowns, watched the spectacle as my momma flailed on the ground like a tragic lunatic. From my hiding place, my only prayer was that his flashing beacons turn off. So selfish was my shame that my sole concern was that our tangled affair wouldn't be illuminated for all the fine folks of Digby to witness.

On Miss Loretta's last night with us, all the useless angry words made matters only worse. Sookie followed after Loretta from room to room, shouting and cursing down the stairs and into the foyer. I trailed behind, attempting to stop what was inevitable, trying to keep balloons afloat that were always destined to pop.

Sook hollered, "Miss Loretta, you've overstayed your welcome."

"No, Sookie!" I cried out. "Don't do it!"

"Poppy, you'd best go on upstairs to your room," Sook insisted.

"I won't!" I shouted. "I won't!"

Sook gave me a stern gaze. "Yes, you will, missy."

"Poppy, you listen to your aunt. Go to your room."

I looked at them both. "I won't! I'm telling you now, I won't!"

"Loretta, I don't want to do this in front of the child."

"Sook, just say your peace. Just say what you've come to say."

Aunt Sookie followed Momma into the kitchen. Gripping the back of a chair with quaking hands, my aunt yelled. "Loretta, it's no secret that you're out mining for a vein every night. Look at yourself! You're wastin' away to flesh and bone." Sook's stare stayed fixed on Loretta's hollow, graying eyes. "You've been warned, and I will no longer abide such behavior under my own roof. It's time you gather up your belongings and clear out."

I shouted, "No, Sookie!"

"Poppy!" Sook set her sights on me, burning a hole clean through me. "I'm too old. I won't fight you, too. This ain't your battle."

But it *was* my battle—a war I'd fought for as long as I could recall.

I yelled at her, "I hate you, Sook! I'll hate you forever!"

"Poppy, your aunt Sook is right," Loretta scolded. She then turned her weary eyes to the floor. "I've gone and overstayed my welcome. It's time I move on."

"No, Loretta," I pleaded. "No."

The room went quiet. A ceasefire had been called.

"Then, I'll go with you," I said. "Let me come."

Loretta spoke to Sookie, but her every word were meant for my hearing. "Goodness, no. What would I do with a child taggin' along? You'd only slow me down, Poppy." Miss Loretta never turned, keeping her eyes fixed on Sook. "I ain't got the patience to tote a child all about the country." She slowly lowered herself into one of the kitchen chairs like the weight of her words were too heavy to bear.

"You're a gawd-damned liar!" I hollered. "I don't care what either of you say, I'm comin' with you, Loretta! I'm packing my case."

"No, Poppy," she insisted. "You ain't goin' nowhere. I got no use for extra baggage."

I kneeled by her chair and took her hand. "But, who will take care of you, Miss Loretta? Who will tend to you?"

She couldn't meet my gaze.

"Momma? I'll fix you hot meals every day. I can take care of you."

Standing, Loretta smoothed her skirt with the palms of her hands. "I'm a grown woman. No one takes care of me." She cleared her throat. "Besides, there's a fella in Oklahoma City who fancies me. He works the oil fields. He's got real potential. I wouldn't stand a ghost of a chance if he finds out that I'm burdened with children. Especially a child with your peculiarities." She attempted a laugh and turned to face me. "If he took one look at you, he'd certainly head for the hills."

"You're a liar." I said. "You're a gawd-damned liar! There's nothin' waiting for you in Oklahoma City. You're a gawd-damned liar!"

Loretta adjusted the collar of her blouse and reached for her purse. She found a powder compact and checked her reflection in the small, round mirror. "Poppy Wainwright, you've gone and lost all your manners."

"You're lyin', Loretta!"

Her eyes welled, but she fought back any tears. Straightening her spine, she replied, "Poppy, you'd best remember just who you are. You haven't been raised to speak to your momma in this uncivilized manner." Miss Loretta walked to the doorway. "Now excuse me. A proper lady knows when to leave a room."

A bloated, pale moon hung above the magnolias when Momma met the yellow taxi at the curb. I watched on from the porch as a young, handsome, obliging man helped her with her scuffed Samsonites. He tipped his hat and opened the car door for her, like a respectable gentleman does.

I reckon, Loretta would never truly unpack her Samsonites for any time longer than the shortest spell. Instead, she'd keep traveling those empty miles, tempting fate at every turn. I wanted to call out to her, but I remained silent on the stoop. Like a river of stones, my momma would run wild through the countryside, bruised and battered from her journey down the rocky backroads—loving men without a vein of kindness, begging the night for any affection, and asking nothing of God.

Aunt Sookie called from inside the house, "Poppy, come on, and I'll whip your scrawny ass at a game of checkers."

I never knew where Miss Loretta was bound. Most likely another dusty town where liquor flows free and menfolk are as horny as toads. I'd have to wait for another day, when my momma tired of smoky taverns, calloused fellas, and useless desires.

"I'm comin', Sook," I said. "I'm comin'."

I waved until the cab's taillights turned off Digby.

Sook hollered, "These checkers aren't gonna play by themselves."

"I'm comin', Sook."

It seemed to me, life never gifted folks all they yearn for. I reckon, you gotta just hold on tight to what is yours until it all falls away or until the red tail lights travel clear out of sight.

For a string of nights, I dreamed that Miss Loretta was in the belly of a whale. God swore to keep her there until she got herself on the straight and narrow. My momma lived in the great beast's belly for the longest spell, until one fine day, after she had healed herself of her cravings, the Lord smiled upon her. He knew Miss Loretta had truly changed her wicked ways. The giant whale then swam near the shore, belching her onto the beach of Tybee Island.

I was there waiting for her with my grandma Lainey. We three walked along the sandy shores of Tybee. The repeating tides washed up on the beach to greet our bare feet. Loretta and Grandma Lainey sat side by side. Not an angry or cross word spilled between them.

My momma's war was over. Her eyes were crystal clear, and she folded into Lainey's arms like a baby who longed to be held by her momma.

———

"And so, she just left?" Pearl asked with a baffled expression. "She's gone, just like that?"

I shrugged my shoulders up to my ears. "It's what she does, Pearl." I said. "For as long as I can recall, Miss Loretta is either co-min' or goin'. I can't keep track."

Pearl wished aloud, "Gee whiz, just once I'd like my momma to try and see if her luggage would fit into a taxi cab's trunk."

We shared a laugh.

"I'm real sorry, Poppy. I can't see no good reason why a momma would do her youngins this way," she said. "If the Holy Lord is just and fair, it seems he'd bring down an angry thunderbolt on any momma who would do such a thing."

I remarked, "Mrs. Tucker don't do you right by you neither, Pearl."

She thought on it for a spell. "I reckon not."

Turning my head to the open window, I replied, "I suppose, if I went searching deep in dark places, I could find a way…"

Through my open window, a family of cicadas homesteading in the magnolias serenaded the heavy August night.

"What?" Pearl asked. "What did ya say, Poppy?"

In a hushed whisper, quieter than God's voice, I said, "I reckon I could find a way to hate her."

Pearl's green eyes opened wide, fixed on my mouth, like I'd muttered the filthiest words.

She studied me for the longest while and slowly nodded her head up and down.

Sookie called from the bottom of the stairs, "Poppy, it's time for bed. Take your bath, and then shut them lights off!"

"OK, Sook," I hollered. "Can Pearl and me have a bedtime snack?"

Sookie griped, "All y'all are eating me out of house and home. I believe all of Savannah must have a tapeworm!"

Pearl asked, "Does Jackson know that your momma left?"

"Nope. Not yet," I answered. "We're gonna go to the movies on Saturday."

Pearl inquired, "Poppy, you gotta tell me. Does Jackson ever get frisky at the picture show? Tell me!"

"He's a perfect gentleman."

"Dang! That ain't no fun. Does he put his arm around you? Do you share a popcorn? Do you two get lovey dovey?"

"Hold your horses. I'll tell ya everything. But, first, I'm gonna take me a bath."

"Do you promise?" Pearl was downright gleeful with the prospects of some romantic gossip.

"I promise. You go to the kitchen and fetch us some of Donita's oatmeal cookies. They're on a platter, next to the fridge, wrapped in cellophane. I'll hop in the bath quick."

The rising steam from the clawed tub fogged the entirety of the small bathroom, clouding the mirror and tiny window. I slipped my dress from my shoulders, and it fell to the floor. I tossed my trainer and panties to the side and tested the rushing water from the tub spout with my big toe. Slowly, I lowered myself into the hot water and rested my back against the cast-iron tub. I shampooed my hair and with a bar of soap, then lathered up my face.

Soaking in the warm water, I thought about Jackson—the way the spark in his eyes made me smile. I recalled our first kiss in the spook house.

I rinsed myself off and was reaching for a towel when Pearl entered through the unlocked door.

Giggling, she announced, "Miss Pearl Tucker, at your service, Madam." She walked in carrying one of Sookie's tarnished silver serving trays, with Donita's oatmeal cookies, all neatly arranged, and two full glasses of cold milk. Searching through the tub's steam, she glimpsed me standing nude before her.

Stopping dead in her tracks, Pearl's mouth went agape. She stood stunned in the open doorway while I scrambled frantically, reaching for a towel.

CHAPTER 29

———◆———

"PEARL?"

She stood slack-jawed.

"Are you OK?"

"Poppy Wainwright, you got yourself a tallywacker." Her face was drained of all its color. She backed from the bathroom, still balancing her tray of treats.

"Pearl! Wait! I can explain!"

I rushed, slipping into my pajamas, and found Pearl sitting on the end of the bed, the tray of cookies still resting on her lap.

"Poppy, you're a dadgum boy!"

I held my finger in front of her mouth. "Shh!"

Aunt Sook shouted from downstairs, "You two deviants shut those damned lights off and get to bed!"

With my index finger still on Pearl's pursed lips, I called to Sookie a goodnight.

The television in the sitting room went silent, and we listened on as Sook moved about the house, pulling closed draperies and turning off lights. She began the slow climb up the stairs and finally reached the top. We followed the sound of Sook's shuffling and the tapping of her walking stick jabbing at the floor boards.

She switched off the crystal sconces in the hallway, and then we heard her bedroom door shut.

Scratching her mass of ruby ringlets, Pearl whispered again, "You're a dadgum boy."

I asked, "You ain't mad at me, are ya, Pearl?"

"You're a boy, Poppy Wainwright," she repeated again, this time only to herself, like she was trying to untangle the thoughts in her head.

"Pearl, I'd just die if you was mad at me."

She pondered on it. "Nope. I ain't mad. But I reckon, some folks are gonna feel like they've been hoodwinked. But I don't have no bone to pick with you."

I sat by her side on the edge of the bed.

"I'm so sorry, Pearl," I said. "Back in Mountain Home, the other kids knew me as the troubled boy. When I arrived to Savannah, all y'all were so kind to me because you just saw a girl."

"Geeze, you're awfully pretty for a fella."

"Thank you, kindly," I said.

"Dang! I ain't that purdy on my best day," she complained. "Don't seem fair."

"That ain't true, Pearl. You're pretty as a picture."

"Poppy, how long have you been a fella? I mean, were you borned a boy, but decided to become a girl?"

"Yessum," I answered. "I know it don't make a lick of sense."

"So it's your intention to be a full-fledged, bonafide girl?"

"Dunno, Pearl. I suppose so. I haven't traveled far 'nuff down that road to know what's comin' around the bend. I just want to be who I feel I am in my innards."

Pearl's silence answered back.

"It's beyond my reckoning, Pearl. It's just sumphin' I feel in my gut, like knowin' when somethin' is right or wrong. Or the notion that you're meant to be a person, but the mirror tells you somethin' different."

"Poppy, I wanna be an astronaut, but I ain't makin' no plans to walk on the moon anytime soon."

I fell back onto the bed. "I dunno, Pearl. If you believed the moon was the single, solitary place where ya could breathe, maybe you might start lookin' for yourself a rocket ship."

"I suppose so."

I could see she was contemplating her next question. "What in tarnation possessed you to put on a dress for the first time?"

"I ain't got no idea," I replied. "I'm just as vexed as anyone."

Giggling, Pearl fell back onto the bed next to me. A full belly laugh erupted between us. "Poppy Wainwright, I do believe this is biggest thing that's ever happened in Savannah since the old spinster Mabel Atkinson grew herself a moustache."

"Huh?"

"Yessum. Miss Mabel had herself a full beard and a fine handlebar 'stache. She'd wax it, groom it, and stroke it while she rocked on her front porch. She'd twist her long whiskers between her two fingers, like she was rolling herself a ciggy."

We laughed out loud.

Sookie called, "Hush up, you youngins, and turn off the lights!"

"Yes, ma'am."

I reached and switched off the lamp.

Pearl lowered her voice to a whisper in the dark, "Old Mabel Atkinson would arrive to the church in her Sunday's finest lace and satin dress with pearls strung around her neck and diamond bobbles hangin' from her ears with a full dadgum black moustache and beard growing wild from beneath her powdered nose."

"Pearl, that can't be true."

"Is too," she replied. "I swear on a stack of Bibles. Poppy, your tallywacker has got Mable Atkinson's beard beat by a country mile." Pearl went quiet for a moment and then asked, "What's it like to have a pecker?"

I shrugged my shoulders. "I don't pay it no never mind," I answered. "Miss Loretta says it was Mother Nature's little mistake, but she told me Mother Nature made up for it by blessing me with fine bone structure and a keen sense of panache."

"Are ya gonna tell folks?"

"I reckon it's just a matter of time. Everyone will know."

Pearl pondered the dire possibilities. "Poppy, some folks aren't gonna be none too pleased."

"Yessum."

"Jackson?" Pearl's mouth went slack-jawed. "Jackson Taylor? Holy moly, Poppy! What in tarnation are you gonna do about Jackson?"

"Shut your mouths, you juvenile delinquents!" Sook bellowed.

"I dunno, Pearl. I dunno," I whispered. "I'm worried sick. I never meant for none of this hubbub to happen. It was never my intention to ever hurt him."

She rested her head deeper in the pillow. "Oh, Lordy. That's a heap of trouble."

"Pearl, it's an aching lonesome," I said. "Believing those affections offered to all the other girls won't never be offered up to me. It's a mean kind of knowing."

"Poppy, I ain't got no long line of beaus at my door neither."

I smiled. "Your turn is comin'. I just know it. Until I met Jackson I was scared I wouldn't never get mine."

We laid side by side in the dark.

"Poppy?"

"Yessum."

"Do you whizz standing upright like a fella or sittin' on the commode like one of us girls?"

"Mostly, I take me a seat."

She confessed, "I'd give my left arm to be able to pee standin' upright."

In the light of a sleepy Georgia moon, Pearl turned to me. "Poppy, your secret is safe with me." Turning an imaginary key to lock her pink lips, Pearl slid the invisible key in the front pocket of her flannel pajamas. I'll take it to my grave."

"Thank you, Pearl," I replied. "Maybe Sook and my grandma Lainey were right. Maybe I should steer clear of folks and stay well inside Sook's gate."

"That ain't no way to live."

"I reckon not. But I could save myself and everyone else a big heap of a mess if they ever find out."

"There ain't nothin' fun about being tidy—no joy in being clean." Pearl grinned. "And it's a heck of a lot more fun outside of old Sook's front gate. Let's go get messy together!"

We chuckled.

"You children stop your gawd-damned yappin'," Sookie yelled. "If I have to get out of this bed, I'm gonna fetch me a leather strap and beat the tar out of both you."

Pearl smothered her giggles with a pillow.

"Good night, Sookie," I called out in the dark.

CHAPTER 30

Port Wentworth, Georgia

IT WAS THE FIRST TIME Donita Pendergast had taken notice of the front door.

She'd woken earlier that morning after falling asleep on the couch, waiting on Rodney's return home from the night before. The television was still on, and Rodney was nowhere to be found. Donita sat upright, wiped sleep from her eyes and surveyed the small sitting room. Rodney's polished trophies lined the mantel, and framed photographs of the attractive couple were nailed about the plastered walls. A pretty vase with some paper flowers sat on the side console table, the same glass vase Donita had pieced back together with glue after Rodney had busted on the floor in the midst of one of his enraged assaults.

In the mirror over the credenza, she viewed her reflection. She sighed at her weary appearance. She needed a brush to tame her tangled mess of hair. An extra five pounds would do her diminished frame some good. Donita was comforted to see that the bruise just above her left cheek bone had healed sufficiently and could be camouflaged with some foundation.

Two antique brass candle sticks, a gift from her mother, sat on the coffee table. One evening, when Rodney was on a bender, he'd taken one of the lovely holders and beat Donita's skull until she bled out on the carpet, finally losing consciousness on the kitchen linoleum. Later she cleaned her dried blood from the brass, unwrapping strands of her auburn hair caught in the tiny brass screws.

Donita considered the hand-stitched curtains hanging over the small windows. She recalled the exact Wednesday afternoon at the Piggly Wiggly when she admired the bolt of blue fabric—it reminded her of the color of the sky. Living with Rodney Pendergast, Donita had learned to keep her windows shut and drapes drawn closed. Curtains were a necessity to stop any passing folks from witnessing the goings-on of the godless marriage playing out inside the tiny rooms.

Donita surveyed the meager room and noticed for the first time the house's front door.

He had purchased the modest home while she was visiting her folks in Richmond. Upon her return to Savannah, an excited Rodney covered his palms over her eyes, eager to surprise his blushing bride. Donita stumbled blindly through the door's threshold and walked directly into the front room. When he uncovered her eyes, she gasped, admiring the new wall-to-wall carpet and the lovely red brick fireplace.

Hugging his neck, she kissed him over and over again. "It's more than I could've ever dreamed of, baby."

Rodney walked her through the tiny kitchen with shiny appliances and new avocado Formica counters. From the window over the kitchen sink, Donita's view was a lovely meadow of golden grasses. She walked all about the house holding Rodney's arm, but Donita never took notice of the paneled front door on its hinges.

Sitting on the couch on this particular morning, Donita thought to herself how just outside that simple door, a rusty train passed by the house three times a day—once in the morning, around half past nine, and twice in the late afternoons. The row of passenger cars linked behind the chugging engine carried folks who were heading somewhere far from Savannah. Were all those folks leaving Georgia searching for someplace better than the life they were living here?

She walked to the front door and twisted its knob. With a slight bump of her hip, the wooden door swung open wide onto the front porch. Sitting back on the upholstered couch, Donita took a moment to enjoy the view of the rolling green pastures across the gravel dirt road. In the distance, she could see groves of live oaks and a blue sky stretching from here all the way to there.

Donita Pendergast had woken on that Friday morning with an aching forehead, stiff bones, a troubled heart, and a head full of regrets. Like too many mornings before, Rodney was out somewhere creating a ruckus or in the arms of a willing Southern blonde. There were bills to be paid, clothes to be laundered, and dishes to be washed, but unlike those other mornings, on this particular day, Donita Pendergast saw an open door.

———◆———

CHAPTER 31

I SUSPECTED IT ALL STARTED with a single smoldering ember.

Like a piece of kindling buried at the bottom of a doused fire, our sworn secret started sparking deep inside Pearl's belly. The news of my willy was combustible. I reckoned there wasn't no way she could contain the fire.

"I swear, I'll never tell another livin' soul," Pearl had promised. We locked pinkies, and she skipped out the front gate.

Nedra Sue picked up Pearl on the sidewalk out front of Sook's place, and off they drove with the fire sparking inside her gut. Pearl waved widely from the little bug as they sped up Digby. A summer wind blew in through her open window, stoking the spark, igniting the flicker into a red-hot glow.

It was later that Pearl conveyed how the fervor of my pecker burned to a blaze.

It seemed by the time the tiny Volkswagen had turned onto West Jones Street, the combustible secret burned free from Pearl Tucker's tummy.

"Poppy, ain't no real girl," Pearl confided to her older sister in the car. "She was birthed Samuel Wainwright."

"What?" Nedra looked over once and then again, nearly veering her speeding bug directly into a horse-drawn carriage trotting up ballast stone street. "No way!"

"Yessum. It's true," Pearl confirmed. "But zip it, keep quiet!"

"Far out!" Nedra celebrated with an extended honk on her car's horn. "That's so dang cool! The instant I met that little radical rebel I knew she was part of the revolution!"

Needing gas, Nedra pulled her Volkswagen into the service station on the corner of Market Street. While filling her tank, she happened across Brody Banks, a teen from her second-period geometry class, who stood pumping fuel into his Dodge pickup.

"Hi, Brody!"

"Howdy, Nedra Sue."

"Did you pass Miss Haynes's quiz?"

"Hell no!" The Banks boy swiped his stringy hair from his eyes. "She's a ball buster."

Nedra called over to him, "You ain't never gonna believe what I just heard! It's the craziest damned thing ever! You know Poppy Wainwright, the kid who moved into old Sook's on Digby?"

"Yessum. The little girl from Arkansas?" he answered back. "She's a friend of my little sis, Tallulah."

Nedra lowered her voice to almost a whisper. "Well, that little runt is actually a boy!"

"Huh?" Brody's eyes grew as wide as two shiny silver dollars. "You're fuckin' kiddin' me." He scratched his forehead. "Can't be true. No fuckin' way!"

Old Jack Paul, who owned the station, called from an adjacent pump, "Mr. Banks, cursing is a sure sign of a lack of intelligence. And cussing in the presence of a young lady displays a serious lack of character."

"My apologies, Mr. Paul." Brody whispered back to Nedra, "No fuckin' way!"

"Yessum. It's true!" She giggled. "Isn't that so cool?"

"That's fuckin' crazy!" The Banks boy stood dumbfounded. Petroleum overflowed from his car, spilling onto the pavement.

"Catch ya later, Brody." Nedra waved, hopped in her bug, and took off toward home.

It seemed the hearsay of my hidden, hooded hotdog continued to spread like a wild fire.

Later that evening, after heads were bowed and grace was said over the Banks's family supper table, Brody Banks unceremoniously announced, "Old Sook's kin from Arkansas, the little whippersnapper? She's actually a fella."

Mr. Banks nearly choked on a piece of fried chicken. Gathering his composure, he asked, "Excuse me, son? Could you repeat that?"

The entire Banks family went silent, patiently watching on as young Brody finished devouring his buttered corn on the cob.

The Banks's matriarch cleared her throat and dabbed the corners of her mouth. "Son, would you please explain yourself?"

The boy took a swig of his orange soda pop and repeated, "Yessum, the little gal who moved into Sook's place on Digby. Well, come to find out, she ain't no *she* at all. She's a fella. Aren't you friendly with her, sis?"

Little Tallulah went pale. Her mouth went cotton dry and her lips turned blue.

Hyperventilating at the table, Tallulah suffered a full-fledged asthmatic episode. The Banks's fine supper was cut short when it was necessary to rush little Tallulah to the Mercy Medical Emergency Room. She sucked the mouth piece of her inhaler while her panicked parents loaded her into the family station wagon.

The hot chatter of my popular pecker burned to a bonfire, spreading through Savannah like a raging forest fire in the sweltering days of August. Come the following morning, the youngest Banks boy, who also happened to deliver the *Savannah Morning Press*, felt obliged to distribute a burning ember to every doorstep on Digby.

Pedaling by each home, Brody greeted the early risers with a paper. "Good morning, Mrs. Calvert. Here's the morning edition!" He smiled. "Did you happen to know that young Poppy Wainwright, Sook's niece, is really a boy? Have a fine day!"

"Mornin', Mrs. Atkinson. I hope you're having a pleasant morning." Brody waved as he tossed the newspaper on her front lawn. "I ain't sure you've heard, but come to find out the young, orphaned Wainwright gal ain't no gal at all!"

As Carl McAllister sauntered out to the sidewalk to fetch his paper, the youngest Banks hollered, "Good mornin', sir."

"And a fine mornin' to you, Mr. Banks!"

"Here's your newspaper, sir!"

"Thank you, son."

The boy tossed the rolled paper, sending it sailing in the air. It landed at Carl's socked feet.

"That's a mighty nice throw, Brody. I'm sure that strong arm of yours will be a fine addition to the Savannah High baseball squad next season."

"Thank you," the boy called as he pedaled by. "Sir, ain't sure if you've heard the news, but it seems old Sookie Wainwright's niece ain't her niece after all. She's her nephew!" The young boy steered his Schwinn onto West Jones Street and pedaled out of sight.

Mr. McAllister's mouth went dry as dust. His tongue went limp. He stood slack-jawed, paralyzed on the sidewalk in his flannel pajamas. Carl went to beckon back the young Banks boy, but the words wouldn't come. Instead, he abandoned the morning paper on the curb and walked slowly back to the house, scratching his noggin.

Like some tasty treat, the yummy news was nourishment for the hungry ears of the silver-haired ladies in the squares of Savannah. The ancient women resting on the park benches in Forsyth and Colonial Square gobbled it up.

The gossip of my goober was like some miracle tonic for the old men in Johnson Square, causing them to jump to their feet, stretch their boney knees, and go about spreading the word of my piddly pickle's presence. The townsfolk repeated the news to anyone within earshot. The patrons in Leopold's and Delia's Diner fed on the scandalous chatter.

Pearl Tucker had let the cat out of the bag, and it had scampered from square to square, scurrying to all corners of Savannah.

Like a string stretched between tin cans, word of my peculiarity traveled to the faithful flock of the Savannah First Baptist Church.

As I entered through the open doors, the congregation's voices dwindled to only hushed murmurs. I took my place in the back pew. The elderly ladies whispered in one another's ears, suspiciously looking over their shoulders at me. Behind white lace gloves, the news of my puny peepee journeyed from pew to pew. Before the last chime had rung in the steeple, summoning all to Sunday service, my willy was the congregation's sole worry.

When Donita entered the hall, she spotted me from across the chapel. Waving wildly, she scooted by down the pew and took her regular spot at my side.

She greeted me with a big hug and a *howdy*. With her cordial disposition, I wondered if the gossip hadn't yet found its way out past the railroad tracks.

The pastor welcomed the congregation and led us in "Just a Closer Walk with Thee." Sharing a hymnal, Donita and I sang along.

As the choir rejoiced, she leaned in closer to me. "Well, Miss Poppy Wainwright," she nudged and winked, "aren't you a bundle of surprises?"

I felt my pulse pounding like a drum in my ears, and my knees went weak and wobbly.

Donita and I took our seats, and the pastor took his place behind his pulpit. Clearing his throat, he prepared himself to address his parishioners. But on this particular Sunday it seemed our minister was uncertain of his sermon. As he readied himself, fidgeting with his notes, the front doors of the church swung wide open.

The scandalous sight of Mr. Daryl Turnball and Miss Sookie Wainwright walking arm-in-arm over the threshold of the First Savannah Baptist Church left the devout congregation God-smacked. The twosome entered, cackling like they'd just heard the punchline to a tawdry joke. But it was the obscene spectacle of the pair's attire that brought gasps from the sanctuary. The elderly women of the church feigned fainting and the deacons grumbled in utter disgust.

Daryl wore a blush-and-champagne striped seersucker suit and a top hat. His white shoes were spit and polished, and he wore a white rose pinned to his lapel. Aunt Sookie was draped in full-length white fur and wore red satin gloves up to her elbows. Her feathered headdress blossomed with pink plumes of feathers, and her neck, ears, fingers, and wrists were smothered in garish costume jewelry.

As the pair sauntered in, Daryl winked at the handsome altar boys, and Sook smiled broadly, waving to the appalled congregation like they were her admiring fans. When they spotted Donita and me, they pushed their way down the pew and took a seat next to us. Sookie pulled a fan from her purse and complained loudly to the congregation, "It's hotter than fuckin' Hades in here!"

The church went quiet as a tomb.

Folks settled themselves, and the smiling pastor welcomed the unexpected guests, "I am so very pleased to see Miss Sookie Wainwright has joined us on this glorious day. It is a rare occasion but a welcomed one, indeed. She's been kinder to this church than any of you could know. Her quiet generosity has been a blessing throughout the years. And I see my dear old friend, Mr. Daryl Turnball. I have asked Daryl to stop by and visit our church many, many times. Just the sound of the music coming from his ice cream truck brings smiles to my five youngins' faces. My children are more delighted to see Daryl everyday than they are to see my ugly mug arrive home. I'm overjoyed to see his smiling face among us this morning."

The minister then opened his leather Bible, cleared his throat, and preached from the book of John.

He spoke of the Lord's benevolence to a wanton woman.

The preacher looked to his congregation and his tone took a serious turn. "Brothers and sisters, it's the church's foremost obligation to reach a compassionate hand to the troubled. It's our promise to the ages to lift up the downcast and disheartened."

The pudgy preacher recounted the story of Jesus on the Mount of Olives. He spoke of how early one morning, Jesus came to the temple, and crowds gathered around him. When the scribes and Pharisees brought to Jesus a shamed, adulterous woman, they forced her at his feet, reminding him that under Moses's law, the immoral woman should be stoned. But Jesus kneeled down and remained silent for the longest while.

The pastor described to his hushed congregation, "With his finger, the Lord wrote in the dirt, as though he had heard them not. But when the scribes pressed our Lord for his judgement of the adulterous woman, Jesus finally lifted himself up and spoke to the gathered crowds, 'He who is without sin among you, let him cast the first stone.'"

Sweat soaked through our preacher's button-up. He pounded a closed fist on his pulpit, jarring the slumbering from their naps. "Judgement is not ours, my brothers and sisters! Judgement is not ours!" He pointed a rigid finger out over the pews of believers. "And I tell you now, if there are any of you sitting in this sanctuary preparing to cast stones at another member of this faithful congregation, you'll be answering to the Almighty." The pastor drew in a deep breath. "And make no mistake, you will also be answering to me!" His fist pounded the pine pulpit once more. "I will not abide the weakest among us to be treated with anything less than kindness and compassion. Inside these walls is a holy refuge, this is not a room for condemnation! Can I get an *amen?*"

The shell-shocked congregation muttered among themselves. The stodgy gray men complained low in dissention, while the offended church ladies rapidly fanned their flushed cheeks.

It was the singular voice that sounded from the back pew. Jumping to her feet, Donita proclaimed, "Amen!"

In unison, every head pivoted to the back row of the sanctuary. Donita turned a crimson shade of red and returned to her seat.

After the closing prayer and the collection plate was passed along the rows of pews, Sook, Daryl, Donita, and I walked from the chapel. I assisted my aunt down the front steps and into her Buick.

"Thank you for comin' Sook," I said. "I really do appreciate it."

"'Twas nothin'," she replied.

"You'll forever be a mystery to me. Why would you give money to the church? I thought you were of the belief that all Christians were charlatans?"

"They are! Self-righteous bastards all of 'em! A bunch of busy-body know-it-alls. But raisin' children in these tryin' times is like sailin' a ship in troublesome waters. Youngins need an anchor and a compass to guide them true north," she said. "It's a real pity that the church is bogged down in such bullshit, but the way I see it, the alternative is a frightenin' affair. Now I have to go home and take me a long hot bath. I have to scrub off all this mendacity. I'm covered in filthy mendacity! How 'bout you Daryl?" She elbowed Mr. Turnball. "Are you coated in the grimy soot of mendacity?"

"Yes, ma'am." He tipped his hat and winked at me.

Mr. Turnball rode shotgun in Sookie's old Buick. The sound of his panicked squeals could be heard all the way down the lane as she drove the opposite direction down the one-way road.

"Poppy Wainwright, is it true?" Donita asked under the shade of an elm. "I thought we were good friends. How could you not have said somethin'?"

I shrugged my shoulders up to my ears. "I reckon it's some scandalous secret for most folks, but when you've walked about in my shoes, it's no big deal."

Donita laughed, "In a city like Savannah, it's a great big deal!"

"I suppose so," I replied. "Pearl Tucker let the secret slip. I can't blame her. I should've known something like this was too big for Pearl to keep locked up in that little body of hers."

Donita asked, "What about Jackson Taylor?"

"That's a whole heap of trouble. He won't return my calls. I gotta run and find him. I suspect he ain't never gonna speak to me again."

Donita offered, "We can load your bike in my trunk and go track him down together, if you'd like."

"No, thank you, ma'am. I've made this messy mess," I replied. "I best go clean it up myself. Old Sook says telling lies is like sleeping in a barberry thicket. You won't never get a restful night's sleep, and you're certain to wake up with thorns in your backside. I reckoned I'm harvesting a patch of stickers from my rear for not being forthright with the other kids right from the start."

"Well, you be careful, baby girl. I don't want any harm to come to you."

I pedaled myself up Gaston Street to Forsyth Square in my search for Jackson. Forsyth was crowded with tourists admiring the splashing fountain and snapping pictures of the oaks, but there was no sign of Jackson.

Over on Montgomery Street, in Franklin Square, I found Constance and a few of the other girls near the swings.

Constance's little pink finger pointed in my face. "You ain't no real girl. You're a nasty, disgustin' boy, Poppy Wainwright!"

"Is it true?" Little Tallulah's two magnified eyeballs looked baffled. "Are you really a fella?"

"Yessum. It's true," I answered back. "I'm real sorry for not being more forthright."

"It's a sin against nature!" Constance hoisted her hands high on her hips. "My momma says you can powder yourself up and put on as many frilly dresses as you wish, but that don't make you no girl. And what's more, you're never gonna be one!"

Pearl came peddling up to the rescue on her rusty bike. "Hey, Poppy, I've been huntin' all over Savannah for you!" She turned and greeted the others. "Howdy, Constance, Tallulah."

Constance huffed, "Pearl, I'm suspectin' you knew all the while that Poppy here was a boy! It's downright disgustin'!"

Pearl dropped her bicycle on the grass and walked a direct line to Constance. "Shut your mouth. You may be a real girl and all, and you may be a hell of a lot prettier than Poppy here, but..."

I looked to Pearl with a puzzled expression.

Pearl shrugged her shoulders. "I'm sorry, Poppy, but this ain't no time to be dilutin' ourselves in hogwash." She turned back to Constance. "It's true you may be prettier than the rest of us with your long locks of silky hair, but Constance, you're ugly in places where Poppy is beautiful."

"You're hateful, Pearl Tucker!" Constance barked.

"No. I'm just truth tellin'. I suspect the Lord burdened you with your repulsive skin condition to even the playin' field for the rest of us!"

Constance sniffled as the pack of boys led by the McAllister twins sauntered up to the swing set.

Pearl continued, "Sure, Constance, all your teeth are pearly white and in perfect, straight rows, and God gifted you with glistening green eyes, but Poppy Wainwright has more kindness in her pinky finger than you have in your entire perfect body!"

Constance gave a slight tilt to her head and offered up a pretty pout. Her little lips pursed into the shape of a perfect, pink heart.

All the gathered boys sighed at the sad sight, offering Constance their unwavering support and devotion.

"Ain't true, Constance," a skinny boy with dirty bare feet the color of coal consoled her. "Pearl Tucker don't know what she's talkin' about."

Another older kid with a mouth full of metal advised, "Constance, don't you listen to Pearl. She's just jealous."

"Yup. Don't believe a single word," Tommy McAllister remarked. "Pearl Tucker is just pea green with envy."

Constance worked up a single translucent tear. The collection of concerned admirers moved closer to her side as reinforcement.

A few of the older boys came sniffing. They walked in closer behind me. I could feel their breath on the back of my neck. One of the boys gave me a hard push, and I stumbled into the chest of another kid, who shoved me over to the McAllisters.

Timothy and Tommy moved in like two attacking alley dogs—one to my left, one to my right.

"Is it true?" Tommy scoffed. "You're a sissy boy?"

The other McAllister hocked up some snot, spitting it at my Sunday shoes. "I always knew sumpthin' didn't add up."

The rowdy boys strutted about me like fighting cocks, kicking up dust, pecking at me. Not a one was willing to admit that we'd become fast friends since my arrival to Savannah. Not one of them was courageous enough to be kind.

Timmy McAllister reached to grab my shoulder, ripping the seams of the sleeve of my cotton dress.

"Oh, look, you ripped his pretty little dress," one of the other guys mocked.

"McAllister, you'd best step back." Pearl's round face was as red as a beet, and her two fists were balled up behind her back. "I'd hate to send you home to your momma, crying with a busted lip." Pearl took a big step in front of me. "I'm warnin' you assholes to let her be."

"Wainwright, you're a faggot!" one of the boys jeered.

The others snickered.

Timmy uttered, "From the second I set my sights on you, I knew you was a fuckin' pansy."

Little Tallulah stood up from the grass, dusting off her back-side. "I don't wanna stick my nose where I ought not." She pushed her magnifying spectacles further up on her nose and went thumb-ing through the well-worn pages of her notebook.

Finding a specific page, Tallulah held out the open pad, show-ing all of us her hand-written inscription. She announced, "The Golden Rule instructs us to always treat others as we wish to be treated."

In front of the McAllister boys and the other fellas, Tallulah held out the single page for a closer examination.

Tommy scoffed, "If you're suggestin' that we give this little per-vert a pass, then you're barking up the wrong tree."

Without taking a breath, the little wisp of a girl replied, "What I'm suggesting is, if you fellas don't wanna be treated to an ass whippin' by my older brother and his buddies from over at the high school, you assholes best step back and let my good friend Poppy pass by."

A few of the girls gasped at little Tallulah's cursing. The boys seemed to rethink their positions.

Little Tallulah gestured to me with a friendly nod. "Poppy, if you ever find yourself in a pinch, you just let me know. My brother, Brody, and his buds know how to treat a lady and won't stand for this kind of disrespect."

"Let's go, Poppy." Pearl cautiously led me through the circle of kids. "I've had enough of this bullshit!" Holding my hand, Pearl led me through the cluster of boys and over to our bikes.

Pearl and I pedaled from the park, speeding through the gates of Franklin Square. There, off by himself, I spotted Jackson. He sat in the shade of a hackle berry tree. I called out to him, but he remained still, resting his back against the tree's trunk.

Constance yelled, "You're a freak of nature, Poppy Wainwright!"

As Pearl and I sped on to Market Street, the collection of kids jeered and mocked behind us.

"Thank you, Pearl!"

"Poppy, this whole dust up is all my fault," she confessed. "I'm real sorry."

"Ain't nothin," I said. "It was bound to become common knowledge."

"No, it was dead wrong of me. You left a treasured secret in my care, but because of my loose lips, the shit has done hit the fan."

"Ya think?"

"Yessum," she answered back. "You'd best run for cover. The shit is gonna start flyin'."

CHAPTER 32

———◆———

SOOKIE'S NERVOUS INDEX FINGER REPEATEDLY tapped on her chin as she considered my dire circumstances. "So, tell me, missy, now that your pickle is out of the jar and this news has made its way into the clear light of day, just how in tarnation are you fixin' to deal with it?"

"Ain't sure."

"Well, I haven't the vaguest notion how folks around here are gonna sit with all of this hubbub." Sook fidgeted with the collar of her blouse.

I asked, "Sook, am I a freak of nature?"

"A freak of nature?"

"Yessum. Constance White called me a freak of nature."

Sook cleared her throat. "Well, I reckon so. But you've come from a long, proud lineage of freaks. You know your precious grandma Lainey? The one who you believe walked on water? When we was just youngins, no more than your age, I walked into her room and caught her sniffing her own undies."

"Nu-uh. That ain't true," I said.

"Yes, ma'am," Sook cackled. "Your pious grandma Lainey was gripping a pair of her own bloomers and was sniffin' them like they was one of Dixie's Queen Anne, long-stem roses."

"That ain't true." Laughter erupted from my belly.

"The sooner you understand that there ain't no saints walking about on this green earth, the better off you'll be. Every last one of us is equal parts good and evil. Look at your Miss Loretta. You won't find a kinder heart, but goodness knows your momma ain't got the good sense the Lord gave her. She's one card shy of a full deck. My daddy, your great-grandpa, would play with his pecker during church service, right in the third-row pew! He was sweet on a young, fiery-haired girl in the Sunday choir. While she was singing "How Great Thou Art," my daddy would slide his hand into his trousers and yank his johnson. When Pa cried out, rejoicing during the pastor's sermon, folks believed my daddy was moved by the spirit, but it had nothin' to do with the Almighty. It was that red-haired soprano in the choir who brought Papa to his knees. Child, do you understand what I'm sayin' to you?"

"Yessum. One of the McAllister's said that I was a faggot."

"Oh, he did, did he? Well, that chaps my hide. I'd like to slap the stupid out of them boys. And I certainly wouldn't put stock in nothing those two hooligans have to say. God help him, if I catch him out of the street, I will wash his mouth out with Borax soap. Tell me, which one of those little bastards was it?"

"Ain't sure."

Sook seemed to be growing more agitated as she spoke. "Whether you choose to love Jackson Taylor or a gawd-damned lawn rake, it ain't no one's concern."

"Thank you, Sook. But why do you reckon folks get so upset about sumpthin' that don't concern them none?"

"Pay them no mind. You can't change folks' minds if they don't have ears that are willing to listen. Folks of strong faith hold tight to what they believe to be true. Their beliefs are cooked in the pie at a young age."

"Yessum."

"I suspect folks will have to pass on before the times will truly change," she remarked, "Velvet and ignorance has lined many caskets. Don't waste your breath trying to teach people nothing. My late poppa use to say, 'Sookie, never go about trying to teach a hog to sing. It's a waste of your precious time and annoys the fuck out of the hog.'" My quivering aunt touched my forearm. "Do you understand?"

"Yes, ma'am," I answered. "I reckon how folks feel about my peculiarity shouldn't concern me, since I'm never gonna teach those hogs to sing."

"Yessum!" She slapped her knee. "Now then, go get my pellet gun."

"What?"

"You heard me. Fetch me my pellet gun. You'll find it hidden in the back of the coat closet, under the staircase. Hurry up now!" She waved me on. "You can sit around here all day and mope about, but Missy, there's nothin' at the end of that road. So stop your belly achin', put your big girl bloomers on, and go fetch my pellet gun, then come upstairs to the attic."

I cracked a grin. "Yes, ma'am!"

I located Sook's rifle in the back of the closet, hidden behind some worn wool coats and dusty hats. Sprinting up the tight stairwell into the attic, I found Sookie spying through the slightest gap in the window shade.

"Gimme that!" She seized the rifle, pumped it four times, and then slid the gun's barrel through a crack in the open glass. Over her shoulder, out the window, I could see Timmy McAllister resting on the summer lawn. He was occupied with picking his nose while munching on a box of Cracker Jacks.

I whispered, "Sook, this ain't right."

"Shh!" she silenced me and took aim. Steading her quaking hands, she squeezed the trigger. "That little fucker is all mine."

The first pellet nailed Timmy on his right shoulder, sending the Cracker Jacks box flying into the air. The second clipped his left ear. By the time McAllister understood he was under attack, Sookie had pumped the rifle again, and the third BB nailed him right in the center of his forehead. Grabbing his ear, Timmy hollered, "Momma, I'm under fire!" He darted for the shelter of their house, crying out, "I've been shot! I've been shot!"

The old woman vigorously pumped the rifle again and zeroed in on her fleeing target, nailing a bawling Timmy in his back as he ran screaming through the screen door.

The McAllister house went suddenly quiet. Sookie remained motionless, looking down the barrel of the rifle.

I said, "You're crazy, you can't...!"

"Shh!" She silenced me.

After a spell, Dixie's head appeared from the screen door. With a scalp populated with pink curlers, she cautiously looked in both directions. Just when she felt safe to step into the light of day, Sook pulled the rifle's trigger, sending a pellet whizzing across Digby and shattering a glass hummingbird feeder suspended near Dixie's door. Colored water splattered Mrs. McAllister, and she returned shrieking into the safety of her house.

"Sook," I repeated, "that just ain't right! Come next Sunday, I'm gonna ask for the congregation to pray for your lost soul."

With a satisfied smile, Sook replied, "I'm only doin' the Lord's work!"

CHAPTER 33

"I'm LEAVING MY RODNEY BEHIND," Donita announced. "If Poppy is brave enough to show all of Savannah who she really is, then I figure that I should step up. I need to be brave, too."

"Well, good riddance. Hallelujah!" Sookie rejoiced. "It's high time! Daryl, fix this little lady a banana split! It's my treat!"

Sookie, Donita, and I stood at the counter of Daryl's truck window.

Mr. Turnball exclaimed, "Oh my, I'm not called upon to create my split-banana extravaganza often, but on this auspicious occasion, it will be my pleasure!" Daryl went to the back of his truck and started preparing his ice cream delight. Placing two ripe banana halves in a plastic dish, he scooped half a dozen creamy mounds of ice cream on each side—two scoops of strawberry, vanilla, and chocolate. Daryl then smothered the decadent dessert in caramel and chocolate sauce, added a generous squirt of whipped cream, and then finished off by sprinkling the split with salty peanuts.

Mr. Turnball presented the dish to Donita from over the counter. "Congratulations, little lady. Here's to your liberation!"

She eyed the treat. "I can't eat all of this."

Sookie jested, "Child, it could be a long spell before another man offers you a meaty, ripe banana with nuts. I suggest you enjoy it, given the opportunity."

Donita covered her mouth with a nervous hand. "Sook, the things you say."

Daryl leaned his elbows on the counter and rested his chin in his palms. "So, how did Mr. Pendergast respond when you announced that you're plannin' on splittin' the blanket?"

"No, I haven't breathed a word to Rodney. I'm fixin' to break the news to him soon," Donita replied. "I'm working up my nerve."

Sookie piped up, "Child, you've hooked your wagon to a man who cares more about his animalistic carnal desires than he does his blushing bride. I believe the aerosol fumes have polluted his mind, and the Beefeaters gin has soaked his heart. There ain't no reasoning with a lost soul who's not clear of mind. You best be careful."

"Mr. Pendergast doesn't seem to me to be the understanding sort," I said.

"Yessum," Sook agreed. "You'd be wise to steer well clear of a hot-headed, crazy man. There's no telling what such a scoundrel will do."

"I'm fixin' to pack up my belongings and leave the house this weekend. Rodney will be out with his buds."

Daryl asked, "Excuse me, Donita. I don't want to be presumptuous, but isn't your Rodney heading off to the penitentiary in the near future? Can't you simply wait it out and save yourself all the fussing and fighting? Just leave the son of a bitch when he's locked up behind bars."

"I can't." She anxiously looked to us as though she was searching for answers in our eyes. Donita shook her head back and forth, beginning to unravel. "I just can't wait, Sook. I can't wait another day. I can't. I can't."

Mrs. Pendergast covered her face with trembling hands.

Sookie wrapped her arm around Donita's shoulder. "Breathe. Calm yourself, child."

"Sookie, I can't go back there!" Donita began wrestling with the tiny pearl buttons on her blouse's sleeve. In a desperate, breathless voice, she cried, "I won't survive another day in that sinking house." Starting at her wrist, she rushed to unbutton her sleeve.

We watched on as she unfastened each tiny, delicate button, finally leaving her left forearm exposed up to her elbow. A white bandage was haphazardly wrapped over slices to her skin. Several gashes lining her forearm had bled out. The white gauze absorbed the crimson red. Donita extended her arm to Sook as though she was offering up a gift.

Sookie took Donita's trembling hands in her own and in a most tender voice, asked, "When did Rodney do this to you, child? When did that monster do this to you?"

Donita seemed to be folding into the smallest of nothing, falling toward the ground. Daryl and Sook caught her in their arms. "No, Sookie." Her slight shoulders shook uncontrollably. "It wasn't Rodney. He didn't do it. He never touched me."

———————

I was awoken by the sound of pebbles striking against my window glass. Scrambling from my bed, I slid open the window to the night and peeked out into the dark yard.

"Poppy, down here!" I recognized Pearl's voice.

"Where are ya, Pearl?"

"I'm here."

I searched the lawn until a beam of yellow light from her flashlight blinded me.

"Get on down here."

"OK, OK." I pulled on some wrinkled clothes from the floor, laced my sneakers, and climbed out the window. Tiptoeing across the shingled roof, I treaded carefully, vigilant not to alarm Annabelle or wake Sookie.

Wrapping my legs around a column, I shimmied down a porch post, where Pearl's hands guided my feet to the top of the railing.

"What's goin' on?" I asked.

"Shh! Follow me."

"Pearl, it's the dead of night," I replied. "If Sook finds out, I'm gonna be in big trouble."

"I gotta show you something. Trust me."

"Where are we off to?" I asked.

"We gotta go into town."

"Sook ain't gonna be none too pleased."

"I'll get you back home in no time."

The two of us took off up the path and out the gate. Pearl stopped in front of the McAllister's place and trespassed over their fence.

I asked, "What in tarnation are you up to?"

"Shh!" Pearl crept on tip toes up the McAllister's path. Pulling a jackknife from her front pocket, she opened the blade and began cutting Dixie's prized, long-stemmed, white roses from their bushes.

"Oh, Lordy, Pearl, you're gonna get skinned alive," I whispered.

"Shh! I got better use for these flowers," Pearl announced and continued to scalp every last blooming snow-white rose from its stalks. She gathered the roses in her hand, making a glorious bouquet the size of the Georgia moon.

After Pearl had pruned Dixie's bushes clean of every rose, she snuck back out the gate.

"Let's get goin'!" She signaled for me to follow, and we ran up to Wilmington.

"Pearl, what do you have up your sleeve?"

"Hush up. If you do less talkin' and more walkin', we'll be there in no time."

We boarded a city bus at Montgomery; all the while, Pearl wore a serious expression and spoke not a word as the bus made its way to the Broad Street stop.

"Come on." Pearl signaled and jumped off, running ahead of me, carrying her full moon of roses.

When we arrived at the iron entry gates of old Laurel Grove Cemetery, Pearl gestured for me to follow her deeper into the graveyard.

An old wall constructed of gray stones and mortar was stacked over six feet tall and ran the perimeter of the dark cemetery. Black moss grew in and around each stone and marker. When the trees rustled in a night wind, the heavy oak branches shuffled like approaching feet. The two of us hid low like thieves behind a nearby vault, watching to see if the coast was clear.

"Pearl, I'm scared," I confessed.

"Ain't nothing to be scared of. It's like a garter snake. The dead are more scared of you than we are of them."

"Ya think?"

"Yessum," she replied. "I hear scripture says that they're just waiting around for the Lord's rapture. They're only biding their time. They ain't got no beef with us."

I was relieved to hear Pearl's thoughts on the dead.

I asked, "You ain't planning on diggin' up some buried carcass, are you?"

She grabbed hold of my hand. "Just come with me."

As we walked further into the shadowy ancient cemetery, Pearl took a deep breath and announced, "The dead ain't got no time for us." I suspected she was reassuring herself.

Handing me the bouquet of Dixie's roses, Pearl pulled her metal flashlight from her back pocket. "Just keep quiet."

"Why in tarnation are we here?" I asked and followed behind as she pointed her light deeper into the graveyard.

"I got sumpthin' I gotta show you."

"Couldn't you have shown me in the clear light of day?"

"Naw, some things are best kept in the dark."

Pearl led me deeper into the cemetery, down cobblestone lanes.

Turning to me with a serious expression, she said, "You have to swear on your life that you're gonna keep quiet 'bout this. My momma will beat me raw with a leather strap if she finds out I've brought you here."

"I will, Pearl."

"Promise?"

She pointed her beam of light directly in my face to confirm my sincerity.

"I promise."

We walked down narrow cobbled streets of family grave markers, chiseled headstones, and ornate mausoleums. Carved grieving faces, trumpeting angels, and granite cherubs with frozen smiles watched our passing. Wild cats silently lurked in and out, always following near, stalking our path.

Pearl slid between two gravestones, and I scooted right behind her through the narrow space. She hopped over an iron fence, and I lost her in the dark.

"Pearl?" I called out, "Where'd you go?"

"Hurry up, slow poke," her voice beckoned to me. She flashed her beam of light.

I found her standing among a small gathering of modest gravestones under an oak tree. Pearl placed her flashlight on the ground. Getting on her hands and knees, she cleared leaves from a small, nondescript granite marker. Mud had settled in the stone inscription, and an empty bronze flower vase embedded in the center of the stone was bent toward the ground. She found a stick to her liking and scratched caked mud out from the script.

Wiping her hands off on the sides of her skirt, Pearl picked up the flashlight and pointed the beam of light to the inscription. She declared, "This here is my pops."

In the yellow light, I read "Aaron James Tucker."

"Pearl, I don't understand. I thought you said your daddy had run off to Tulsa with some lady in fancy feathers?"

She shook her head. "Naw. Ain't true. None of it's true. He's been here sleeping all the while, deader than a doornail."

I asked, "There never was no pretty lady? No chickadee on a swing?"

"Nope. I was lyin'."

"No tail feathers?"

"No."

"Why so, Pearl?"

She shrugged her shoulders. "Momma felt it was best."

"How come?"

"Not sure. I reckon one lie begets another and then another. I suspect momma wanted pops to just disappear like one of his magic tricks. But the truth is he went and got himself beat. Momma believes it was on account of pop's sinful wicked ways."

I looked over to her. "Pearl, I just don't understand."

She took a seat on the slab of stone. "Poppy, folks say my dad was light in the loafers. The queer type." Pulling some wild dandelions growing near the marker, she cleared the modest resting place. "He got himself in a heap of trouble with some fellas one night in an alley over in Richmond. The next thing ya know, my daddy got his skull crushed in like some melon. And now, Pop rests here, six feet under. Momma didn't want the shame weighing down on us, so she shipped him here in a poor man's pine box. Momma had Pops buried without a proper funeral, not a single prayer or scripture. Nothin'. I reckon that's why bad luck has shadowed us like a mean tree from that day on." She rubbed her hand over the face of the smooth stone and turned to me, peering hard into my eyes. "Poppy, don't you go huntin' for trouble. It may come huntin' for you. One person dead for such desire is plenty."

I watched on as she tended to her daddy's lonely marker.

"Now, gimme those flowers."

I handed her the blossoming white roses, and she began arranging them in the metal urn. One after the next, little Pearl placed each rose, creating a glorious bouquet that would've even made Mrs. McAllister proud.

Brushing off the last leaves from the stone, Pearl admired the grave. "There ya go," she replied with a satisfied smile. "Good night, Pa." For the briefest moment, she rested the side of her face on the cold stone's surface as if it were the softest pillow. "Sleep tight." Pearl kissed the granite marker and looked up to me. "I've tried and tried to square this in my mind, Poppy, but I can see no good reason for such cruelty."

"I'm real sorry about your pa."

She shrugged her shoulders. "It ain't nuttin'. But you'd best watch your step, Poppy. Folks won't take kindly to your sort. Steer clear of dark alleys."

"I will, Pearl."

"You promise?"

"I swear."

We hooked our pinky fingers.

Pearl took my hand, leading me from the cemetery. "Let's get on outta here."

The two of us hoofed it all the way back home.

———

CHAPTER 34

I KNEW TROUBLE WAS BREWING when I first took notice of the cluster of neighbor ladies percolating down the lane. Filtering out from their screen doors, they gathered on the sidewalk. Dixie McAllister emerged from her front door and took the lead of the crusading battalion of beehives, marching in our direction. They staked their position at our front gate, standing three-bouffant deep with their hands on their hips, shaking their heads disapprovingly. They stood in solidarity with an abiding conviction for all that was righteous, decent, and holy. Not since the confederacy had surrendered Atlanta to Sherman's army had so many angry Southern women taken to the streets.

Sook and I sat on the porch, playing a game of checkers.

"Sookie Wainwright, it's imperative we speak to you," Dixie called from over the fence. She wore a delicate, white pillbox hat that resembled a dollop of whipped cream resting on her mass of teased hair.

My aunt remained engrossed in her next board move.

"Sookie. I know you can hear me." Dixie approached the gate and hollered out again, "Sookie Wainwright, are you listening to me?"

Sook surveyed the checkered board and threatened, "Dixie McAllister, I'm giving you fair warning. If you trespass on this property, there's gonna be hell to pay."

Dixie huffed, returning to the circle of ladies. They pow-wowed, strategizing their next move.

"Yes!" Sook jumped two of my red plastic pieces and exclaimed, "King me!"

Outside our gate, the ladies carried on like it was some hell-dousing prayer meeting.

"It's an unholy perversion!" Mrs. Calvert held one white, gloved hand into the air, crying out, "It's a blatant sin against our Lord's will!"

Another woman, whom I recognized from the Piggly Wiggly, insisted, "Someone must rescue that precious little boy from that house of sin!"

Dixie preached, "I ain't sure what this god-forsaken world is comin' to, but we mustn't allow this abomination to abide here on Digby!"

Maudie Perkins announced, "It's the godless communists!"

"Communist?" asked Dixie.

The collection of Christian crusaders all turned their eyes to Maudie.

"Yes. It's the communists!" she repeated with a fervent conviction.

"Shut up, Maudie." Dixie dismissed her.

Feigning interest on our checker game, from the corner of her mouth, Sookie whispered, "Poppy, listen up. If those fools pass through my gate, I want you to go in yonder and fetch your great granddaddy's musket off the mantel."

"I will not," I refused.

She spoke in a murmur, "Child, you listen to your Aunt Sook. Go get my gun!"

"Sookie, have you come completely unhinged?"

"I won't kill 'em," she declared. "I'll aim right over the top of their heads. I'm gonna scare those nervous hens all the way back to their coop."

"It's finally happened, Sook. You've come completely undone."

Dixie hollered, "Sookie, it is imperative that I speak with you concerning that sweet child."

My old aunt fought to rise from her chair. "You'll do no such thing, Dixie. If you step one foot onto my property, your skinny ass will be full of buck shot."

"Sookie," I said, "let her come on in and say her piece. Let's be done with it."

Arms crossed tight, Sook grumbled low, deliberating with herself. "OK, Dixie, it's against my better judgement, but you may come and speak your mind. But only you. I don't want all those clucking chickens pecking in my yard."

Dixie fought with the gate latch.

I hollered, "Mrs. McAllister, you gotta jiggle it, and give it a firm kick."

With a bump of her pump, the gate swung open. Dixie grew uneasy as she entered the yard. She smoothed her cotton skirt with the palms of her hands and started a determined pace up the sidewalk.

Stepping onto our porch, Dixie appeared as if she were approaching the lion's den at the Savannah Zoo. She cleared her throat and nervously fiddled with the collar of her blouse. "Good mornin', Sook." She nodded her head at me. "Poppy."

"Dixie, say what you've come to say, and then leave us be."

"Sookie, you know I'm not one to stick my nose where it ought not be, but I believe I must speak to you about the disturbing news that has recently come to my attention." As she spoke, her left eye began to twitch about.

Sook asked, "I reckon, you're speakin' of Poppy?"

"Yes." Dixie gathered herself. "May we speak privately?"

Sook signaled for my exit with a wave of her hand. I gave a smile and nod to Mrs. McAllister and went on inside.

Sookie cautioned, "Dixie, I'm giving you fair warning, I ain't certain how any of this is any of your concern."

"I'm fretting about the little precious boy's welfare."

Sookie growled like an old bear as she rocked, "Dixie McAllister, don't mistake my silence for hospitality. I may look calm and collected, but in my mind, I've already kicked your skinny ass all the way to Charleston and back."

Dixie paid her no attention and started up. "I've always had an uncomfortable feeling in my gut that sumpthin' wasn't right with that child. When she arrived, I said to my husband, Carl, something ain't right with that child."

"Is that so?" Sook bit down on her jaw. Gripping tight to the arms of her rocker, it appeared that old Sook was holding herself down in the seat.

Another anxious convulsion caused Dixie's teal-coated eyelid to twitch nervously about.

"Yessum," Mrs. McAllister replied. "I said to my Carl, why has Sookie got that sweet little girl locked up in that big house with no proper schooling?"

"Dixie, the child has proper schooling. I suspect Poppy could run circles around your two Neanderthals."

Mrs. McAllister clutched to her breast. "My heart breaks for that confused little boy."

"Oh, Dixie. Calm yourself. I believe you've been touched by this heat, or are you plagiarizing Tennessee Williams with all this bullshit?"

Dixie yanked a delicate hanky from her breast pocket and dabbed her dry eyes. "That poor child," she slobbered. "It just breaks my heart." Waving her lilac hanky about, she looked as if she were starting the stock car race over at the county fair.

"Ah, horse shit!" Sook declared. "Dixie, if you're gonna start blubbering, could you take your tears over onto my lawn? My grass needs a good watering."

"Sookie Wainwright, you're heartless." Her left eye winked involuntarily. "That poor child is confused. He needs to come to know the Lord."

Sook asked, "Dixie, are you winking at me?"

"Don't be ridiculous, Sook. It's a condition brought on by all my worry. My poor nerves are frayed with all this blatant sin and perversion."

"That child is off to church every Sunday morning. I suspect Poppy could quote scriptures as well as any redneck pastor in Savannah."

"It's just plain wrong what you're doin' to that precious boy."

"Dixie, not that it's any of your concern, but the child arrived on a Greyhound bus from Arkansas in a lace dress. And I'm not of the mind to go telling Poppy what she's gotta wear or what she ain't gonna wear." Sookie pointed her cane to Dixie's tiny hat. "I certainly can't prevent you from comin' out in broad daylight with that there ridiculous hat. I can't stop Poppy, neither."

Mrs. McAllister ignored the insult. "Sook, I am only suggestin' that perhaps living here with you ain't the proper place for a child with such oddities."

"Poppy!" Sookie called out to me.

"Yessum."

"Haul your tail feathers out here. Dixie McAllister wants to discuss your proclivities."

"Yes, ma'am." I arrived from the screen door and took a seat in the chair next to Sook. I asked. "How are the boys and Mr. McAllister?"

"Poppy, Dixie ain't here for neighborly niceties," Sook replied. "Word has traveled through all of Savannah about your peculiar situation."

"Yessum."

Dixie kneeled at my side and took my hand in hers. "Child, you understand that I'm just heartsick about your circumstance." Her left eye convulsed about.

I asked, "Are you feeling OK, Mrs. McAllister?"

"Poppy, Dixie wants you to put on some britches and stop dressing like a silly girl."

"Why?" I asked Sook. I turned back to Dixie. "Why so, Mrs. McAllister?"

"Child, it's a sin against all of nature."

Sook interrupted, "Dixie here, is fretting about your soul's salvation."

"Oh, I see. That's mighty kind of you. I appreciate your concern. But my soul is in fine condition. I can't explain why in tarnation I'm wired this way. I suppose the good Lord will shed some light on it when I arrive at the pearly gates. But I've known it deep in my gut for some time. I was fortunate enough to be reared by womenfolk who let me be just who I am."

Dixie cleared her throat. "Child, sometimes your elders are supposed to provide the guidance to keep you on a straight and narrow path. Perhaps it isn't in your best interest to be gussied up like this. You should be a proper boy like my angelic little Tommy and Timmy. That is who the Lord intended you to be."

"I don't know nothin' about God's intention," I said, "but I was a real sad case before I understood just who I was—a pitifully sad case. Miss Loretta ain't never been much of a momma, but I reckon she saved my life on the day she first dolled me up. My grandma Lainey was a God-fearing believer, and when she saw how much happier I was, even Lainey determined to let it be."

Dixie took her a deep breath.

"The child has got nothin' more to say on this matter," Sookie announced. "She's made her decision, and I don't believe for a single, solitary second that it has been an easy one. No child wakes up one morning and invites such disappointment and ridicule. Besides, being a woman these days ain't all that fun. It's a particular kind of fool who enjoys ratting their follicles into giant gawd-damned bubbles." Sook pointed to Dixie's grand teased yellow bouffant, "Nothin' I could say would stop you from runnin' around town dressed up like some Christian clown with your minefield of makeup! Poppy ain't gonna listen to me, neither."

Dixie nervously fingered the bleached fringe about her face. "Why, I've never been so insulted in all my life!" Her anxious left eye twittered.

"Oh, sure you have, Dixie. Don't underestimate yourself. And for God's sake, stop winking at me!"

"Sook, don't be ridiculous," Dixie snapped back. "It's just a silly tic."

Her eye, rapidly twitched again.

Sookie remarked, "I'm not casting aspersions on anyone's sexual proclivities, but Dixie, your particular preference ain't my cup of tea." My aunt toyed with her. "For the past year, my place has been at full occupancy with its share of sexual deviants. I got no room for a carpet-munchin' lezbo, too!"

Dixie's attempt to control her twitching was futile. "Sookie Wainwright, you know full well I love my Carl."

"OK, Dixie. Don't get your bloomers in a bind," my aunt taunted. "I'm just sayin' if you're hankering for a big slice of hairy cherry pie, you need to keep walkin' seven doors up and to the right. I believe old Alice Faye will accommodate your particular appetite."

Dixie's disgust was palatable. "You're a vile woman, Sookie Wainwright!"

"You've said your piece, Dixie. Now, kindly get your skinny ass off my porch. You have three seconds to get back onto Digby Street, or your backside will be full of buckshot."

"Sookie Wainwright, you need to get yourself some help. This whole sordid affair is an abomination." Dixie contorted her pink mouth in disgust. "It's revoltin'. You are an embarrassment to all of Savannah!"

Old Sook slightly elevated her right hip and floated a gaseous air biscuit.

Wholly offended, Mrs. McAllister rapidly fanned the sulfur scent. "Sook, you are rude and crude and vulgar!"

"Dixie, I believe you've gone soft in the head," Sook replied. "You're not firing on all cylinders. All that yellah hair color has turned your brain to corn mush."

Mrs. McAllister huffed and started for the gate. "And don't think for a second that I don't know that it was you who shot my sweet little Tommy with a BB gun."

Dixie fought with the front latch.

I called out, "Mrs. McAllister, you gotta wiggle the thingamajig!"

Cackling, Sookie hollered, "It wasn't Tommy!"

"What?" Dixie looked over her shoulder as she labored with the rusty latch.

"It was the other one!" Sook stood from her rocker, and called out to her, "I shot the booger picker!"

———

From my bedroom window, I caught sight of Jackson as he paced outside our front gate. He wore a tight-lipped, solemn expression with a serious brow.

"Sook," I called from my bedroom door. "We have ourselves some trouble brewing."

I watched from my open window while Jackson lingered on the sidewalk.

From downstairs, Sookie hollered out the screen, "Mr. Taylor, I do believe you've spent more time contemplating my front gate than any living soul in Savannah."

Jackson ducked low behind our hedge.

I darted from my room, dashed up the hall, and tripped down the stair treads.

Sookie shouted out, "Son, you're wearing out my pavement. The county ain't gonna be none too pleased when they gotta re-pour my sidewalk because of your pacing back and forth."

Sook snickered. "Boy, you ain't hiding from no one."

Jackson slowly rose, reappearing over the top of the hedge. He nervously waved to Sook.

"Are you comin' up to the house or ain't you?"

I hid behind the door and whispered, "Please, I don't wanna talk to him. Tell him I'm gone, Sook."

She hollered out, "I'm certain Poppy will be pleased to see you've come by. Come on up, Mr. Jackson."

"Sookie, please!" I pleaded. "I just can't! I don't wanna talk to him now. He must be so angry with me."

Sook shook her head. "I warned you about that little red-haired demon-child. She's nothin' but trouble!"

"Not now, Sookie."

"If Mr. Jackson has a bone to pick with you, he had best remember you are a respectable young lady. You hear me? He must treat you with the utmost respect that any young lady deserves."

"Thanks, Sookie." I grinned. "I reckon I gotta clean up the mess I've made."

She squared my shoulders with hers. "Just take a moment, child, to right yourself."

Jackson fought with the gate latch and walked with a direct gait up the path. His sneakers were untied, and his straw-colored hair was untamed by a brush. He skipped the treads of the porch steps and rapped his knuckles on the front door.

"Well, good evenin', Mr. Taylor."

"Evenin', Miss Wainwright. Is Poppy here?"

"Yessum. She is, but…"

I walked from behind the door. "Hello, Jackson."

"Good evenin', Poppy." He nodded his head but couldn't meet me eyes. "May I speak with you?"

"Yessum."

Sookie wore a concerned expression. "Poppy, I'll be right in the kitchen."

I walked on to the porch, where Jackson had taken a seat on the swing. He gestured for me to join him. "Come sit for a spell." Patting the wooden seat next to him, he smiled.

As soon as I sat near his side, I began pleading my case. "I reckon you're boiling mad at me, and you have every right to be. If I ever believed that you and I were…" I stuttered, "Jackson, it wasn't never my intention to hurt you."

"Poppy, you never—"

"I know none of this makes a lick of sense, but for someone like me, having a boy like you come a calling was…" I stopped myself, turning my eyes to the floor. I wanted to run, escape all the way back to Mountain Home, and find my grandma Lainey in her rocker, waiting on my return. "I just never thought this would happen. Jackson, I never wanted to bring shame on you."

"I ain't ashamed of nothin', Poppy. I told my momma 'bout this whole dust up, and she said it's a dishonest thing you've done."

"I swear, Jackson," I said, "everything happened so fast."

"Poppy, I need you to be quiet for a spell." He folded his hand over mine.

"Yessum," I agreed with a nod.

"My momma said that it's a dishonest thing you've gone and done. She believes it was wrong as wrong can be. But then she asked me if I thought it was your intention to hurt me." Jackson's hand still rested on mine. "I told my momma, Never! Poppy Wainwright wouldn't ever do such a thing." With his untied sneaker, Jackson gave a push, and the swing started a slow, slight rocking. "Poppy, I'm not the sort of fella who hankers for another fella, but I've been thinkin' hard, and I wanted you to know how I've come down on this matter."

Jackson wore a pleasant expression. His gentle eyes were the color of the greenest meadow. But, all at once, I wanted to cover my face to shield Jackson from seeing me overcome.

He took my head in his hands. "Poppy, don't you cry a single tear. Don't you do it!"

"I won't," I said. "I promise, I won't."

"You see, I'm just not the sort of fellow who's lookin to settle down with another fella." Jackson cleared a lump from his throat. "I'm not castin' no aspersions, but if I was *that* sort of fellow, I'd choose you, Poppy. I'd always choose you."

"Jackson, what if it was just you and me?" I asked. But my useless words floated from my lips, lighter than a leaf carried on a breeze. Like my hopes for us, they lifted from the porch and were lost in the warm night.

Jackson never answered.

I looked to him. "I truly appreciate you comin' here. It was dead wrong what I did, and you've been nothin' but kind to me. I'm as sorry as I can be."

I felt awkward and stupid and small.

"Poppy, I swear, if you were my girl..." He stopped himself, stood from the swing, and dug his hands deep in his pockets.

The silence widened until no words could bridge the distance.

"I'd best go now," he said.

Jackson walked the path to the front gate and waited for the longest while before stepping onto the sidewalk.

I wanted him to turn around. I wanted to tell Jackson that I'd be anyone he needed me to be, if only he'd stay. But he took off sprinting up Digby.

Sookie came shuffling on to the porch, taking a seat next to me. "It's comin' on a summer shower," she reported.

"Yessum."

"Poppy, it's the nature of this old world. You can't keep nothin' any nearer than it chooses to remain. The sooner you come to that understanding, the sooner you'll appreciate those who choose to stay close."

"Yes, ma'am." I nodded. With a momma like Miss Loretta, I knew too well it was plain foolishness wishing wishes that burned like paper.

Sook reached to me and rested her trembling hand on my knee. "You will learn that some folks hold a tender place in your heart but ain't got no place in your life."

CHAPTER 35

Pendergast Auto Repair
101 Eisenhower Drive, Savannah, GA
RODNEY PENDERGAST WOKE EARLY ON that particular Friday morning—
a dead man walking.

At the breakfast table, he complained to Donita that his eggs
were over scrambled and that the strips of bacon were undercooked.

"I can't stomach this shit!" He pushed back his breakfast and
pounded the little table with his balled fist. The fragile plates,
bowls, cups, and saucers quaked at the sheer brute force of his
anger.

Skittish, Donita rushed about, attempting to appease him.
"Baby, let me fry you up something else. Flap-jacks? How about
some biscuits and gravy?"

Rodney snapped, "No, I ain't got time! I'll just go to the shop
hungry."

On that particular morning, scrambled eggs should've been
the least of his concern.

Rodney Pendergast should've savored his breakfast and enjoyed the aroma of his coffee, because Rodney would be deader
than Lincoln by supper time.

He made his early drive to the auto shop. He picked up the morning edition of the *Savannah Press* and purchased a pack of ciggies at the A&P. He placed the "We're Open" sign in the front window glass, slid open the two garage doors, and sorted through the cash register drawer. He perused the sports section in the newspaper while squatting on the toilet and enjoyed the colored pictures of a *Playboy* magazine he kept hidden above a ceiling tile in the office. His attorney phoned, conveying a few details of his upcoming criminal trial. The top-notch lawyer his folks had hired was well respected and had advised Rodney to take the plea deal— twenty-four months in the Savannah County jail and a $65,000 fine—but Rodney wasn't having none of it.

An aging Southern belle who wore white stockings stopped by the shop, and Rodney serviced her and her carburetor. After she drove from the shop with her chassis lubricated and engine running smoothly, Rodney waited in the front office for an hour or so, just watching the morning traffic speed on by.

But Rodney understood there weren't any paying customers coming in. All of Savannah had cheered him on from the high school bleachers. They had wished for big things for Rodney over at University of Georgia, and even after he had failed to make the cut in college, townsfolk patronized his new auto and paint shop. But now the citizens of Savannah had watched on in silence long enough as their golden boy answered to the courts for his crimes. Savannah's patience was being tested. The locals had read the bold, disgraceful headlines of Rodney's legal woes. They had heard the scandalous whispers of his addiction and the damning rumors of his brutality to his young bride. His affairs were far too messy for civilized Savannah society. By this particular Friday morning, all of the townsfolk had grown weary of Mr. Rodney Pendergast's sordid conduct.

Out of regard for Rodney's respected parents, Rosemary and Charles, the townsfolk had patronized Rodney for an oil change or a new coat of paint on their jalopies. The great ladies of Savannah would take their automobiles in to Rodney's shop for a tire rotation and a buff and polish. But those days had long passed. Rodney knew full well that the shop was a losing proposition. It was bleeding money like spilling blood through a cut vein.

He stared at the silent phone on his desk until noon, watching and waiting on any potential customer's call. He gobbled up the packed lunch that Donita had prepared for him. All the while, a voice was beckoning to Rodney from the back of the shop. He blared Lynyrd Skynyrd from the mounted speakers, but no matter how loud the radio raged, Rodney could still hear the call.

The aerosol cans lining the shelves in the storage room summoned Rodney. He tried with all his might to ignore them, but to no avail. Behind the locked metal racks, the cans called.

Around two thirty, he phoned another lady friend from his high school hey days—a sweet, accommodating gal who was always more than willing to pleasure Rodney in the office.

By the time her Pontiac drove up to the curb, Rodney was sky high. She discovered him in his office, his work boots kicked up on his desk, laughing deliriously at nothing in particular. The paint fumes caused Rodney to lose his head. The sweet scent allowed him to forget his past. In those lost moments, as the poisonous vapors contaminated Rodney's noggin, he could forget all the disappointments. He could discount Donita's tears and forget the sweet babies who were born too soon. All of Rodney's hopes and unrealized dreams would dissipate, like the aerosol fumes from the paint cans.

His eager lady friend pulled closed the blinds in his office and took the We're Open sign from the store front. Rodney unbuttoned his jeans, dropping them to the concrete floor. He watched the blonde seductively undress in front of him. She then climbed between Rodney's legs, under his desk. He leaned back in his office chair and placed his hands behind his head. The talented, willing lady worked Rodney on her knees.

After the deed was done, Rodney ran her off from the shop. Returning inside, he went to answer the repeating calls coming from the storage room.

Rodney took several deep breaths and then inhaled the metallic red paint. The room was spinning. He dropped his head back, closed his eyes, and let the devil do his work.

My life ain't so bad, he mused with a satisfied smile. It's gonna be a fine day after all.

What Rodney Pendergast hadn't considered—what he hadn't accounted for—was that fate was a fickle thing. Like the Southern belle who loved her man strong on one day and then slices his neck with a dagger on the next, fate could turn on a dime.

After Rodney sniffed a few rounds, he inhaled even more. Spraying the aerosol into a tin bucket, he quickly breathed in the ether. The stinging scent sent Rodney's head whirling, poisoning his mind and igniting his temper.

An old high school buddy phoned up. "Hey, you son of a bitch. Let's go get some beers. It's fuckin' Friday! What do you say we go kick some ass?"

"Hell ya! I'm on my way." Rodney's head was spinning.

Stumbling out to his pickup, he tripped on the pavement. Checking his handsome reflection in the mirror, he thought, it's a fine day for a little hell raisin'.

What Mr. Rodney Pendergast didn't know—what he couldn't have foreseen—was that particular Friday was a fine day for dying.

———◆———

"The coast is clear!"

Donita and I snuck into their small house. Like cat burglars, we tiptoed from room to room. When she was assured that it was safe passage, Donita went about packing up her belongings. Running back and forth from the house, she rushed about, carrying in her arms blouses, skirts, and dresses still on wire hangers. She piled them into the car's open trunk. Picture albums and her momma's Bible were stacked in her backseat.

It was a troublesome thing watching a desperate woman choosing what would accompany her to a new life and what should remain.

I said, "I'm really scared that Mr. Pendergast is gonna come home, Donita."

"No, no. It's Friday, Poppy. Rodney called earlier, and he'll be out all night with his buds. He won't come home till sunrise."

With a screwdriver, she removed a loose floor board in the hall closet and took a meager stash of cash held together by a single rubber band. She frantically went about pulling drawers and opening cabinets, searching dressers and cupboards, scavenging for pieces of her life that could fit in the back seat of a Galaxie.

When the rumbling of Rodney's engine came driving up gravel road, Donita looked over to me with frightened, panicked eyes. For a split second, we just stood in place. She searched my eyes like I had an answer to a pressing question. The little house swayed on its footings. The walls trembled and the trusses creaked.

Donita scrambled about, clearing up the mess, stuffing shoes beneath the sofa, and placing framed photographs back on the mantel.

"Poppy, get in the closet below the stairs," she demanded, "and stay there!"

Hurrying me into a tiny broom closet, she repeated, "You stay put! Don't you dare come out!" And she shut the door.

"What's all this about?" Rodney stepped in through the back-screen. "Can you explain all this?"

"Welcome home, baby. What a lovely surprise having my Rodney home for a Friday night supper." She rung her hands. "You're gonna spoil me, coming home on a Friday."

A single burned-out bulb hung from a wire over my head. I held my breath, crouched low in the tiny space.

"Donita, what the fuck is goin' on here?"

I turned the handle, cracking the door open a sliver.

Donita walked into the kitchen and started readying Rodney's supper.

"I wasn't expecting you, baby. What a treat to have you home." She stood at the sink, tying her apron about her waist. "Let me fix your favorite. How about some chicken and dumplings, honey?"

"I can see you weren't expectin' me," he scoffed. "Are you leavin', Donita?" Rodney walked to her side and took her hands in his own. "Is that what you're doin'? Are you leavin' me?" He brought her quivering hands up to his mouth, kissing both her palms. "Stay with me, will you?"

She broke away from him and walked over to the fridge. "Don't be silly. Have you already been drinking, Rodney?"

His impossibly blue eyes held Donita's. "Baby, why is your trunk full? You've got a carload of stuff out yonder."

"It's nothin'. I'm going to visit Mom and Pa in Richmond," she lied. "Momma called early this mornin', and Daddy has taken a turn for the worse."

"Don't you fuckin' lie to me."

"I'll just be gone for a few days. I wanna help Momma with Daddy. Bless her heart. He's been so sick for so long."

"Come on over here, babe," the handsome man summoned her, but Donita stepped further to the corner. "Come here," he repeated.

"No, Rodney."

He reached for her, but she swatted back at his hand.

"Please."

"Donita, come here," he attempted a sincere note. "I'm real sorry about your daddy."

"I just want to get my stuff and go," she pleaded. "Let me be, Rodney."

He reached for Donita again, but she moved behind the counter. "I just wanna go. Please, baby, let me go."

"Donita, just settle yourself." His voice was calm, but his stare was hard. "You've gone and got yourself all flustered. You're free to go." Rodney's words were soothing, but his anger was palatable. "I ain't holdin' you here like some prisoner." With a wave of his hand, he stepped aside to let her pass.

When Donita made her move, Rodney jumped to frighten her. Snickering, he warned, "Get your fuckin ass out of here. And I best not ever find you snoopin' 'round her again. You hear me, you crazy, fucking bitch?"

"I'm leavin'. It's done, Rodney. It is done," she repeated and then called out to me. "Poppy, you can come on out and go get in the car."

I slowly exited the closet.

Rodney turned to find me. He snickered, "Well, I'll be gawd-damned."

I asked, "Are you gonna be OK, Mrs. Pendergast?"

"It's OK, Poppy." From the kitchen, Donita's eyes tried to comfort me. "Everything is gonna be just fine. Grab your stuff, and let's go."

Donita cautiously reached for her purse on the counter.

With the backside of his hand, Rodney swung, striking her the side of her face. Her purse flew across the kitchen.

She stumbled about the room, dazed by the staggering blow. Holding to the counter, Donita moved toward the back door, but Rodney was there.

I screamed for her to run, but he took hold of the back of her skull.

"Let Poppy go. Let the child go!" Donita pleaded. "Poppy, take yourself out of here right now."

He gripped Donita's hair and walked her face directly into the refrigerator door. She yelped, like a hurt animal. Still clutching the back of her skull, he slammed her face again and then again. Blood splattered about the white refrigerator door.

Picking up her small frame, Rodney dragged Donita into the sitting room. Her limp body seemed to float over the floor, her sandaled feet skimmed the carpet. Holding her trembling chin with his thick fingers, he shouted, "Look at this gawd-damned mess of a house. You're a worthless piece of shit. Ain't you?" He brought her face nearer his own and slapped her cheeks lightly, toying with her.

Donita gasped for air through a broken nose. Crimson red smeared her face. She wasn't expecting the devastating punch; when Rodney landed the blow to her cheek, she was left flailing to the floor. The hit caused blood to spill from Donita's mouth, staining the front of her apron.

Through running tears and blood, she begged, "If you ever loved me, let the child go. Let Poppy leave this place."

He picked Donita up like a doll and spoke directly into her face. "I say who comes and who goes in my own gawd-damned house," Rodney raged. "It's my gawd-damned house, and I don't want no fucking freaks here." He dropped her to the floor, and with both hands flipped the coffee table. The glass vase with paper flowers shattered on the floor.

Donita withdrew, crawling behind the sofa.

"So, you're a fuckin' fairy?" Rodney directed his fury toward me.

I stuttered, "No, sir."

"You look like a gawd-damned fairy to me," he scouffed. "It ain't no wonder that you're a damned faggot. Your momma is a doped-up fucking whore."

"Stop it, Rodney. That's enough!" Donita pleaded as she attempted to pick herself off the ground. "Let Poppy go."

"It just so happens your momma came by my shop a few months back sniffing for drugs and a good time. She wanted to get serviced." He ran his dirty hands through his black hair and smirked. "Of course, being a fine Southern gentleman, I obliged her."

"Please, stop, Rodney."

"You're a liar!" I hollered.

He chuckled. "Kid, it ain't no lie. Your sloppy momma left my shop a satisfied customer. I believe she even said I had real potential."

"You're a filthy liar!" I repeated.

"Yessum. I was just being neighborly. And let's say your momma and me bartered for the services rendered. She left a trinket for my tip." He walked over to Donita and ripped the small rose pendant from her neck.

Donita pleaded, "Just stop, Rodney."

He tossed the delicate necklace at my feet and then made a rapid movement in my direction as though he was gonna pounce. Instead he laughed. "Are you frightened, kid?"

"No."

Rodney snickered. "Funny...for a minute you looked like some pretty, scared little girl."

"You're a pig!" Donita lunged at him, clawing at his face, but Rodney caught her forearm. His grasp muscled her arm back down to her side.

I ran into the kitchen and searched the cupboards while the two scuffled. When Donita screamed, he covered her bleeding mouth with the palm of his grimy hand. She bit down on his fingers and he hollered out. Throwing her back to the ground, with the heel of his work boots, he kicked Donita's chest. Attempting a scream, only an aching loathsome sound erupted from her throat.

With one swing, Rodney Pendergast dropped to the ground with a thud. I gripped to the handle of a frying skillet with both my hands.

I ran to Donita and helped her to her feet. Still gasping for air, she clutched to her chest with terror-stricken eyes and a bloody heaving mouth.

I squared her shoulders with mine. "Breathe, Donita. You gotta breathe!"

After I had talked her back from her panic, she and I stood, facing each other.

She asked, "Are you OK, Poppy?"

"Yessum."

Rodney's body laid limp at our feet. The summer night was still as a grave.

She looked over to me. The running blood from her nose saturated the front of her dress.

"I believe, he's dead," I uttered. "I killed him dead, Donita."

"God help us."

"You're bleeding really bad," I told her.

"Are you sure you're OK, Poppy?"

"Yes, ma'am," I answered. "What are we gonna do? I killed him."

Donita reached over with her sandaled foot and nudged his limp shoulder. "I'm gonna get you outta here."

I said, "I suspect we should call Sheriff Delany."

"No, no! Let's go." She grabbed her purse and my hand, pulling me out of the door.

Donita battled with her key in the ignition. "Let's leave this God-forsaken place."

She was shifting the car into gear when Rodney came stumbling out from the house, gripping one of his golden trophies. He swung wildly at the car, striking the window, shattering the glass into thousands of glistening puzzle pieces.

I screamed for Donita to go, but Rodney hoisted his torso onto the car's hood. Using his trophy, he repeatedly struck the front window shield. Donita punched the gas and the car lurched forward. Slamming the brakes, she sent Rodney sliding off the hood. He hit the pavement with a thud. She cut the steering wheel and accelerated the automobile, but Rodney was there, standing in our headlights. She pressed the pedal and struck him. Rodney's body fell in front of the car's path, and she accelerated again.

I felt the car roll over his body, crushing his chest under the weight.

The spinning rubber tires spit up gravel and dust. Her hands gripped to the steering wheel.

She hollered, "Hold on, Poppy! Hold on!"

There was no stopping Donita Pendergast; she was leaving Rodney behind.

CHAPTER 36

———◆———

THE UPSTANDING FOLKS OF DIGBY Street were ever vigilant of the comings and goings in their neighborhood of privilege. Proud and protective, they stood watch over their prestigious, historic homesteads. From behind their window blinds, they peeked suspiciously when a loitering stranger wandered on to Digby. They took special note of any suspect automobile cruising down the lane. They listened for any unfamiliar voice and took notice of every changing wind.

On a particularly warm August night, well past midnight, not a soul on Digby thought it odd when Mr. Daryl Turnball's muted ice cream truck drove down the street, headlights darkened. Not a single neighbor ventured outside into the night when Daryl parked in front of old Sook Wainwright's ramshackle.

On the evening of Rodney Pendergast's disappearance, the fine families of Digby slept soundly while three shadowy figures unloaded a cumbersome cargo from Turnball's aluminum ice cream freezer. In the light of a half moon, not a single porch light burned as three cloaked silhouettes seemed to be midnight gardening at old Sook Wainwright's place in the ungodly hours, when only ghosts and goblins haunted Savannah's streets.

When Rodney didn't appear for his hearing at the court-house the following Tuesday, Sheriff Delany presumed Rodney had skipped town. He notified old Judge Cleveland that they had a runner, who left Savannah rather than face the charges filed against him.

Sheriff Delany came knocking on our front door, prepared to ask a grieving Donita a round of questions. But when the sheriff arrived and saw the bruises along her arms and her beaten, swollen face, his tone turned surprisingly soft. Sheriff Delany postponed his interrogation, respectfully tipped his hat, and let Donita be.

As the sheriff was departing, he came upon Sookie, who was busy tending to her rows of vegetables.

"Sook, your garden looks mighty fine this year."

"Thank you, kindly, Bernard," she replied. "The secret to a flourishing vegetable garden relies solely on the quality of the ma-nure in the soil. This patch of earth has the finest bullshit in all of Savannah." Sook shoveled her spade deep in the dirt, near the vicinity of Rodney's buried skull.

The sheriff looked to the sky. "On such a fine day as this, it's hard to imagine that the paper is reportin' a hurricane could be headin' in our direction."

"I ain't never trusted a blue sky," Sook replied. "It can change in a blink of an eye."

"I suppose so."

"Did you ask your questions of Miss Donita?"

"Yessum. Poor child," the sheriff sighed and shook his head. "If you happen to hear or see anything suspicious, Sook, could you give me a call?"

"Yes, sirree."

Not a single soul in Savannah thought it odd when Rodney Pendergast vanished without a trace. The truth be told, most townsfolk were tickled pink to see him long gone.

It would seem that luck had turned in Donita's favor.

It was said that Savannah slept on her deceased. Unmarked graves were her calling card. Stacks upon stacks of unclaimed corpses lay buried below the city's many streets, sidewalks, and squares. But luck was a fickle thing. It turned like a wicked wind. Folks believed Rodney had blown out of town, but outside Donita's second-floor window, his spirit beckoned to her. The muddy earth couldn't smother his calls.

Indeed, Savannah may have slept on her dead, but the grand old city traded in ghosts who haunted her ballast stone streets at nightfall, crying out for vengeance, demanding their day of reckoning.

———◆———

CHAPTER 37

THE ANGRY STORM BLEW IN from the coast. Newscasters on the television reported the eye of Hurricane Clara would miss Savannah and make landfall nearer Saint Simons Island. But it was not a week earlier when old Sookie had predicted the hurricane's arrival just off Ossabaw Sound.

She surveyed the clear blue sky and sniffed the wind. "Dontcha listen to no TV weatherman. It's blowin' up a mighty storm, and it's comin' our way. She has her eye set on Savannah."

I said, "Sook, the newspaper reports Clara is gonna miss us."

"Child, mark my words, Miss Clara is comin' for a visit."

She and I went about closing shutters, bolting up doors, and securing belongings. By early evening a howling wind blew in heavy, black clouds blanketing the sky. Come midday, town folks gazed to a troubling sky, certain it would fall from its sheer weight.

By the following day, strong gusts had ripped a dozen giant oaks in Forsyth Square from the muddy ground and tossed them back to the earth. Their mangled roots lay bare and exposed on the wet pavement. Picket fences, garbage bins, and children's toys were strewn about the streets.

Donita remained hidden away, locked in her room upstairs, so lost in her sadness, I wondered if she was frightened by the powerful, raging storm or if she was even aware of its wrath.

Wind rattled the window glass in their frames, and the downpour found its way in through every nook and cranny of Sook's old place. Leaks sprung from the haphazard wood shingles. Dripping water fell from the corridor ceiling and trickled from the tin panels in the kitchen. A seeping drizzle leaked from the beamed ceiling in the dining room and pooled on the long mahogany table. The rain found its way from the attic, through the innards of the walls of the upper level, escaping in a stream down the brass chain of the great crystal chandelier in the foyer. It drizzled into a tin bucket in the center of the marble floor.

Sookie's old house seemed to be weeping under the weight of the storm. Pots and pans were scattered about the house, collecting buckets of its tears.

By dusk, as Sookie and I sat for supper, a torrential downpour fell like drapes off the house's eaves. The authorities warned us townsfolk to move further inland. Sook determined that we would stay put. Our quaint lane resembled some lonely, deserted place.

Annabelle squalled about the house, whining at the wicked weather. She aimlessly roamed the hallways of the leaking house, pooping a trail of pellets. They dropped from her backside onto the oriental rugs like tiny green gumballs spilling from a candy dispenser at the Piggly Wiggly. The storm intermittently interrupted our electric, so Sook and I opted to watch God's fury from the thin cracks of the boarded-up sitting-room window.

Lightning struck nearby. The bolt was so powerful, I felt it down deep in the soles of my shoes. Unnerved, Annabelle ceased her constant crying, warily peering at the creaking, plastered ceilings above her.

"It's gonna be a long night," Sookie warned me. "This storm ain't gonna let up. I'm goin' off to bed and try and get some shut eye."

I agreed, "Me, too."

I helped Aunt Sook up the stairs, and we traveled our separate ways along the long corridor.

"Good night, Sookie." I called to her before she disappeared behind her paneled door.

With the storm raging outside my window, I tossed and turned in my bed throughout the night, tangled in bed sheets.

Well past midnight I heard Donita leaving her room, her slippers moving on the wood-planked floor. I suspected she was off to fetch her some late-night leftovers, but with the sound of our front door opening, I knew that something was afoot.

Slipping from my bed, I snuck to my shuttered window. I attempted to spy through the slivers in the glass, but heavy rains slapped against the panes.

White lightning splintered across the night sky, breaking the black into fragmented pieces. I strained to see through the invading rain, pouring off the shingled rooftop. The gutter pipes rushed like muddy rivers, and the wind whipped the giant magnolias. They bent and swayed like great soaked beasts, battling against the violent thunderstorm. The squalls snapped the electric poles like matchsticks, and the hallway sconces sputtered once and then went black.

When lightning illuminated the yard, I spotted her below. There, in her dressing gown, Donita moved about the yard like a haunting spirit. Gusts of spiraling winds whipped her hair and tore at her night dress. Steeped in mud, she battled the wrathful wind and falling water. With balled fists, I struck the window glass, fearing she'd be lifted from the earth and carried off like Dorothy to Oz. I shouted out her name.

She moved through the yard, lurching toward Sook's garden bed, staggering against the storm. She stumbled nearer to Rodney's resting place.

"Sookie!" I screamed, running out my door and down the darkened corridor. "It's Donita! Sookie, hurry!"

Descending the stairs, I leaped four treads at a time. The front door stood open wide with Annabelle screeching at the invading wind. The gales whipped the swag drapes, and the downpour blew through the open door, soaking the front Oriental rug, wall tapestries, and oiled portraits. Water collected in puddles on the marble floors, and the old, heavy crystal chandelier swayed to and fro.

I ran to the door and hollered, "Donita, you're gonna get yourself killed! For heaven's sake, please come inside!"

Disrobed, Donita stood naked as the night under a raging black sky. Her arms stretched open wide. The hard, falling rain covered her like an anointing—her head tilted back, her face washed by God's angry tears.

"You're gonna drown!" I rushed to the edge of the stoop. "I'm beggin' ya. Please, come on in!"

But Donita stood like a stone over Rodney's grave, her bare backside exposed, her eyes searching the heavens, the dark bruising on her thighs, hips and forearms revealed to all of Digby. Rodney's fury marked her body up and down like the foulest tattoos. In the flashes of cracking light, it appeared Donita was looking to the angry sky for any sign of her Savior's return or Satan's chariot coming to hasten her away.

Aunt Sook rushed out onto the porch, pitching a conniption fit. "Donita Pendergast, get your ass in here! You're gonna catch a death of cold." Sook cobbled down the front stoops and out into the storm. She put her arms around Donita's frail, naked torso. "Baby, you come with me."

She studied Sook's mouth as though she was speaking in some foreign tongue.

Aunt Sookie squeezed Donita's shoulders, until it appeared that she had come back to us. "We're goin' on inside! You hear me?"

Donita slightly nodded her head.

The rain fell in sheets. The magnolias moaned low in the tempest of the swirling thunderstorm.

"Poppy, grab her dressing gown, over yonder!"

I ran, snatching up Donita's sopping wrap from the muddy ground and placed it around Mrs. Pendergast's bare shoulders. We walked her back into the house.

Mrs. Pendergast was a puddle in the foyer floor, dripping wet, sniffling and snorting, her perfect ringlets reduced to soggy, limp strands, curtaining her weepy eyes. Sookie went about toweling her off, but there wasn't any stopping Donita's sobbing.

"Poor child," Sook consoled her. "Go ahead and let it go."

Her bawling continued without a breath.

"You're gonna be fine. You ain't the first woman to kill her husband, and you certainly won't be the last."

"Sookie!" I said "That's not helping matters none."

My old aunt shrugged her shoulders and continued to dry off Donita as if she were buffing an automobile's chrome bumper.

"Let's get you dry and into the kitchen. Poppy will heat up some hot tea in the kettle."

Donita sat at the table, her eyes still spilling over with tears, wetter than the falling rain. Her mournful cries were louder than the wind howling outside our door. Annabelle's snout sniffed near her side, attempting to comfort her grieving.

Sookie squared Donita's shoulders with hers. "Child, you're gonna be just fine. Are you listenin' to me?"

Donita's bewildered eyes struggled to focus on Sook, studying her mouth as she spoke.

"Poppy is gonna take you upstairs and tuck you into your bed," Sookie declared in a clear, matter-of-fact tone. "You need to rest. Do you understand me?"

Donita nodded dumbly.

"We'll handle this tomorrow. Some aches and pains are too tender to tend to in the dead of night."

My aunt gestured for me to escort Donita upstairs to her waiting room.

I have been of the belief bacon frying in a skillet cured any ailment. The hiss and pop of a crisp side of bacon sizzling on the fire could remedy any infirmity plaguing a body. A side of bacon brought peace to a trouble-stricken soul.

In all my days spent standing in front of a gas stove, it seemed the aroma of frying pork flesh attracted folks from their sleeping quarters, beckoning them downstairs, still dressed in their bed robes and flannel pajamas, hunting a single slice of healing bacon. Hot, buttered flap jacks, biscuits, and white gravy could bring a smile to the corners of a hungry mouth, but a slab of fried bacon lessened the load of a heavy burden and lightened a solemn spirit.

Come the next morning, the men of Digby had already taken to the streets, boarding up broken windows and racking up the debris left behind in Hurricane Clara's path. Carl McAllister came knocking on our door earlier that morning to confirm all was safe and sound.

Standing on the front porch with Mr. McAllister, Sook surveyed the damage of the stately homes up the lane—shutters hung from their last nails, window glass blown from their frames, and gutters torn from their siding. But it seemed Sook's old antebellum had survived the storm's wrath with only the slightest of damage.

"Carl, tell your Dixie, if she don't get that house of hers cleaned up, I'm planning on turning her in to the town officials."

Carl just smiled and winked at Sook.

She thanked him for coming by and gave him a basket of warm buttermilk biscuits for his hungry boys.

Strips of bacon were frying in the skillet when Donita made her way down into the kitchen; her weakened body appeared ready to give way. She cautiously held the walls for support, entering the room with an uncertain smile. "Mornin', Poppy. Mornin', Ms. Wainwright."

"Child, we're accomplices in a crime." My aunt sipped coffee from her steaming mug. "You can call me Sookie."

"Good morning, Sookie." Donita nodded her head. "Thank you both for taking care of me last night."

"'Twas nothin'," Sook replied. "Have yourself a seat. Your coffee has been saucered and blown. Poppy, I'm certain Donita must be famished."

From the stove, I announced, "Breakfast is comin' up!"

"I ain't sure how I can ever repay you both for your kindness."

Sook dismissed her with a wave of her quaking hand. "Poppy's flap jacks will heal whatever ails you."

"Thank you kindly, but it ain't necessary. I'm taking myself down to the county jail and turning myself in. I've made up my mind. I'm gonna walk myself into Sheriff Delany's jailhouse and turn myself in to the authorities."

Sookie thought on Donita's pronouncement. "Well, let's not say just yet what you're gonna or not gonna do this mornin'. We got ourselves a dead man under my garden, and I suspect that rotten son of a bitch got exactly what was comin' to him. Let's let that sleepin' dog lie."

"I can't do that, Sook," Donita insisted.

"In case you've forgotten, Donita, we've all got an iron in that fire. Fruity Daryl Turnball might not protest being locked up in a maximum-security prison with a bunch of deviant, tattooed convicts, but you are far too fragile, and I'm entirely too gawd-damned old to be imprisoned behind iron bars," Sook replied. "Besides, I'd miss *The Guiding Light!*"

"Sookie, I killed him dead," she stuttered. "It's a sin against God."

Aunt Sook's tone turned stern. "So is leavin' this child in the hands of Georgia state authorities." She gestured over to me. "I promised my younger sister, Lainey, a long, long time ago that I'd be accountable for the safety of this child. If anything should happen to Poppy, I'd have to live the rest of my days with the knowing that I hadn't kept my pledge. Lainey and I never saw eye to eye on much, but I plan to see my promise through. So, unless you'd like to find your carcass next to your late Rodney, I suggest we leave it be."

Donita nervously took a sip of her coffee and glanced over to me.

I shrugged my shoulders up to my ears. "Sookie would be mighty displeased if she was to miss her *Guiding Light.*"

"Miss Donita, the way I see it, that boy was mean to his core," Sook said. "And from what Poppy has told me, if Rodney had his way the other night, it would've been you buried six feet under right about now." Sookie shuffled to the cupboard and took out her mason jar full of spirits.

Unscrewing the lid, the old woman grasped the moonshine and took a full swig. Her lips puckered. Wiping her mouth with the back of her forearm, she slid the jar across the wood's surface. Donita caught the mason jar before it tipped over the table's edge.

Sook offered, "Go on. Have yourself a sip."

Donita suspiciously regarded the glass jar as if it were bottled sin.

"Child, the Lord ain't keeping score. He never did."

The slightest smile turned at the corners of Donita's mouth. She tilted back the jar, swallowed hard, and had a coughing fit.

Aunt Sook chuckled. "Nothing good ever comes from hitching your wagon to one person for a lifetime," Sook declared. "Marriage is like a deck of playing cards. When you first wed, all you need is two hearts and a diamond. After a spell, all you need is a club and a spade."

Donita scratched her forehead.

For the remainder of the sweltering summer, Donita said good-bye to what was known. She grew stronger with each passing day.

She chose not to join me to church on Sunday mornings. I'd call up the stairs to her before I pedaled off to service, but I never received a response.

I asked Sook if she thought that Donita had buried her faith when she buried her Rodney.

"No, child," my aunt replied. "I've witnessed it many times. Folks of faith are odd creatures. They go searchin' in the darkest places until they see the light. And then they'll follow their faith out from the darkness. It will take some time, but she'll come 'round. Donita Pendergast will be back in the comfort of a pew any day now."

Aunt Sookie and I moved Donita into the ramshackle on Digby Street. She occupied the third bedroom on the right, nearest to mine.

It only seemed fitting that Rodney and Donita's tiny place out past the railroad tracks was lost in the storm. That night, the roof succumbed to the Hurricane Clara's violent winds. The trusses snapped, the plaster walls buckled, the window glass shattered, and the little house was flattened.

Daryl Turnball hired Donita to stock his traveling truck with fresh homemade cookies, cupcakes, and other scrumptious pastries. Donita's Delicious Delights was boldly emblazoned in pink letters across the back of his musical van.

When Daryl first drove up the curb with his newly decorated truck, Donita jumped and squealed with excitement.

Daryl asked, "So what do you think, Sookie?"

Old Sook shook her head. "I didn't think it was possible for your ridiculous jalopy to be any queerer. Now it's as gay as a pink pony farting gawd-damned fairy dust!"

Donita smiled. "Don't listen to her, Daryl. It's lovely."

When she wasn't baking, Donita spent her days tending to Sookie's garden as though it were her own. She worked the soil and tended to the rows of ripening vegetables. I reckoned it brought her peace of mind.

On her knees, there in the patch of ground, I suspected Donita believed she could be nearer to her sweetheart. In her own way, among the tomato bushes; stalks of corn; and crops of carrots, cabbage and cucumbers, Donita could still take care of her Rodney. But it wouldn't ever be easy for Donita. Rodney's restless spirit called to her from below the rows of radishes. He was always near her. If she passed a dark-haired man on the sidewalk with deep blue eyes, she'd lose her breath for the briefest moment. When

Sook reported the final score of the Friday-night Savannah High football game from her evening paper, Donita would turn her face from us.

When blue days took a hold of Donita, we'd lose her to some place remembered. I'd reach for her, touching her arm, attempting to bring her back to us from some mournful memory.

I understand that life don't never make living easy. Fine, happy days were made bittersweet by regrets and unanswered prayers.

One afternoon, on a blanket spread out near the beach on Tybee Island, Donita and I picnicked on her yummy potato salad and cucumber sandwiches.

"Poppy, how are you gonna go about living here in Savannah with all the hubbub?"

"I suppose most folks think I'm a sad case," I replied. "But I don't need to go searching to the far ends of the earth to find a home. This is my home. Besides, it seems to me that everyone spends their days searching. My momma travels from county to county, lookin' for something she won't never find. My grandma Lainey was always searchin' the heavens for her chariot on to glory. I suspect every soul goes about hankerin' for their rightful place, their slice of the sky. I just happen to be a fella doin' my searching in a yellow dress and wearing a bracelet of genuine pearls."

I held out my wrist, showing off my pearl bracelet.

Donita admired the jewelry. "It's so lovely, Poppy."

"It was a gift from Jackson," I said.

"Have you ever heard from him?"

"Never," I replied. "When I think about him now, I almost never get sad. I suspect Jackson won't come 'round no more."

Donita poured freshly squeezed lemonade from a silver Thermos.

"Jackson deserved the truth," I confessed. "It was selfish of me to deny him the truth."

"Poppy, boys will grow up to be men, and girls become women. You understand that season is coming for you?"

"Yessum."

"As children, we can play games for a spell, but life requires adults to make choices, hard choices," Donita remarked. "Your body is gonna be changing soon, and being Poppy will become harder."

"Harder for who?"

"For you," she answered. "You'll have to work a heap harder to convince folks you're Poppy and not Samuel."

I could see Donita was treading softly, frightened that she was delivering some dire news that I hadn't considered. "Poppy, I'm not sure you'll be able to disguise all the changes as your body grows. Folks will be mighty spiteful. They won't take kindly to you being different." Donita looked at me from across our picnic spread.

"I understand," I replied. "My momma once told me that my daddy had himself a thick, full moustache. I suppose it's only a matter of time before my upper lip starts a-itchin'." I smiled, trying to reassure her. "For thirteen years I've been raised by the Wainwright sisters. Just as sure as my daddy's family tree grew a crop of fine respectable moustaches, my momma's tree is a long line of stubborn, strong-willed women—strong as any oak. None of them bent when the wind blew hard. I'm a Wainwright," I declared. "Don't go worryin' yourself none 'bout me."

Donita's shoulders eased, and a slight smile played at the corners of her mouth. "OK, Poppy, I won't worry." She tentatively reached over and touched my hand. "I'm sorry about you being burdened with this, Poppy. Maybe you and I, together, with the Lord's help, can beat it."

I shook my head. "I ain't tryin' to *beat* nothin'. I'd welcome the Lord's help, if he's agreeable. I'm just tryin' to find me a place where folks won't fret so much 'bout it. Maybe they can find a kind place in their hearts to let me be."

THE FINAL CHAPTER

―――――◆―――――

"WHAT IN TARNATION ARE YOU two delinquents doin' up there?" Sookie called to us.

I hollered down, "We're just doin' some thinkin'."

From my shingled perch, Pearl and I watched on as Aunt Sook and Donita tended to the garden below. Donita hoed a straight row while Sook came up from behind, planted a seed, and gingerly covered it with rich, fertile soil.

Annabelle had forced her wet snout through a generous gap between two white pickets, angrily hissing, spitting, and snapping at the passing tourists on Digby.

Pearl declared, "My goodness gracious, Savannah is lovely from up here."

"Yessum," I said. "On some days, it looks just like a watercolor souvenir from one of the sidewalk painters over on Forsyth Square."

Across the way, Dixie McAllister was hanging out her boys' matching shirts and trousers on the line to dry, while Carl read his newspaper, smoking a pipe.

The sun was setting low below the magnolias. A September breeze blew in from the water, cooling the last days of August.

"It's a lovely place, indeed," I agreed.

"I must confess," Pearl remarked, "there's plenty of ugliness in a world painted with such pretty colors."

"Ain't true," I said. "There's far more lovely about than ugly."

"Where do you reckon your Miss Loretta is at?"

"Ain't sure, Pearl," I answered. "I suspect she's kicking up dust and raisin' hell somewhere. But when she's weary, Loretta will come huntin' for me. Maybe there's a taxi cab bringing my momma home to me right this very minute."

"Our gawd-damned lunch ain't gonna make itself!" Aunt Sook hollered. "You and that red-haired demon child get your asses off my rooftop, and get into the kitchen."

"OK, Sook," I said, turning to Pearl. "We'd best get movin'. She's a mean grizzly bear when she's hungry."

Pearl's bony elbow nudged my side, and she gestured down the road.

"Holy moly," she gasped.

Up the sidewalk, with a clean, straight part in his hair and a spry step in his gait, carrying a bouquet of yellow daffodils and a box of chocolate-covered peanut clusters, came Mr. Jackson Taylor.

With a determined stride, Jackson walked a straight line in the direction of 22 South Digby.

Acknowledgments

———

To MY SISTERS, CHRISTI AND Lori—thank you for your friendships.

To my parents, Loran and Alice—thank you for everything.

Team AH—Brittany, Kurt, Brandon, Lauren, Jessie, Sean, Kennedy, Jackson, Eric, Lee, Coutny, Hallie—y'all better hope this novel sells like hotcakes, or there's no inheritance when I bite the dust. The party will be over!

My gratitude to Patty Griffin—thank you for the inspiration. Darlingside, Stevie Nicks, Robert Ellis, Iris Dement, the Avett Brothers, Ricki Lee Jones, Lucinda Williams—thank you for all the music.

Thank you to Will Freshwater, Lisa Horan, Frederick Feeley, SA Collins (Baz), Jeff Adams, Patti Comeau, Anita Locke, Tara Catogge, Ross Brown, Brian, Bruce Trethewy, Janet Mason, Cassie Dandridge Selleck, Marcia Ford, Shannon Roberts, the Editorial Department in Tucson, the Novel Approach, Wrote Podcast, Brittan, CreateSpace, and so many others. The most pleasant surprise of my journey into the publishing industry was the support

I've received from the community of writers, reviewers, publishers, bloggers, and podcasts. Thank you all!

To my grandmothers, Lucille and Beatrice. Your fingerprints are on every page of this manuscript. Thank you.

About The Author

———

MICHAEL SCOTT GARVIN IS AN award-winning custom home builder and interior designer. His design firm, Michael Scott Garvin Studio, has designed and built a number of custom homes throughout the Southwest.

A Faithful Son, his debut novel, was a 2017 Independent Publisher Book Awards winner, a 2016 Beverly Hill Book Awards winner, a 2017 Indies finalist, and a finalist at the 2016 New York Book Festival. It was also voted Best of 2016 for The Novel Approach. At the International Book Festival, Garvin sat at the Table of Honor.

Aunt Sookie & Me: The Sordid Tale of a Scandalous Southern Belle is his second novel. Michael Scott Garvin's third novel, *The Last Winter*, will be released in the summer of 2018.

CPSIA information can be obtained
at www.ICGtesting.com
Printed in the USA
LVHW08s0123170918
590353LV00006B/155/P